THE DRINKING WELL

Neil Miller Gunn was born in Dunbeath, Caithness, in 1891, the seventh son of nine children. His father, James Miller, was a fishing skipper, his mother, Isabella, a domestic servant. At the age of twelve Gunn went to live with his married sister in Kirkcudbrightshire, where he was privately educated in preparation for Civil Service exams which he passed in 1907. After brief spells in London and Edinburgh, where he became aware of new political and philosophical thinking, he was appointed Customs and Excise officer in Inverness in 1911. During the first World War he began to write but it was not until 1926 that his first novel, *Grey Coast*, was published. His first commercial success came with *Morning Tide* (1930).

In 1937 he became a full-time writer. The next twelve years were his most productive, including *Highland River* (1937), *The Silver Darlings* (1941), *Young Art and Old Hector* (1942), *The Green Isle of the Great Deep* (1943), *The Key of the Chest* (1945), *The Drinking Well* (1946) and *The Silver Bough* (1948).

His writing also extended to journalism and he wrote articles for American and British publications, including the *Scots Magazine*, in which he argued for the preservation of the Highland way of life.

Later years were spent at Kincraig and Dalcraig on the Black Isle. He was heavily involved in Scottish Nationalism and grew increasingly fascinated by Zen Buddhism, discussed in his unconventional, spiritual autobiography, *Atom of Delight* (1956). This was to be his final book. He died after a short illness in 1973.

Neil M. Gunn

The Drinking Well

Introduced by Alan Spence

Polygon

This edition first published in Great Britain in 2006 by
Polygon, an imprint of Birlinn Ltd

West Newington House
10 Newington Road
Edinburgh
EH9 1QS

www.birlinn.co.uk

ISBN 10: 1 904598 89 7
ISBN 13: 978 1 904598 89 3

The publishers acknowledge subsidy from the

Scottish
Arts Council

_E_

Typeset by P␣   ␣ingshire
Printed   ␣ire

To My
OLD FRIEND IAN
and the sheep farm on the Grampians,
not forgetting the little black diary

CONTENTS

Introduction

It's almost 30 years since I first read *The Drinking Well*. I'd only recently discovered Neil Gunn's work, not long before he died, and I worked my way eagerly through all of his books, not systematically or in any kind of chronological order, but randomly, as I could get my hands on them, for the sheer joy of reading them. On the surface, the books worked as good old-fashioned stories, traditionally realistic – nothing experimental or modernist about them – grounded in the farming and fishing communities of North-East Scotland. But what was endlessly fascinating was what was going on behind the narrative – more than symbolism, rather glimpses of another, hidden story, another reality, a spiritual dimension to the lives he depicted. This inner search came to inform his work more and more, culminating in his final book, his 'spiritual autobiography' *The Atom of Delight*. And while some of his earlier readership were happy to follow him on his journey, others were unwilling or unable to make the effort.

The vagaries of literary fashion in these last three decades have meant a further ebb of interest in Gunn's work, and only the most popular and accessible of his books have remained in print. That's a great pity; he's a seminal figure, and new generations of readers (and writers) should have the opportunity to have their lives enriched (as mine was) by reading him. It's a cause for celebration, then, that his novels are being reissued in this new edition from Polygon.

Gunn himself once spoke of a quality he admired in the great writers he read – he said their work was 'companionable'. (He was referring at the time to *Siddhartha* by Hermann Hesse.) And I found myself returning to *The Drinking Well* as I would approach an old friend, full of anticipation tinged with a little apprehension. What if the book hadn't aged well? What if I felt distanced from it, felt it no longer spoke to me as it once had?

I needn't have worried – it was all there, on the first page, drawing me in, reminding me just how well Gunn could write. It begins with an *aubade*, an evocation, mystical in its intensity, of the morning light dawning over the Highland landscape, a description so beautiful and so precisely observed it takes the breath away. Then there's a beat, a change of pace, and this:

> But man himself, the queer fellow, had blinded windows. He kept his face shut until the mood moved him. He went about, creating or killing on his own, and what he would be up to next was a thing the light never knew.

After this arresting and generalised statement of a theme, there's another shift as the light moves on through a scatter of homesteads and steadings, picks out with sudden clarity the face of a woman, gaunt and weary, staring out through her window. And with that the story moves into the specific, the real, the actual lives and sufferings of these folk in the here and now of this place, this time. It's masterly, the movement from meditation on the eternal, through a moment's insight into the nature of man, to the everyday, real time; and it's handled with apparent ease, great art concealing itself.

I was hooked, and ready to read on.

The Drinking Well occupies an interesting place in the development of Gunn's work. Originally published in 1947 (though written a year or two before) it falls between the early popular novels, like *Morning Tide* and *Highland River*, and the later more 'difficult' works like *The Other Landscape*. Like its companion piece, *The Serpent*, published a few years earlier, it deals with a young man from a small tight-knit Highland community, leaving to seek a new life in the city, then making an ignominious return. (*The Drinking Well* has its origins in an early short story by Gunn, entitled 'The Man Who Came Back'.)

The novel is divided into four sections, or movements: 'At Home', 'In Edinburgh', 'Back Home' and 'The Drinking Well', charting the journey (literal and metaphorical) of the central character, Iain Cattanach. Iain is the typical 'lad o' pairts' beloved of Scottish novelists – bright, doing well at school, destined to 'get on'. This, in the nature of such things, means getting out, making a success in the wider world of the big city (in this case Edinburgh). Driving him towards this goal, towards making a better life for himself, is his mother, whose gaunt face is the one we see in that opening scene, staring bleakly through the window.

And the life that has been endured by Iain's parents has been a harsh one, eking out a living from the land.

> A complicated life, which a man had to carry on his two feet, ready to outwit the adverse chance, capable of hanging on against superior force, ert or inert, active or drearily wearing. When the blow could not be avoided, it was taken. The man went on again.

The irony is that this life is depicted by Gunn as rich and full, vividly real. There are memorable passages describing Iain at work with his father at the lambing – one particular scene stands out, in which his father takes a dead lamb and skins it, then clothes another lamb, whose mother has died, in the dead lamb's skin. With a little coaxing and cajoling the dead lamb's mother accepts the motherless lamb as its own, and the life goes on.

There are wonderful set pieces celebrating what Gunn himself described as 'ploys' – the recurring theme of fishing for salmon, which in Gunn's work became iconic, a motif for the search after wisdom; the sheer joy in living and in celebrating life and love. The ceilidh scenes are full of energy, and there are few better evocations of the transcendent power of traditional music.

The female aspect is strong in this world Gunn creates. There is Iain's burgeoning, half-denied love for young Mary, a girl he's known since childhood. There's the timeless, enduring, practical wisdom he senses when he overhears his mother and grandmother talking.

At the beginning of life and at its end, they were there, handling the unbearable with competent hands, doing little things, material things, with knowledge in their eyes, moving about, silent or speaking as the need demanded. They were there, with the awful progression of the minutes in their hands.

And there's another kind of wisdom again in the character of Mad Mairag, dismissed as daft but possessed of a different kind of insight, beyond the merely rational, gifted with 'the second sight'. Her character is another Gunn archetype, like Dark Mairi in *Butcher's Broom*, in touch with the land and the old ways, and with the drinking well of the title (an actual, physical, well, but one that clearly stands as a symbol of that other life, that depth of meaning).

So in spite of its grim economic necessities, the world that Iain is to leave has an Edenic, pre-Fall quality to it – it is in a real sense a community, a way of life aeons old. But inexorably the story unfolds, becomes more complex. Iain's mother has been ill and her condition worsens. She has in the meantime pleaded with the local estate factor, Major Grant, to use his influence in the city to get Iain 'a start' – an apprenticeship in a law office. When she dies – the loss described with beautiful, moving understatement – Iain feels beholden, committed to honouring her wishes. So going against what he himself really wants, he moves to the city and another life.

Gunn's account of Iain's sojourn in Edinburgh has its origins in his own experience as a young man preparing for his Civil Service exams in that same city in the years immediately before World War I. It all rings true – the exhilaration of city life, the grandeur of the city itself, but also its squalor – Gunn met poverty and deprivation on a scale he had never encountered before.

Iain can be overcome by the spectacle of the Castle on its rock against a dramatic evening sky.

Iain was caught into history, with echoes of ancient battles and riding horsemen, and he felt in himself the smallness of individual life against that which endures.

But he also has to return from such contemplation of the sublime to his drab rented room and a parsimonious landlady who stints on his breakfast rations! Initially, because of his background, he's the butt of office jokes. But with his innate intelligence and wit he more than holds his own, in fact he makes a positive impression on the senior partners in the firm. There's one colleague, however, a clerk by the name of Smeaton, whose attacks on Iain are vicious and cruel, born of snobbery, an assumed sense of his own superiority. Iain simmers, keeps his anger in check.

And there's more to his life than work: he eases into an affair with a young girl, Morna, who works in the office; he falls in with a crowd whose ideas – political and artistic – he finds stimulating. The intellectual climate of the time is vividly rendered in brilliantly sustained arguments and counter-arguments in the smoky pubs of the Old Town. Perhaps a modern readership might find the dialectic heavy-handed, might wish for it to be more integrated into the telling rather than rendered into lengthy exchanges of dialogue. But in that sense it is a novel of ideas – ideas about which Gunn himself was passionate. It's worth bearing in mind just when the novel was written, immediately after World War II. Behind Gunn's love of life, his search for light, was a profound awareness of the darkness, the forces of destruction latent in each individual and in society at large. These ideas were not being discussed in the abstract, but with a sense that the future of the planet depended (as it does now!) on finding solutions.

Gunn was avowedly socialist, committedly nationalist – he was instrumental in the establishment of the Scottish National Party, was a sane, calm, moderating presence, working in the background to bring together warring elements, enable them to find common cause. To one party member he wrote, 'Disruption or internal quarrelling has not only been Scotland's curse but has come too perilously near to being her death.' He was described as 'the ideologue – even the mystagogue' of the party, and could get to the heart of the arguments with succinctness and clarity.

So young Iain enjoys the cut and thrust of the bar-room debates, and he comes to his own realisation, his own synthesis, a sense of the challenge facing him and his generation:

> To do things themselves in their own land and to be allowed to do them. Not to be frustrated from outside but to be inspired from within. For they knew their own land as no others could know it. And it was what folk knew, what they knew in their blood, as he knew his own music, that excited and interested them.

It's this creative element, the triumph of the human spirit, that fires Iain. There's a wonderful evocation of a particular night when the talk and the drink flow, with a great sweep through history, politics, art, psychology. Jung's notion of the collective unconscious is invoked, it's argued that 'a Scot ... is most highly creative when he is flowering from his own unconscious root'. Cutting across the argument comes a crude sawing at the fiddle by an old street musician, and the incongruity reduces the company to laughter. But Iain is moved in a way he can't explain. He goes outside and speaks to the old man, borrows his fiddle, tunes it up and launches into what becomes a virtuoso performance, drawing a crowd and eventually attracting the police who move them on for blocking the traffic. It's a remarkable, heightened piece of writing, Gunn at his best, and the scene ends with Iain turning to see his companions staring at him, saying nothing.

The incident becomes distorted in the telling, turns to vicious gossip, and from this point on, city life stifles Iain. His lack of money – he's getting by at bare subsistence level – means he can no longer socialise. In fact he's eating so little his health suffers and he collapses in on himself. On his return to work he discovers Smeaton is suppressing information relating to a case involving Iain's home village, which will result in friends of Iain's being cheated. There's a confrontation, an outburst of violence, and Iain's life in the city is over.

Initially Iain is unable to tell his father and grandmother what has happened. He acts as if he has simply come home for a while to recuperate after his illness. The land restores him, and there's another powerful set piece in which he displays great strength and courage in struggling to save his father's flock in a winter storm. Inevitably, however, the story of his misadventure spreads after reaching the ears of the Major through his connections in the city. What is worse, the news convinces the Major that Iain is worthless, and revives his suspicion that he was implicated in an earlier incident in which the Major almost drowned. Iain's father is ashamed and turns from him, pushing him away. Iain is the man who came back, and an air of failure and defeat hangs over him.

In this section of the novel, again the set pieces are brilliantly handled – the rescue of the sheep, a near-fatal accident involving Iain's father. Gunn is incomparable when it comes to portraying the enormous weight of the unspoken – saying the unsayable, and the intensity of the family relationships, the sheer power of the emotions are quite overwhelming (all the more so for being understated). There are further turns in the plot leading to a denouement in which somehow, miraculously, the strands come together, and there is at least the hope of resolution, redemption. (We'll leave aside the fact that the instrument of such redemption – at least in practical, political terms – is an unlikely *deus ex machina*!)

In a final coda Iain is reunited with his first love, Mary, and healed by the old spaewife Mairag. They return, literally and symbolically, to the drinking well, the source of life. Mairag's exhortation is simple: Love the land. It's as pure and clear and basic as that. Love the land, and all else – political, social, cultural – will follow. It's a remarkable message of hope, a suggestion that the good ultimately triumphs, love is the strongest force, the light really does prevail.

Alan Spence
August 2006

PART ONE

AT HOME

ONE

The morning light was clear behind the mountains. It drew the horizon in flowing lines, in swift descents, in up-flung jagged edges, and picked out a small group of pine trees as it might a handful of prehistoric men.

Then it was over into the river valley, drawing and defining with singular care, using silver-point and shadow with a freshness that sent a wash of fragrance through the air.

The breath of dun and red cattle became visible along the river flats, and two horses, standing at a gate, caught the morning in their eyes and on their manes. Scattered sheep on a slope were white as quartz boulders. Invisible oyster catchers shot arrows of dark sound and everything was held for a moment in a far memory of breaking seas. Then a curlew fluted and the hills came back, the familiar slopes, the river pools, and the freshness of the morning was a shiver in the blood.

When the light had dealt with its own, it became more curious. Now it was seeking about the scattered home-steads, the steadings, the places defended against assault, the roofs, the closed doors, the rowan tree. Through chinks it caught the red comb of the cock that crew, the cow that mooed to its dancing calf, and the horse that stirred and clomped in its cobbled stall.

But man himself, the queer fellow, had blinded windows. He kept his face shut until the mood moved him. He went about, creating or killing on his own, and what he would be up to next was a thing the light never knew.

So it watched, from window to distant window, until at last a blind was drawn aside by a bony hand and a woman's face came staring through the glass.

It was a gaunt face that had not slept well; its weary

thought or concern was like a kind of anger that had taken to living in the firm bone structure behind. The morning light paused on the blue sunken eyes. The eyes turned away and the light entered the farm kitchen quietly.

From lack of sleep or hidden internal trouble, the woman moved slowly. Gripping a stool, she dropped to her knees and began stirring the yellow peat ash with a long poker. Red embers came glowing out of the ash. She built the embers together with a heavy tongs and set warm, hard-dried peat around them. Leaning forward, she blew on the embers, but the flame would not come, so at last she had to waddle on her knees for the hanging bellows. A collie dog uncurled and went under the table. Soon the flames were licking the edges of the new peat and she got to her feet, hung up the bellows, and carried the black iron kettle to the small back-kitchen. Two collie dogs followed her. She opened the door and they slid outside.

In a little time the kettle was boiling, for she had put only a jugful of water in it. Having brewed herself a strong cup of tea, she sat on the small stool before the fire and drank it slowly and meditatively. The tea refreshed her and she went about her business of putting the kitchen straight with some purpose. She was not a tidy woman, and blew the dust from the high single shelf of the mantelpiece with an automatic indifference. Sometimes she paused and stared at nothing for her mind was preoccupied.

By the time the porridge pot was on the boil, her husband appeared. He was a middle-sized man, no taller than herself (so that one thought of him as a little smaller) but round-chested and strong. His hair was more grey than brown but still thick. His beard, an inch to two inches long, suited his weathered face, giving it a compactness and dignity. Taking a black briar pipe from the mantelshelf he carefully tapped ash from the bowl and lit what tobacco was left in it. As he puffed, he gave his wife a quiet, unobserved look; then, without a word, he went out.

From the dresser she brought a bowl of eggs and began wrapping each one in pieces of paper taken from an empty cardboard egg-box. In the middle of this task, she stopped and, leaving the kitchen, came back with a young man's shirt and undervest which she carefully draped before the fire to air. Then she completed the filling of the egg-box.

The yellow-faced wag-at-th'-wa' clock struck six times. She looked at it and stood thoughtfully. Then taking the aired clothes with her she went to her son's bedroom and, opening the door, said in quiet tones, 'It's time you were up, Iain.' She pulled the winding cord of the little yellow blind, lifted his old underclothes and left the fresh ones in their place. 'Iain!'

He mumbled, turned his flushed, eighteen-year-old face and blinked. 'What time is it?'

'After six.'

He mumbled and lay.

'Now don't go to sleep again.'

When she had closed the door, he turned over and went to sleep.

Presently her husband came back into the kitchen. 'What little wind there is is against him,' he said. She stood, listening, then went and roused her son again.

By the time he appeared, his father was eating. She gave him a long mother's look as he sat down to his plate of porridge and bowl of milk. 'You'll need your time,' she said. 'It isn't good for you to be tearing into the road on that bicycle.' She spoke dispassionately, standing by the fire, and he did not answer.

Before the two had finished their porridge, she poured three cups of tea and set a boiled egg by Iain's plate.

'I don't want an egg.'

'You need it for your journey,' she answered.

His young face caught a troubled, impatient look. His hazel eyes grew dark as his hair.

Her fair hair was now bleached and lustreless. She was a woman in her fifties and the silence waited for her. At last she spoke. 'I have been thinking over it. There could be no harm if I went and saw Major Grant, heard at least what he had to say.'

Her husband expressionlessly finished his porridge. Iain gulped a spoonful and his face hardened. But neither spoke.

'So I may as well go to-day,' she concluded.

Iain drank the milk out of his bowl and got up.

'Eat your egg,' she said.

'No, I'll be off,' he answered. 'Need my time.'

'Iain! Are you against me going?'

Gathering his school books, he did not look at her. 'I don't mind,' he muttered.

'Answer your mother,' said his father.

'I don't care for an office,' he muttered, hitching to his back the khaki knapsack into which his mother had packed the egg-box, stockings and other belongings.

'It's not what you care for in this world,' she answered. 'It's the best we can do for you – that's all that matters.'

He neither answered nor looked at her as he lifted his books and went out.

TWO

The father stared for a moment at his hands on the table, then drew his pipe from his waistcoat pocket and put an inquiring finger in the bowl. Laying the pipe on the table, he took a short plug of black tobacco from his jacket pocket and a knife from his trousers' pocket.

The woman, waiting for the kettle to boil again, glanced at him.

'I'll go and see Major Grant this morning,' she said. 'I know he's at home.'

Holding the plug in the fingers of his left hand, he slowly and methodically cut flakes from it, dropping each flake from the blade into the cupped palm below the plug.

'Have you nothing to say?' she asked.

'What is there to say?' he answered.

'Surely you know your own mind.'

'There's the boy's mind. He does not seem very anxious.'

'What does he know about it? As long as he gets fiddling and singing – that's all he thinks about. There's nothing for him here.'

He continued cutting his plug. She stared at him, solidly and quietly sitting there. Her voice rose a tone.

'What is there for him here?'

'Just the land,' he answered.

'The land! Yes, a bonny land! Struggle and poverty and never getting out of the bit! Have you not had enough of it yet?

'It'll have to do me my day.'

'Yes, your day – and mine.'

A bitterness in her tone brought a glance from him.

'I have slaved to save the others – and I'll save him, too.'

'You sound bitter, woman,' he answered quietly.

'Bitter! You sit there and say that to me! Would James, your son as well as mine, be a doctor in Canada this day, but for me? Would William be making the money he is making in the United States, but for me? Would Shiela be married in London, but for me?'

'They have all gone. That is true.'

'Gone! . . . Did you want them to stay? Were you not proud to see them getting on? Do you think I didn't know your hidden pride when James became a doctor? And now you cast it up to me that they're gone!'

'I don't cast it up to you.'

'What then are you doing? Do you think I can't read your mind, after thirty years?'

He laid the plug of tobacco on the table, but kept the knife with its upthrust blade between the thumb and first finger of his right hand. Slowly, with the heel of the right palm, he began pounding the flakes in the cup of the left palm. It was like a ritual.

In the silence he said evenly, 'You know I don't cast it up to you.'

'But you did. You said they were gone – as though you would rather have had them beggars about the door.'

'I was thinking about yourself. You slaved too hard for them.'

'Slaved too hard for them! That's all the thanks I get now! That's all! That's everything! They're gone!'

He teased the bruised tobacco with his finger-tips.

'You should have taken it easier,' he said.

'Easier! And what would have happened then? They would have got on whether I had pinched and saved or not? Wouldn't they?'

But her derision did not rouse him. Calmly gripping the inverted bowl of his pipe in the crook of the left thumb, he scraped the dottle from it on top of the teased tobacco. Then he tapped the empty bowl on a knuckle and blew sharply through the stem once or twice.

'Wouldn't they?' she cried.

'I'm not saying that,' he answered. 'I was thinking of yourself. You worked yourself too hard.'

'And if I hadn't worked myself, who would, I should like to know? Is that all you have to say about it – now – at the end of the day?' Her right hand pressed strongly under her left breast and she sat down on the stool.

As he brought the bowl of his pipe under the heel of the full palm and began poking the tobacco into it, he looked at her half-averted face, looked over her spare figure and said nothing. Slowly he filled the pipe in the silence, pushing up the final grains from between the fingers, then he dusted the palm and tried the 'draw' of the pipe. Finding it satisfactory, he laid the pipe on the table and began slowly shaving the tobacco dust and dottle from his palm with the blade of the knife. He wiped the blade against his haunch, shut it, and put the knife in his pocket.

She sat quite still, staring into the fire. He got up, tore a piece of paper from an old newspaper, lit the spill at the fire and began puffing at his pipe. On the way to the door, he stopped and, with his back to her, asked, 'When are you thinking of going?'

She did not answer. Turning his head, he looked at her with a sad, troubled expression. Then he went out.

THREE

With his face over the handlebars, Iain swept on, the khaki kitbag on his back, the bag of school books strapped to the carrier. About a mile from the house, a crofter in his late forties, a slight man with a limp driving a cow to pasture, gave him a wave.

'Hullo, Iain! Late as usual!'

'Late as usual!' cried Iain with a gay wave, and swept on. Suddenly he pulled up the cycle, braking fiercely, and leapt off.

'Ewan! I'll remember the fiddle strings,' he shouted.

'Wait – I'll pay you,' yelled Ewan.

'What?'

'I'll pay you now.'

'Right! Friday night!'

On he jumped and into the road he tore. An old woman with a cow on a tether, a man in a cart, a little girl standing in a door, they all gave him a salute of some kind. It was mostly a sheep-farming country, but there were crofts here and there, and on slope and flat ground crops were green. A lovely summer morning, with the clean, fine light of the high lands, an invigorating morning with a slight breeze, and into it he tore head down like one escaping in a mad race.

A small huddle of houses, the merchant's shop with the post office, a church and graveyard, a scurry of hens from his wheels, and he was over the rise and down onto the straight. In the distance, he could now see a lad like himself. Soon he was up behind him and, in a flash, was past.

The boy let out a yell. Iain eased up, turned his head, and laughed.

They cycled wheel by wheel.

'We're in plenty of time,' said Angus. 'What's all your hurry?'

'To get back to school,' said Iain sarcastically. 'What did you think?'

Angus laughed. 'Got all the geometry deductions out?'

'No, one stuck me.'

'The third one?'

'Yes.'

Angus laughed. 'You seem concerned about it.'

'I knew you would get it out – so why should I worry? I was at Kinbeg on Saturday with Ewan.'

'Were you? Many there?'

'Yes. Plenty of drink, too.'

'You didn't drink?'

'They would only give me beer.'

'What was it like?'

'Rotten.'

'Was Ewan with you?'

'Yes. We borrowed Sandy's gig, took the fiddle with us and broke two strings. They were saying I should put Heath in for the sheep-dog trials.'

Angus laughed. 'When did you get home?'

'All hours.'

'Did your mother say anything?'

'Come on!' Iain struck out.

Soon they rounded a bend and saw three cyclists ahead, two girls and a lad, also making for High School after the weekend at home. As they drew nearer, they heard one of the girls singing the song *Mairi Bhan* to a gay rhythm that kept time to her pedalling feet. Cautioning Angus to silence, Iain stood on the pedals and, driving forward full tilt, caught the singing girl's saddle behind and swept her on. She let out a scream. The girl and lad who were a few yards in front turned their heads and the lad swerved. In a moment all four were in collision and thrown off their bikes. Iain landed on his back in the ditch. Angus, who had managed to jump off in time, helped the singing girl, Mary, to her feet.

'I'm all right,' she was saying to him.

'Are you sure?'

'Yes, yes.'

The other lad, Alan, turning from his girl companion, who was also unhurt, strode up to Iain. 'That was a clever thing to do, wasn't it?'

'What was?' said Iain, looking at him directly.

'Banging in like that, you fool!' He was in a white rage.

'You watch your mouth,' said Iain.

'There's two spokes broken,' said the dark girl, Anne, looking at her glittering new machine. Alan turned away to help her.

Iain's face broke in a hard grin as he slowly took the kit-bag from his back. Inside the egg-box was disaster. As he hunted out each yellowed mess of shell and paper and dropped it in the ditch, Angus started laughing.

'It needs more than geometry to solve this,' said Iain.

'Oh, Iain!' said Mary, but she started to laugh, too, in nervous relief.

Soon they were ready again, all except Iain, whose front tyre was flat. He upended his machine on the grassy verge.

'I'll give you a hand,' offered Angus.

'No, you won't.'

'But—'

'Clear out. I'm all right. You need your time.'

Angus did not press his help, and presently he was pushing on in Mary's company, behind Alan and Anne. Iain knew that Angus was soft on Mary.

It was a nasty puncture, near the valve, a small blow-out. He was late for school by the time he reached Kinmore, but at the corner of the street, where he turned up to his aunt's house, Mary was waiting and signalled to him.

He leapt off.

'Here,' she said. 'Here are your eggs.' She held out a brown paper bag.

'But—'

'Never mind. My sister has plenty. She *knows* your aunt.' Her manner was hurried, a little confused, as if Iain might refuse to take them.

But Iain had no idea of refusing. 'Oh Mary, this is great! It was worrying me to death what to say to her. She's got to keep me till Friday!'

'Hurry up. You're awfully late.'

'I won't forget you for this. Look, I'll stick them in the box.'

'Do that. But I'm off.'

'Yes, yes. You run.' He looked at her. She smiled, turned away, and ran.

FOUR

The small drive was contained by a narrow plantation of pines. As Iain's mother walked by the straight tree boles, she glanced sideways at them. The stone house came into view, with its two bay-windows and rose climbers. On the outer edge of the gravel grew more roses in bloom, guarding a small lawn with shaped flower beds.

She paused and breathed heavily, her right hand instinctively feeling for hair and hat. It was an old-fashioned black hat. The clothes hung loosely on her. She had the air of one who has not been dressed in her best clothes for a long time.

A woman of forty in a gay, skimpy wrapper came up from the garden carrying flowers and a pair of scissors in gloved hands. She saw the visitor and waited.

'Good morning, Mrs Cattanach.'

'Good morning, Mrs Grant.'

'I hope you are keeping well?'

'Yes, thank you.' They shook hands. 'We are all well, thank you. I hope you are keeping well yourselves?'

'We have nothing to complain about.' Mrs Grant was gracious enough but firm, with an eye for her visitor. There was a moment's pause.

'I was wondering if I could see Major Grant.'

'I think so. He's about somewhere.' There was another pause. 'You would like to see him specially?'

'Please. I would.'

'It's about estate matters?'

'Well – it's about—'

Mrs Grant waited.

'It's about – my son.'

'Is that – uh—'

'Iain.'

'Iain? Oh yes. Nothing wrong, I hope?'

'No, I hope not.'

But Mrs Grant hardly noticed the deep, sunken glint of humour.

'Very well. I'll see if I can find him.'

She ushered Mrs Cattanach into the room which Major Grant used as his office for estate business and told her to take a chair.

Of their own accord Mrs Cattanach's eyes roved over the room, while her ears kept listening for sounds within the house and her lips parted. The writing table was laden with papers, some folded and neatly tied, others flat; a shallow wicker tray overflowed; opened letters lay on the blotting pad in front of the curved back of the swivel chair; behind the chair, a solid iron safe; above the chair, on a shelf, a black japanned box and the brown leather backs of three ledgers. But Mrs Cattanach's eyes came back to the papers, as though their hidden importance fascinated her.

Then she heard footsteps and straightened herself, wetting her lips, pressing her hand under her breast, and drawing a deep breath. The door opened and Major Grant came in. She got up.

'Please sit down, Mrs Cattanach.' He shook hands, and she sat down while he went round to his swivel chair.

He was a slim, sinewy man with a quiet manner, a clipped moustache and neatly brushed hair, grey above the ears. His homespun grey tweed was well cut and his stockings, hand-knitted, had plain tops.

'Well, Mrs Cattanach, and what can I do for you to-day?' he asked in a level, friendly voice.

'I came to see you, Major, about my son.'

'Iain, is it? What's he been doing now?' He moved the letters aside, waiting.

'Nothing. It's – it's – he's—'

'He's fond of fiddling and we all like that,' he helped her, lifting his eyes in a slight smile. 'They also say he will be a good lad with sheep.'

'So they say. But – I was wondering if we couldn't do something for him. He's over eighteen now.'

'You mean you wouldn't care for him to carry on – your place?' He looked shrewdly at her as she dropped her eyes to the nervous hands in her lap.

'No,' she answered, lifting her eyes frankly. 'I would not. There's nothing for him there.'

He gazed out through the window. 'That's a pity,' he said.

'You know how it's been. The struggle is – difficult.'

'I know.' He nodded absently. 'Since the War, prices have collapsed. Farming was always a struggle, but now – I know it's bad. It's a pity. It drives out the best lads.'

'Yes, that's it. There's nothing for them but struggle – with nothing at the end of it.'

'Um.' He turned his eyes on her, then dropped them to the blotting pad. 'You certainly have helped your family. I have often wondered how you managed it.'

'It was not always easy. And sometimes I had to ask help – where it was not easy to ask.'

He nodded. 'Iain is at Kinmore High School.'

'Yes. He goes on the Monday morning and stays with his aunt till the Friday night. She is my husband's sister and we give her what we can, from the land.'

'I see. Your husband manages the place himself.'

'Yes. We have some good neighbours. And – there's plenty of labour, when there's anything for it. Iain helps – and can stay off school when it's absolutely necessary.'

'But you don't like him staying off?'

'No. I don't encourage it.' She returned his faint smile a trifle awkwardly. 'I want him to get his school certificate, the Higher Leaving Certificate. With that, I felt, he could – could – get something, in an office, perhaps.'

'I'll be frank with you, Mrs Cattanach. I think your husband is about the finest tenant we have on the estate. I should have liked to have seen your son following him. Perhaps – so should he?'

'No.' She shook her head firmly, and her features took

on their graven strong lines. Major Grant looked at that lifted face with a compelled curiosity.

'I have done my best for them. Iain is the last. I want to see him – getting on – like the others.'

'Why?'

She looked straight back at him. 'Why? Surely it is natural that a mother should?'

'I suppose it is.'

She shifted her eyes from his face, without lowering them. 'There is nothing for them on the land.'

'You don't like the land?'

'No.'

There was a pause.

'Is it really the land you don't like?' he asked.

She turned her eyes on him and her face hardened in reserve. But she began to breathe heavily as if she might break out or break down.

'I don't mean to be curious,' he explained in a detached way. 'But when I see the best mothers driving their sons, their own flesh and blood, away, I sometimes wonder.' He squared a letter on the blotting pad thoughtfully. 'It's a problem. It's perhaps the world's greatest problem.'

She did not answer.

He leaned back. 'For, you see, it's not the men – it's the women – the land depends on finally. That's the conclusion I have come to, after all these years.'

The slight smile touched his features again, but she did not respond.

'However, that's not helping you now. Is there something you think I can do for your boy?'

'I'm sorry to trouble you with our affairs, Major. It's not easy – but I was wondering – if it was possible for him to get into an office – an office like this?'

'I'm afraid – not, Mrs Cattanach. As you may have heard, William is leaving me – in fact he has gone – but the new lad has been engaged. Many, as you can imagine, have been after me about it – long before this.'

'I only heard about one boy, Alan—'

'Yes.'

'Then I'm too late?'

'I'm afraid so.'

She sat quite still for a moment, then got up.

'I have been taking up your time. I hope you will excuse me for coming.'

Her courtesy and dignity were complete. The slight old-fashioned bow brought him to his feet. She was making it easy for him to open the door.

'Please sit down, Mrs Cattanach. No harm in talking it over.'

She hesitated, for courage uses up energy, and she had taken a heavy blow. Talk would drain the strength that might still take her home.

But he waved his hand to her chair and she sat down.

'What made you think of him coming into an office like this?'

'It's the only one I know. And—'

'Yes?'

'I thought he might get on. He knows about land.'

'I see.'

'And I thought he would be able to stay at home.'

'So you *would* like him to stay at home?'

'It's a matter of expense.'

'You mean, you would like to send him to college or something like that, but you haven't – it would be difficult.'

'We haven't the money.'

He thought for a moment. 'There's a way it might be done fairly cheaply.'

She looked at him.

'Don't let me raise false hopes. But I should like to help if I could. As you know I am factor for this estate. It's a big estate, with the fishings and shootings. We have our law agents in Edinburgh. They are a very important firm in the legal world. Normally there would not, of course, be the least chance of your son getting in there. I know the senior partner, Mr Cunningham. He was shooting here last year. The laird, Mr Henderson, had him up. We had some long talks about land and its management. I could write Mr Cunningham.'

He paused over a sudden thought and his vision narrowed distantly. Then he looked at the woman in his cool way, curious how she would react to what he was going to say, as though she might be some sort of test case.

'Perhaps I should tell you – and I rely on you to treat it as confidential – that Mr Henderson is beginning to have ideas about the land. He comes from an old family but he made his money in the Colonies. He bought this estate some years ago as a sporting estate, but since his wife died he – well, he farmed in a big way in the Colonies, and apparently his interest in the land is reviving again and he may be going in for politics. Nothing is settled, but it is possible that he may spend more money on the farming side of the estate here. In that case, quite a lot may be done in putting things in better shape, buildings and fences and so on. That might help; so if Iain stayed on he might not find things so difficult – as your husband has done.'

She shook her head, without looking at him. He could see that she considered what he had said as a dangerous distraction, something like a trap. A smile touched his eyes.

'Might not that help?' he asked.

'No,' she said involuntarily, shaking her head again.

'You don't believe in what landlords might do?' he probed.

Now she was distressed. 'It's not that,' she managed to say. 'It's more than fences or ditches. It's – it's everything.'

'Everything? You mean money?'

She nodded. 'Life,' she said.

Now he grew afraid she was going to break down, for she was breathing heavily, as if the word 'Life' had nearly choked her.

'Well, I thought I would just mention it to you,' he remarked in easy tones, leaning back.

She looked at her knees, where her hands were working. Then he saw the effort she made; she clearly had courage and persistence. She lifted her face and looked at him. It was flushed, with a wild gleam in the eyes. 'You said you might write Mr Cunningham.' Her smile did more than plead, yet was not intrusive. She was a remarkable woman.

'Yes, I could write him – and interest him, I think. There might not be an opening in his office at once – but there just might, in time. Anyway, I could write him, if you like.'

'That would be too much.'

'Not at all. The trouble is that Iain wouldn't get much salary. A few shillings a week. He would need help to keep him there.'

'Yes. I understand. I know what lodgings cost.' Her long fingers were bent against her knees. The light in her blue eyes was now hot.

'It has this advantage,' continued Major Grant. 'While working at the office he could also, if he liked, attend classes at the University. That's always done. It's done by all law students, rich or poor. And if your son got his school certificate, his Higher Leaving Certificate, then certain University fees would be paid for him – as you know.'

She nodded. 'I know.'

'There is a certain sum to pay, when one qualifies as a law agent – about £50 to £60, I think. But even if your son did not want to qualify, did not attend the University, he could still train as a clerk and might get a factor's post in the country. That's where Mr Cunningham would help.' He looked at her. 'Though I am factor here, I am not a qualified law agent.'

She had nothing to say. Words were lost in the turmoil of her thought.

Curious again about the way she had dismissed his references to what the landlord might do to the land – for this was occupying his thought at the moment – he could not help asking, 'You would not wait a while yet, just to see what Mr Henderson intends doing to the estate? He is not – the usual landlord. He has Colonial experience. There might be plenty of work for a time.'

'I am sure he is a very fine gentleman,' she agreed politely.

The dry smile almost lit his face. Here was the real

problem that Mr Henderson would have to deal with! Sinking money in draining and fences might be all right for a landlord with money to burn and with an eye on political life, but it would hardly bring about a revolution in Balmore! He drew his letters in front of him and slowly lifted his face. 'You would rather I wrote Mr Cunningham about a place in his office?'

'Oh yes,' she said.

'Very well. Talk it over with your husband. Remember, I can promise nothing. And I should be obliged if you would meantime keep all this to yourselves.'

'We'll do that. I hardly know what to say – how to thank you.'

'Say nothing, till we see what happens.' He pushed the pad from him. 'You – or your husband – can let me know what you decide.'

'I have decided now.'

About to rise, he paused and looked at her. 'I think, perhaps, you had better talk it over with your husband and your boy. Your boy must do us credit.'

'Yes, Major, he must do you credit. He will.'

She got up and swayed slightly. Gripping the back of the chair, she steadied herself.

'You are not feeling well?' He went towards her. 'Sit down and I'll get my wife—'

'Please – no. I'm all right.'

'But I will—'

She detained him, her fingers on his arm. 'If you please ... Now I'm fine. Just a small dizziness.' The smile came into her sunken eyes in profound acknowledgement, then she bowed to him again, ready for the door.

He opened it, and, as she went out, he shook hands.

'I hope you will be all right?'

'I will be very happy – thank you.'

She went.

He closed the door quietly and turned to watch her passing beyond the window. A strange power in her ... something wild about the eyes ... wings beating from a trap ...

Tall and straight she went, and the ill-fitting, loose clothes, ludicrous upon her, gave her a certain stateliness. Past the tall pines . . . out of sight.

FIVE

Duncan Cattanach pulled his horse to a standstill. 'Whoa, there, lass!' The jolting cart stopped and he dropped the rope reins on his knees. Leisurely he surveyed the countryside as he drew his pipe from a waistcoat pocket which kept the bowl right side up. But as he lit it, his eyes scanned sharply, through the tobacco smoke, the road that came from the pines about the factor's house. The face of the house was partly visible. There was no-one on the road.

Away beyond the factor's house, where the hillside slowly fell back, he caught the roofs and gable, the old square tower, of the mansion house, once the stronghold of a Highland chief. It stood on a terrace, thickly wooded, the many kinds of trees thinning out to birches on the slopes behind, then to heather and high deer-stalking country.

But his eyes were defeated in their search, and clearly he felt awkward sitting there doing nothing, so he busied himself making a more comfortable seat by stretching the front shelving across the cart.

This was better, and he caught up the reins. But once more he looked towards the factor's house, now with a certain impatience, a troubling of his brows.

About fifty yards along, his wife was sitting against a bank by the roadside. An understanding of his veiled concern came into her face in half-amused derision. He would not like anyone to think that he was looking for his wife – least of all would he like her to think it. Openly to come for her in a cart! . . . so he would just be passing, as it were!

A motor-car bearing down swiftly on the cart, hooted fiercely. Cattanach drew his horse into the roadside. When the car had passed, his wife was going along the road in front of him. He stared at the apparition, brows gathering, then whipped his horse with the end of the reins.

Presently she turned. 'Is it you?' she said.

He drew up. 'You've got back?'

'Yes. Where were you?'

'I was just down at Altnacraig with some potatoes. I didn't see you on the road.'

'I was resting.'

'Are you tired?'

'I am. Could you give me a lift?'

'Get round behind.' He jumped down and in a stern voice said to his horse, 'Stay there now!' Then he unpinned and lifted out the back door of the cart. 'It's a bit high for you.'

'I'll manage.'

She could not manage, and without more ado he stooped, put an arm round her legs, and heaved her up. She scrambled in on all fours, her hat falling over her eyes. Then she sat on the bottom of the cart, pushing her hat straight, her face flushed and laughing.

He pinned the door on, without expression, went round to the front of the cart, hopped with one knee onto a shaft and caught the reins.

'You'll be more comfortable sitting here,' he suggested in the same even, laconic voice.

'Wait, then.' Like a doubtful sailor, she got over the shelving and sat down, facing front. The hat was troubling her. She took it off and dropped it in the cart. 'That's better. And it's more like a cart.' The derision in her voice was almost gay.

He pulled the reins and they went ahead.

'I told you,' he said, 'that you could have had the trap. It's a long way.'

'You were right. The road was longer than I remembered. However, I have enjoyed it. It's so long since I have been anywhere.'

He did not answer.

'Are you not wondering how I got on?'

'Well?'

She glanced sideways at him, observed the dour, impersonal mood – this adventure with the cart did not help him – and smiled to herself.

'I have every hope of being able to send him to the University.'

'What?' He drew the horse up abruptly and turned to her.

'I said to the University.' Her smile was charged with triumph.

'But you can't send him there – we've no money.'

'We have no money – but I'll send him.'

'What do you mean, woman? What have you been doing?'

'Nothing that will stain your fair name, Duncan. Don't be afraid,' she suggested, drawing out her triumph, playing with it.

He stared steadily at her for many seconds. 'If I thought you went there' – his head nodded sideways towards the factor's house – 'to get help, to get money, to make beggars of us, I'd—'

'Yes?' She held his look.

'I'd drive straight there now – and make you take your words back.'

She was now staring at him. His voice had hardly risen, but it had gathered an elemental power.

Her stare broke in a short ironic laugh as she glanced away from him.

'You would make me take them back?'

'Yes, I would make you take them back.'

'You think you could?'

'Speak, woman!'

'You think he's the sort of man who would give me money? Why do you think he would?'

'Don't anger me!'

'You think Mrs Major Grant, with her flowers and her gloves on her, would be anxious to pay for our boy's education?' She met his steady eyes. 'You think – that I would be the person – to go before them on my knees, like a beggar? You think that?'

He broke away from her wild harsh challenge, caught up

the reins, and set the horse going. 'God knows what I'm to think,' he said, staring ahead.

She smiled to herself again, her face flushed like a girl's.

They drove on, and she began to look at the cultivated fields, at the land around her, with a detached almost pleasant interest.

SIX

Iain saw Angus and Mary cycling ahead, but before closing in on them he started ringing his bell furiously.

Instinctively they swerved to the side of the road and turned their heads.

'Thought I'd warn you,' he shouted, shooting past. They laughed.

'Iain!' called Mary. 'Wait!'

'Can't you see I have an engagement?' he called back.

'What engagement?'

'Wait and see.'

He kept ahead of them and presently Alan and Anne came in sight. Iain stood on his pedals, shot forward, and just before closing on the two in front let out a blood-curdling yell. They swerved wildly, one to each side of the road, and Iain rode in between them, straightening himself and slackening speed.

'Getting home, Anne?' he greeted her pleasantly.

'What a fright you gave me!' She was a dark, good-looking girl, and swayed becomingly, as if all the breath had been knocked out of her.

'Suppose you think that's funny!' said Alan, now on Iain's other side.

Iain turned his face to him. 'Funny? I was merely giving you polite warning of my approach.' He turned to Anne. 'If I don't give you warning, I'm a fool. And if I do, I'm funny. Now I think that's funny, don't you?'

Anne lowered her lids and said nothing.

'Showing off like a fool.' Alan, pale and trembling with rage, was trying to contain himself.

'That's twice he's called me a fool. Do you think I'm a fool, Anne?'

She did not answer.

'Or do you think Alan's a fool?'

'Don't be silly,' she said.

'Ah! I can see this is no place for me.' He shook his head. 'And there I was, banking on you, Anne. I suppose I'd better go ahead?'

'Sooner the better for you!' said Alan.

'He's threatening me now, Anne. Do you think he might throw me in the ditch?'

'Don't be silly, Iain,' she said sensibly, and just a little frightened.

'Get out!' yelled Alan.

At the shout, Iain swerved expertly, caught Alan neatly with his shoulder and sent him headlong into the grassy ditch.

'Good-bye, Anne,' he called, smiling and waving a hand. 'Farewell.' And off he went at speed, the song *Mairi Bhan* laughing in his throat, bursting forth with verve and glee.

It was Friday evening and he was home for the week-end.

As he came by Ewan's croft, he swung off the main road and down the rough cart track to the long low cottage with its tarred felt roof, which once had been thatch. Ewan came to the door of his workshop, pulling a shaving of wood out of a short plane, a small thin man with a clever-looking, clean-shaven face. As he moved he limped, and his face lit up in a merry smile.

'Home again!'

'Home again,' repeated Iain.

'And glad of it!'

'And glad of it.'

Ewan laughed, and the clear quality of his voice increased its warmth.

'No troubles?'

'Not one. How have you been doing? Anything on? Oh, I've got the fiddle strings – an E and an A.'

'Good for you! And how much was that?'

'One and six. Old Alie said they were a special make. The very best.'

Ewan looked at the transparent packets. 'The same make – but he's merely put them up a penny.' He smiled. 'That's Alie!'

'He said the price was put up last week.'

'Perhaps he's right. Everything is going up. Put them on the fiddle – it's hanging there – and I'll just finish this little job. And look – here's the money.'

'Och, never mind.'

'A wealthy young fellow you are,' said Ewan, forcing it on him.

'What are you doing?'

'Mending an old cart for big Andrew. It's a new one he needs. But as he said himself, "I'm trying to keep the where-withal to bury myself!"'

They laughed, for Ewan had a gift of mimicry.

While Iain was tuning the two new strings, Mary came and stood in the door.

'Hullo, Father!'

'Hullo! Back again to worry your poor old father. How did you get on?'

'Fine. How did you manage without me?'

'Very poorly, Mary. I took a stitch in my right side on Tuesday – or was it Wednesday? – and on Thursday it was catching my breath here. This morning it was creeping in on my heart—' His clawed hand was searching for his heart when Mary called: 'Father, don't!'

His dolorous voice silenced, Ewan shook his head sadly and went on planing. Then he glanced up quickly, winked at Iain, and they all started laughing.

'Tune up, Iain – and Mary will give us a song. Isn't it lovely to find laughter in the world?'

'I'm going to milk the cow.'

'Mary!'

But she was gone.

'Never will you get a woman to do the thing you want her to do at the time you want her to do it – or very rarely,' said Ewan.

Iain, with the top part of the bow, began playing the tune

Mairi Bhan, lightly and crisply, an exquisite, distant, dancing measure. Then, suddenly flooded by energy, he gave it the full bow to the same time – and as suddenly dropped it back again into the distance.

Ewan had stopped working and, as Iain lowered the fiddle, he said, 'Boy, Iain, you have made that tune your very own!'

'They're stretching,' said Iain, tightening the two new strings.

'An extraordinary thing,' said Ewan. 'It's an ordinary song – and you make it dance like a green fairy on her toes.'

'No,' said Iain. 'But I see what you mean.' His face was slightly flushed, his head up, hearkening to his thumb plucking the two strings.

'For it's a queer thing that some of our saddest folk songs – and God knows they can be the saddest in the world – have somewhere, away behind them, the fairies on their toes in a lost green world.'

'Perhaps that's why they're sad,' said Iain.

Ewan looked at him. 'Out of the mouths of babes—' He shook his head drolly, then, staring before him, began singing the song slowly over to himself, quietly, in his clear tenor voice, as if hearkening to its sadness and despair.

Iain began to play the notes behind the voice. As the voice stopped, he played on, then held a note – and as it died, out of its silence came the far-away dancing measure, nearer, nearer, till it was in the shop, vigorous, full-bodied, and Ewan, snatching up his plane, began conducting and dancing grotesquely to it at the same time.

At the height of the fury, a crofter's head was poked round the door, heavily moustached, over sixty years of age, and as it gaped in solemn astonishment, it shouted 'Hooch!'

Fiddler and dancer stopped. Then Ewan dropped his plane.

'Were you wanting anything?' he asked the face solemnly.

'Yes. I'm wanting my cart.'

'Is that all? Come in.'

Andrew McAndrew came lumbering in. 'Well, of all the

carry-ons in the broad light of the day! At your time of life, Ewan, I thought you would have more sense.' He shook his head.

'You think I'm beyond repair?'

Andrew eyed Ewan: 'Are you going to say – like my cart?'

Ewan's mock solemnity broke and he began laughing. Andrew turned to Iain with a wink, clearing his mouth of moustache with the back of his hand. 'He thinks he's clever, but I got him that time.'

Iain hung up the fiddle.

'I saw your father west yonder,' continued Andrew, 'rounding up some sheep.'

'Oh Lord, I forgot!' Iain made for the door.

'Ay, you forgot! One of these days you'll be finding your-self—'

'In the cart,' said Iain, and out he went.

But as he was putting the khaki bag over his back, he paused, listening. From the byre, next door, Mary's singing voice fell faintly on his ear. Tip-toeing to the door, he looked in. She was milking the old dun cow, and to help the beast let down her milk, was singing softly, *Cronan Bleoghain*, the rhythm keeping time to the pulling of the teats and the dancing of the milk-squirts in the bright tin pail. It was one of the old traditional milking songs that Iain liked and he leaned against the door jamb, watching her. Her head, tilted sideways, was against the cow's hide.

Presently she moved and saw him.

'Hullo!' she said. 'Not home yet?'

'No. But I'm going.'

'High time.'

'I know.'

She started milking again. 'That was a fine thing to do.'

'What?'

'Knocking Alan into the ditch.'

'Me?'

'Why do you do it?' She was looking into the pail.

'He asks for it. He's so important.'

After a minute, she asked, 'Is that the only reason?'

He looked at her averted head sharply. Then he laughed in his nostrils. 'If you have stopped singing, I'm off.'

She went on milking, without looking up.

'So long! See you Monday,' he called.

She stopped milking and listened to his movements outside. Then he was gone. She dropped her brow against the cow's hide and her hands fell idly over her knees.

SEVEN

'What's been keeping you?' asked his mother, as he entered at the kitchen door.

'Nothing,' he answered, dumping his school books on the table and slinging the khaki bag from his back.

She looked at the school books and quickly back at him.

'How did you get on this week?'

'All right.'

'I've been trying to keep it warm for you. Sit in now. You must be starving.'

His place at table was all ready and when he sat down she came with a steaming plate and set it before him. Then she brought a pan from the fire and with a spoon picked out the best of the potatoes, those which had burst their jackets. 'I thought they were going to be ruined.'

He did not look at her and began to eat.

'Is it good?'

'Yes, it's fine.'

'Be eating, then. You need it.'

From the fireplace she turned to his khaki bag and began emptying it. A yellow stain on the egg box caught her eye. As she paused, he gave her a quick side glance. He had done his best to remove the stains. She opened the box.

'Did some of them get broken?' she asked.

'Broken? She didn't say.'

'In that case, they weren't broken.' She laughed harshly. 'Had they been broken you would have heard about it!'

He went on eating.

'Perhaps she broke them herself.' This made her laugh again, with warm malice. 'Did you get an egg at all?'

'Yes. Just as usual.'

'Tell me, Iain. Does she give you proper food?' The maternal concern in her voice disturbed him.

'Och, not too bad.'

At this lightening of his voice her manner became still more friendly, as if she were hungry for her son's trust.

'She's a mean one if ever there was! But never mind. It's your last year.'

He did not answer.

She remained silent for a little time, then in a restrained voice said, 'You must get your Leaving Certificate – without fail.'

He went on eating, with a confused warmth in his face and a faint knitting of the eyebrows that made him look like his father.

She seated herself on the stool and with the tongs placed a peat on edge against the flame. 'You'll do your best?'

'Yes,' he mumbled.

'It's all I ask you.' Then she turned her face to him and in a light enticing manner, said, 'Great things may come of it, if you do.'

But he did not look at her. 'What things?'

'I went and saw Major Grant.'

'Oh.'

'Iain – why don't you help me? I'm trying to do my best.'

He was disturbed, confused, looked almost angry. 'What is it?'

'It's this, Iain. If you get your Certificate – you may be able to go to the University.'

The hand that brought the fork to his mouth hesitated and a piece of potato fell back on the plate. The fork retrieved it.

'Wouldn't you like to go to the University?'

'I don't know,' he mumbled.

'Listen to me, Iain. For it's only your good I'm thinking of. You know that.' She looked across at him. 'You know that, don't you?'

He made a confused sound of assent.

'All I have ever wanted to do is help my family – out of

this. I have managed so far. I am not going to fail with you.'
Her voice gathered strength. 'I know – and you don't. I have
got to help you – while I can.'

'Where's the money to come from?'

Her voice softened again and her eyes caught the light.
'Is it only the money that's troubling you?'

'I don't want you to be spending more money on me.'
His manner was awkward, his voice abrupt.

'It won't need so much money.'

'You need it for yourselves. I don't want to go.'

'Don't worry about the money, Iain. I'll manage. I managed
before. Only – you'll have to get your Certificate.'

'Don't want it,' he muttered.

'What's that? What don't you want?'

'Want to help Father. That's all I want.'

'You want to be a shepherd to your own poverty-stricken
father. That's all you want, is it?' She got up, the bones clear
in her face, her eyes flashing.

He laid down his knife and fork and pushed his plate
from him.

She controlled herself. 'Oh, why do you make it difficult
for me? Can't you see that I am trying to help you, to help
you away from all this – this poverty and drudgery – from
morning till night – without end – without anything for it?'

He did not speak.

'Why have I always to fight?' The wild strange note had
come into her voice. 'Always to fight, against silence and
dourness, against everything that drags and drags, drags
down, like the mire of the land at my feet.' She breathed
heavily for a little while, then brought the back of her hand
against her nose, sniffed, and swallowed. Wisps of hair had
come over her brow and she drove them back. She sat down
on the little stool. 'You'll have to forgive me,' she said quietly.
'I'm not so strong as I was.' She stared into the fire.

He wanted to get up and go out but could not move. His
mother in this mood disturbed him profoundly.

'I went and saw Major Grant,' she said to the fire. 'He
was very kind.'

He waited.

'Do you remember,' she asked, 'a Mr Cunningham, who was up here from Edinburgh at the Big House – with the laird?'

'Yes. I gillied for him.'

Her face turned to him and brightened. 'Did you? Was that the time you stayed off school for the deer-stalking?'

'Yes.'

'Are you sure it was Mr Cunningham?'

'Yes. It was he who gave me the pound in a tip.'

'Did he?' She got up. 'Did you like him?'

'He's a bit particular – but he's all right. Why?'

'Oh, Iain – it's into his office in Edinburgh you may be going!'

He looked at her.

'Listen to me, Iain. I went and saw Major Grant. There's nothing for you in his office. But far greater than that – he said he might get an opening for you in the law agents' office in Edinburgh. They're terribly high up in the legal world. Writers to the Signet. No poor boy gets in there. Mr Cunningham is the – the – senior partner, the biggest one in the firm. He is the laird's friend. And now you tell me that you know him! Oh, I'll have to tell Major Grant that. Mr Cunningham will remember you. This is more than I had hoped for, ever.' She began to move excitedly. 'You'll take a little more, Iain. Look, there's more in the pot.'

'Don't want more.' He got up.

'Where are you going?'

'Where's father?'

She looked at him steadily. 'Iain, don't you see what this means? You'll be there in that grand office – and getting paid. And while you're working, you can attend your classes at the University. They all do that. If only you get your Certificate it will cover the fees – the University fees – and out of that office you can step into a position like Major Grant's. You can be a gentleman. Think of it, Iain – a gentleman, like Major Grant. No longer slaving away here like your father.'

'I think Father is just as much a gentleman as Major Grant.'

She looked at him – and laughed. 'Yes, yes, we're all gentlemen! Only some can afford to live like gentlemen – and others like dirt.'

He made for the door.

'Iain!'

Staring at the vacant door, she stood like one enraged and bereft. Her right hand came under her breast and pressed hard. Slightly doubled up, she went and sat down. 'I'm losing hold of myself,' she said aloud. 'I get angry too easy. I can't help it.' She shook her bowed head – and lifted it. 'But I'll have my way. I'll cheat the hungry mire. It can't beat me. Nothing can beat me.' She breathed heavily, staring in front of her. Then her stare narrowed as if she were indeed seeing someone or something in the guise of death. Her eyes closed and, with a small moan, her head and body drooped towards her knees.

EIGHT

Iain went out through the steading blindly, past the pine trees huddled on the round knoll, past the corner of the grey dyke, and along the path by the base of the hill.

Presently a distant whistle stopped him. Through the dusk of the summer evening, he saw his father, a small still figure, directing that living world. Grey specks on a slope above rushed together as if an eddy of wind had blown them. Then his keen eyes picked up the moving dog. Another whistle and the earth sucked the dog under.

The stillness that was the silence of the mountains now held everything, and far away the purple-dark peaks stared upon the world of the west, whither the sun had gone, leaving a wake of molten silver in the sky.

Not what he saw, but something in it, made him turn round, as if he were still a little boy of six or seven and the silence was coming up behind him. The mushroom of black pines stood by his home. Deserted his home looked, isolated, as though some prehistoric giant, bending down from the height of the sky, had set it there, together with the low outhouses, piece by piece, from between finger and thumb.

High the sky was, in a lucent blue, and over in the east floating islets of white cloud were stained with red.

When he looked ahead again, the shadow seemed to have deepened about his father's world. His father himself was like the stump of a dead tree, a solitary stump, dark against a low island of green grass. The stump moved, and but for something solid about its girth, it might have been the figure of a small boy.

Not far from the figure, its ordered grey-stone dykes like a giant's signature at the base of the hill, stood the empty sheep fank.

Iain went on. A wash of sound came from the Grey Mare's Tail and, glancing up, he saw the waterfall.

In a little while he stopped. The sheep moved down past him, but slowly now, cropping as they went. The dog was flat in the heather, head up, watching the figure down below. All was going well, so the dripping tongue was out in its breath-dance between the white teeth. But the eyes were watchful, and clearly the brain behind had thoughts of its own, for it stole a look at a sheep that stood on the brink of the small ravine through which the hill burn flowed. The red tongue went into the mouth and the long muzzle narrowed. Eyes switched to the figure below, but no order came.

Iain saw Heath gathering himself, making up his mind to act on his own, but discreetly. For well Heath knew this fool of a sheep, this ramstam baaing ditherer. A nip in the flank was in the offing. Iain waited.

But despite the hard bone of its head, the sheep knew something of all this also, and turned away from the ravine, nose up, in a sort of bewildered yet important stagger, following the others, but by no means docile.

For the first time Heath's eyes rested on Iain, and Iain could have sworn that the old dog smiled.

It was for Iain a first smile of recognition, and the heather moved as the tail switched once. Then the eyes were on the figure below again.

His father was now coming up the path and Iain went slowly to meet him. Before they actually met, and to ease the impact of the meeting, Iain looked back. Heath, having decided that work was over, had got up and was quietly approaching. The young dog, Mat, was rushing up on Heath and, in the exuberance of having completed a successful round-up, made a playful pass at the old dog's ears. But the old dog was not amused.

His father paused and, after slowly sweeping his eyes around, said, 'They'll do there fine.' His voice was casual and friendly, as if they had been together on the hill all day.

'Fine,' Iain echoed.

Then his father glanced at him directly. 'You've got back?'

'Yes.'

They walked on, and presently Iain said, 'I met big Andrew. He was after his cart.'

His father smiled. 'I told him he could have ours.'

'I think he'll have to have it yet,' said Iain.

'It's a new one he needs right enough,' agreed his father. 'I sometimes wonder if Ewan gets his money back itself.'

Their voices were unstressed, unhurried, in the quiet of the evening, and the faint humour was the greeting between them.

'He can't get much more,' Iain thought.

'I don't know that I ever remember times being so bad for the hill sheep farmer,' said his father. 'It's not only the bad prices. It's what you have to pay for everything – especially the wintering of the sheep.'

Not often did his father talk to him in this grown-up way, and Iain was moved.

Then his father said simply, 'I doubt it's done, boy.'

The words hit Iain's mind a dark blow. He could hardly breathe from surprise. Leagues of distance between them were closed as his father looked at defeat, at it and all round it. Bewilderment and nearness scattered all words from his mind, and somewhere his father's head bowed.

'There have been hard times before, they say,' murmured Iain.

'I know. I know,' said his father slowly, his head always up, his eyes level along the slopes and the great distances.

They walked for a little way in silence.

'But times have changed,' added his father. 'The world is no longer what it was, since the great war.'

And finality came down like a darkness.

They walked on.

'Has your mother been talking to you?' asked his father in the same voice.

'Yes,' mumbled Iain, his heart caught and held.

'And what do you think?'

'I don't know.'

'You'll have to know,' said his father thoughtfully. 'Don't you want to go?' he asked after a little while.

Iain did not answer.

'You better make up your mind,' said his father. 'Don't you want to go to Edinburgh?'

'No. I don't want to go particularly,' answered Iain, his eyes flashing ahead from the petulant mood in his face.

'What have you against it?'

'I don't care for it.'

'Is that all?' asked his father, and the simple question, because it held no irony, was terrible as a vision of all life.

Iain could not speak. The little question now had something in it that made him feel like a child.

'It's a good chance for you,' said his father evenly. 'And your mother is set on it.'

Rebellion stirred in an inner congestion. He was no child; he could fight.

'I would rather stay here,' said Iain, and added on the next breath, 'and help you.'

Iain could not look at his father, but from the sound of the breath in his father's nostrils, he felt that his father had smiled in weary irony. But his words when they came were friendly. 'I'll try and manage without you, boy. Don't think of me. I have had my day, and, with health, I'll carry on for a few years yet, God willing. Don't think of me.'

Something distant and austere about his father, something finished, wrung his heart.

'I could help you,' said Iain, his voice thick with moodiness. 'I don't want to get on.'

'Surely you want to get on?'

'I don't want to get on in the world,' said Iain in a rush.

'You can't start life like that,' replied his father. 'If you do, life will become too much for you, it will get you down. It's a struggle at the best. At the worst . . . it's something I would not like you to know.'

'I don't care for that kind of life,' said Iain doggedly.

'You're not frightened of it?' asked his father quietly.

'No, I'm not frightened of it,' answered Iain, his heart suddenly pierced, the harmony torn.

'You better make up your mind,' said his father. He stopped. The dogs stopped and looked up at him. 'I'm going over to see Geordie about to-morrow.'

They stood for a moment, then his father walked away.

NINE

Seven men sat about on the grass, clipping wool with hand-shears off the sheep between their legs. Now and then a sheep struggled but, as its legs were in the air, the clipper found no difficulty in subduing its energy.

The day was good and the work going ahead happily amid a tremendous turmoil of baaing sheep and barking dogs. Little boys were tripping over fleeces; a man's head sweated above the mouth of the great bag slung to its gibbet; old Willie, with his hot tar and marking iron, was doing his best to show he was not getting deaf. Iain, 'drawing' sheep to the clippers, was bathed in sweat. Jokes were tossed about, for communal work of this kind had its air of ancient fellowship. Thus together men had gone on expeditions, or hunted, or fought, or cut fuel, or sailed away to far lands.

'Off!' said Andrew, and the newly-shorn sheep rose white out of its old grey fleece. Like its own ghost, it started baaing for a lost world – saw the lost world and bolted, leaping ludicrously at every few strides over invisible walls or ditches.

'Right, Iain!' called Andrew.

But Iain was already cornering the old barren ewe which had threatened to cross the ravine under Heath's eye.

As he came to grips with the ramstam brute, there was a struggle. She was heavy and in good condition. Heath's muzzle went down and he crept nearer, as if a nip in the right place now might square a long account. Several heads turned and smiled as Iain's face grew congested in the wrestling match.

Iain got his hold, but the ewe, thrusting from her hind legs, staggered him. It was a moment of wild embrace, with Iain's hands slipping and the brute frenziedly trying to break away. Her muzzle came across his face and he bent his head back.

'Don't be bashful, Iain!' called Geordie. 'Get your leg over her.'

There was a laugh from the clippers, and even his father paused to cast a glance at him.

'On her back, Iain,' suggested Andrew, taking a lazy stride forward. 'Will I help you?' He spread his arms in an exaggerated gesture and turned his head to say something to Geordie when Iain let the ewe go. She got Andrew fair between the legs and he went over like a pole.

Six clippers, sitting about on turf stools, gave laughter its mouth.

Andrew rolled slowly over on his face.

'Are you hurt?' asked Iain.

'You young devil,' said Andrew, pushing himself up on one arm and rubbing his head. 'Don't you know yet how to put a ewe on her back?'

'She put you on your back whatever,' said Geordie.

The laughter now was merry, and into it walked two of the crofters' wives and Mary, carrying baskets of food.

'What's wrong with you?' asked Andrew's wife, seeing him get up off his knees.

'Surely, as his wife, you've seen him at his prayers before now?' asked Geordie.

'I have,' she answered. 'What was he praying for?'

'What do men pray for?' asked Geordie.

'Mostly for their bellies,' she answered. 'Where's the fire?'

'Iain!' called Cattanach.

'Right!' said Iain, and off he went.

'Go with him, Mary,' said Mrs McAndrew. 'You're hardly old enough yet to hear Geordie's prayers.'

Below the fanks, Iain was tearing old heather runts from the ground. Mary passed him, carrying the kettle, and, getting to her knees, dipped it in the stream, emptied it, and filled it once more.

Between old smoke-blackened stones, Iain was building his fire, lining it with bits of last year's peat and placing the dry withered heather in the heart. His hands were careful and intelligent.

When Mary came to place the kettle on top, Iain waved her back. 'Wait a bit.' He added, 'It's no good lighting a fire unless you have enough stuff to keep it going.'

She glanced at his stooping figure. 'Will I get some more heather?' she asked.

'See if you can get a bit of wood,' he suggested.

At once she turned away, her eyes quick and eager. Soon Iain had his fire ready and, getting up from his knees, saw Mary coming round the wall with an old batten which had once been part of a gate.

'You're a marvel,' he told her in his frank, friendly way. He put a match to the heather and, taking the strip of wood, laid it against a boulder and jumped on it. He fed the broken pieces into the blaze and presently had the kettle balanced on the stone edges.

'Anything more?' she asked.

'Yes. Bring another peat.' He pointed to the small mouldering black pile in an angle of the stone wall.

She quickly brought it and he broke it up. 'The less smoke—' he began.

'The more heat.'

He glanced sideways at her.

'I have heard you say it before,' she explained.

He laughed. 'I suppose I often bossed you.'

'Always.'

'But you didn't always let me off with it.'

'Far too often – for your good.'

He laughed again. 'As children, we had good times here, right enough. Remember the time you fell off the tree and I thought you had broken your neck?'

'And I ran home bawling. Go on.'

'Because Angus was bawling.'

'You weren't bawling anyway.'

'I was scared stiff at what your father might say.'

'That was why you ran after me and told me to shut up and not be a fool.'

He chuckled. 'I think Angus always had a bit of a soft side for you.'

She started back from a swirl of smoke and rubbed her eyes. 'I'll go for the tea.'

'It's not nearly boiling yet.'

'It's singing. I can hear it.'

'That's always one thing you could do.'

'What?'

'Sing.'

'Glad I could do something to please you.'

Squatting before the fire, he fed it carefully. 'You did not do it to please me. You liked doing it.' He brushed his hands and looked around. 'Good being here, isn't it? Instead of listening to old Baldhead and his quadratic equations.'

'It's lovely.'

'Think of you as a schoolmistress. C-A-T cat. The cat sat on the mat. The cat caught a rat. Good cat.'

'Perhaps I won't catch a rat.'

'On any school mat?'

'I hate the brutes.'

He laughed and she joined in his mirth, swaying where she sat on the grass. She was now a little erratic, excited, with colour in her cheeks. Her hair was a light brown, with sun-smitten parts and her warm skin had freckles. She was like one who had come all alive out of the background of heather and moss and grey walls and green grass. The brown water of the stream had caught her reflection as she stooped with the kettle. Her hair, cut short, had fallen towards the water, and for a moment her face had come to meet her out of the stream.

It was easy for Iain nowadays to make her feel like that face in the stream, approaching eyes and mouth – to shiver and vanish at a touch.

A female head rose behind the wall. 'What carry-on is that you're having and us waiting here for our tea!'

'It's just on the boil!' called Iain.

TEN

'Make a poem on that tree! Make a poem on that tree!' chanted the children in unison.

Mad Mairag stood staring at the tree. It was a young aspen, and something in her aspect as she stared at it silenced the children, for it did indeed look as if she were 'seeing things'. Then she withdrew her eyes and muttered to herself.

A boy shouted: 'She can't make a poem on that tree!' The oldest was not yet thirteen, and the girls' voices rose shrilly. 'She can't make a poem on that tree!' All the voices shouted in excitement and derision. 'She can't make a poem on that tree!'

The old woman shook her head. 'No,' she said, 'I can't make a poem on that tree. No, not on that tree. Never, never, on that tree.' She stood in such profound dejection that clearly she had forgotten them.

But once again the leading boy broke the silence, crying, 'Why not on that tree?'

With a quick jerk of the head, like the jerk of a hen's head, she looked at them, and some of the girls gave a squeal and started back a pace. 'Do you know,' she asked them, 'what tree that tree is?'

They stood silent, for none of them knew the tree's name.

She suddenly pointed at it. 'Look at it. There is no wind. The evening is calm and warm. Yet it shivers. Do you see its leaves shivering there, while all other things are still? Even the little birches have gone to sleep. But it shivers.'

Her head began to nod. 'It will never forget. Some say it will never forget because of the great crime it did. But I know it will never forget – the great crime put upon it by man. To this day it shivers, remembering, and always, to the end of time, it will shiver.'

Then the bold boy asked in a gruff voice, 'What crime?'
But this time no voice echoed him.

She looked at the boy, and kept looking at him, until his
body twisted. Then she said, 'That is the tree, from which
they made the cross, on which they crucified Christ.'

All the children grew very still, and when the old woman
walked on, none followed her.

'She seems to have silenced them that time,' said Ewan,
as Iain returned from the shelter of the bushes beyond Ewan's
garden.

'She did.'

The children saw the two men gazing towards them, and
suddenly they began running away, as if caught in guilt.

'I was waiting for them to begin tormenting her. But she
silenced them all right,' said Iain.

'I heard most of it.'

'How did the tree come to be there?'

'Some bird must have dropped it – to remind us of our
sins!'

They smiled.

'Do you think she's mad?' asked Iain.

'Mary doesn't. She even goes to see her sometimes. I think
she's a bit queer – but quite harmless. They have been talking
about lifting her.'

'Who?'

'The authorities.'

'Have they? Because she's – off her head?'

'Well, yes, and she lives all alone. It's over three miles as
you know to her place at Achmore. When she was a girl,
there were seven crofts there. The old folk died or were
cleared out. But she refused to budge. That's her land, her
earth. She has delusions about it.'

'Has she?'

'She says the dead come out of the land and speak to her.'

'So I've heard,' murmured Iain, staring into distance. Then
he stirred. 'All the same – I don't know. We have a master
at school who gives us English poetry about the earth and
trees and flowers. But I have heard Mairag say things that

stuck in my mind, that will always stick. The English master would laugh at them as poetry. Her rhymes are too simple. Childish.'

'Like the aspen tree?'

'She didn't make a rhyme about the aspen tree. It was suddenly – too terrible – for rhyme,' said Iain.

'She mentioned Christ?'

'Yes.'

'A pity. If they hear she has mentioned Him to the children, they will lift her sure.'

'But the children won't tell. That's the queer thing. We never told grown-ups.'

'There is always one who tells.'

They stood silent for a little as the shadow of Judas passed.

'Anyway it will be a handle for Major Grant,' added Ewan. 'He wants her cleared out. Come on in and give us a tune.'

As Iain lifted the fiddle off its nail, he asked, 'What do you think of Major Grant?'

'Better than most factors. I'll say that for him. He's fair and he's decent – unless you get on his wrong side – then he can be merciless as the old factors who drove the people from the land.'

Iain played a few bars of an old Gaelic song, swelling the long-drawn notes with sadness and heart-longing, then stopped abruptly.

Ewan looked at him.

'My fingers are all wool, after the sheep.' Iain hung up the fiddle on its nail. 'I think I'll get home to bed. I'm pretty tired.'

'Mary should be home soon, and perhaps one or two with her. It's early for bed. Cheer up, man. What's happened to you at all? It's a poor night when we can't have a tune and a song.'

'No. I think I'll be going. They'll be waiting for me at home.'

'Nothing wrong is there, boy?'

'Well, no, but . . . Major Grant . . . my mother went to see him about me.'

'Good lord! – they didn't catch you poaching?'

'No.' Iain smiled wryly. 'Not yet!'

'Phew! Thank goodness! I've told you before, my boy, to watch your step there. He's death on the poacher.'

'That's half the fun.'

'It'll be no fun. Think of the effect on your father, not to mention – your mother.'

Iain met Ewan's eyes. 'She's taking care of that.'

'How?'

'She went to see him. You know the Edinburgh firm of lawyers for the estate?'

'You mean, Mr Cunningham—'

'Yes. Major Grant thinks he can get me a job in the Edinburgh office, if I get my Leaving Certificate.'

'No! Boy, aren't you going to land on your feet! Isn't that the great news!'

'You think so?'

'Of course! Heavens, man, it's the chance of a lifetime. A firm like that will be able to plant you as a factor anywhere. You'll have a job like Major Grant's in your pocket.' Ewan was delighted with the news. He laughed. 'Lord, you'll be raising my rent yet!'

'I'd sooner raise the dead.'

Ewan looked at him. 'What are you glum about?'

'I don't want to go into an office.'

'No? You don't want the moon! Now, Iain, be sensible. You're a bright lad. Given half a chance, you'll make your way in the world. Here's the chance. Take it with both hands and go ahead.'

Iain remained silent, his face moody, intolerant, staring through the door.

'Look, Iain,' continued Ewan reasonably, 'your mother knows. See what she has done for your family. It's a credit and an example to the place. There's nothing here for you – nothing here but struggling away, with damall at the end of it. And if prices go still lower – debt and poverty, and the shame of poverty. You don't understand that yet. You're young. But one day you'll marry; you'll have a family. You'll *know* then.'

'I don't know,' muttered Iain.

'Yes, you'll know all right. Only the bright ones feel the struggle and shame of poverty. Leave the land to the dull minds. There's always plenty of them. They'll take the punishment – and go on taking it.'

'I don't think my father is dull – nor you.'

'Perhaps', answered Ewan slowly, 'that's why we know.'

'You're good enough for me.'

Ewan looked at him. 'You're not frightened of going to this Edinburgh office?'

Iain swung round on him. 'Frightened? Who said I was frightened?'

'I don't mean frightened in that way.'

'What was I going to be frightened of?'

'You know I don't mean—'

'You said it,' muttered Ewan, turning away, 'and my father said it.'

'Hey, wait a minute.' Ewan caught him by the shoulder and pulled him round. 'It isn't like you to be a fool.'

'Oh, it's all right.'

'Now, cool yourself, Iain. Be sensible. Tell me – why don't you want to go?'

'Why should I go?'

'To get on in the world. Take Major Grant—'

'Well, take him. He may have his car and be important on the County Council and have power over us – what's that to me? I want to be with you, with the people who work, who make things and grow things.' There was fire in Iain's voice.

'I know,' said Ewan gently. 'But life does not work out like that.'

'Why not? Why shouldn't it?'

'Because it doesn't. Because the money is not in it.'

'Money! Money isn't everything.'

'I agree. But it's this much: in October your father will take his lambs and his cast ewes to the sheep sales. He will *have* to take the price he is given in the open ring. Prices have been falling – steadily. He can do nothing about it. Just nothing.'

Iain stared moodily through the door. There were footsteps and Mary came in.

'Hullo!' she called brightly. 'What's up?'

'Having an argument,' said her father cheerfully.

'Well, I must be off.' Iain had hardly looked at her, and though he spoke brightly enough, the mood of the argument was deeply upon him.

'Wait a minute, Iain—' began Ewan hospitably.

But Iain was on the move. 'I must be going. Good night.' And he walked out.

Mary glanced at her father, whose face was thoughtful.

'What's wrong?' she asked.

He regarded her in a speculative way. 'Didn't you hear us?'

'I heard – a little.'

He nodded. 'He is being given a first-class chance in Edinburgh – and he doesn't want to take it.'

She was silent for a moment, then removed her eyes from her father's face. 'Why?'

'Because he wants to stay on the land.' With an ironic gleam, a certain bitterness in his chuckle, he turned away.

ELEVEN

As Iain entered the kitchen that night, he found his father and mother sitting before the fire. The lamp had not been lit and the flickering tongues of flame on the peat made the gloom dance.

His mother's face turned to him. 'What's been keeping you, Iain? You must be tired.'

'No. I'm all right.' His voice was level, without colour.

'I'll light the lamp,' she said brightly, now on her feet.

'I'm going to my bed,' he answered.

'Sit down,' she said. 'Your father and I have been talking about you.'

Iain sat down. His father, who had not turned his head, kept on smoking.

His mother's manner was kind and friendly, almost ingratiating. He knew she had been getting things to go her way.

'We've just been talking over what Major Grant said. The more I think of it, the more I am certain it will turn out as he said. For even if there should not be an opening when you get your Leaving Certificate, there's bound to be one sooner or later. There must always be some finishing and some starting in that great office in Edinburgh. It's certain.'

Iain did not answer.

There was silence for a little time.

She turned her face to her son, and in tones troubled and beseeching, asked the question: 'You'll go, Iain, won't you?'

And he answered levelly: 'Yes, I'll go.'

She drew a deep breath that quivered as it was released. 'I knew you would.' She was deeply moved and could hardly hide it.

'I'm a bit foolish sometimes, and not so strong as I was,' she excused herself, though indeed she had not broken down in any way, shown nothing beyond the profound inner stress. 'Now I'll be able to tell Major Grant. Your father and I have settled how it can be done – even if I'm not here. That's everything now – except the one thing: you'll have to get your School Certificate.' She looked at her son. 'You'll do that?'

'I'll try,' he answered.

'You can do no more. Now I'm happy.'

Iain got up.

'Are you going to your bed, then? Look, your lamp is on the dresser.' She went quickly for the lamp and brought it to the fire.

His father lit a paper spill and touched the wick with it. She put on the funnel and he took the lamp from her hand.

'Good night,' he said.

'Good night, Iain. A good sleep to you.'

'Good night,' said his father calmly.

As Iain went out, she stood looking after him.

TWELVE

His school books were scattered over the bare table in his bedroom. The fading summer light came through the small window by Iain's shoulder and picked out some of the titles: *Virgil, English History, Algebra* ... An open book exposed a Euclidean Theorem, diagram and proof on one page and *Deductions* on the other. In front of him lay an *Exercise Book*, its ruled pages innocent of writing. Iain once more pushed a slip of paper in front of his eyes. On it was written: *Give a short account of either* (a) *the English Wars of the Roses or* (b) *Slavery, and Britain's part in its abolition.*

The choice seemed difficult. Iain's brows knitted dourly. For the last month he had been studying with deliberate concentration. Before he had passed his word to his mother that he would go to Edinburgh, he had not greatly cared whether he got his Higher Leaving Certificate or not, had not thought much about it, had been in the mood to do his school work reasonably well and leave the rest to chance or luck. Now his pride was affected almost to a perverse degree. The very fact that deep in him he did not want to go to Edinburgh, and hated more than ever the idea of going because he was driven, made it at the same time absolutely imperative for him to get the Certificate.

His mother knew this. His father knew it. There is a hidden pride of the hills that cannot accept defeat except on its own terms. What would happen in face of defeat, he did not know. None of them knew.

His head lifted and half-turned, listening. From very far away came the sound of a bagpipe playing a march. His mind taut as the silence, he tried to catch it as it swelled thinly, and faded, and finally died away.

He squared himself to his task and, dipping his pen in

the old-fashioned inkpot, wrote the word 'Slavery'. But the light was going. He rubbed his eyes, looked at the window. He had better get the lamp. But he sat still. For now, far away the pipes had started playing a reel. Distance thinned the dancing measure to an exquisite fineness. It stole into his blood, with rhythm of wildness and mirth. The hand that held the pen began just perceptibly, as from a faint but precise pulse, to keep time. The hand shut slowly against the rhythm, the other hand came up and caught the top of the pen-holder, the nib dragged its trail of ink over the written word, and in the fight of the two hands against the rhythm, the pen snapped. The door knob turned and his mother entered, carrying the lighted lamp.

'You'll be straining your eyes,' she said in kindly concern.

His hands fell, covering the broken pen and the paper.

'It's all right,' he answered in that expressionless voice which had become habitual.

She laid the lamp on the table and lingered.

'Are you sure you're not working too hard?'

'No. It's all right,' he muttered, impatience in the movement of his shoulders.

'Perhaps – you would be the better of going out for a little.'

'I don't mind.'

The light showed the hollows in her gaunt face, the burning maternal feeling in her eyes. She withdrew, closing the door quietly.

He looked at the broken pen and the smudged page. He ripped the page from the copy-book and began tearing it up, his face drawn and bitter. His eyes wandered over the books. He got up.

For a little he stood quite still on the middle of the floor, then he screwed down the wick of the lamp and blew out the flame.

As he entered the kitchen, his mother was sitting alone on the small stool before the fire. She straightened her body and turned her face. Something in her loneliness, in her secret illness, caught at his heart.

'You're going out, Iain, after all,' she said, as if pleased.

'Go out for a bit,' he muttered, turning away and taking his cap from the back of the door.

'Maybe it will do you good,' she said. And then, as if suddenly all life was something more than she knew, she murmured to herself and to life, 'I don't know.'

He moved out and closed the door quietly behind him.

THIRTEEN

It was almost dark before he approached the wooden hall where a dance was now in full swing. Song and dance and recitation; a local entertainment or ceilidh to support the funds for the district nurse. He stood back as he saw Major Grant and his wife come through the crowd at the door, get into their car, and drive off, having graced the occasion for a suitable length of time.

'Come on, Iain! Where's your fiddle?' Voices rose at him as he came among the young men about the door.

'At Ewan's,' said Iain, pushing his way slowly through.

'What? Not going to play to-night?'

'We'll see.'

In the hall, the piper had swung from an eightsome to a foursome reel, and now the hot dancers were lining up, were off, threading the maze, curved arms aloft, exuberant young men saluting with a 'hooch!' and setting to a new partner. Alan to Mary, Angus to Anne. He picked up their foursome at once. Alan had oiled his dark hair; it was gleaming. He danced correctly, with a studied grace, and Mary danced before him, danced lightly, and caught his arm as they came to the swing. No attempt to swing her wildly, but, on the contrary, and at the proper time, withdrew his arm, clapped his hands once, and began the swing the reverse way. Then they were threading the maze again, and now Angus set to Mary and danced before her and she before him, and when they came to the swing, Angus crooked Mary's arm firmly and swung as if life and love were more than elegance. Mary's laughter was shaken like her hair. The dance over, Angus saw her to the long seat where the women sat, and made his little bow, and turned, wiping his neck, towards the cool entrance door along with the other men.

Iain at once began to back away. An instinct not to get caught gripped him like a secret hand. Then a hand did grip him, an eye winked, and a head gave a slight backward nod. Iain followed Hamish MacPherson round the corner of the hall.

'Going in?' asked Hamish, a strong dark fellow in his early thirties.

'Don't think so.'

'Fine! Listen.' He looked about him and whispered, 'I saw three fish this morning in the Rock Pool.'

'Thinking of calling on the factor?'

'It's two hundred yards below the factor's house, as you know. You saw him leave in the car for his bed. Finlay, the keeper, is in there dancing. The thing is safe as a church.'

Iain stood still, hesitating. He was terribly tempted. The wildness and danger of the night. They cried to him.

'It's what you need, to clean your blood.'

'I don't know,' muttered Iain.

'Lord, think of it – the whole river to ourselves! And what a night!' The suppressed glee, the excitement, reached into the night, raced into it, had a laughing strength of mockery and delight.

A woman's voice began singing the Eriskay love song in the hall.

'I'll pass the tip to Hughie,' whispered Hamish. 'After the next dance. We'll meet at the Cairn.'

The singing voice caught the ear of the night and the two men found themselves listening, held by something coming out of their own land, their own tradition, out of the river of their own blood.

'She can sing, can Mary,' said Hamish, the listening smile on his face, his voice at once tender and appreciative.

Iain did not speak. He could see Mary, singing from where she sat on her seat, simply, naturally. Everyone was listening inside, all the faces; out here the walls were still, the grey dyke, the dun bushes lower down, the night and the spaces of the night.

'You'll come?' whispered Hamish.

'Yes.'

'I'll slip off. Better not be seen together.'

Quietly Hamish moved round to the entrance. Amid the tumult of applause, he slid his way in beside Hughie, a crofter's son, who did occasional work on the estate and was sought after in the stalking season by sportsmen who knew something about the hill.

Even now, when Hamish gripped his elbow his reaction was characteristic. He side-kicked Hamish and paid no attention to him. At once Hamish began looking around inside the hall, moving his hand from Hughie's elbow to another man's shoulder as if to get a better view. 'Take your partners for the Barn Dance!' sang out the M.C.

As the men crowded forward, laughing and chattering, Hamish dropped five words into Hughie's ear, and then swept on for his partner.

FOURTEEN

Iain waited for them at the Cairn.

First Hughie came: 'What a night!' subdued excitement and love of the night in his voice.

'Where's Hamish?'

'I thought he would have been here.' Hughie chuckled. 'Finlay is keeping an eye open.'

'What makes you think that?'

'I smelt it. Hamish is quick, too! He came in through the door and caught my arm. I gave him a side kick. He never even looked at me. He felt at once that Finlay was near. So he started blindly shoving me aside to get onto the floor!'

'Was Finlay near?'

'Yes. At our backs.'

They were talking in undertones. A voice said, 'What are you shouting about?' Hamish stood beside them with a sack on his back. 'Come on, while the going's good!' He spoke with confidence, with a jaunty delight. A whiff of whisky came from his breath.

'You've been drinking,' said Hughie.

Hamish laughed softly upon the night. 'Dan-the-trapper asked me out to have one – just when I was wondering how I could get clear. He's now finishing the bottle with Jimmy Macdonald in Andrew's barn. Come on.'

They set off for the river, going single file. A milky haze was over the sky and here and there a star shone faintly. Hamish set a smart pace, for it was not very dark, as though a slim moon had risen somewhere, or an afterglow from the summer's day still dwelt in the high air. A clean, fresh night, with now and then a tang of scent that went straight into the blood.

A peewit swung up, crying. Hamish stopped and cursed

it with a soft intensity. As they stood, they heard the noises of living things, and the earth itself was not asleep but lying quietly, with all her secret brood alive. Even the bushes in their sleep seemed watchful and hid under their skirts sudden scurryings and rustlings. A tiny stream sang, the song that haunts the mind and won't stop. Iain's eyes were moving about him, his hearing drawn fine as a bat's cry.

The river was near when Hamish stopped.

'You go straight on with the bag,' he said, 'and I'll go up and round by the bridge. You'll find the coil of string on top, tied to the net's back line. Wait till you hear me whistle. Fix a stone to the string and heave it over. Right?'

'Right,' said Hughie, and Hamish disappeared.

Iain and Hughie came by the pool and, after much hearkening and careful scouting around, they settled.

'Not a soul in the world!' said Hughie, feeling for the coil of string.

'Wait a bit,' said Iain. 'Plenty of time.'

Hughie laughed and forbore hauling the net out of the bag. Iain was trying to get his ears used to the sound of the water as it rumbled over boulders into the pool, so that they could readily pick up a new sound.

'Hearing things?' asked Hughie with sly but friendly humour.

'No,' answered Iain.

'Queer, all the same, the things you do hear when you listen.'

'On a stunt like this, you come alive.'

'I suppose that's it.'

'As if you didn't know!'

They smiled in friendship, in warm adventure.

'It's good, this,' said Iain, confidence coming around him as his senses tuned themselves to the moment and to the night.

'Nothing better,' agreed Hughie. 'I wouldn't swop a night like this for a king's ransom.'

'If we're caught – you'll have to swop it for much less!'

'I'd have to clear out. And my parents depending on me!'

'And if Finlay even whispered to Major Grant that I was suspected – oh lord!'

They laughed softly, but still hearkening, vividly aware of movement and sound and silence.

'And you can't even take a bit of salmon home with you,' said Hughie.

'I know. It's pure madness,' said Iain.

'Danger.'

'Yes – and more.' Iain peered around him, his eyes going from one shape to another, to the pool, lifting to the sky, while his fingers of their own accord felt round the ledge of rock like a blind man's feeling a face.

Hughie's fingers had found a stone under the water, in shape like a big matchbox, and were now tying an end of the stout string round it.

A whistle came across the pool and they went into action. Hughie got the coil of string ready, stood up, whistled, and heaved the stone so that it would pass over the dim figure on the opposite bank. Presently he felt a jerk on the line and said, 'He's got it.' Iain picked up the net and they started moving down the ledge of rock to where the pool, broadening slightly, grew fairly still. On their knees, with great care, they paid out the net as Hamish hauled from the other side.

Like small dark otter heads the corks went across the pool, like living things with their arrows of water. Sometimes Hughie stood upright, lifting the net against the sky to clear a ravelling and ensure that the rounded lead sinkers would draw the net to its natural wall. At last a jerk came along the back line. The net had reached the other bank, the river was spanned.

The moment of all moments had come, and suspense squatted in its own hollow. Each of them had a hand on the back line, waiting for the swimming salmon to hit the net. The surge of the river came from the pool's throat, rose into the still night, and their listening pierced it, hearkening for other sounds in between it and beyond it, but hardly consciously, for the stream of their instincts ran into their hands, ran so finely, so expectantly, that breathing itself was all but suspended between their open lips.

This was the moment of ecstasy before the act. This is what they always remembered as the state of delight and of freedom, for at this point a million hunting years distilled their drop of pure being.

When expectancy could draw itself no finer, the signal came to their hands. Small tugs at the back line – tug-tug – tug-tug – and they felt the fish nosing into the net, knew the shape of the fish, saw it with an inner eye and eased the back line a little, and then the pool's face was riven as the silver body rose above the surface and thrashed within the' loose light meshes of the net.

Carefully but firmly they drew in the net, for the salmon had meshed near their bank, and now the thrashing white body was on the pool's edge, was drawn clear, and they fell on it. A sharp rap on the dark nape, and Iain pulled away the fish, gleaming against the sky's light. They had their moment of adoration, then he went up over the bank with it.

Confidence now rose like laughter. They were freed – the deed done – and nothing had come at them out of the night.

'Fifteen pounds,' called Hughie across the pool in an almost open voice.

'Good lads!'

And the net was being drawn away again, drawn back by Hamish whose voice had echoed their gaiety.

Once more the net was set and they crouched on their heels by the water's edge, waiting. But expectancy has lost its first tension, and now, having sunk deep into the mood of the night, they chuckle at quick, small jokes, at words thrown like pebbles, at a picture of Finlay, the gamekeeper, leading his partner to the dance. Because they love the night so much, they feel friendly to Finlay, to those having authority, to everyone, for have they not stepped beyond *that* world into *this*?

So subtle with mystery and wonder is their mirth that presently it knows why the pool has gone dead. The wise fish have seen or felt, have become aware of dark danger, and are keeping their distance from its otter's teeth.

'I'll go and stone the top of the pool,' spoke Hughie. He had hardly finished when the voice from the other side called, 'Stone it.'

'Great minds think alike,' murmured Iain, squatting now squarely and taking the back line between both hands.

'I'll shift them!' declared Hughie.

Iain laughed softly.

Hughie stepped lightly on to the rock ledge which swept up towards the throat of the pool. It was a narrow ledge some two feet above water with wide cracks and crannies in the rock wall that rose behind it eight to ten feet.

He had taken three or four paces along this ledge when an extraordinary thing happened to him. His body sidestepped into a cavity in the rock wall and stood there keyed to a quivering pitch. It was not that he had consciously heard or seen anything. 'Suddenly I felt something coming,' was the only way he could explain his action afterwards. For, as he added, 'If I had seen or heard anything, naturally I would have given the signal.'

A figure was suddenly there between him and the pool. The figure stopped. He could have touched it with his hand. Then he smelt it, smelt tobacco from its tweeds, and in an instant knew, from the smell and the shape of the head, of the cap, that it was Major Grant.

Slowly the head moved and peered along the margin of the pool. At that moment, Iain must have moved, for above the noise of the tumbling water rose a distinct crushing and crunching of small stones, giving his exact position away.

Major Grant took one wary step forward, stooping slightly – a second step – an arm began to go up, with something in its hand – light-coloured metal – and Hughie realised, as if it had already happened, that an electric torch was about to flash fatally on Iain.

Quicker than his thought, Hughie charged the body. Major Grant half turned to get a hold, and the electric torch shot from his hand. It described an arc and landed against Iain's neck, bounced off, and struck through his hands to the ground. Full-length, Major Grant pitched into the pool. As his body hit the water, he let out a terrific yell.

Iain grabbed the torch like a weapon. But he did not move at once. Crouching, ready to jump, he waited the onrush of his enemies. A voice was now yelling from the other side: 'Stand! I'm seeing you! I know you!' It was the voice of Finlay the keeper.

Iain leapt onto the ledge, but now the voice in the pool was making weird and drowning sounds. All at once it choked and went under.

A wild fear touched Iain. A swift look around and he pushed forward the catch of the torch. Its beam struck the water, travelled, caught a white face rolling in the salmon net and realised it belonged to Major Grant. The face rose spluttering and gurgling, then dipped under as the meshed arms and body wriggled futilely. In his dive from the ledge, Major Grant had hit the wall of the loose net and brought it up about him. The man was drowning.

Iain leapt back onto the pocket of shingle and, dropping the lit torch, began hauling on the back line. Swiftly he drew in the heavy body to his feet, dragged it clear of water and the folds of the net.

The body squirmed slowly and lay still. Iain caught it under the arm-pits and was heaving it up when it began to retch and vomit. Instinctively he dropped it again to make the retching easier.

There was no desire in him now to fly, to escape. Only one wild desire, and that was to drag the body away from the pool. He got his grip, and was about to heave when a fierce yelling stopped him.

The keeper was crossing the river, wading across the tail of the pool. Iain recovered the torch and swept its beam on him.

'I'm coming!' yelled Finlay.

And all in a desperate moment Iain realised that the gamekeeper was, in fact, coming. He laid the torch on the ground, so that its beam shone on Major Grant's head and shoulders, leapt onto the ledge and ran along it out of sight.

FIFTEEN

Stealthily he approached the lighted window. A violin was playing *Mairi Bhan* in the light dancing time that Iain had made his own. The music ceased, and as the violin started again on long, sweeping notes, Iain tapped on the pane.

At once there was silence. Ewan could be heard coming to the door, where he stood peering into the dark.

'It's me. Anybody in?'

'You! What on earth? . . . there's nobody in. Anything wrong?' Ewan caught Iain by the arm. 'Why, you're wet!'

'Hush!'

In the lamplight, Ewan looked at him.

'The river,' explained Iain, feeling his arms with a strained smile.

'What happened?'

'We were caught—'

'Do you mean you were caught by Finlay?'

'And Major Grant.'

Ewan's mouth opened as he stared at Iain.

'They came on us,' explained Iain. 'Major Grant – he was thrown into the river.'

'Good God! Boy, are you mad? This bursts everything. You mean – they saw you – they—'

'I don't know,' said Iain. 'We were poaching the Rock Pool with a net—'

'Who?'

'Three of us. We had landed a fish. The next I knew – a man's body went splash into the pool and an electric torch hit me in the neck.'

'Was it shining?'

'No.'

'Then?'

'Then I heard him drowning. I switched on the torch. He was caught in the net.'

'You mean Major Grant?'

'Yes. I hauled him and the net in. He lay. Then I heard Finlay – he was on the other side – coming across the tail of the pool – shouting. I left the lighted torch by the Major's head – and cleared off.'

'Cleared off?'

'Yes. After a time, I thought I'd creep back. But I heard Finlay's voice. He was with the Major.'

'Did you hear the Major speak?'

'No. But I felt Finlay was speaking to a living man.'

'Let us hope to God he was! Why on earth did your pal heave the Major into the river?'

'I think – to save me.'

Ewan was lost in wild thought, staring into Iain's face. 'Do you think *you* were seen or known?'

'Don't know.'

'Then you'll come with me this instant. You've been here with me to-night, you understand? Take that fiddle. You'll play.' Ewan stuck his cap on. 'Come on.'

'But—'

'Dammit, man, have you no sense? Don't you know that this may mean a trial for murder? Do you want to kill your mother, too? Have you just no dam' glimmering of sense in you at all?'

'Don't want to go,' muttered Iain, reacting dourly against Ewan's mood, for he had never seen him like this before.

'No?' Ewan's sarcasm was sharp as a knife. 'You feel you would rather not?'

Iain turned for the door.

Ewan caught him by the shoulder and swung him round. 'What's wrong with you?'

'Nothing.'

'Thinking only of yourself?'

'No. There's the other two.'

Ewan's mood swiftly changed. 'Forgive me, Iain. The thing angered me. God knows whether we can do anything about

it or not. But this is the only way for you. They'll find *their*
way. Trust them.' He felt Iain's arms and breast. 'You're not
very wet and it doesn't show. Come on.' He screwed down
and blew out the lamp-flame.

By the time they were approaching the hall, Ewan was
making bright talk. There was the usual bunch of young
fellows cooling off before the door.

'Hullo, Iain – where have *you* been?'

'He came over for the fiddle – and make way for it, for
if you harm that fiddle it will be the end of you,' declared
Ewan.

Amid the laughter and back-chat, the M.C. appeared,
craning his neck. 'Thank goodness!' he called. 'They're
wanting a Petronella, Iain. Come on.'

'Righto!' said Iain.

'Partners for a Petronella!'

Through the rush for partners, Iain threaded his way to
the platform. As he tuned the strings, he cast an eye over
the dancers. Alan was piloting Mary. Angus came in a rush
with Anne. The two lines strung down the floor, men facing
women.

'Right!' called the M.C., and off went the tune and the
dancers.

Though his time seemed slow to him and the violin unre-
sponsive in a hard, wooden way, Iain knew he was playing
correctly, knew his time was right and each note clear. As
he looked down the instrument to his dancing fingers, he
presently experienced a strange satisfaction in this mathe-
matical playing. What was wrong with the usual country
player was a tendency to slur the notes and scrape the gut,
to care nothing for a continuous precision and clarity, so
long as the dance-beat was given forth with the rhythm of
a hammer. Imperceptibly, with a perverse exactitude, Iain
slowed the time, making the dancers move with greater care,
with less abandon, forcing them to give whatever grace – or
lack of it – was in them, for the dance itself, like most of
the old country dances, had grace and pattern, a social
pattern, and the need for courtesy.

Then the lids of his eyes lifted slightly and he looked down the hall. Alan was doing the superior courtier. And Mary danced before him, at each cardinal point of the compass, until they had completed the circle and, taking hands, went down the room and back.

Iain shifted his eyes – and his fingers tripped, the notes went wrong, but his bow kept the beat, the beat, and now his fingers were flying again and a wave of heat was coming up over his body. For there was Hughie, with the sword-dancer's grace, the sway and the rhythm, the feet that touch lightly, oh, the incomparable grace, inborn and alive, and trained over the steel blades. The wave of heat, of inspiration, went up into Iain's fingers, into his bow, into the fiddle, and the dancers heard, and some faces turned, and Hughie executed an intricate Highland fling step before taking his partner's hand and dancing her down the floor.

Ewan, at the door, let out a deep breath.

'He's all right now,' said a voice by his ear.

Ewan turned and looked into Hamish's eyes.

Hamish nodded. 'Sometimes Iain plays all right. Other times – he plays well.' His voice had the deliberation of a drunk man conscious of his sober wisdom.

A merry, dark fellow laughed. 'You've been drinking, Hamish.'

Hamish turned slowly and looked at him. 'Me drinking? Where was I drinking?'

'I wish I knew!'

'Too late, my boy.' Smiling with slow good nature, he turned to Ewan again. 'Going to dance, Ewan?'

'Are you?'

'Yes.' Hamish nodded. 'You and me – we'll give them an exhib-ishon dance.'

'That's the stuff!' said the merry fellow. 'Wait till we get the M.C.'

'You know I never dance,' said Ewan.

'You're never too young to start as the girl said to her mother.'

'You come home with me,' said Ewan, 'and I'll get my

dancing pumps on. We'll have a cup of tea – and then we'll show them a step or two.'

'Why the cup of tea?'

'Because it's all I've got.'

Hamish nodded judicially. 'That's fair. You make it a bargain?'

'I do.'

They shook hands.

Sallies followed them through the door, but Hamish was now talking in what was meant to be confidential tones. 'I – I have had a drop. First – there was Dan-the-trapper. He – he had a bottle. Then – but listen, and I'll tell you the whole trouble about drinking.' He paused, his back towards the dark wall of the hall, against which Ewan saw the black shadow of a solitary figure. 'Never,' continued Hamish weightily, 'drink whisky out of a bottle. There's only one thing worse.'

'What's that?'

'Drinking it out of two bottles.' He lurched on with a laugh.

Ewan caught up with him and took his arm. 'You must have been drinking all night to have such a skinful.'

Hamish paused. 'All night? The night hasn't started yet.' He turned as if to make back to the hall, but Ewan firmly led him on.

'Oh, all right, all right,' muttered Hamish, 'I'm coming.'

They went on in silence for a bit.

'Trouble about you, Ewan,' said Hamish, 'is that you haven't got the sporting instinct.'

'The what?' asked Ewan suspiciously.

'The sporting instinct. You can only think of tea. Tea!' He laughed. 'High heaven, it was a good night!' He rolled on.

'Where have you been?' asked Ewan in a low, sharp voice.

'Drinking,' said Hamish, in the same hilarious tones. 'I'm drunk. And it's a good man who knows when he's drunk.' He paused and looked up at the stars, but Ewan had the feeling he was listening. 'What about a smoke?' He fumbled in his pockets.

'Wait till we get home.'

'Right.' And off he went again. But before turning down to Ewan's cottage, he appeared to slip – and lay with his ear to the road.

'Get up,' said Ewan.

Hamish got up with a grunt, and at the door, in a low, clear, sober voice, full of suppressed mirth, said, 'That was Finlay standing by the hall.'

Without a word, Ewan took him into the kitchen and screwed up the lamp. Hamish's eyes shone in the light. They turned on Ewan. 'Would you like a cut of salmon?'

Ewan stared at him.

'It's all right,' said Hamish. 'I saw you take Iain to the hall. Don't worry. Finlay was so busy helping the Major home that he had to leave the net and the salmon behind him for the time being. So I thought I'd save him all bother. I dumped the bag under the hay in your barn.'

Ewan sat down. 'Listen Hamish: this is going too far. I don't mind what happens to you – or to me – but when it comes to a lad like Iain, then I draw the line. Dammit all, don't you know that his mother wants him out of this, that Major Grant has promised her to get him a job in the estate's legal offices in Edinburgh? The chance of his lifetime – and you would wreck it – perhaps have wrecked it. And very nearly committed murder.'

'Nearly – but not quite.' Hamish's eyes glittered. 'So Iain is being pushed off, too! They all go. All the lads of spirit.' He laughed.

'It's no laughing matter.'

'I agree.'

'I don't mind a bit of sport, but—'

'What sport? When you talk of sport, folk think of fishing salmon, shooting grouse, or stalking deer. Can you, or me, or Iain, fish or shoot or stalk? You know we can't. Yet we have been here all our lives, and our people before us for generations. This is supposed to be our land – yet if we try for one fish in our native river, we're for it!'

'I'm not talking of the right or wrong of it—'

'Well, I am. I don't grudge the wealthy their sport. All we ask, those of us who work the land and rear sheep and cattle, is our share. Do we get it? When we try they hunt us like criminals, like dogs.'

'I know. But that's the law, the law of the land, and if—'

'And if I'm caught, I'll pay. Do you think I don't know?'

'I was thinking of the boy,' said Ewan in a quieter voice.

'Do you think I'm not thinking of him?'

Ewan got up and stuck the kettle in the fire. As he limped to the dresser for cups, he said, 'There's no need for words between us, Hamish.' But Hamish had turned to the door, moving with the quietness of a cat. Ewan stood still, listening. He heard the door open. No sounds came from outside. Then Hamish returned.

'We were speaking a bit loud,' he said. 'And Finlay is out for any scrap of evidence he can find.' He smiled satirically.

'Do you think he has any?'

'The only evidence for a court is the net and the salmon. It was too dark to identify anybody. He has no case – and knows it. He has sworn he'll get me. This night won't make him any less keen.' Hamish chuckled softly to himself.

Ewan was inwardly profoundly relieved, but as he put two cups on the table, he asked, 'For all you get out of it, do you think it's worth it?'

'What do you think I get out of it?' Hamish, who had sat down, looked at Ewan with his dark, smiling, penetrating eyes.

'For the sake of a bit of salmon—'

'I don't care much for salmon, as it happens, and I never sold a bit in my life.'

'I know. You give it away – as a treat to an old woman – or a poor fellow like myself. But – is it worth it? I mean—'

'You mean you're still thinking of Iain. Now listen to me, Ewan. Why do I do it? Why does Iain do it? Because it's the only sport they have left us. It's adventure. Out there the night comes alive about you. Your blood comes alive. All your senses grow sharp as pine needles. It's a glory just to be living. You're on your toes. You could walk – you could walk on the river water!' He leaned back, realising the impossibility of telling anyone how he felt, and smiled through narrowing, watchful eyes.

Ewan poured water into the teapot and set it to toast by the fire. Hamish hearkened to the night outside.

'You like it strong?' asked Ewan as he poured the tea.

'Strong and scalding hot,' said Hamish.

'The hillman's drink.'

'Better than whisky, Ewan – most times.' He blew on the tea and took a mouthful. It was certainly hot. 'Boy, that's good!'

'Drink up, then. There's a whole pot here.'

Hamish lifted a face of glimmering humour. 'You're upset a bit, Ewan – and that's not like you.'

'Well, I was upset. Iain has come round about here since he could toddle. I know what you mean, Hamish – but it's no use.'

'Don't think that I'll try to keep the lad from going away. I'll egg him on. There's nothing for a bright lad here. The women know that. And the men grow silent – like Iain's father.'

'That time he lost three hundred sheep in the snow – it crippled him.'

'And finished her,' said Hamish. 'My god, a woman can get a hatred of the struggle!' He chuckled harshly.

'Iain does not want to go,' said Ewan simply. 'But – he does not understand life yet. He'll make his way. Then he'll understand his mother – and those of us who did not stand in his way.'

'You think so?' Hamish, his elbows on the table, his head sunk between his shoulders, looked across at Ewan.

'Yes,' answered Ewan.

'You're an older man than me, Ewan, but I have been away. Listen. If you think that Iain will forget the land, the sheep, his father slaving here alone, the river, a night like this night, his fiddle-playing with you, our old songs and

Mary singing them – if you think he will forget that, and be glad to forget it, because he has become a clerk, a legal man in an office – you're wrong, wrong right in to where the marrow crawls in the bone.' Hamish stared at Ewan, then drank off his tea, shoved his chair back abruptly and got up. 'It's time we got back to the hall. Come on.'

The story of Major Grant's narrow escape from death created a great stir in the district. Something unlawful and desperate about the event lay upon thought like a drowned body.

Mothers cautioned their children or spoke in such a way in their hearing that an air of horror rose from the Rock Pool. They were told never to go near the river, so after school two or three boys would steal by hidden ways to look at the poacher's ledge, to walk upon it, and even to peer into the water, until suddenly they felt that the air was listening and the grey rock behind watching, whereupon they would walk away unhurriedly, as though the whole place had nothing to do with them, then take to their heels.

By his friends, Iain was never even suspected. It was taken for granted that between his first appearance in the hall, when he had been asked to fetch his fiddle, and his second appearance with the fiddle and Ewan, he had been in Ewan's house. For he was in that house of an evening more often than in his own, and Ewan was his friend. Weren't they at the music, whenever they got the chance, work or no work?

Ewan put it like this: 'Iain and I were playing away here. He told me when he came in that they had asked him to bring his fiddle, so after a time I thought we had better put in an appearance. I don't usually go, for dancing is not in my line. However, this dance was for the local nursing funds, so I went. It was while I stood looking on at the dance that Hamish spoke to me. Now I wouldn't say that Hamish was drunk. He might have had a good shot in him, but he could walk. But what I don't believe is this – that Hamish could have poached a pool in that condition and got away with it. I just don't believe it. To believe it is to make a fool of Finlay – and Finlay, on river or hill, is no fool.'

Hamish was helped by others and without any asking on his part. Dan-the-trapper may have had no very clear idea of exactly how long Hamish had been in his company, but he asserted it was 'a long time'. When pressed, he was prepared to admit it might well have been hours.

'What's an hour, or three hours, even to a man dancing?' asked Dan.

Iain's mother postponed her call on Major Grant for nearly a fortnight.

'I did not want to trouble you sooner,' she said reticently.

'That's all right. I'm still here.' He smiled in his dry, distant way.

'We were more than sorry to hear about it. It was a great shock to the place.'

'The place manages to keep its secret pretty well.'

'No one seems to know,' she stammered.

'And those who do won't tell.'

'It's getting – like that.'

'Getting?' He smiled, picked up the flat ivory paper-cutter, and looked across at her. 'I don't suppose *you* know?'

Her eyes opened. 'Me? No. Surely you don't think I know?'

'No. I don't think so.' His eyes dropped for a moment and lifted again. 'Supposing you did know, would you tell me?'

Distress came into her face. Her fingers moved nervously on her lap. 'That's a hard question.'

'You're an honest woman, Mrs Cattanach. There are, however, some bad elements in this place. But I'll catch them yet – whatever it costs. I'll root them out.' His voice was very clear, very incisive. 'I wouldn't even say that I won't yet be able to prove who were in this business. It will be a nasty day for them when I do.'

'It was a dreadful, dreadful business.' Her voice was low.

'However,' and he leaned back, 'that's my affair.' His tone became more normal. 'Well, I suppose you have come to see me about Iain?'

'Yes, Major. We have been thinking over it. Indeed, there was no thinking to do. We are just overcome at the thought of your help. If you could do what you said, my husband and myself would be more than indebted to you always.'

'And Iain?'

'He is now studying harder than ever before.'

'I see . . . Well, Mrs Cattanach, I'll write Mr Cunningham. I'll tell him the position. I'll explain that the examination is some months ahead yet. In an office that size, the more time the better.'

'I don't know how to thank you.'

'That's all right. As I said before, your husband is one of our best tenants – a man who always pays his dues and knows how to keep his own place. We want more of that kind, and I'm only sorry that there isn't a son like him to follow him.'

'I – I am sorry, too, Major,' she said haltingly, 'but – I am only trying to do my best by my own.'

He smiled drily. 'And the best isn't here?' He shoved the blotting pad from him slowly. 'Very well.'

She got up.

'I'll let you know when I hear from Edinburgh.'

She hesitated.

'You can take it,' he said, 'I'll do my best for him.'

She flushed slightly. 'Thank you. He's my son.'

'I understand. Good morning.'

They shook hands and she went.

SEVENTEEN

The winter that followed produced for Iain some rare memories.

If Major Grant's face in the net came gaping through a dream, in the daylight it served but to quicken his senses, or quicken in particular a sort of visionary apprehension of natural things about him. Sometimes there was the taint of guilt. This darkened his sight for a moment, giving to the shape of a bush, the face of a pool, a waiting criminal air. But the quickened senses only rose all the higher for the check. At the back of everything, he *had* saved Major Grant's life. And if he was ashamed to admit it openly to himself, still – there had been that loveliness in pure chance! A gift, from pure chance, of freedom. It helped to still the early tumult over going away, gave at moments a fine detachment to the mood of acceptance.

Then one day, while he was in school at Kinmore, Major Grant called in person on his parents with a letter from Mr Cunningham intimating that there would be an opening in his office next year which would be reserved for Iain. Whether he manages to take a college degree or not, said Major Grant, he will get a job from that office. Mr Cunningham says that the more local factors there are who have a real knowledge of a tenant's needs, the better it will be for everyone. The present times require more than ever a new harmony between landlord and tenant. If Iain proved the right kind of lad for the work, he might, in the special circumstances, be helped by a weekly wage beyond what was customary in the matter of apprentices. Mr Cunningham had remembered Iain personally.

This news had a marked effect on Mrs Cattanach. It quietened her. For days she moved about as if she had come through some profound ordeal and was now able to look on the world with clear eyes. Her voice lost its harsh, strident note. Smouldering discontent, sharp angers, left her. Sometimes she stood quite still, but plainly she was not thinking or planning, for all of a sudden, with a sigh or a surprised look, she would 'come to herself'.

Her health seemed to improve also, as though the core of her internal trouble had been a misery which she had had to grip with her bony hand. Now if her thin forearm and hand came across her body, the pressure was more gentle, as if applied against the quiet surge of an emotion rather than a bodily ill.

Cattanach himself, too, was caught up in this acceptance, and there came upon the whole house a quietude that was not unpleasant. It was not a complete relief, a conscious and happy ease, because it had the air of an interlude, of an oasis reached – perhaps the last oasis. Man comes to the time when all is shorn from him, everything, including the burden.

Iain spoke more naturally to his mother, actually volunteered the information that he had done better in his last quarterly exams, than ever before. But it was out-of-doors that he came to himself and all unconsciously stored memories which had little to do with human relationships but which, when they recurred, were sharp and clear as the pattern of frost.

The Christmas holiday was the window which remained open on that time. The weather was brilliant and the small streams as they ran down to the river kicked up drops which froze into slender icicles. In the morning the grass, crisp and full of sparkles, gave under his feet with a brittle hiss-hiss. When he looked back he saw his footsteps coming to him.

Round about ran the imprints of other living things, crisscrossing bare-cropped green mounds, disappearing into rabbit-holes, vanishing under low bushes. Here where many rabbits' feet had beaten a path through the skin of frost, a faint purple shone from the path itself, a colour seen in the western sky when the sun has sunk and the very chill of the evening foretells, through the colour, another day of sun and frost.

A harsh scurry, a yelp – the young dog Mat was off, and Iain's heart gave the hunter's beat.

Swift the eyes then, sharp the breath in the nostrils, instantaneous and sure the feet. And when movement vanished, the listening ear searched and followed like another kind of sight.

His home was settled in this landscape, fixed. The hoof-marked mud around the outhouses was frozen. What had been sodden and dreary was firm and healthy. The cock, vastly astonished, skated on a grey film of ice. When his mother came out with the tin dish to feed the fowls, they flapped their wings to help their slithering toes. And the slanting sun hit them with its thin fine light.

Inside the byre, the air was warm from the breath of the two cows. As they mooed and turned their heads, their eyes shone expectant, waiting for the armful of hay or straw, or, with noisy breaths and restless feet, for the more eagerly desired sliced turnips. Their mouths slavered.

'Stand over!' And Iain slapped a flank, his fingers tingling from the ice-cold yellow turnips which he had chopped in the cutter.

Pleasant thus to feed the brutes, the cows he knew, whose milk he had drunk for years, whose calves had sucked his hand, whose names came naturally to his lips as any girl's. Gruff his voice telling them to stand over, rough and friendly

'Couldn't you feel she was at your feet, ye old fool?' he addressed Jess when the kitten was seen going about on three legs. Kittens liked Jess, but she had an awkward habit of standing on their toes.

In the stone-walled field near the house grew the crops: potatoes, oats, turnips, and beyond the cultivated ground a slow-rolling area of bog hay.

All that was grown here was entirely for home use. Milk, butter, eggs, oatmeal, and a frosted swedish turnip for the table. The rest was for the stock, and all cash came from the sale of the stock, including wool, and an occasional sheep skin.

It was a straightforward economy, simple in its outline, yet forever complicated by hazard or chance. Weather was the great unknown. A bad growing season and the corn might hardly be worth cutting; a wet harvest, and much of the hay might blacken and rot. But taking season by season, and the eager hand that did not miss the good day, the corn was cut and gathered, and the hay built into stacks, those stacks that were more precious than all other feeding. For when the snow came heavily upon the mountains, when one day it came down into the valleys covering heather and grass with its white sheet, then the Blackface sheep, hardy scroungers as they were, could not find enough to live on and had to be fed the soft bog hay.

A stormy winter was hard on the sheep. A cold, wet lambing season had its deaths. The struggle against nature was difficult enough, but the good farmer who knew his beasts and could smell the weather could out-fight nature in the long run. Against prices which hit him below subsistence level, however, he had no way of fighting and had to take the blow as it was arbitrarily given.

A complicated life, which a man had to carry on his two feet, ready to outwit the adverse chance, capable of hanging on against superior force, ert or inert, active or drearily wearing. When the blow could not be avoided, it was taken. The man went on again.

The hill farm carried about five hundred ewes, the normal hirsel for one shepherd. Iain remembered when his father also carried another hirsel on the grazing of Torglas, lower down on the west side. A hired shepherd looked after it, and in the February of the sudden great snowstorm, when a man could hardly breathe in the fineness of the driven flakes, had lost over three hundred sheep, smothered under the snow, smothered and never found until the dykes were emptied in the thaw and the dead sheep were seen to have been eating their wool.

He had given up Torglas after that, in the need to cut his losses and realise some ready cash; for James, Iain's brother was at Edinburgh University studying medicine, and his mother had been scheming to send William there also. In this she failed.

It had been a bad and difficult time with scenes of bitterness that pierced like rusty nails, but in the end Cattanach, in debt, had settled down to his one-hirsel farm which he shepherded himself, getting and giving help, and paying for labour when he had to. In a sense this suited his character better, for he came from the old native economy, where each man ran his own croft or sheep, helped by the family. It was not fundamentally in him to own many places and have them run by others. Life to him meant having beasts and crops under his own eyes and hands, working with them, knowing them, and being responsible for them.

Still, he had stepped down in terms of money and all worldly reckoning. There was that in his history. Though yet again, and in all the circumstances (he had been unfortunate in his shepherd, a good man without the true hill sense) he carried a distinction among the many who were worse off in the countryside.

In his sixty-fourth year, he moved about the steading or on the hill with a certain deliberation, a lack of haste, that, continuously observed, was curiously impressive. For Iain did not feel that the deliberation had its root in age, or was even deliberate, but rather that it was a final steadying of the whole man, and in this Christmas weather, as they found themselves out together in the frosted air, with the hill-tops white and bright, the hay dry and warm to the touch and mustily fragrant, he would now and then have a consciousness of friendliness to his father, of a delight in helping him, steadied in a wordless responsible way by his father's steadiness.

Then again, there was no exhausting this feeling, for it had to do with a constantly increasing knowledge. Iain would see his father looking at a sheep, and would know that his father knew this sheep, knew it with the understanding but objective regard a doctor has for his patient. And just as a doctor knows all his patients and sees how different they are one from another in appearance and illness, so did his father know his sheep. He did not require to search for some distinguishing mark; he knew them by appearance, individually.

'I don't know, boy, but I'm afraid she's going that way.' The quiet voice seemed to be speaking to itself as much as to Iain, but the eyes were keen, watching every movement of the ewe, detecting something half-hearted in the nosing of the hay, until Iain himself, by a subtle sympathy, realised that the sheep was in truth going 'that way', that presently it would not turn up but would wander by itself to some lonely spot, and would stay there, standing, until it could no longer stand, and, lying, would slowly die.

Sometimes his father would illustrate information with stories, reminiscences, in so simple a manner that it became vivid and memorable. For example, when he had once asked him about the sheep disease called *braxy*, his father not only told him about it, its varying and often terrible incidence, how sheep left perfectly well in the evening would be found dead in the morning, but gave the names of farms and shepherds, adding his own notions, from specific experience, of the causes of the disease itself, contrasting braxy in the old days with braxy to-day and defining a difference in terms of the stench left on the hands from the skinning of the dead sheep. Folk ate braxy mutton in the old days though they didn't now. He described how the sheep was disembowelled and the part that had been lying on the ground cut away, and Iain realised how lucky the shepherd was who found the dead sheep still warm, for that made the drawing away of the blood easy. There followed a final picture of a shepherd's house, with braxy mutton hanging plentifully from the kitchen rafters, and his father calling there as a young man for breakfast. The mutton had first been compressed and left for a time in the running water of the burn. After that it had been salt-cured, and then, like bacon, strung up until needed. The woman of the house had boiled it, before cutting it into thin slices to fry with the bacon. His father had enjoyed his breakfast. There were six children in the shepherd's family then, and they had all turned out handsome men and women. 'Many a shepherd's big family in the old days,' concluded his father, 'was brought up on braxy mutton.'

In the short days, there was plenty to do, and Iain rarely left their own ground or spoke to anyone. For the first time in life, he was conscious of a pleasure in his own company. This was so new, so abnormal, that sometimes he smiled to himself when alone, and felt like the furry things that scampered, or the weasel that stuck its head up, sensing the air, clean and avid, with white throat and long, reddish brown body; or in the twilight, standing arrested, he merged for a moment in the closing world, with a robin's notes falling, like the music of a final reflection, amid the brittle frost.

At night he studied.

EIGHTEEN

He sat the examination for the Higher Leaving Certificate in March and did, he believed, fairly well. In May there would be the oral examination, and then, some time towards the end of June, the final result would be declared.

His school friends had been astonished at his burst of studious energy, but when it got known that he was all fixed up for a job in Mr Cunningham's offices in Edinburgh, his energy was understood.

If there were a few heart-burnings or jealousies over this amid struggling parents, they were not shown, for Iain was well liked and seemed in these spring days to be full of a greater gaiety and life than ever before. They admired, too, the way he helped his father, for the weather completely broke during the lambing season, a sharp fall of snow turning, under sou'-westerly gales, to driving sleet. The hill-burns roared white and the flat lands grew sodden.

For a short spell the weather might take off, but his father was never deceived. And he knew the ewes that would need help. And he helped them, helped the frail bleating things into a roaring world that must surely blow the life instantly out of them but did not, and succoured the mothers, and wiped the blood and slime from his hands.

There was one attitude of mind in his father that never failed to give him a feeling of assurance and strength, and that was the way his father dealt with loss. For example, one day his father came on a dead lamb. Without showing any surprise or vexation, he examined it and explained to Iain that the first rush of milk from the mother is strong, that the lamb had had too much of it, that the milk had curdled into lumps in the lamb's stomach and had there generated gas, which had swelled the stomach against vital organs and so stifled the lamb.

Iain could see, and feel, that the lamb's belly was swollen, but he could not help wondering if his father's description was really true. He had heard a lot from his schoolmasters about accepted beliefs and superstitions which science now smiled upon.

But his father had his knife out and was bending over the lamb. A few quick sure cuts, the stomach lay open, and there, showing white in a green fluid, were the lumps his father had spoken of. They were like small lozenges of cheese, with sharp edges, and could be nothing other than curdled milk. The blade of the knife turned over one or two curiously and tried their consistency. A steady look for a little while – and that was that. Then his father began skinning the lamb.

They had hardly noticed the mother-ewe, though her behaviour had been restless and anxious. Circling round them, she had kept up a short intimate bleating through scenting nostrils. Now his father looked at her and said to Iain in even, natural tones, 'Go home for the lamb.'

Iain set off at once and returned with a lamb whose mother had died that morning. His father had the skin ready and began dressing the living lamb in it, saying 'Come away, now,' as he steadied the little forelegs and shoved them through the foreleg openings in the skin. A vague memory came upon Iain of having once been dressed thus by his father. The tone of the voice recalled it. There had always been a reluctance, a difficulty, in poking his own legs into the little trousers. An access of warmth touched him.

'There now!' said his father. The lamb staggered slightly, under the extra skin, but not very much, going towards the ewe. But the ewe was wild and suspicious and kept looking at the men. However, she lowered her nostrils and sniffed the lamb. Swiftly raising her head, she cried shortly and anxiously – and sniffed again. The lamb began to stagger round her hind quarters, uncertainly, but not without intention. The ewe moved off in an abrupt, strange way.

His father lifted the skinned lamb and they began walking down the slope. After a little, they stopped and looked round.

The ewe was standing, her head twisted towards this strange offspring, sniffing it still with a wild surprise. But the lamb was concerned only with direction – and at last it found the way.

'They're all right now,' said his father.

He dropped the skinned body into a hole and broke some earth over it with his boot.

In all this, there was never for a moment a suggestion that a ewe and a lamb had been lost in the sense that money had been lost.

'She'll accept it now?'

'Yes – once the lamb has taken her milk.'

Presently the skin would be taken off the accepted lamb and life would go on. Death and life – here on the hillside. As he walked home with his father, there was a warmth of wellbeing in his body, and in his eyes the silent glimmer that accompanies the memory of a legend told long ago in childhood.

Often he came home sodden and weary, but his mother always had dry clothes ready for him. Had he been only half wet, a little tired, he might have felt a dreary misery in the work. But out of exhaustion came a deep languid satisfaction. And all the time he knew that this would be the last season he would help his father, the last months of working contact with the earth at home, so he gave himself with a dawning sense of manhood and responsibility in which selfishness or self-desiring would have been like the carry-over of a childish petulance.

Then as the leaves broke out on the young birches and the earth began to breathe, his world was shaken by a look he saw in his father's eyes. It happened one Saturday evening, after they had eaten, and his mother got up to leave the table. She stumbled slightly, as if her foot had caught in something, as indeed it had, but as she left the table, his father's eyes secretly followed her.

Iain knew that look, and in a moment its still, objective searching had him by the throat. His own eyes at once followed his mother, the growing thinness of her body, a quietness about it, going away. He found he could not breathe, and the kitchen was translated into some new silent place, arrested and still.

His father got up in the usual way and took his pipe from the mantelshelf. There was a scurry round Iain's heart, and then it began pounding heavily. Rising from the table, he went as naturally as he could into his bedroom. There, he sat on the bed, staring through the little window into the softly falling dusk.

The dusk deepened as he sat unmoving. He heard his mother's footsteps, her voice. She was lighting the lamp. She might, out of habit, come through with the hand lamp for him, the light on her face. Always coming through the door there, with the hand lamp, its light on her face.

He got up and began whistling under his breath notes of no particular tune, whistling them through his teeth in an unconcerned thoughtless way. Out through the kitchen, taking his cap from the back of the door, casually outside. Along the road – and there was Ewan's cottage. He stopped. He could not call. Perhaps Ewan was alone – but there was no light in the workshop. He left the road and went down by the bushes, but stopped again, turning round to listen. His eyes saw the aspen tree, but could not tell whether there were leaves on it or not. Two women's voices now coming along the road, talking in earnest tones, low and controlled, not to be overheard, but heard so clearly by Iain.

'Ay, she's wasting. She is that. I got a shock when I saw her.'

'It's terrible like the way old Tom Munro's wife went. But I wouldn't say it. Save her from that!'

'Save her indeed! For she did not spare herself.'

'Never. It was always the family, the family. It was too much and it bred a bitterness in her.'

He heard his own name mentioned, but the voices were growing indistinct; they faded.

In the silence, the beating of his heart became audible again. It died down and he stood curiously drained and without thought. Then his eyes glanced about him, stared through the bushes at the cottage. He knew now he would not go in. If Ewan came out, he would stay hidden where he was, not speak to him. He wondered where he would go and thought vaguely of lonely pools on the river.

Mary came out, carrying a tin pail which shone brightly for a moment before the door closed. She was in a hurry, for it was more than half dark now. He gave her time to settle down to the milking and then, drawn in a way he could not understand and half struggled against, he went towards her softly singing voice.

'Is it you?' she cried.

'Am I blocking your light?'

'I'm late – but I did not want to light the lantern. You gave me a start!'

He moved in round the jamb of the door to let her have what glimmering of light there was. The pallor of her face became just discernible. Suddenly he could not speak.

'I can't see you now,' she said.

'I'm here, all the same.'

'Where have you been?' Her voice had quietened, touched by something in his presence.

'No place in particular.' He heard his own forced tones, their awkward affectation of his usual light-hearted way of speaking.

He knew she had turned her eyes downward to the pail. The silence grew and suddenly he felt a strangeness, there between them in the byre. It was something that had to be defeated, broken through.

'As a matter of fact, I heard two women speaking – out there on the road.'

'What about?'

'Oh, just gossip.'

The milking had stopped.

'Tell me,' he said in the intolerable silence, 'what was it old Tom Munro's wife died of.'

'Cancer.'

The word, dropped so quietly, grew until it filled the byre. Its growth choked him. He had to move. With a stupendous effort, he said 'Was that it?' His body lumbered out. 'I must be off. I'm late.'

She dropped the pail from between her knees and with a small sharp animal cry, quickly reached the door.

Noiselessly his body passed beyond the garden dyke and the dark bushes.

NINETEEN

Hughie McIntosh, who competed at Highland Games, both in bagpipe playing and dancing, had given Iain an old chanter. He became very devoted to it, put in hours of time practising on the hillside, the dogs with him, the sheep grazing.

In this way he was able to avoid his home and the queer quietness, with its terror of death, that sometimes came upon him there. These were the last days of June, too, and the results of the Higher Leaving Certificate examination should be out any time. Whatever happened, he was finished with school for good. All that part of his life was over.

In these long summer days there was not much to do. The crops were rooted and the lambs frisky. Sometimes as he piped and a few of the lambs raced and jumped, he would glimpse them over his puffed cheeks; a glimmer would come into his eyes, a suppressed humour, like a young satyr's, and he would take the chanter from his mouth and switch drops from its stem.

One afternoon as he was playing in a dell, where birch trees grew, ferns and bracken, he heard a voice crying his name. It was Mary's voice. He got up but could not move to meet her, suddenly afraid. His breathing thickened.

'Here!' he called.

She came over the shallow crest and saw him. 'Oh, Iain!' she cried, and threw her arms up and came running. 'Iain, you're through!'

A weakening went over him and only in that instant did he realize how profound his anxiety had been about the result of the examination. To have failed would have been a final, a fatal blow to his mother. Now he was through.

'No?' he said earnestly, foolishly, looking at her happy impatience, her abandon. His eyes were growing bright.

'Yes, you are! I'm just from Kinmore! Isn't it lovely?' Mat, the young dog, was frisking about her. She caught his forelegs as he jumped and singing the notes of a reel 'Ta-ra-rum – ta-ra-rum – ta-ra-rum – ta-ra-riddle . . .' began dancing with the dog.

Iain suddenly gave a shout, a terrific *hooch!* and, linking Mary's arm, let the notes rip and swung her; let her arm go and danced wildly in front of her; linked the other arm and swung the opposite way. It was suddenly a frenzy, a breaking down of thought, a madness of release, of delight. A reel breaks the mountains open. The lambs scatter. The young birches blaze green fire in the sun. The grass shimmers. Mary slips, her laughter lifting to a sharp cry, but Iain has her, grips and swings her, up against him, crushes her in his arms and kisses her. She hangs for a lost moment, then breaks away, gasping for breath.

Iain stands dead still, breathing heavily.

She puts her hair back, flushed, wildly confused, not looking at him; she turns away.

There is a crackling from approaching feet. Iain looks over his shoulder. Angus!

'Angus!' shouts Iain on the instant. 'Heard the news?'

'Yes. We're through.'

'Good boy!' Iain shook hands with great warmth. 'Hurrah!' He was delighted; he was carrying it off; he had to tear through Angus's queer look some way. Angus had seen them and was white to the lips. 'And Alan? Is he through?'

'Yes.'

'Good for him, too! Another toss in the ditch for that!'

Iain laughed, as if everything that had taken place were part of this merriment, this exuberance. 'Why you looking so glum?' he asked straight into Angus's eyes.

'I met your father. He asked me to tell you – to go home.'

Iain's face grew still and his eyes piercing. Mary turned fully, her lips parting in a wild, frightened look.

'Did he?' muttered Iain, lifting his eyes from Angus's face and staring into the distance.

'Yes.'

'Well, I'll go.' He walked away, forgetting them, without a look.

TWENTY

He walked along towards the house, gazing straight ahead. His feet never stumbled and Mat, after looking at him once or twice, dropped in behind his heels.

The house was still, terribly still. The green of the group of pines was a funereal dark. Feeling, alive in his face, in the glance of his eyes, like pain, threatened to come through, but he choked it back and his features took on a dour, unyielding look.

There was his father, standing at the door in an aimless way. Iain went steadily on. His father looked at him. 'She's asking for you,' he said in quiet tones, removing his eyes.

Iain went in through the door. His grandmother met him. She was a small woman, tidy in her person, comfortably stout, and did not look like the mother of the thin woman now dying in the spare bed in the parlour. When she spoke, her voice was gentle and her eyes kind with understanding.

'She's been asking for you,' she said.

He stood, without a word.

'Angus was here. He told your father you had passed your examination. Glad we are to hear that.' She smiled, as if there was no hurry, no need for haste now.

The awkwardness in his body was a torture to him. It threatened to break, to burst. He feared seeing his mother.

'Yes, laddie.' She patted him on the shoulder, but sensibly, with calm understanding. 'We did not tell her you have passed. It will please her. Take your time, Iain, and calm yourself.'

Her voice helped him and he straightened himself.

She went before him and opened the door. 'Here's Iain to see you,' she called cheerfully.

Iain entered and turned towards his mother, who was

propped up against the pillows, a white knitted jacket buttoned over her breast. The grandmother stood a moment, then went out and pulled the door quietly behind her.

'You've come to see me?' said his mother. Her eyes were large in her gaunt pale face, and something of banter or challenge in her voice steadied him.

'Yes,' he answered, and did not know where to look.

'Sit down,' she said. 'Surely you can spare me a little of your time now.'

He sat down, knowing she was accusing him, knowing in his heart that he had been trying to avoid seeing her. Her eyes had their own queer smile.

'What were you doing?' she asked.

'Herding the sheep.'

'Always the sheep. Always . . .' Her eyes lifted to the window and her thought began to wander. 'Always – that.' It was, however, memory speaking in her rather than bitterness. Her voice, though not very strong, had the strange remoteness, wildness, which he had known these last years. It frightened him a little, as though any moment it might break out in a wild, incoherent way.

She suddenly looked at him. 'I am glad to see you, Iain. I wanted to tell you something.'

Her smile was simple and friendly, almost confidential, like a young woman's. This lifting of her expression away from death eased him. He met her eyes for a moment.

'I wanted to tell you that you have helped me these last months,' she said. 'You have reconciled me. I did not want to go away, hard and bitter.' Her eyes glistened and feeling welled up and choked her, but it did not affect her thought. Her voice grew younger. 'I have seen the leaves coming, and one day, Iain, I saw them, as I saw them long long ago. I am glad of that.'

Her eyes were on the window. Suddenly she smiled in a knowing way. It was the expression of a young girl, who would make silly jokes. He saw her brain was affected. And though this lacerated him, like the stab of a knife, something in his own youth understood the something she had lost and was finding again. Terrible, terrible, and shameful somehow, but he knew, and could have cried out down the long ago. The cancer now had got its roots in her brain.

'Why don't you come to see me?' she asked, looking at him again in a natural way.

'I was coming,' he answered.

'Were you?' Her voice was husky and her hands now moved over the bedclothes.

'Yes – I – heard about the exam.'

Her hands steadied and her eyes grew very large. He could see her mind coming through the roots of her disease, coming up to this hour.

'I passed,' he said.

'You passed!' Her voice repeated the words, with heightened pitch. Her hands lifted from the elbows and clapped once – twice – with little sound. 'You have won, Iain! We have won!' She was gay. 'And now you'll go to Edinburgh. You'll ride away to Edinburgh.'

She was making a story of it. Triumph was in her voice. A young triumph – but somewhere in it were the eyes of his mother, and they triumphed also. Something in it, too, of the woman who had decided not to make this a sad occasion – and had forgotten all decision in the natural moment. A light in her eyes, light-hearted and terrible; a laughing gleam from the bared surface of an agony that was now hardly felt.

'Oh, I'm glad!' The gleam threw a vindictive flash from the very heart of her pleasure and she looked at her son as if she would draw him into her mind.

'I only just heard it,' he said, smiling awkwardly, unable to look at her.

'And you were coming to tell me!' Nothing could make her happier than that, or could at the same time make her sense of conspiracy more complete. 'I have everything ready for you – everything washed and ironed and laid away. Your granny knows where they are.' She paused a moment, wrinkling her brows. 'You'll be going now – a month to-morrow.'

'Yes.'

She nodded. Then, as if the words were spoken inside her mind and she was repeating them slowly, she said, 'A month to-morrow.' She flashed her eyes suddenly on her son, her features stiffened, her upper lip drew tightly down over her teeth, her chest began to heave and her left hand came up to cover her face, the spread fingers moving, as a stifled convulsion of sobbing broke through.

Iain rose and stood. Tears were running down his cheeks. 'Mother!' He put a hand out to stop her crying. She caught it and clawed weakly at it, pulling him to her. He fell on his knees and buried his face in the bedclothes. She tried to lift her head as her thin, hungry hands moved through his hair, then her head fell back, and her hands caressed him and came away, leaving him.

He got up. Her eyes were closed and her breath came heavily through her parted lips. Before he went out at the door, he turned round and found her eyes wide upon him, and in them a profound and tender smile, but with the gleam in it, the wildness, and the tragic knowledge.

TWENTY-ONE

Five days after that, his mother died.

They were hard days, for his mother's mind became more and more erratic. At night, lying listening in his bed, he would be terribly moved when he heard her singing songs from her childhood, little childish songs, in a thin cracked voice.

The past would then come back upon him, not his own past, but, as it seemed, the past of the world that was also her past. From far away it came and children ran down it, laughing.

In an instant this past, with its fleeting pictures, by the pressure of his emotion, would swell outward as a cry swells, and he himself within it would silently cry out. But he could not command it, could not sweep it away, and it would swell as the sky swells its blue arch over little green fields, and he would see the fields and the burns that wander by them with wind in the bushes hanging over the water.

Beyond fear and terror, a queer clairvoyance was in all this for him. It was like a face that looked at him from the far verge of the landscape, a young woman's face, white, with knowledge in the eyes. But the face was no face he knew, and he could not see it properly, but knew it was there; for if he but tried to look, it grew large in a transparency that faded away, as birds' cries fade away.

And somewhere there he met his mother and understood, even though he paused not a moment to understand, so terrible in its beauty and innocence was that place.

Sometimes, too, he would hear the two women talking away. Occasionally his mother's voice would lift and crack, but his granny's voice was always sensible and calm. It's not that his granny's voice was humouring his mother's fancies.

It was more than that, and it was the 'more' that searched him out. She was the mother talking to her child, hardly listening at times because her hands were busy; chiding now and then, but prepared to explain over and over. There was something so normal about this, so assured, that it gave Iain a conception of women which he never afterwards forgot.

At the beginning of life and at its end, they were there, handling the unbearable with competent hands, doing little things, material things, with knowledge in their eyes, moving about, silent or speaking as the need demanded. They were there, with the awful progression of the minutes in their hands.

He got his short sharp vision of the tragic heart of life, from which all songs of innocence are distilled. And though, like a boy maddened by restraints, he turned to break away, still it was there; the voices went on.

During the day, he spent all the time he could outside. Mrs McAndrew came in to help and thus relieved the strain on his grandmother, who, however, seemed to need no great spell of sleep so long as she could doze off now and then for an hour or two. Mrs McAndrew was a capable woman, full of good sense and good cheer, showing little of the mournfulness with which many of the countrywomen liked to indulge themselves; though when the district nurse called, Mrs McAndrew would hardly let her off from the flow of her low-toned conversation, with its facts and observations and warm gossip.

His father kept near the house, attending to the cows, bringing peats for the fire, mending broken things long neglected. Sometimes, from a distance, Iain would see him and experience a sharp blinding in his vision. The solitariness of his father was too defined, and once in a surging moment that rose from nowhere, he wondered, passionately, why his father could not go and speak to his mother, so that all would be clear between them and resolved.

On the last night, there were moments when he felt something like this was in fact happening. Iain wakened to the sound of his father's voice in the parlour. How long it had been there he could not know. His own bedroom was small and the partition between a matter of lathe and plaster. Thus he could clearly catch the tones of a voice, the sympathy or feeling in its pitch, even if he could not catch the words.

His father's tones were even and gentle, unhurried. He was like one coming to the end of a fatal story, but only a story, for there he was himself, talking, and the hour was what it was, and he was looking after her.

There came a queer husky mumbling, hardly audible, and then he heard his father say quite distinctly, 'Yes, Seonaid.'

The speaking of her name pierced Iain sharply. All his father's calm was there and his steadiness, and the spoken name was like an old vow.

Iain felt his body rise up in a moment of crisis. There was a long silence. Then he heard his granny's voice go from her sharply to a drawn-out tremulous, 'Ah-h-h.'

Blood drowned his hearing and he sank his face in the pillow.

Presently the door opened and his father came into the room. Iain could neither move nor speak. His father remained still, then walked to the little window and stood looking out on a world all quiet and fresh in the summer dawn.

TWENTY-TWO

The day before Iain left home his father suggested, 'You'd better call on a few of them and say good-bye.'

It was an old custom, and though Iain had felt a bit shy about it to begin with – for times and manners had changed a lot since the Great War – he did call at a few houses, and the folk were so kind, so pleased with his call, that he had the greatest difficulty in getting away without breaking bread, without eating something. He joked and laughed, passing the visit off in the gayest way. And when they pulled his leg, he had his answer.

'When you come back as the factor, Iain, you'll know what I'm wanting,' said the man of the house.

'Mairag's croft as a sheep outrun, is it?'

The woman of the house laughed, but the man added, scratching his chin, 'If you could make it the whole of Achmore, you would make a job of it.'

'No, no,' said Iain. 'I'm keeping that for wintering the deer.'

'In that case you needn't bother, for the deer winter there whatever – when they're not eating our turnips.'

'Will you listen to him?' said Iain to his wife. 'As if his handful of sheep mattered against the noble stags on the hill!'

Handshakes and crying of good wishes, and he was off to the next leave-taking.

Suddenly he found himself liking it. There was an old country warmth in it, near the heart. It was nearly six o'clock before he noticed the time.

A restlessness had come upon him now. He had taken tea in two houses, because before he had known what was happening, it was there on the table. So he did not go home.

All at once he felt a need to be with himself for a while. Their certainty that he would 'get on in the world' had something irksome in it, deep in his mind. Once or twice when he had suggested that he would as soon stay at home among good people, they smiled back at his politeness, his modesty. Never for a moment could it occur to them that he meant it.

Extraordinary, the power of a common belief, the force of suggestion. He felt himself being carried away on it, like a stick on a stream. Something a little frightening about it, and, somehow, sad.

So he went to look at some of the lonely places, where no people were but only memories, ghosts of days, of boyhood. The day-dream; the heart in the mouth and the feet running. Grass and rocks; small birches and heather; sheep tracks. Hidden places, where one could sit and listen.

He sat and he listened, but by trying to listen he couldn't hear. The small singing birds dropped their notes among the leaves. The light came down from the sky. But a veil was drawn, and everything was seen and heard on this side of it.

From the Rock Pool, a certain grey power touched him, but what his eyes saw was hard and material, withdrawn and ominous within itself. It warned him to keep off. That stirred him a little, and his expression twisted, taking the challenge. But he passed on.

In the Dell, where he had been playing the chanter when Mary came with her news of the exam., his heart did give a beat. He stood still and an amused half-satiric smile stayed on his face while his eyes glanced here and there.

Angus had seen them go mad for a minute. But for the news Angus was bringing – what would have happened?

What happened between them, when he left? Mary had been quiet enough afterwards, as if avoiding him, refusing to sing when her father pressed her, on the plea that she had something to do. Once that had suddenly angered him.

Between Angus and herself, he had sensed trouble. That had made him feel guilty, for Angus had never hidden his feelings for Mary.

Well, it couldn't be helped. Pity Angus had seen it, all the same. Always he had had a certain feeling of responsibility for Angus. And Mary – Mary was Ewan's daughter. They had run together since childhood. She was like a sister.

The thought of her running made him lift his eyes to where she had appeared. All at once he felt she was going to appear. He waited, listening tensely. When she did not come, he walked up to the crest. She was not there; not anywhere. He found himself slightly light-headed, dry-mouthed, and walked away with a curious, half-shamed, illicit feeling.

He walked a mile without consciously knowing where he was going. No clear thought in his mind, nothing definite, only a turmoil to walk away from, even as he bore it with him. Then he realized he had gone over the shoulder of a hill, following a slanting sheep-path. The broad valley had vanished. He was on the way to Achmore.

That brightened him and lifted the sky. He would go and call on Mad Mairag! So perfectly did this suit his mood that he all but laughed aloud.

Soon there was Achmore, green in its hollow, with smoke from Mad Mairag's thatched cottage. Lonely the place looked, but with a loneliness that touched his spirit. No interference of worldliness, of 'getting on', here. This was beyond the world.

As he drew near, he could see the parallel rigs of the old croftings, grass green, which had once been cultivated by human hands. The ruins of the little houses lay scattered about, hardly even skeletons now. The hunch of one gable wall looked like a smashed shoulder. Its head was buried, all their heads were buried in their own mounds.

The tethered white nanny-goat bleated, and the kid ran to its side. How nimble the kid, how sensitive and cream-white, with its agate eyes and quivering nostrils. Pagan-lovely out of a story of fawns and magic – now there in the flesh.

He became aware of someone behind him and turned. Mairag was in the door.

'They're my watchdogs,' she said.

She looked like a witch, with wisps of grey hair poking out beneath a round cap with fluted edging. The cap made her face look round. The eyes were dark and alert, not so much suspicious as watchful, waiting for the humour in him to show.

He turned his shoulder to her, looking back at the goats. The goats were watching him with their characteristic reserve in complete stillness.

'Is she a good milker?' He did not know what to say, and from instinct treated Mairag in a natural, courteous way, without stress or exaggeration of any kind.

'She is that.'

He felt her eyes on him all the time. 'You will be Seonaid Cattanach's son?'

'I am.' He turned, smiling.

'I would know you on her,' she said, and he found his right hand in both of hers. She did not shake it so much as give it short impulsive squeezes.

'I would that. I see her in your eyes. Come away in. Come away.' She bustled in before him, shushed a big tortoiseshell cat from an old-fashioned rocking chair, and set him in it. The chair rocked and he quickly gripped its round slender arms.

She spoke continuously, and he knew it was the way she spoke to herself when moved. 'Indeed I was at her wedding. And a slender, lovely girl she was. And she laughed and her voice was high, and her glances were bright as the sun on the water. She was like a viking's daughter.' She caught his right hand which still gripped the chair, and bent to him in a confidential courtesy. 'Now you'll have a nice cup of tea.'

'No, I just looked in—'

But already she was off. A chain, with a hook on the end of it, came down the chimney. On this hook she hung a big black kettle. An old-fashioned wooden structure bulged out over the fireplace from the gable wall. He had only seen one chimney-piece like it before, and that was in a long-deserted cottage where the roof had fallen in, leaving the curved rafters like bare ribs. He had then noticed the big wooden tie-pins, fixing the ribs to the uprights. He now observed things hanging from their ends. Time began to dissolve and suddenly he saw his mother's eyes over him as a child in her lap. This was going back far beyond what he had hitherto believed was his earliest memory. He moved and the chair rocked.

It was a small room, and the big wooden bed against the wall, opposite the fireplace, filled a large part of it. The bed was hung with faded cretonne, dark red and white, above and below. There was little of the bright cleanliness so often found in the houses of solitary old women. Odds and ends everywhere, and things shoved into dark corners, but cosy and clean enough. She probably gave her face a lick with a wet flannel clout once a week before going to the shop. Her eye caught something in the bottom of a cup. She blew it out.

He could not let his mind settle on anything, for his mother's eyes had been bright. The kettle, always murmuring by the fire, was now boiling, its spout of steam coming straight out with remarkable force. The cat had jumped up on the bed. Everything had its own life.

She kept on talking, but now and then paused in what she was doing, out of a special consideration for her guest. As she swilled the hot water round and round in the brown earthenware teapot, she inclined her head to him. 'It was kind of you to come and see me, for not many living come now.' Then she hurried off with the pot to empty the swill outside.

He remembered the popular saying that the dead came out of the land to speak with her.

'I came,' he said, 'because I'm going away to-morrow.'

'I remember you now as a little boy.' She looked across the table. 'You would be teasing poor old Mairag.' Her smile was bright but enigmatic.

He felt himself flush. 'We didn't – we were just wanting to hear you—'

'Some of them would say things that hurt me. Often, when I got out of sight, I would run home.'

'I'm sorry for that,' he mumbled, chewing her hard oatcake. 'No-one meant to hurt you.'

'Some of them did.' She nodded with a sideways nod.

He thought of the way she would run, waddling, the hurt in her heart. She was known to be eighty years, because she had been getting the Old Age Pension for ten.

'But och! the bairns,' she added with a laugh, recovering in a moment like a child herself. 'I remember!'

'It's the lines of poetry you made,' he explained, spreading butter.

'Bairns are between the one world and the other, and they love the one, but they feel they are made for the other, and whenever they feel that – they must show off.'

He glanced at her, and found her eyes waiting in cunning merriment.

'Is your tea to your taste?'

'Yes, thank you.'

'Perhaps you don't like the goat's milk?'

'I do. It's very good.'

'And how do you think you'll like Edinburgh?'

'Who told you I was going there?'

'You would wonder!' She smiled slyly, enjoying his surprise. 'It's not much I don't find out – one way or another.'

'I give it up!' he replied, trying to be jocular.

'Do you want to go?'

'Well – what is there for a young fellow here?'

She kept her eyes on him. 'There's the land, the bonny land of your country.'

'Much good you get out of the land nowadays!'

'All life comes up out of the land.'

'Maybe. But it doesn't give you a decent living.'

'It will give you everything, but on one condition.'

'What's that?'

'That you love the land.'

She was like a witch laying incantation on him. He moved restlessly. 'You can't live on love,' he almost cried.

She shook her head slowly. 'You cannot live without it – and those who went away – came back to it.'

He muttered, moving his shoulders.

'You're frightened of these things,' she said.

'What things?' he asked abruptly.

Her expression slowly lightened.

'That's what the bairns will be asking me. So I tell them I see the leaves dancing on the trees, and the flowers laughing on the potatoes – *and the little path going to the well.*'

He made a vague sound of acknowledgement, for her voice had dropped in speaking of the well.

'There's grass now on the little path – but it still runs to the well,' she added.

'What path?'

'The path that goes to the old drinking well.'

'Where?'

'Out there.'

He could not speak for a moment. 'But that's because you're only using it yourself.'

'Perhaps so,' she said, and looked at him out of the corners of her eyes.

'I don't know what you mean.'

'The bairns know – but they like to be frightened.'

'Frightened at what?'

'The feet that go to the drinking well.'

He finished his cup and she got up and brought the teapot. 'You still like me to make verses!'

'You're teasing me.'

She laughed, quick merry cackles under her dark glancing eyes. But she did not sit down at table again. She stood listening, and he glanced at her.

'The feet are coming,' she said, little above a whisper.

There was a catch at his heart.

'What feet?' He started up, but she put her hand on his shoulder.

'Didn't you hear Nancy whispering to her little one just now?'

'No.'

She looked at him with a humour that, being deliberately veiled, seemed quite mad. 'Do you know what I can hear? I can hear the feet keeping time to your heart. Listen!'

Nancy the goat bleated loudly.

She laughed and went to the door. 'Yes, there she is!'

Iain got up and looked through the little window. Mary was coming down the slanting path to the house, a brown wicker basket slung over her arm.

'Is that you, my sweetheart? Come away!' cried Mairag.

'I'm late,' called Mary. 'Did you think I wasn't coming?'

'Well did I know you would come, if come you could. Come in now, come in, and see who I have got for you.'

Iain was on his feet and Mary stopped as she saw him. 'You!' she said.

Mairag laughed with delight, like a clever child who had pulled off a joke, glancing from one to the other. The cat had come back to the rocker, so she pushed it off again. 'Now, my darling, here you are, and I'll make a new cup for you in a minute.'

'I have been going the round,' Iain explained, and sat down.

Mary lay back in the chair and it rocked. She laughed and gripped the arms, her face vivid and fresh, warm with life, her hair shaken back and free. As Mairag leaned towards her, the contrast between youth and age caught Iain in an uncanny way, as if the veil over Mairag's talk were momentarily withdrawn and a strange revelation glimpsed. His eyes went back to his plate, and the bright easy talk of the women, as Mary emptied her basket on the dresser, set him apart with his tangled feelings.

'So you've been doing your round of farewells,' called Mary, turning from the dresser with an assurance that did not help him.

'Yes. My father thought it the proper thing to do.'

'And was it your father sent you to me?' asked Mairag.

'No,' began Iain, and got no further, because the women laughed.

'Mairag is having her own back on him now,' said Mairag, 'for many's the time he teased me, the rascal.'

'Did he tease you badly?' asked Mary.

'He did indeed. Many's the time I thought I'd tell his mother on him.' She glanced from one to the other, with a quick movement of her head like a bird's, as if waiting for them to see the point and laugh.

Mary laughed and released her.

Soon fresh tea was on the table, and Mary was sitting between them, facing the small window. She seemed to have complete confidence in herself and in her power to deal with Mairag. 'Where were you to-day?' she asked Iain naturally, as she ate, and at once life was on its normal feet.

He told her in an off-hand way and she accepted his manner.

'Does it make you feel sorry about going away?'

'Oh, I don't know,' he answered largely.

She drank her tea. 'That's lovely tea,' she said to Mairag, glancing towards her. But Mairag was staring somewhere between them, her lips parted. At once Mary turned her eyes on the window. 'I like looking out of this little window,' she said in a clear, loud voice. Then she looked directly at Iain. 'She's just thinking to herself,' she explained, and smiled.

Iain felt uncomfortable, for Mary had made no effort to lower her voice. Deep in her smile, too, was a queer knowledge, a half-wonder if he understood.

'I'll have to be going. I didn't go home for tea.' He looked at the table and pushed his plate slowly from him.

'They'll know you would get food wherever you went.'

'Suppose so.' He looked out of the window.

Mary's eyes rested on his face, and withdrew. She drained her cup.

As Mairag began to mutter to herself, Mary got up. 'Thank you very much. That was a grand cup of tea,' she said in a high voice.

'What!' said Mairag, blinking, 'You're not going?'

'Yes, we must. It's getting on, you know.'

Iain was now in the middle of the floor.

'Here's my basket,' called Mary brightly, picking it up.

Mairag's hands came on the table and she leaned back, looking at them. They stood, arrested. 'Achmore will not be left desolate,' said Mairag in a chanting voice. 'You're going now, but you will come back.'

'Of course we'll come back,' cried Mary quickly.

'I know you will,' said Mairag. Her face gradually melted into a tender smile, but she made no effort to get up.

'And thank you again,' said Mary, who seemed anxious now to be gone, and made a move towards the door.

Mairag arose. 'It's a handsome young couple you are, and youth on you like wild flowers on the green pasture.'

'You're not that old yourself,' Mary rallied her.

Mairag shook her head, but now the cunning smile was coming into her expression again. She glanced at Iain.

'Good-bye,' said Iain.

She took his hand in both of hers. 'Will I tell her about the feet I see running to the well?'

'No, I wouldn't if I were you,' said Iain.

She looked into his eyes. 'God keep you – till you come again.'

TWENTY-THREE

'I think she's daft,' said Iain, as they went on their way.

Mary did not answer.

'Quite mad,' added Iain.

'I don't think so,' said Mary quietly.

'No? All that talk about feet going to the well. Do you believe that?'

'Yes,' answered Mary, quietly but defiantly.

'You mean she sees things? . . . That's what I mean. Clean daft!' He laughed.

Mary did not answer. It was she now who seemed constrained, with Iain free and getting his own back.

'Do you think she sees the dead?' he asked, almost brutally.

She remained silent.

He glanced at her. 'Do you go to see her often?'

'Occasionally.'

'You'll be getting like her, if you don't watch!'

'I might get worse.'

'You seem annoyed.'

'No, I'm not.' Then she added, 'What did she say to you that annoyed you?'

'Me annoyed? I'm not annoyed. I'm just amused. But you better watch yourself.'

'I can do that, thank you.'

He was amused.

They went on.

'And she's cunning, too,' asserted Iain. 'She's not so simple as she looks.'

'Nor so daft.'

'One for me!' Iain stumbled. They kept their faces front and went on as if they were at a walking match. 'You seem to know her.'

'I do, a little.'

'How?'

'She lives in her own world.'

'That's clear enough,' agreed Iain, scoring again.

'In that world, everything has its own life, and behaves in its own way.'

'Even the dead?'

'Even the dead.'

'That's what I say. Can't you see that she's imagining these things? It's pure imagination.'

'The English master says that pure imagination is very rare.'

'And *he* ought to know!' Iain seemed delighted with his stroke. 'Especially about the mighty dead!'

Mary smiled at this thrust at the dry English master in the High School, and the tension between them eased a little.

'Why are you against her?' she asked.

'I'm not. It's just that – she's queer. I was never with her alone before. I began to feel things crawling about.'

'They weren't crawling.'

'No?' He looked at her sideways.

'You felt the happiness of old days and quick feet running. You know you did. To begin with, it makes you feel a bit frightened. But afterwards – you understand.'

'What?'

'I cannot tell you,' said Mary, 'if you don't know.' She wanted to tell him. 'Her way of looking cunning and playing tricks – that's her fun. It's like a game. She lives in that place.'

'What place?'

'Where things are bright and – and happy. I can't explain. Once, looking out of her window, I saw the light on the grass. Have you never seen the light on the leaves of trees? . . . I can't tell you . . . Once – after leaving her – I felt a little frightened – I ran. And as I ran I began to laugh. Anyone would have thought I was mad. Then suddenly the world here, and everything, was beautiful.' She stole a glance at him, but now the fun had left his features, which were gathered in a hard, intolerant way.

'You should stop going to see her,' he said.

His harsh voice, with the obvious thought behind it, made her wince.

They walked on in silence.

'Will you stop going?' he demanded.

'No.'

'It's nothing to do with me, I'm only warning you,' he said, after another hundred yards.

She remained silent.

'Does she talk to the dead?' he asked, satirically.

'Regularly,' she answered, without expression.

'Hmf! I told you!'

'Perhaps she finds the dead better company than many of the living. I go down this way. Good-bye.'

She left him at once and went walking away alone.

He stood still, with the extraordinary feeling of being bereft of all his senses. Anger swept amazement away and darkened his sight. Then quite clearly he saw her walking, head up, not looking where her feet were going, and he knew that she was terribly hurt. He began to stumble on with a harsh laughing expression, and the fact that their paths diverged slowly did not help him. It would have been just as quick for him to have taken her path. They both knew it.

This was monstrous. She began to descend. The valley was coming into sight. Feeling trapped, he stretched himself on the heather.

Nothing would come into his head except blind emotions that twisted him about. He got up and went on, with the feeling of being watched or hunted. Presently he was whistling through his teeth, but with eyes alert. When he reached the Dell, he sat down, glancing around with relief.

That had been a mad afternoon if you like! Mad as Mairag! His mouth opened in a twist to help his listening. Some warblers were chirping away. His eyes looked for them – and saw the leaves. Everything was very still. Ferns were growing out of a bank, spreading and showing themselves; different from the bracken, whose broad fronds curved over

to catch a glisten of light. Suddenly the Dell was pierced by
a ringing song. The song over, a tiny brown body flitted
swiftly, here, there; a fern frond moved, and the wren was
gone. The whole fern-face looked at him from the shadow.

Two hours later he approached Ewan's cottage. He knew
he was late, knew Ewan would have been waiting for him,
but he was taken aback by the number of fellows in Ewan's
shop. There was an overflow of girls in the house.

'And where on earth have you been?' cried Ewan.

'What's on? A wedding?'

'We were wondering if it was your funeral,' cried Hamish.
Hughie was there, too. Angus. Even Alan, dark and smiling.

Iain realized that they had gathered to give him a send-
off, but he did not let this appear, met the banter and the
chaff with a rising challenge, with rising spirits, till his fingers
were flying over the strings of the fiddle and, in the darkening, dancing was going on everywhere. Dan-the-trapper
had a bottle of whisky. Mary was flushed, hurrying to make
tea, ordering the girls about. The girls had baked cakes and
scones and brought them along.

Everyone did what he or she was asked to do. Mary sang
three times.

At four o'clock in the morning, Ewan proclaimed that he
had a duty to perform.

'Here in the country,' said Ewan, pressed in upon by eager
faces which threw enigmatic glances at Iain, 'we take a thing
as we find it. If it's a fiddle, it's a fiddle, and it's enough for
us if it's there, hanging to a nail, without coverings or wrap-
pings.'

'Naked,' nodded Dan, out of the warm glow of many
drams.

'But we can't go abroad in that way,' continued Ewan.
'We have to cover the fiddle up, or the bridge might get
knocked down, the sound posts slip, and the music be no
more. And that was why we put our pennies together to buy
a case for Iain's fiddle. We hope it will always protect the
music for him, the music that only he himself knows how
to play. We give it to you, Iain,' concluded Ewan, lifting the

case from the chair behind him, 'with our best wishes for your health, wealth, and happiness.'

Iain took the case across his forearms, looking at it while the warm blood flushed his smiling, deeply embarrassed face.

'You're holding it Iain, boy,' said Dan appreciatively, 'like your first-born.'

The laughter helped to cover Iain's embarrassment. 'Thank you very much,' he muttered. They saw he was deeply moved.

'Many a good hour you have given us,' said a man's quiet voice.

At that, everyone cheered, and they pressed round Iain and shook hands with him.

Voices laughing as they went into the dim morning. Ewan shook hands with him at the door, and Angus. And there was Mary, her soft hand in his, her face lifted. 'Good-bye, Iain.' Her hand pressed his, fluttered like a wing, and was gone with herself into the house.

Hamish and Hughie saw him to his home.

'What a night for the river!' said Hughie.

'The morning is here,' said Hamish.

They stood for a long moment and saw the morning coming behind the hills. Then Iain, alone, turned to the closed door.

PART TWO

IN EDINBURGH

ONE

The sun was carrying on an aerial battle with the vapours produced by its own heat. Silent explosions, molten red at the core, sent wreaths curling upward in fantastic gyres.

Riding this primeval warfare, its dark battlements showing immovable amid the wreaths, was the Castle, high on its invisible rock.

As he stood gazing up at it from the West End, Iain was caught into history, with echoes of ancient battles and riding horsemen, and he felt in himself the smallness of individual life against that which endures.

Dark it looked, forbidding, and grimly triumphant.

A near church rose from its ghostly gravestones to thrust a spire at the hidden sky. Reformation and persecution, the Covenant and bloody martyrdom. But the eye lifted from the spire to that great Castle which over-topped it, broad-browed in stone, contending with the sun and its fiery elements, dominant, and, even as he watched, taking the sun's first shafts and splintering them on turret and keep.

Jostled, he moved on, and heard, for bugles, the clanging of tramcars, the grinding of their wheels as they took the curve, the hooting of dark, squat, swiftly-moving motor-cars, and glimpsed pale faces over shoulders before they hurried from one safe spot to the next, as a man leaps from one boulder to another in a dangerous current.

Along 'the first street in Europe' faces went intent and hurrying, though late, late. But here and there, apart, walked men in dark morning dress and hard hat, with umbrellas furled tight as walking sticks. With an intent yet leisurely air they proceeded, naturally unaware, with a fine negligence, of that which had been created for, and existed under, their governance. As the Castle took the elements on its stone brows, so did they the street on their uplifted, clean-shaven faces.

The girls walked swiftly on high heels, *click-click*, with perfect complexions, and lips red as raspberry juice. The very restriction in their movements gave them, by its artifice, an unapproachable air. They were continuously overtaking him, and he tried to throw off his slouching walk and become one with the many. But when he quickened his pace he merely went at a great rate, felt foolish, and fell back upon his country stride.

When his eyes dropped to the hurrying silken legs, the calves shook back at him from each impact of the high-heeled shoes with an abrupt arrogance. The young men strode more smoothly but also with quick steps for there was nothing to trip over. No-one looked at the ground, not even the large church dignitary of great years on gaitered legs advancing jerkily like a black tower.

Ten o'clock at last and the time had come. The queasy feeling spread in his breast as he turned off Princes Street, unknowingly buttoned his jacket, and assumed a vacant expression. He had passed the door an hour ago, but now it seemed to be guarded by a man in dark-braided uniform and peaked cap, with a heavy grey-sandy moustache, and sharp eyes under strong eyebrows.

'What do you want?' asked this soldierly man as Iain hesitated.

'I – I have a letter,' said Iain, trying to speak casually while producing the letter unhurriedly from an inside breast-pocket.

'You passed here before?'

As Iain did not answer – he had his memory of pausing and staring at the brass plate – the peering eyes lifted from the envelope and gave him an assessing glance. Then they turned away and the man walked into the vestibule. As he opened a door, he saw Iain behind him.

'Waiting an answer?' The look now travelled over Iain's greyish-green tweed suit. It had been made in Kinmore by District Councillor Magnus Grant, a genial man who believed that youth needed room in which to expand. A good cloth, thick, hairy, and with plenty of wear.

Iain's discomfort was increased by a glimpse of men's faces and bodies in the room beyond the door which his interlocutor held open.

'Yes, sir,' Iain replied. 'I am—'

But the uniformed man, having found his spectacles on the long counter, now perused the letter's superscription more attentively.

'For Mr Cunningham. Is this urgent?'

'Well—'

'Where are you from?'

'From home,' answered Iain.

There was an audible chuckle from a corner of the room and a general air of arrest.

'I can see that. But who do you represent?'

'I would like to see Mr Cunningham, if you please,' replied Iain, his tone hardening.

'Have you an appointment?'

'I have come here – to work.'

'To work! Do you mean you are the new apprentice?'

'The letter—'

'Why didn't you say so?' He turned his head. 'Mr Lindsay – this appears to be the gentleman you are waiting for.'

A young man of about Iain's own age came to the counter with negligent dignity, accepted the letter, and raised his eyebrows. 'Shall I take him to Mr Cunningham now, sir?'

A rumble of laughter rolled round the desks.

'You take him to—' The sentence drowned in its own soldierly growl.

'Yes, sir.' Mr Lindsay came round the counter, bowed slightly to Iain, opened the door – 'If you please—' and closed it on a gust of laughter. 'This way,' and he led Iain on, pushed open a door, and let it swing to after them. They were in the lavatory.

'This', said young Lindsay, with perfect manners, 'is the council chamber of the male staff. Here all matters of dispute are resolved, sometimes to the shedding of blood. As a meeting-place of the waters, it is convenient. What's your name?'

'Cattanach.'

'Mine is John Lindsay. Where do you come from?'

'From – near Kinmore.'

'What school did you go to?'

'The local school.'

'You didn't go to a public school?'

'I thought all schools were public schools.'

John Lindsay smiled. 'In Scotland they are. It's a point! What does your father do?'

'He's a sheep farmer,' replied Iain, his colour darkening in confusion and the beginnings of anger.

'A sheep farmer.' Lindsay nodded.

'What's yours?' Iain asked belligerently because he thought the question rude.

'A lawyer,' answered Lindsay. He looked at Iain frankly. 'There are certain things you have to know about an office like this. The first is that you don't address old Corbet as sir, unless the occasion warrants a degree of irony. He is our unique commissionaire and general factotum. He will help you. I, of course, am an apprentice like yourself. I'll now introduce you to Mr Cunningham and the two other partners. Then to the clerks. Most of them are decent enough fellows. Two of them are—,' and he used a lavatory word with sibilant calm. 'But you'll get to know them. Shall we go along now?'

Iain followed, bewildered, in a sinking dismay. Lindsay's manners and detachment, his natural air of ease and breeding, veiled an appraisement which Iain could not fathom but which left him with the feeling of having appeared as the complete country bumpkin. The queasy feeling of apprehension spread outward in a slight trembling of his muscles, rendered none the less agreeable by a dumb, smothered anger.

Lindsay paused, on a sudden thought, opened a door and ushered Iain in before him. There were half-a-dozen typists in the room. As by magic, each clattering machine stopped and all faces looked at him. They were the faces he had seen on Princes Street, selected and arranged on slim chairs, hatless, coatless, and in colour ranging from corn-blonde to raven-black. Somewhat dazed, he caught the edge of the small counter and gazed at his hand.

'Oh, Miss Lennox,' called Lindsay.

'Yes, Mr Lindsay.' A girl in her early twenties came up.

'The old man in?'

'Yes. I'm just waiting for his ring.'

'May I introduce Mr Cattanach, our new apprentice? Miss Lennox.'

'How do you do, Mr Cattanach?'

Iain shook hands.

Her hair was a tawny brown, her skin wonderfully fair, her features regular with wide-spaced eyes, dark-blue. Though she smiled only towards his eyes, Iain was aware that she had sounded and weighed him, not unkindly but absolutely.

'By the way,' began Lindsay, 'about – uh—'

'I think,' interrupted Miss Lennox, 'if you want to get Mr Cunningham before he starts his letters, perhaps you had better go in now.' While she spoke her eyes were on Lindsay.

He accepted their private and apparently agreeable message, for he smiled. 'I was merely about to suggest that I might introduce Mr Cattanach to the expectant, severally and individually. However – we shall return. Thank you.'

As he closed the door, he said calmly, 'That will give them something to talk about. They like it.' Opposite a door, bearing the name MR. CUNNINGHAM, he paused, and knocked, and, in answer to a summons, entered.

'This is Mr Cattanach, sir, the new apprentice.'

Mr Cunningham looked up from his broad desk. 'I think we have met before.' He smiled as he got up and shook hands with Iain, and the smile gave his smooth professional face a pleasing expressiveness. Of medium height, spare, with deep brown eyes, he was fifty-three years old, but did not look it. As he sat down, he said, 'So you're leaving sheep-farming for the law?'

'Yes, sir.'

'How is Major Grant?'

'I think he is very well.'

The brown eyes caught a quizzing light. 'I suppose you have no idea who it was that attempted to drown him?'

'No, sir.' Iain was not given to blushing. In such a moment, a confused rather dour expression might harden his features, but it could also effectively hide his thought. Now he felt guilt write itself blood-red on his face.

Mr Cunningham withdrew his eyes to Iain's letter.

'It was a dastardly thing to do,' he said, opening the letter, and added, 'I can naturally understand you would feel ashamed of such a thing happening in your own home district ... Major Grant thinks that you might like to concentrate on the estate side of our business?'

'Yes, sir,' said Iain blindly.

'Have you decided to take out classes at the University?'

Iain hesitated: 'I wrote about it – but I don't know—'

'And there's no particular hurry, for classes do not begin until—'

'October,' answered John Lindsay.

'Very good,' said Mr Cunningham. 'We'll have a talk when you have found your way about. When are you ready to begin here?'

'Now, sir.'

'That's the spirit!' He looked at John Lindsay. 'You will take Mr Cattanach around and introduce him and help him all you can.'

'Yes, sir.'

He smiled again to Iain. 'Don't hesitate to come and see me. You have got lodgings?'

'Yes, sir.'

'Good.' He brought some letters before him, then lifted his face again. 'You may find things a bit strange to begin with, but, as you know, it's not always the easy stalk that is the most satisfactory.'

Outside in the corridor, John Lindsay turned to Iain, 'Have you stalked deer with him?'

'Yes,' replied Iain shortly. He felt John Lindsay's eyes walking over his face.

'You were his stalker?'

'I helped.'

Lindsay withdrew his eyes and they walked a few paces to a door inscribed MR FORREST.

'Why', asked John Lindsay pausing, 'did you push Major Grant into the river?'

Iain turned on him. 'I didn't push him into the river.'

'No?' The cool eyes were regarding, with interest, Iain's quivering anger.

'No!'

'Not so loud. Brawls are reserved for the lavatory.' He smiled; then raising his eyebrows inquired, 'All right?'

Iain controlled himself and Lindsay knocked.

Mr Forrest, the second partner, had a notably large, thin, beaked nose ridden by pince-nez, a social smile that went on and off like the pince-nez, and a brow that wrinkled upward in harmony with a slight left-shouldered shrug.

Outside again, Lindsay explained: 'If you hear anyone referring to "The Macaw", you'll now know who it is. Plays the 'cello. String quartet. Mozart. Drawing rooms.' And he walked on to his next door. 'Charming way of putting in the morning, isn't it?' He pointed to the name MR HUTCHESON, said, 'Junior partner,' and knocked.

Mr Hutcheson pushed the chair back with his legs, remarking at the same time, 'It's all right, Miss Galloway,' to the girl who had picked up notebook and pencil. She sat on.

A tall, fair, well-made man in his forties, he looked naturally pleased at the interruption. Having learned who Iain was and where he came from, he asked, leaving his desk to stretch his legs, 'And what's brought you to a place like this?'

Iain smiled back but remained silent.

'What do you think, Lindsay?'

'Ambition,' answered Lindsay calmly.

'You see how it's done?' said Mr Hutcheson to Iain. He spoke with good nature, salted with friendly satire. 'Sheep not paying?'

'No.'

'The real things rarely do. When you get settled in, I want to have a talk with you about that. About farms and sheep. You'll know a bit about it, I suppose?'

'Oh well – a little.'

'Helped your father?'

'Yes.'

'Have you ever thought out why they don't pay?'

'Because—'

'Yes?'

'There's no money in it.'

Mr Hutcheson laughed. 'Lindsay would say that was obvious. He does not understand finality. That right, Lindsay?'

'I reserve comment,' said Lindsay.

'See?' said Mr Hutcheson to Iain. 'My advice to you is to watch these city hoggs. Know what a hogg is, Lindsay?'

'I always like learning, sir,' said Lindsay, 'at first hand.'

Mr Hutcheson laughed heartily. 'Know what a wether hogg is?'

'No, unless it is something shorn to the weather of a superior wit.'

'No, not that kind of weather, Lindsay, and not that kind of "shorn"!'

Iain could not help being affected by Mr Hutcheson's infectious laughter.

'You tell him all about it, Cattanach.' He shepherded them out of the room.

'What's a hogg?' asked Lindsay in the corridor.

Iain, who was now feeling more like himself, answered, 'A hogg is a young sheep.'

'Really. And what's a wether hogg?'

'A young sheep that has been castrated.'

Lindsay looked at him and smiled thoughtfully. He did not seem annoyed. 'An interesting type, Hutchy,' he remarked. 'The sort of man who would like to be doing "real things", but never will. His deeds are all written ones.'

They walked along.

'Well, shall we go in again?'

'No,' answered Iain.

Lindsay withdrew his hand from the door of the typists' room.

'Frightened of them?'

The verb stung Iain. 'I'm not usually frightened.'

Lindsay regarded him. 'I don't blame you, though there are one or two tolerable bits of stuff among 'em. Well, shall we have a smoke before continuing the introductions?'

'As you like,' muttered Iain.

Lindsay ushered him into the lavatory and produced a silver cigarette case bearing his monogram.

'You'll have to get to know the typists, so don't blame me.' He offered his case. As they lit up, he continued, 'Each partner has his typists, just as he has his clerk, senior and junior. There are other three typists, but you seem to have had enough of that genus for the moment. Then there are various departments and sections, cashier, conveyancing, and so on. You'll find it confusing. But it doesn't matter in the least.'

'What have we to do?'

'Donkey work – remarkable only for its variety. Estate duty forms, stock and share transfers, lots of copying work in Trust minute books – sederunt books – and estate chartularies, but traditionally we believe here in an early spell on effete Letter Books, both copying and indexing. I suppose there are more soulless jobs, though I don't happen to know any.' He was examining his hands and in the same toneless voice said, 'Filth.' Going to the nearest wash-hand basin, he manipulated the taps and, as he washed his hands, continued, 'You'll also have to run all sorts of errands. Here you'll find Corbie – your commissionaire friend – very useful. He prefers fetching and carrying when the pubs are open. You may find that useful, if you are given that way. Though I might point out that Mr Dowie – otherwise Bowf – has a rooted objection to breath that breathes strong drink. He is the senior clerk – Mr Cunningham's own. They say he is a Plymouth Brother or perhaps one of Jehovah's Witnesses.' He regarded his dark, pale, good-looking face in the mirror above the basin. 'A cheerful old fellow after his fashion, with a solicitous care for a young man's moral welfare. His sense of responsibility is such that he feels himself occasionally compelled to report delinquency to the high chief. You are warned.' He turned to the white roller-towel, dried his hands, combed his hair carefully, picked up his cigarette. After taking two deep mouthfuls, which he inhaled, he pushed a door open with his knee and shot his half-smoked cigarette neatly into a lavatory pan. 'You are requested not to drop cigarette-ends in the urinal. Shall we proceed?' He continued to hold the door open, and when Iain had disposed of his cigarette-end, he said, 'Please pull the chain.' They then proceeded.

TWO

By this time, Iain was conscious of little but grimly holding on. He could make nothing of John Lindsay, could not tell whether he was elaborately mocking an ignorant countryman or deliberately observing his behaviour as one might study the more curious antics of an unusual animal. His refusal to take offence, even to recognize the surges of dumb anger of which Iain himself had been chokingly aware, contained a politeness which was profoundly offensive. Yet there was nothing one could be certain of. He seemed, in his own cool way, to be quite frank.

Iain drew all his resources inward. The one thing the country had taught him was how to endure. Now was the time for it, as he entered upon the male faces in that large room. Shake hands, say as little as possible, go from one to another, get it over.

Mr Dowie was a big burly man with a full head of hair, grey over the ears but faded ginger elsewhere. He took Iain's hand in a firm grip. His words were at once jocular and cautionary. His eyes, which were not very large, twinkled. 'Coming from the country we will expect you to set a standard of conduct which is often sadly lacking in them who know only city ways.'

'Oh, come, come, Mr Dowie!' said an elderly, tired voice. 'We can't all emanate from the righteousness of the country.'

'More's the pity,' retorted Mr Dowie, his eyes glinting at the slight emphasis on the word 'righteousness'.

Iain felt he understood Mr Dowie, and as Lindsay took him from one to another, the back chat of office humour passed over his head. The short bursts of laughter were more important to the staff than his personal advent, though they all looked at him and had a word of greeting. Except for

Mr Dowie, the old or elderly men were spare and sharp-faced, as though time and their desks had rather withered them and rounded their shoulders.

Hissing the lavatory word under his breath, without any expression or movement of his features, Lindsay approached a man whose back was to them. As Lindsay spoke, the man turned round, accepted the introduction, remarking, 'Ha, the righteous young man!' Of medium height, stoutish, and growing noticeably bald, he laughed a social laugh in quick haw-haw notes, while his eyes took in Iain's appearance. His well-dressed body swayed, caught, as always, in its busy moment of importance, while his hands quickly and neatly squared the documents they held. He was about forty. No-one else laughed and Iain was dumb.

'Righteous my foot,' remarked Lindsay calmly.

'What's that? Haw-haw! You must stick your word in, Lindsay.'

'My defective social sense, Mr Smeaton.'

With his laugh, Smeaton turned from the disconcerting Lindsay to Iain. 'You know all about crofts?'

'Well, I know a bit,' admitted Iain.

'That's more than anyone else in this office does! Know anything about compensation claims for buildings, improvements, and so on?' He shook his papers.

'No.'

'Thought that was your main pastime up there – claiming compensation.'

'No. Not the main one.'

'You also look after sheep? Eh? Haw-haw!'

'Well,' said Iain, in his modest way, 'we know a sheep when we see one.'

A howl of laughter went through the office. Smeaton laughed also, but his face warmed and his green-grey eyes were now glinting on Iain, who, it must be confessed, had not deliberately been guilty of any innuendo.

'Glad you can see yourself,' called Mr Smeaton, hurrying off with his papers.

'Hear! hear!' cried a voice.

Mr Smeaton turned at the door and waved his papers with a gesture, 'Baa!' and out he went.

The office seemed delighted and glances were cast at Iain, whom Lindsay was now introducing to a man named Douglas, quiet, reserved, in his late thirties, with somewhat heavy features but noticeably dark eyes. He stretched himself and pulled down his waistcoat as his eyes wandered from their faces.

Finally John Lindsay introduced Iain to the Letter Book. 'It has to be indexed every morning,' he said, and was explaining the procedure to Iain, when he was called away.

Iain began turning over the flimsy pages, and so became engaged on his first task in the distinguished legal offices of Cunningham, Cunningham and Scott, Writers to the Signet.

THREE

Lifting his hand to the gas tap, Iain had a final look about his lodging. It was a big room with a high ceiling, and his nostrils caught again its mean, bare smell. The air in it was old and tired. It had, too, a peculiar dead silence. Something that had once been life clung about its chairs and lay under the table. The black horse-hair seat from which he had risen had a dull gleam.

Raising his eyes to the mantelpiece, he observed again the heavy green-and-gilt china dolphins, one at either end, whose gaping mouths upthrust sprays of withered honesty bearing ghostly shillings. Hanging between them, and three feet above the grey marble shelf, was the picture, framed in narrow gilt, of a minister of the gospel. It was a greatly enlarged photograph, the black cloth and hair very black and the face pale with a ghostly animation. There was great eloquence in the face, and from the places upon it where the hair grew, Iain knew that this divine had passed with his generation into that beyond where the mysteries themselves assess the eloquence.

The light went out with a plop like a bursting bubble, and over the cold linoleum he found his way to bed. Blankets and sheets had their own dry-steamy smell, but he was very tired and was going to sleep. For he had wandered about the streets, wondered and wandered, and finally just wandered on. From a bridge he had seen streets far below him, and they had seemed streets in a frightening under-world, and he had turned back.

Now he began to wonder about the kind of people who lived there, away down there. The dark stone tenements rose like cliffs, storey upon storey. Once again he had the curious childish feeling of human guilt and crime. These great dark window-pitted walls were ancient with human living, soaked with human deeds, the deeds of that world where he had seen, as he had looked down from the bridge, a girl hurrying across the street and two young fellows running after her.

His own street was mean enough, with hollowed stone doorsteps and the chalk-scrawls of noisy children. But he had got the room for fifteen shillings a week, including breakfast and supper, with lunch on Saturday and Sunday. He was going to get fifteen shillings a week from the office, so that all he had to provide was a meal in the middle of the day for five days out of seven. To-day he had had a glass of milk and buns at a total cost of fourpence. He began to make elaborate calculations. His father had handed him ten pounds with a quiet air, saying that when he needed more just to write. It had seemed an enormous sum. His grandmother had slipped another pound into his hand, with hurried injunctions about keeping up his strength and 'never to go without: mind that'. His landlady had asked for a pound a week – a meagre old maid with a stoop – but as he had made up his mind not to go beyond fifteen shillings, he told her so and turned away. Then she had looked pitiful and asked him where he worked. It had been like haggling and he had hated it. But now, when he had calculated that he could manage for six months without calling on his father, he felt better.

He was very wide awake by this time, and the day's happenings in the office began to stir. During his street wanderings, he had finally suppressed them, banished them. Now Mr Cunningham's question about Major Grant pierced him suddenly like a red-hot spike. He turned over and gripped two fistfuls of bedsheet. It was not the pushing of Major Grant into the river that did this, but the memory of his own blood-guilty flush.

How awkwardly he had behaved! Somehow he had never seen himself as a stiff, stupid country boy. At home, folk welcomed him and laughed, and he could pull legs and give back answers with the best. And make the fiddle fly and the dancers swing.

Awkward and stupid, unsure of his movements, with a

dull wild-beast anger throwing up sudden spirts, and all the time trying to be correct, smiling, saying 'Yes, sir!' – oh, excruciating! – to the commissionaire! And two juniors saying, 'Yes, sir – if you please,' as they passed out laughing, while Corbet blew out his moustaches.

And everywhere, in every black corridor of vision – John Lindsay's face.

He knew now that he was exaggerating everything, overdoing it, but still in this raw pain of feeling, this grotesque sensitivity, this idiocy of vision, he glimpsed something of what seemed the ultimate truth of himself.

They would make a butt of him. They could. He had no defence. They did not really mean to hurt him. All jocular; for fun. The only thing he could do would be to hit a young face hard, to let the country heave up and out and smash the city grin.

His teeth ground shut. The Letter Book was easy. He did not mind how much of that kind of work he got. So long as he knew how to do it. He would do whatever he was told. If he didn't understand quite what he was doing, he would find out in time. Keep himself within himself and give away as little as possible.

He began to calculate his money again. Suddenly he saw the girl sitting in Mr Hutcheson's office. He had hardly noticed her at the time and she certainly had never come into his mind since. But now he saw her completely, sitting alone, with dark hair and soft brown eyes, her hands in her lap and face slightly down. In a moment he saw her as if she sat alone in a great hall, or in a place where all around was darkness, and he was held by the stillness of her eyes.

Something of the mystery behind all eyes, behind all faces, touched him, and hearkening for meaning, his mind got hung up, and he sank out of it into sleep.

FOUR

Three of his letter impressions were badly smudged, but he could read them. Others of last night's batch were so faintly impressed on the flimsy sheets that there were whole phrases he could hardly make out. Too much water on the brush – and too little. Indexing was a laborious business, because he was not always certain of the proper index letter, particularly in the case of public companies, and so spent time hunting up previous entries. He was feeling tired, too, and the taste of that boiled egg was still in his mouth. Half dazed from lack of sleep, he had taken a whole spoonful of egg and swallowed it. The porridge had been thin and the milk blue, and when the lump of egg reached them they began to move around, trying to escape. They were still inclined to move and he felt he would be better if he could empty his stomach. But he was rather afraid of vomiting, for once, as a small boy, he had been sick from chewing a piece of black tobacco and had felt very weak, like death, after it.

There went Smeaton's voice, urgent in its haw-haw way. Iain did not lift his head. Now he was asking Wilson, who was in his third office year and talked of golf and wore a tie with school stripes, what a certain stamp duty was. Wilson replied that he wasn't quite sure and added something about 'the Budget'.

'That's the trouble,' replied Smeaton. 'I must find out. Oh, you, Cattanach!' A few quick strides and he was by Iain's side. 'Would you go along to the Revenue Stamp Office and find out the stamp duty on a verbal agreement. I want to know at once.'

Iain looked blank for a moment. 'The Revenue Stamp Office—?'

'It's at the east end of Princes Street, just beyond the Post Office.'

Iain decided he could find it and got up.

'Stamp duty – the amount of stamp duty – on a verbal agreement. Shall I write it down for you?'

'Oh, it's all right,' said Iain, automatically trying to memorize the words without thinking of their meaning.

He repeated them as he went along the street. 'Stamp duty on a verbal agreement.' The word 'verbal' began to stick out. 'Verbal', he knew, meant spoken, from the Latin *verbum*, a word. How could there be a stamp on a *spoken* agreement? Yet there might be an agreement by word of mouth, which could afterwards be put on paper? There were whole legal phrases in some of the letters he had been copying which held no meaning for him. Everyone knew the law was like that. His stomach was certain of it.

He stood on the edge of the last pavement, opposite the Register House, watching the traffic swing up the Bridges and swirl down Leith Street, or take off on a straight way that lifted to the distant sky. Human beings milled and swirled like the traffic, legions of them. His father was alone on the hillside and Mary was a solitary figure on a path. A newspaper was flicked in front of him. He turned away from the vendor, crossed the street, and found the Inland Revenue office which dealt in stamps.

'Yes?'

'Have you got a list, please, of the – of the latest stamp duties?'

The cool face with the sharp eyes concentrated on Iain. 'What exactly do you want?'

Then Iain plunged. 'The stamp duty on a verbal agreement.'

Iain saw the light change and glisten in the eyes. But the face turned over its shoulder and solemnly called aloud to another face: 'This gentleman wants to know the stamp duty on a verbal agreement.'

A voice with thick unction somewhere said, 'Another mug!'

Iain turned and made blindly for the door, followed by laughter from both sides of the counter.

Presently he found himself in Rose Street, a narrow high-walled cavern, that was Princes Street's back lane, avoiding horses and barrows if not the curses of those who directed them. He was feeling blind and murderous. Never before had he known humiliation of this kind. Never. There had been two or three young fellows in the public office – he had only half glimpsed them – but now he knew they were apprentices from other legal firms. It would be the joke everywhere. Stamp duty on a *verbal* agreement! Oh God!

There was now a queer laugh in his face. A woman cleaner looked after him. A policeman's head, turning slowly on its neck, following his progress, brought him to himself. Before the side window of a shop on Hanover Street, he drew up to look at some paintings, for he would have to think of what he was going to do next.

Two lads, seedy clerks of some kind by their appearance, were contemplating a picture of Christ. The crown of thorns was part of the dark-brown hair and the eyes were closed in dark-brown smudges. The face with its immortal suffering was calm.

'No, I'm not pulling your leg,' said a cheerful Edinburgh voice. 'Stare steadily at the eyes and they'll open. It's a fact.'

'How could they open? I may be from the country, but I'm no mug.'

'Damn it, try it, and you'll see.'

'Have you tried it?'

'Yes. It's a famous picture . . .'

Pursued by the need to get away from himself, Iain had been staring at the eyes. Possibly because his instinct would have been to avoid that face, he now regarded it with a dumb concentration in which there was a strange element of defiance.

Quietly – and slowly – the eyes opened and looked straight at him. Actually he had this feeling of time being taken, of an action that was real and perfectly natural. And in the open eyes was something more than the crown of thorns, the pale brow, the accepted agony, more than they could ever mortally convey. Their sad gaze at once penetrated him utterly and was gentle.

He broke away in a fashion that made the Edinburgh voice call after him, 'Hey, did you see it?' But he hardly heard, went straight across the street, and continued along the narrow lane.

FIVE

Corbet, the commissionaire, saw him coming in a drifting, uncertain fashion, without haste. 'What's kept you?' he asked.

Iain glanced at him. 'Nothing,' and was about to walk past.

'Couldn't you find the place?'

'Yes, I found it.'

'They've been asking for you. You have been away over two hours.'

'Have I?'

'There were letters to deliver, you know.'

'Have you got them?' His manner was calm and distant, his voice indifferent.

The commissionaire looked sharply at him. 'I'll get them.'

Iain waited in the vestibule. Beyond the door, he heard a laugh. The commissionaire came out with a brisk expression and some letters in his hand. He walked, head up, like a sergeant-major. 'This should have been done earlier,' he announced. 'You slip down and deliver that two. I'll meet you here.'

When they met again, the commissionaire said, 'We'll go back this way,' and Iain found himself in Rose Street once more. Before the door of a public-house, the commissionaire paused and looked searchingly at Iain from under his heavy, thrusting eyebrows. 'Could you do with something?'

'I don't mind,' answered Iain.

It was now nearly two o'clock and there was no-one in the pub. The barman came in from a side door, saying, 'Hullo, Bob. Nice day again.'

The commissionaire's manner now changed, as if an invisible starch had been taken out of it all at once. He called the barman Jimmy, and spoke naturally and humanly. When

he asked Iain what he would have, Iain looked expressionlessly along the rows of bottles.

'A beer?' prompted the commissionaire.

'No.'

'A wee port? It might do you good.'

'A whisky.'

'Ghor!' said the commissionaire. He made a joke of it
with the barman, then carried the pint of beer and the small
whisky to a little table in a corner. The barman went out.

'Don't you worry, lad. It's a joke that's played on every
young apprentice,' began the commissionaire, in a warm,
expansive voice. 'Here's the best!'

'Slainte,' acknowledged Iain and straightway drank off
the whisky. It caught his throat.

'Gode, you're quick on it!'

Iain wiped his eyes and coughed his throat clear. 'It's all
right,' he said, in the same indifferent tones.

'You see,' explained the commissionaire, in a confidential
voice gone husky, as he splayed his elbows on the table, 'a
verbal agreement is something that is not written down. You
couldn't stick a stamp on it. It's only spoken. See? It's not
on stamped paper. It's not on any paper. That's where Hee-
haw had you! You get me?' He leaned back, lifted his pint,
then laid it down in order to illustrate the matter still further.
By the time he had finished, his voice had even gained rich
country intonations. Laughter was nodding inward in his
face.

'What did they say to you in the Stamp Office when you
asked?'

'Nothing much,' replied Iain.

A gust or two of laughing breath moved the moustaches.
'Look, now, you want to get your own back. You *had* to go
through it. No-one could help you there. But – give him as
much as you got. That's the ticket. You get me?'

'No.'

'Well, listen. You know young Lindsay? The same joke
was played on him.' Suddenly the commissionaire glanced
sharply and mistrustfully at Iain. 'Did he tell you?'

'No.'

'I thought not.' He nodded, reassured. 'Well, young Lindsay came back after two hours – like yourself – and when he came back, they asked him what about it.'

'Who? Hee-haw?'

'No fear. Not with a Lindsay. Though he was in it. You know who young Lindsay is?'

'No.'

'Ghor!' He then proceeded at length to give the Lindsay history, complete with law lords and its distant link with a titled nobility. With the firm of Lindsay and Ross nothing, it appeared, could compete in legal tradition. 'That', said the commissionaire, 'is the appex.'

'Why doesn't he train in his father's office?'

'Lord love you, that's not done! It wouldn't do. Don't you see? They must go through the mill, all the young sprigs take their knocks with the rest. And they do. There's worse than young Lindsay, even if he does look at you as if you was a specimen.'

A faint light came back into Iain's eyes.

'However,' continued the commissionaire, 'he certainly scored in the end!'

'How?'

'When he came back to the office at last and was asked what about it, he said he had spent the two hours hunting the coffee houses of Edinburgh for a lawyer who knew enough Latin to give him the root meaning of 'verbal'. So far he had not succeeded, but he hoped to pursue his researches at greater length in the afternoon, after which he trusted he would be in a position to approach the Stamp Office with some authority.' Corbet produced a fair mimicry of John Lindsay, then proceeded to explain the joke. 'See? He had never been to the Stamp Office at all!'

The empty whisky-glass was turning to a watery light before Iain's eyes.

'Here, you're looking green!'

'Rotten egg – this morning—' Iain rose, and the commissionaire ran him into the urinal. There he comforted him with practical advice about the need for having all the stuff up when he was at it. 'You were right about the egg,' he added critically.

On his chair again, Iain wiped the cold beads from his forehead. His flesh was trembling, his face of a ghastly pallor. But his lips were pressed back hard against his teeth.

The commissionaire called on Jimmy and they had a confidential talk. The barman returned presently with a cup of hot tea. Three men came in for beer. When Iain had drunk the tea, the commissionaire called a word of thanks to Jimmy, and, outside, squared himself, with a swift glance on either hand.

'Think you can face it?'

'Yes.'

'Fine! Rub your face. I'll go on first.' The commissionaire, with a final back-handed lift to his moustaches, strode away.

'Hullo!' called Smeaton. 'What's kept you?'

'Had to wait,' said Iain.

'Did you get it?'

'No. They asked me back at three o'clock.' He turned to the Letter Book.

'What for?'

'They said the Budget would be sure to be out by then.'

Laughter cackled through the office. Iain sat down, looking weary and dumb.

Smeaton's expression narrowed on Iain's face. 'Are you going back at three?'

Iain looked up at him. 'Do you want me to?'

'Of course!'

'All right,' murmured Iain, 'I'll go.' The tea had cleared away the grey pallor but his face was still unnaturally pale. Obviously he wanted to be left alone, like some dour but sensitive country youth who could not grip the meaning of what was happening around him. Something in this attitude, something genuine but also dangerous, warned Smeaton not to probe further at the moment.

Iain was, in fact, feeling so ill that he was afraid he would have to give in and stagger from the office, perhaps collapse. The shame of that, he would never live down. If only he could manage to hold on till three o'clock, he would then go straight home. He did not mind the joke now.

The whole office, however, was aware of an element of uncertainty, enigmatic and therefore the more amusing. Had Iain given the least impression that he was acting a part, Lindsay would have come under suspicion. But the new apprentice, whatever else troubled his mind, was certainly not acting.

John Lindsay, checking over some newly typed lists of feu-duties in a Church Trust, was rendered thoughtful. In a little while, he strolled over to the table where Iain was working.

'How are you getting on?' he asked.

'All right,' replied Iain laconically.

'If you're not sure of anything—'

Iain, giving him his shoulder, went on with his work.

Lindsay looked at the side face narrowly, at the hand which wrote, then turned back to his desk. Iain's contained enmity had been unmistakable, even to the rest of the office. There was more than one smile at Lindsay's expense.

'Got a lot of change, Lindsay?' suggested Smeaton.

'You may keep it,' said Lindsay, in the tone of one tipping the hall porter.

About three o'clock, Mr Dowie, who had the air of not knowing anything about the current office joke, came bustling along and stopped at Iain's desk. 'Well, young man, and how are you getting along? Let me see your book.'

When Mr Dowie had consulted whatever letter he may have wished to see, he ostentatiously checked one or two of Iain's entries in the index. 'Very good.' He patted him on the shoulder. 'Unlike some of them in this office, you at least haven't indexed a Company under "Secretary". That's some-thing to your credit side.' He gave one or two small bowfs of challenging satisfaction.

Iain kept his face to the table and hardly breathed, for he was afraid that Mr Dowie might smell the whisky, whose aftermath was still in his nostrils.

Now Mr Dowie was asking him if he knew any Latin and it became clear to the office, and to Iain, that the inquisition was to lead to an interpretation of the word 'verbal'. But just then a bell went and Mr Dowie was called aloft.

After the lapse of a few minutes, the commissionaire, with a wink behind Iain's back, said in his impersonal voice, 'It's three o'clock.'

Iain continued working on the Letter Book for a full couple of minutes. Then obviously having completed his task, he slowly got up and went out without looking at anyone.

Ten minutes later the golfing junior, Wilson, returned. 'Sold!' he said. 'Never went near the Stamp Office. Took a tram up the Mound.'

'Well I'm damned!' declared Smeaton.

Lindsay laughed, and for Lindsay to laugh was rare.

SIX

Saturday forenoon found the office full of bustle and subdued excitement. Ledgers thumped on desks, feet strode purpose-fully; there were short outbursts of challenging talk on golf and rugby; there were plus-fours and stockings. The younger men seemed removed from Iain by an extra mile.

'Can I see you for a moment?' asked Mr Dowie, and Iain followed him to his desk.

'Do you know any folk in town?' Mr Dowie's voice was at once serious and friendly.

'No,' said Iain, 'not many.' Actually, apart from those in the office, he knew none.

'You have some friends here, then?'

'Well, I haven't called on any. But—' Iain hesitated, looking diffident and confused.

'No family friends?'

'No.'

'What are you doing with yourself to-morrow?'

'Well – I don't know yet.'

'What Church did you go to at home?'

'The United Free.'

'The United Free Church. Very good. I could introduce you – let me see.' Mr Dowie thought for a moment. 'Yes. Could you come along to-morrow, say about half-past five, to my home? This is the address.' He wrote it down, handed it to Iain, and began to explain the easiest way of reaching it.

'Thank you,' murmured Iain.

'We'll be glad to see you,' said Mr Dowie. 'And we can have a little talk at any rate.' His smallish eyes twinkled in the friendliest way. 'Now you run off and get your work through, and we'll see you to-morrow.'

Iain got back to his copying, aware of an ironic glance from young Lindsay, who otherwise, however, paid no attention to him.

The prospect of this visit weighed upon him all Saturday afternoon. It made the streets more tiresome, lifted the houses above the Mound to a crowded, perilous height, threw its shadow on the sombre Castle rock, and gave to the brass notes of the band in Princes Street Gardens a formal and distant mournfulness.

He did not want his solitude broken in upon, as though to lose its tightness would be to lose his strength, for he did not know the ways of these people, did not know how they behaved socially in their own homes, and so the whole thing would be a strain. He began to resent the invitation, and his resentment did not lessen when he argued that, after all, Mr Dowie was the only one who had offered hospitality. He did not want the hospitality, and, remembering John Lindsay's reference to Mr Dowie's religiosity, he began to suspect its motive, just as he had come to suspect the trick in the picture by which Christ's eyes opened. Presently he was surprised how hot and tired his feet were, how stiff and weary his back and shoulders.

When he sat down on the grass in the gardens, his isolation seemed to draw eyes upon him, eyes picking him out or ignoring him as a solitary. When he could no longer bear this, he went away. The music had no meaning for him at all. Each 'classical excerpt' was a solemn irregular wall of sound, matching in sombreness the dark wall of the rock.

Scrambled egg for tea, peppered and salted. He had said he didn't care for an egg in the morning. He should have said that he didn't care for eggs at any time. But that made him think of the fish he had had last night. At least pepper and salt muted this yellow curdly stuff spread thinly over its slice of soggy toast. He ate it all, but so completely without relish that his stomach returned a protest, in the fume of which his nostrils caught the niff which no pepper could confuse.

'Damn muck!' he said with sudden spite. The blue milk

made the tea a ditch-water black. Though perhaps it was hardly fair blaming the milk! He hadn't seen a potato since he had left home, nor solid meat. He was probably weak from lack of nourishment. As he cut another slice from the white loaf, he felt that the miserable old woman would think she was being robbed. Why should he feel uncomfortable about that? Wasn't he paying for it? She had asked for a pound.

When the dishes were cleared away, he took off his shoes and lay on his back in bed. The images that wandered through his mind were only vaguely defined, but perhaps he did fall asleep, for when he came fully to himself there were shadows in the room and he thought he heard the high distant sound of a train's whistle. He listened to the silence in the room and the near sounds in the street. He had heard the train's whistle going rushing through the gardens, under the rock, when the band had been playing, rushing upon an underworld.

He saw the bandsmen again in their uniforms and the conductor beating time with his baton, inclining his head now to this side, now to that. Sometimes the baton quivered upward; there was a roll and a crash; then the baton began beating time again. It was all very solemn and distant, the figures diminished, and it held now, more than before, some haunted memory of a ceremonial occasion. Though as he had encountered no such scene or occasion before, perhaps it was that the bandsmen and their music were in some formal way the expression of crowds of people, sitting or wandering, laughing or listening, swelling over paths upon neatly shorn grass, around clumps of smoke-darkened shrubs and bright flowers, while the rumble of tramcars went along the great street, and, high on the other side, uprose the Castle of history. In a region beyond thought, the gathering of people in crowds had something strangely sad about it and ominous – but ominous, as it were, for them, too, and none the less so because of the air of holiday which swam about them, about the gardens and about the timeless afternoon.

He got out of bed and from underneath it drew forth his

violin case. He had not opened it since his arrival, and now he thumbed the strings quietly, lest anyone should overhear. Finally he tuned it till the fifths sang in his ear. From this high-up room, he reckoned the children on the street could not hear him.

He began to play *Mairi Bhan*, thinly, with the delicate resiliency of the upper bow. There were a few moments when the tune would not come through to him, when it would not come alive, overborne by this new world, by its multiple and terrible significance. The toes of the tune danced, but they were the toes of a wooden figure with country face, empty, without expression. They advanced and retired, vacantly, without meaning. He whipped more action into them, and they did their best, but now the extra energy came not from joy but from pain. They wanted him to stop, to stop, and he felt he should stop, from very shame, and let the simple country figure, with its idiot's alarm, collapse.

But he would not give in; his eyebrows gathered; his eyes shot anger along the strings, between his fingers, until it curled with the scroll, sustaining itself, lifting the drooping fiddle, in defiance and pride, uncaring who heard or what happened, while the bow responded in length and swiftness. The transformation took place in an instant: the figure burst into life and being, as once, when a little boy, taken in wonder to a travelling circus at Kinmore, he had seen a girl burst through a paper hoop, and there she was like a miracle, acknowledging the cheers, while the splendid grey horse, on whose back she stood, swept round the ring.

Alive and dancing-happy, the country face was vivid now, full of warmth, sun warmth, the body alive to its toes. And behind her, around her, deep deep beyond her, the bodies and faces he had known in his country life and did not need to see, all the influences that were there and in his own blood, surging and sweeping through his blood, sweeping beyond what his fiddle could do, until bow and fingers swept them away, like a wind-whirl of leaves, and of their own accord, without conscious thought from him, out of a need for strength and balance, for mastery, bow and fingers improvised a high flurry of notes – and dropped into the slow measure of the Eriskay song.

But the slow notes – they were too profound, too terrible in their potency. There is a level at which the emotion of naked life can no more be borne, life lifting its face from the emotion of ten thousand years, its girl's singing face, pale with the generations of the dead, and the singing throat of an innocence that at last, at long last, is pure.

He laid the fiddle on the bed and went over to his chair. He was breathing heavily and the convolutions and surgings of the music kept thought away, drowned its doll-like city mechanisms in assurance and pride, its clustering houses and toy bandsmen, its dark walls and rock, its peering windows, its legal faces. And all at once, because he had found his lost kingdom of life, he came to the brink of tears, and had to get up and walk about, with a violence in his head, a longing, and a high-crying immortal loveliness.

Impossible to stay in this room now and out he went. But as his fingers fumbled for the small knob of the door of the flat, he became aware of his landlady in the dark passageway to the kitchen. She was standing at a little distance, quite still, her slight stoop made evident by an uptilt of the features. The pale features alone were visible and on them he saw, coming through their pitiable reserve, a queer uncertain smile.

Hurriedly he got out, feeling hot, lest she speak to him.

She must have been listening, he thought. He all but laughed, and strode on without taking any conscious direction. He was oddly relieved. No need now to worry about his playing, about who heard him. Why should he? They could complain if they liked! He saw her face again – in the shadows, swept into the gloom, her shrunken old maid's body. He had no feeling of pity for it, only a certain triumph over it.

His feet carried him into the old town, where life swarmed and the tenement walls were cliffs. Because he had had that first shrinking fear of it, this was adventure. He buttoned his jacket against theft, against pickpockets and sudden assault. History had been one of his school subjects and he

knew a little about the Royal Mile which ran from the Castle
to Holyrood House. Somewhere stood John Knox's house;
from some window or balcony Argyll's wife had spat in the
face of Montrose as he was being led to his execution. Dan-
the-trapper had a poem about 'the great Montrose' which
he still recited when more than half-seas over. Iain had heard
it first just after midnight on a New Year's morning. Ever
since that boyhood's morning the name Montrose had carried
a splendour. Mary Queen o' Scots. Darnley and Kirk o' Field.
Kings and queens in procession. The houses of the great
nobles. James V wandering disguised as a beggar to see how
the poor lived and thought. The ancient, the stormy, the gay
and gallant and dark and bloody pageant of Scots history.

The lamps were lit and night stood in the mouths of the
wynds and closes. The people were different here from the
people in Princes Street, different in their clothes, the movements of their bodies, their features, the way they glanced.
Women with shopping satchels, intent or argumentative,
forthright or timid, sharp-eyed. Youths in a vennel-mouth.
Cat-calls. A figure slipping past, hurried, furtive. A smell
that had no name, faint, pervasive, sifting through its age-
old blanket. Men going into and coming out of pubs, stop-
ping to argue on the kerb. Oaths – a whipping filthy mouthful.
A laughing group, one stout woman swaying, pushing her
neighbour away from her in playful emphasis. Two policemen
walking along slowly, tall men. A scurry of shrill children.
The two policemen stopped, an arguing group dissolved,
sucked out of sight up a dark close.

Intensely alert, Iain tried to feel unconcerned, but all the
time was ready for what might come at him. At last, however,
he stood, deciding he would go no further. Far better to see
the place first in daylight, so that he might know where he
was, know how to behave, what to say, where to retreat. A
countryman learned the ways of a trap before poking about
in it. Burke and Hare murders . . . nothing of that to-day. It
might lurk about – but it could not happen. The unemployed, the unemployed. The dole. 'The bloody Government,'
said a man's hoarse voice; 'the – Government. Christ!'

He moved on, and stood again, looking back. A figure brushed against him – a ragged old man, head bent, mumbling to himself, taking short blind-like steps. He had his own smell.

Presently something vaguely familiar in the shape of a building made his memory grope after an illustration . . . John Knox's house! Could it be? These stones, that house? The graven face, the long grey beard, the round flat bonnet. The Presbyterian's religious man of destiny. The man who had out-argued, out-faced Europe's loveliest queen, and sent her inevitably to her doom. Short echoes of his history-reading came back, hardly in words, more as an overtone of history's weird music, affecting him as did his own native music at times; all violence spent, the tears shed, but in the air still the high-crying immortal loveliness. How surprised he had been when one day the teacher had told them Mary the Queen's age in her arguments with John Knox. Queen of Scotland at nineteen and by twenty-five shut forever in an English prison. Arguing with John Knox at about his own age, or not much older than Mary Cameron at home!

At thought of Mary Cameron, his eyes switched level and were caught at once by the face of a man upon whom the street light fell directly. Again a feeling of familiarity beset him, and for one wild moment the figure came walking towards him, in disguise, out of history.

Only as the face passed and he saw its eyes did he realize that this was the man Douglas from his own office, wearing a cap with the snout pulled well down. Bewildered, the flush of recognition mounting, Iain stood looking after that secretive figure. Had Douglas recognized him? What was he doing here? Where was he going?

For there was something purposeful about his expression now, a strangeness, a glint in the eye. Iain remembered him best by the way his eyes had drifted from his own face and from Lindsay's at the moment of introduction. That hazed expression, as if the man had not slept well and was keeping them both at their distance, politely but indifferently, was now gone.

An impulse to follow him was dispelled by the soft brush
of a passing body, a whiff of scent in his nostrils. The girl
looked back and laughed, swaying and beckoning with her
head. Nothing very professional about her conduct; more
like a girl out for a bit of fun; beckoning him to come and
follow where Douglas was leading. But clearly she was not
following Douglas, for now she loitered and finally stood
on the edge of the pavement, looking back at him. He turned
away, a turmoil in his breast.

SEVEN

Mr Dowie's welcoming voice rose behind the maid who was politely asking his name: 'Ha, you have found your way!' A peg for Iain's hat, and now a door was opening into a large room. He breasted the faces and the frocks. 'This is Mr Cattanach, all the way from the Highlands. My wife.' Iain shook hands and a stout motherly woman beamed at him. 'It's very good of you to come.' There were three daughters: Elizabeth, Agnes, and Joan. He shook hands with them in turn. Joan was about his own age, the other two older. 'This is Miss Galloway, whom you have met.'

'Yes,' said Iain, and 'Yes' said Miss Galloway, her dark face melting in an attractive smile. Her brother was there, Mr William Galloway; also two sons of the house, one of them in a law office, Frank, and the other not in a law office, Jack. And there they all were, standing. 'Sit down now!' said Mrs Dowie, and Iain looked at his chair to make sure it would be there when he sat on it, and they all sat down.

'And how do you like Edinburgh?' asked Mrs Dowie.

'Fine, thanks,' answered Iain.

'You haven't had time yet to find your way about properly, of course.'

'No, not much.'

'Do you think you will prefer the city to the country – or is it a bit early to ask you that?'

'Well,' replied Iain, 'I don't know.'

'Give him a chance,' said Mr Dowie. 'And I would like you people to understand that every countryman doesn't want to come rushing to the city. Isn't that right, Mr Cattanach?'

'Well – I don't know.' Feeling goaded to add something

this time, he added: 'They're different in many ways.' He was smiling all the time.

'As an effort in understatement,' remarked Elizabeth, 'you have said it.'

The girls laughed, and so the concentration upon him was for the moment broken. As a business woman of thirty, Elizabeth had her point of view. She was fair and firm and liked saying things in a crisp, laconic way, as if this household of hers needed it. She liked, too, the laughter that followed her sallies, but at heart she was probably good-natured.

'I think the Highlands are wonderful,' said Agnes, who, in view of her elder sister's responsibility for the astringent, could afford to indulge her romantic nature.

'So do I,' said Miss Galloway.

But unfortunately for Iain, the talk disclosed that he had never been to Appin, had never taken the wonderful train journey to Mallaig, had not seen the Coolin mountains in Skye, even from a distance, and as for the Hebrides—

'Like Mother,' Elizabeth suggested, 'you prefer to behold the Hebrides in dream.'

Again the situation was eased, but Joan, the youngest, who had not yet spoken, now asked feelingly, 'Are you a good sailor?'

'I don't know,' answered Iain. 'I have never been on the sea.'

'Haven't you?' Then she added solemnly, 'You haven't missed much.'

There was great laughter at this. Behind the laughter were regions of family intimacy, of a private social humour to which Iain had no key. When Mr Dowie suddenly got up and bustled out, there ensued an increase of activity in all regions, positively a condition of abandon in which two or even three voices spoke at once, each raising itself in order to be heard. At this point Mrs Dowie, beaming, arose and murmured that she must 'get the tea'.

As the door closed behind her, a piece of music fell off the piano. 'Oh goodness!' declared Elizabeth, looking sharply over her shoulder at this effort of the inanimate to join in.

For a while Iain was completely, if not impolitely, ignored. In some way, indeed, his dumb presence excited them to a social mirth that fed on itself. It was really difficult for them, because nothing could be done about him, and this of itself kept laughter on the bubble. Moreover there had been feminine speculation about him, given a certain shape by Miss Galloway, and now here he was himself. Somehow it was all temptingly amusing, particularly when Elizabeth, recognizing her duties as hostess in the absence of her mother, said that Mr Cattanach must think them very rude in their allusions to people whom he did not know and Iain replied politely, 'Not at all.'

But Joan had her large china-blue eyes on him, because his solitariness, as of a hill bird, roused her sympathy. The smile that froze on his face, the eyes that did not know quite where to look, something particularly about the eyebrows, the way they gathered, giving the eye-glints a certain wild if baffled quality – rather aristocratic, she thought – attracted her secretively, for she knew that she alone understood him. She hated the sea, but loved her picture of mountains and woods and hawks and other birds. Her latest treasured quotation, which explained all life, spoke of the soul as a bird in a cage.

'Joan,' said Agnes.

'Yes?' Joan looked at her.

'Nothing,' said Agnes and, amid the laughter, Joan knew she had been 'staring'.

Frank said something about Agnes's 'drop kick', but Elizabeth refused to have 'the men' talking 'rugby shop'. 'You don't play rugby, do you, Mr Cattanach?'

'No,' answered Mr Cattanach.

'What do you play up there?' asked Jack, in an effort at a natural voice.

'Shinty, mostly.'

'That's a man's game, if you like,' declared Jack.

'It's a kind of hockey, isn't it?' asked William Galloway.

'I have never seen hockey played,' replied Iain, 'but I understand there is a similarity.'

'Take it from me,' said Jack, 'hockey is merely the feminine form of the man's game, which is shinty.'

'You can swing the club all round your head, can't you?' asked Frank.

'Well, you swing it,' said Iain.

'And let out a roar and charge!' added Frank.

'Sounds dangerous to me,' said Elizabeth.

'Did you ever get hurt?' asked Joan.

But this concentration upon him got broken by the ringing of a hand bell. Elizabeth arose.

Mrs Dowie sat alone at one end of the table, with her teacups and silver service before her; Mr Dowie at the other. Cold meat and salad were served. Iain took both milk and sugar, and Joan moved her bread plate to give him plenty of space for his cup and saucer. In a few words, Mr Dowie thanked the bountiful Giver. Iain had a momentary difficulty when his large stiff napkin slipped to the floor. Joan, with a quite romantic eagerness to help him, brought their heads into sharp collision. Iain said he was sorry and flushed very deeply. The whole table was amused, and Joan, forgetting as usual to think before she acted, showed a pink tongue-tip to Agnes's eyes.

'Joan!' said her mother.

'Well, it's sore,' said Joan, rubbing her fair crown.

Iain began eating meat for the second time in one day, and even swallowed the slices of tomato which he disliked.

The meal over, the ladies fled to get ready for church, for as Mr Dowie had remarked, looking at his watch, 'We are cutting it a bit fine.'

After a time Jack, who had obviously been hearkening to internal household noises, said to Iain, 'I think the way is clear now.' He adventured, followed by Iain, and found the bathroom unoccupied.

Mrs Dowie thanked Iain for his visit and hoped that he would come back very soon again to see them, then she shook hands with him. Mr Dowie also shook hands: 'Now that you have found your way, don't stand on ceremony, young man.' Elizabeth shook hands, then Agnes, and finally Joan, whom Agnes watched.

Now they were on the street, and William Galloway changed places so that his sister, Morna, was between them.

'Did you enjoy your visit?' asked Morna.

'Yes, thank you.'

'You know they're Methodists, of course?' said William, speaking now in a man-of-the-world voice. He was twenty-four.

'No, I didn't know.'

'Old Dowie – very kind man. Does a lot for children in connection with his church – treats and so on.'

'Oh,' said Iain. 'He's very kind.'

'Yes. Believes that a truly religious man should be joyful.' He smiled.

Iain did not quite know how to take this, so he said nothing.

'I think Joan very amusing sometimes,' declared Morna, 'don't you?' She gave him a fleeting glance. She looked shy and soft, as if she could retire into herself very deeply. This made her darkly attractive and inviting. And her smile had its gleam. She was almost quite different, somehow, from his imaginary picture of her.

'Yes, I do,' he replied, smiling also.

'Here,' said William, in an even more manly voice, 'sure you want to come to church? It was Mr Dowie's idea. He rather landed us.'

'Yes, thank you. He asked me to come along.'

'I know. But if you want to beat it – now is the time.'

'What William means,' explained Morna, 'is that you mustn't come if you don't want to. If you *do* want to, then we'll be very glad to – to take you.'

'I thought I had made that clear,' remarked William with brotherly sarcasm.

The church bells were now ringing, and something at once solemn and hollow in their high tumbling sounds very nearly freed his wild instinct to escape, but he thought of Mr Dowie. William glanced across at him.

'As long as I'm not troubling you,' said Iain.

'Please don't think that,' said Morna. 'William imagines everyone is like himself.'

'My modesty,' said William.

There was quite a small crowd going in at the door, and William, pausing abruptly to make way for an elderly lady, butted Morna back against Iain. 'Sorry,' she whispered, with an upward glance. 'Not at all,' murmured Iain, looking over her head.

The father and mother and two younger sisters were already in the pew. There were faint smiles from the parents, and side-long looks from the young girls at intervals.

Iain listened to the service with a translated sense of unreality. Sometimes he had deliberately to move to defeat the hypnotic effect. The high vaulted spaces held vacancy and distance, resounding and ascending when the great organ pealed. And even when the organ ceased, the sustained notes lingered, and he found his eyes travelling upward under the iron of his brows.

Outside on the pavement, Morna introduced him to the family as a new arrival at the firm of Cunningham, Cunningham and Scott. More talk. Friendly invitations. A last smile from Morna, and Iain found himself alone. Automatically he removed his hat and wiped his brow with a palm. But his brow was quite dry.

EIGHT

'You get runs like that,' said Corbet, the commissionaire. 'Great thing is to get the damn lot done.' Square-shouldered, with peaked cap, jutting eyebrows and upright carriage, he took the pavement on his bows. Iain saw his eyes glance from side to side before he put about into Rose Street. The post had been exceptionally heavy.

'Jimmy' – Iain recalled the barman – 'make it a port instead of a glass of beer.'

Jimmy smiled. 'Can't manage the beer?'

'No,' said Iain.

'So long as you keep off the whisky!'

'I'm promising nothing!' Iain picked up his change, and carried the pint and glass of port to the corner, where Corbet was elbowing himself into comfort.

'Ho,' said Corbet, eyeing the port with amusement. Down went half the pint. He sucked his moustaches. 'You'll have to learn to take beer. That's a funeral drink – for women. Binds you up – you'll never go wrong on beer. Now . . . watch him!' Corbet had interrupted himself to indicate with a glance a man at the counter who was swilling the dregs of a bottle of beer into his glass. 'Know why he does that? To get the yeast at the bottom. Loosens him up.'

Iain sipped his port and found its sweet fusty flavour attractive.

'That's one thing you have got to watch – constipation.' He eyed Iain. 'You find the change of life and grub putting you off your regular?'

'Well – it's a change,' admitted Iain.

'You watch it, my boy. Ghor! I could tell you a few things about that.' Whereupon he began to tell them, straight from early army days, and even included a civilian who, unaffected by horse pills, finally nearly killed himself by eating a pound of green apples. 'Talk about a burst drain!' He shook his head. 'It was serious.' He became solemn, almost awed, in memory. Then he gave Iain 'a few tips', winding up his discourse with the reflection: 'Man was never meant to sit on an office stool. When I see all of you on stools; the girls on stools; everyone on stools, all over the city, stools – no wonder it's the first thing the doctor asks.' His clean-shaven cheeks might have been oiled, with a rosy tinge glowing in the yellowish skin. 'How long you been here now?'

'Just over a month.'

Corbet winged his moustaches. 'Like it?'

'Oh, not too bad.'

'Afraid you were never made for it,' said Corbet. 'Otherwise you wouldn't be sitting here drinking with a poor old commissionaire. Ghor! What would Bowf say if he knew!' He laughed huskily, and slightly in wonder. 'Not but that I have known a few of them in my time. How old do you think I am?'

'I couldn't say.'

'Make a guess.'

Iain thought he might be a little over fifty, so he said, 'Fifty.'

'On my next birthday I'll be sixty-five.'

'I don't believe it.'

'It's true all the same. Not that many know that, so I keep it to myself.'

'You haven't been troubled about stools,' said Iain, and saw Corbet laugh properly for the first time.

'Here, have another!'

'No,' said Iain. 'I'm late as it is.'

'Late for your landlady! Ghor!' He went to the counter and had a joke with Jimmy, who suggested that he was leading the young fellow astray. Iain did not want the drink. Already the wine was in his head for his stomach was dead empty. But Corbet had helped him with the heavy mail; had obviously taken a liking for him, had given him many useful 'tips' and saved him more than once from making a fool of himself. The contrast between Corbet the commissionaire, the man who smartly saluted Mr Cunningham, said 'Yes, sir!' like a sergeant-major, and eyed callers with an omniscient eye, and Corbet in the pub held a warm humour.

At first, Iain's vanity had secretly resented the way Corbet appeared to take it for granted that he was different from the others, not of their kind, for surely the difference must be very clear indeed before Corbet, the expert, would presume on it. But now he didn't mind.

Iain thanked him for the port and lit a cigarette. 'I suppose you'll know a lot about the fellows in the office?'

'I know enough – to talk to you about it.'

'That chap, Douglas?'

'Exactly. Easily the most brilliant man in the office. Swept the board at college, first-class Honours and medals and all that. Nothing to touch him at Scotch history. Knows more about the history of Edinburgh than any man alive. They say he's writing a book about it, in blank verse or drama or something. God knows. Anyway, after taking his M.A. he started on his LL.B. But something went wrong. Went off the rails for a time and never went back. And now there he is – finished.'

'How, finished?'

'Well, there he is fixed. He'll stick in that office till he pegs out. No ambition. Finished.'

'Is he married?'

'No.' As Corbet shook his head he expelled a humoured breath. 'Between you and I, I have seen too many faces in the morning not to know when a fellow has been on the tiles. Queer – that clever fellows should go that way.'

Iain was silent, remembering his night glimpse of Douglas's face in the Canongate.

'And that's what I want to warn you about. Take Heehaw, again. He's just a bloody snob. His people have pots of money. But he hasn't the brains. Once he had tea with a duke. He went through the office next day like a seidlitz powder. Ghor!' Corbet drank. 'He's a qualified law agent.

But do you think men like Mr Cunningham, Mr Lindsay, any of the real firms, would offer him a partnership at any figure? Not on your life! But he still hopes.'

'Young Lindsay doesn't seem to think much of him.'

'No. Young Lindsay knows. He's the real stuff. No flies on that lad. Wouldn't be surprised if he goes to the Bar. Already he talks like a bloody judge. He could put on the black cap and look well in it.'

Iain laughed.

'But what I'm warning you about is this. Make up your mind now not to stick in that office. You were never cut out for a clerk. I don't know your private affairs, and I'm not asking, but I take it you can't put a thousand or two on the table even for a modest partnership, even if you got the chance?'

'Quite right.'

Corbet nodded. 'I'm only telling you what I would do myself – if I had your education and the chance. At the end of four or five years in that office, you'll still not have the experience of dealing with a case from beginning to end yourself. Very well. When you qualify, clear out – into a small office. There you'll have to do everything yourself. *Then – after that –* start on your own. Not in this city of lawyers. But somewhere in the country, where you know folk and their ways. That's my advice to you.' He finished his beer.

On his way home, Iain felt slightly drunk. Now and then he experienced difficulty in subduing a laughter that bubbled up. Corbet's picture of the old fellows in his office – fixed, finished – was so true that it seemed fantastic. The idea that he might become one of them! It was so impossible – and so queerly possible – that it was frightening in its mirth. Almost his ghost could feel its reality. Like something walking behind him. And when the motor siren screamed at his back like the ghost in action, he leapt. But even the grinding brakes carried the car beyond him and he did not wait for comment.

He laughed over the scrambled egg, over the black specks of pepper – thousands of them – and forked them into his gullet. That would sober the port, the sly port that laughed in his belly after sending the fume to his head. He gulped his tea; drained the tea-pot. He thought his landlady was never coming to clear the table. When at last she came, he pretended to be busy. Then he got on his back in bed and stared at a reality which Corbet had drawn for him. Years – years of office work and study – then some day – perhaps – a struggling 'man of business', in some country town, as 'the appex'!

He had never seen it like this before, never in the body, living, from year to year. That it might be his body was strangely meaningless and frightening.

NINE

Iain could smell autumn in the air. High above the streets
the atmosphere was clear away up to the chill blue of the
sky. The nuts would be ripe in the Dell. All along the valley,
under to-day's sun, his father, Andrew McAndrew, Ewan,
Hamish, Dan-the-trapper, men and women on croft and farm,
would be busy cutting and stooking the grain. If the weather
held, there would be a good harvest.

After spells of dismal uncertainty, of endless argument
with himself, he had decided to take out classes at the
University. The extra cost might not be a great deal, but why
should he come on his father for anything? He felt himself
a grown man, capable of taking on a man's job. His father
had striven enough in this life. By the time Iain might ever
hope to be in a position to help him, he would probably be
beyond help. If ever, in this life, his father was going to get
any real help now was the time when his energies were
waning.

There were many small things, too, in connection with
money spending which nagged at him. Not only boots and
clothes, but certain fees. There was that personal document
he had seen in the office. It disclosed a payment of £54 17s.
6d. Only by this payment was the owner of the document
entitled to charge legal fees. Before he could start on his
own, Iain would have to pay a similar sum. If he wanted to
practise as a Writer to the Signet, he would have to be in a
position to put down about £700. That was the real difference between solicitor and W.S. No question of superior legal
knowledge arose. It would represent a difference in status
between himself and Lindsay. Odd word, 'status'!

But the argument was won by his mother; and behind his
mother now was his father. So he had compromised with

himself, saying he had better take the classes and then wait to see how things developed. Meantime he had managed to buy second-hand textbooks on Roman Law and Constitutional Law. Preliminary readings had not excited him; had, in fact, curiously brought back the heavy dragging feeling that had accompanied certain school tasks; only now the feeling was more solidly weighted.

Darkness was filling the city as he came down from the high streets near the Castle towards the Art Galleries. As he was rounding the steps of the lower building on to Princes Street, Douglas passed along. Iainfollowed him. Beyond the face of the building, after pausing a moment, Douglas turned right into an open space where a public meeting was in progress.

Iain took up a position close to but just a little behind him. He was surprised to find that a man like Douglas was prepared to stand and listen at an open-air meeting. Iain himself had found these meetings among the more extraordinary features of city life. He had no money to go to picture-houses and, anyway, had not formed the habit. But here on the Mound he had many a night found hours of entertainment. There was one socialist orator who was particularly apt in invective. At his best, he did not argue, he illustrated, drawing pictures, for example, of well-known capitalists juggling with innumerable directorships all specifically named, until his pity for the poor fellows could almost be felt, and then finding the relief of comedy in etching the happy lives of the care-free down-and-outs, the houseless, the destitute. He had football matches between mixed teams of capitalists and landlords with the old earth as the ball, and every kick the poor old earth got, swarms of unnecessary creatures, like maggots, like lice, were knocked off it into limbo. And there was no hope for those knocked off. For standing in each goal was a parson, guarding the only way to the eternal net.

His listeners liked this sort of imagery. One night he had created a really shocking fantasy on the subject of prostitutes. The number which he asserted came fresh onto the streets of Edinburgh, of Glasgow, of London, each year, were so vast, that their swarming thousands came up through far dark streets of Iain's mind as legions, as whole armies of the damned, terrible with venereal banners.

Iain was so used to different speakers on different subjects that for the first few moments he hardly listened to this new political voice. He was conscious of Douglas's near presence in a troubling way, for he did not want to intrude, was not sure that he really wanted Douglas to see him, yet felt the relationship between them, even if it was only of the office, as something isolating them in the crowd, and was warmed a little by the knowledge that Douglas also wandered the streets.

Douglas was now listening very intently and Iain became aware that the speaker was talking about Scotland. At first he thought he was a socialist but very soon references to 'London control' made it clear that his real concern was self-government for Scotland. He had facts and figures about unemployment, housing, infant mortality, the slump in Scottish industries, indeed about the whole Scottish economic scene, which, when contrasted with the relevant facts and figures for England, sounded very shocking.

Iain liked this matter-of-fact way of dealing with the ancient subject of Scottish nationhood. Where he would have felt shy of an outspoken patriotism, of references to Wallace and Bruce, Flodden and Bannockburn, he could listen to this statement of an economic argument and find a wonder, at times a thrill, in its newness, in its air of being grown-up in an actual world. The speaker was certainly not more than thirty. He had little of the old socialist orator's wit and drastic imagery, but he did have some quality of earnestness, of vision, that was curiously disturbing. It was as if, after hundreds of years, a pair of new eyes were looking at a naked Scotland.

A real discovery, and pleasant somehow. For no-one at home, or anywhere else as far as he knew, saw or spoke of Scotland in this way. It was always 'the country' or 'this country', a place that wandered away down to the English

Channel, and across to a bit of Ireland, and vaguely faded into distant parts of the globe. Where the English talked of England quite naturally, the Scots referred vaguely to 'this country'. He remembered a joke about that during a Burns night at Kinmore. Only when those at home got worked up over some such celebration as a Burns night, did they wax patriotic and eloquently dig Scotia out of the past. Never, at any such gathering, did he hear of Scotland quite simply and naturally as a place that built ships and factories, reared sheep and cattle, bred scientists and poets, under the skies and on the land that he knew from day to day.

And the speaker, as if aware of the particular condition of the minds about him, made it clear that he was not blaming the English. Why blame them – when the fault lay 'in ourselves'? If the people of Scotland wanted to take their derelict country in hand, to govern and rebuild it, no power on earth could stop them from doing so – and certainly not the English! Scotland had the resources, she had the wealth, she was capable of developing one of the most perfectly balanced and richest economies in Europe. Yet what did we find everywhere? – unemployed, stagnant yards, derelict areas, slums, depopulation, with the young men and the young women leaving the crofts, leaving the farms, leaving the sea, to emigrate or to come to a city like this. What do they come here for, when here we need more fresh meat, more fish, more food, when half our population, as statistics show, are underfed, are starved? Draining the countryside of its finest blood, sticking a butcher's knife in its throat, and accepting the corpse as an act of God. But then we are such a religious people, said the speaker sarcastically, with such a reputation among the world's greatest fighters! ... Yet once upon a time we *were* great fighters, as that old Castle on its rock could tell. Once upon a time we were religious. Once upon a time this was a capital city, a famous city. Now what is it? – an Anglo-Scottish burgh, an inflated legal office, its influence on the human spirit gone, its creativeness vanished, its glory dead.

Question time was lively, for there were a few socialist

hecklers who said that the solution of the bread-and-butter problem must come before all other considerations, national or cultural. Very well, answered the speaker, join us and ensure that the bread and butter will come, not in some vague international hereafter, but now in this our own country. We had relied on other people getting bread and butter for us – with tragic results. Why not stop whining, and have a shot at getting the bread and butter for ourselves?

The argument was lively, and when the speaker retorted, 'You'll never do anything, comrade, until an English socialist first does it for you,' there was wordy uproar. But presently something did emerge that stuck in Iain's mind.

Mention had been made of deer forests, run by wealthy sportsmen from outside Scotland and covering some three and a half million acres of Highland country. There was nothing new about that, nor about the way in which the old Highland economy of rearing sheep and cattle had been disastrously broken up at the time of the evictions, when the people were brutally cleared off the land. But now a man in the audience, talking in a quiet Highland voice – and its quietness, with a hint of bitterness, had everyone listening in a moment – wanted to know if the speaker knew what he was talking about in this matter of rearing sheep and cattle on deer forests.

The speaker assured the questioner that he knew quite a bit from personal experience, for his own people had come out of the Highlands. Then, after shortly tracing the history of crofting and hill farming, from the old economy through the evictions, to sheep, and then to deer, he got down to what might be done for hill farming, particularly hill sheep-and-cattle farming, to-day. He referred to the latest results by experts carrying out experiments on such land, whereby the grazings were enriched, the winter feed increased, and generally the stock doubled. This interested Iain acutely.

'And who is going to do that for us in the Highlands to-day?' asked the ironic questioner.

'Listen,' answered the speaker. 'Have you noticed that you asked who is going to do that *for us*? Not – how are *we ourselves* going to do it? In the very form of your question you exhibit the fatal psychology which has landed us where we are, and which, in particular, has landed the Highlands where they are. No wonder the women of the Highlands drive their clever sons from home, into offices, into school teaching, into pulpits where they can comfortably wag their pows, anywhere – so long as it is off the land, for which their menfolk refuse to fight. Not, perhaps, that we can altogether blame the men. For who would support them in the fight? Would London, whose financiers rent the deer forests? ... But – had there been our own men here, to support us in our fight on croft and hill and sea, then the story might indeed have been a very different and a gallant one, for, given a cause and a lead, the Highlanders have shown themselves among the great fighters of the world. They showed it in the Great War. It could still be a gallant fight – and a successful one – were this city the centre of our government, the focal point of our inspiration. But it is none of these things. It is still beautiful, but at its core, where creation should live, it is null and void.'

Iain had forgotten Douglas, but now the rattle of a money-box drew his eyes, and he saw Douglas slip a large silver coin into it, and at that moment Douglas saw him.

As Iain was getting his penny into the box, Douglas spoke to him, and in a little while, the meeting over, they were walking along towards the east end.

TEN

That was a strange and memorable night for Iain. In after years it often came back, dark, magnificent, ghostly. It was a difficult night to tell about, because it belonged so much to the realms of the imagination. But on that night, that midnight, with a three-quarter moon navigating a sky upon which great clouds were advancing, Iain was introduced by Douglas to the Royal Mile.

Extraordinary the change that had come over Douglas from the first early quietude of manner, that natural rather cool voice asking him what he had thought of the speaker, as they walked along towards the huge hotel with the lit-up clock in its tower.

'You think he knows about sheep farming?'

'I think he knows a bit,' replied Iain.

'But not, perhaps, at first hand?'

'I don't know,' said Iain. 'It's not so easy – when you're dealing with the actual sheep on the actual land. You can't compel buyers to give more than they want to give.'

'Why not?'

'Well – how can you?'

'Couldn't you refuse to sell unless you got your price?'

'No, you couldn't do that.'

'Why?'

'Because you've got to live.'

'Why?'

'I don't know,' replied Iain, his voice hardening, for he felt that Douglas was now making fun of him.

'It's the perfect answer,' Douglas agreed. 'But if I go into a shop on this street and ask for any article, or into that hotel for drink, or food, or even for your delightful hill mutton, I have got to pay the price they demand. If I don't pay their price, I don't get the mutton.'

Iain remained silent.

Douglas glanced at him. 'You can't explain the difference?'

'Yes, I can,' said Iain, in a voice that he strove to make cool though he was feeling hot. 'It's not the same at all. They know in that hotel they can get the price for their mutton. If they couldn't get it, they wouldn't stock it. That's all. They would still carry on.'

'But the sheep farmer has mutton only? I see your point.'

'It's more than that,' said Iain. 'When the autumn comes, the hill farmer must sell the usual lambs and sheep, even if he doesn't need the money, and the buyers know that.'

'Why must he sell?'

'Because he hasn't the winter feed for them.'

'Ah!' said Douglas. 'Check! In fact, checkmate!' He gave a small pleasant laugh, and suddenly Iain liked him, as if, at that moment, Douglas had admitted him to his company. They turned, right, beyond the hotel and began going up the Bridges.

'Do you drink?'

'Not much,' replied Iain.

'Beer, I suppose?'

'No, I don't like beer.'

'Don't you? What do you drink?'

'I can take a glass of wine – but I don't drink.'

'Your distinctions are sound. You take wine but you don't *drink*.' Douglas chuckled with pleasure. 'All the courtliness of the Royal Mile before it changed from a demesne to a rabbit warren. Contrast in this city to-day the difference between *he drinks* and *he takes a glass of wine*. The feminine glass of wine! Yet claret was the drink of the nobles who vied at hanging or beheading one another up there at the Mercat Cross and finally were so tough that they murdered Scots history and dubbed their performance "the end of an auld sang".'

If there was something a trifle learned about the diction, it did not at all strike Iain as affected or condescending, but rather as a sort of elaborate negligence upon an ironic under-tow, upon a mocking strength, that was coming queerly alive in the man the nearer they approached the old town.

Soon they were in the heart of it, and though the descent was neither so crowded nor so varied in its human interest as it had been on the Saturday night, yet this, for Iain, gave somehow to the tall dark buildings a darker life of their own, a more powerful effect in menacing stone.

Douglas paid no attention to his surroundings. He had reverted to sheep farming, and continued to ask questions as if in some way this talk, by its elaborate normality, kept the surroundings in their proper place. At last he paused, and Iain stood as at the bottom of a great well, hearkening to a recapitulation of his own description of the working differences between Blackface sheep and Cheviots. Then Douglas turned a corner, pushed open a door, and entered a pub. This pub had its small saloon, and within the saloon a narrow tiny chamber, with a fixed table and wall seats on either side. There was no-one in it as Douglas switched on the light. 'Good! Take a seat.' And in a little while he returned with two glasses and a half-bottle of claret.

While preoccupied with pouring the wine, holding it against the light, sniffing it, Douglas was making some contrast between it and burgundy, calling one 'the wine of kings' and the other 'the king of wines'. His face, lifted against the naked electric bulb, had gathered now a certain force, all the more striking because the features themselves were not clean-cut but slightly heavy, lumpy, rather slumbrous. The dark eyes, however, had a glow. The face smiled, with a scholarly courtesy which the eyes mocked, and waited for Iain's verdict on the wine.

Iain realized how special was the occasion for him, and when the wine searched his mouth and wrung it dry of all pleasantness, he controlled his features, showing no more than the ghost of a twinge, and said, 'It's curious.'

'You don't like it?'

'I don't know,' said Iain. 'It's warm – like cream.'

'Cream? Is cream always warm?'

'No,' replied Iain, 'but – somehow – you always think it's warmer than the milk it's taken off.'

'Ha!' nodded Douglas. He raised his glass to Iain. 'Your palate has discrimination.' He took a fair sip and appeared to crush it inside his mouth as though it were a purple berry – then let it go. After a few moments, he breathed again. 'My God, it always surprises me!'

His surprise was so real, showed such awakened pleasure, that Iain knew he was in the presence, for the first time, of a connoisseur. Douglas nursed the glass in his hands, while saying, 'The temperature is almost perfect.' He could not leave the glass alone. He sniffed and drank some more, then pushed the glass a little distance from him with his finger-tips, as if defeating a hungry impulse to gulp the lot. He expatiated on the wine, not thoughtfully but well, a running commentary of fond dalliance, which he interrupted on the off-chance that Iain might again say something apt this time on the matter of bouquet.

And Iain genuinely did his best, sniffing carefully before remarking, 'It's got a nice smell.'

'Smell!' Douglas threw his face aloft. 'God!' It was an invocation, however, not in horror but of translunary wonder, and it may have been some measure of the man's deeper nature that Iain, realizing from the very sound of 'Smell!' that he had erred in his choice of word, was yet not unduly dashed and even smiled, if a trifle warmly.

Clearly things like this did not often happen to Douglas, not, anyhow, at such a chosen moment. But he composed his inner shakings, and with gleaming eyes suggested that, technically speaking at least, wine did not smell. Wine might have fragrance like a rose, but – but—

'Could not smell like carrion,' suggested Iain.

Then Douglas let his laughter out, and drained his glass.

'Carrion was a damned good word,' he said. 'Anything more explicit might have come back on the wine.'

As they were finishing the half-bottle, the door opened and a face looked round. Douglas got up. 'Come in, Maitland. Here's a colleague of mine who knows all about sheep. Mr

Cattanach, Mr Maitland of the "Board". Know what the "Board" is?'

'At home, it's still the Board of Agriculture,' Iain answered.

'Right first shot,' declared Douglas. 'Cattanach is positively uncanny in his first shots. He even smelt out the claret.'

'Not really?' said Maitland, raising his eyebrows and looking at Iain.

'No.' Iain shook his head, smiling like a shy country youth. 'He put me on the scent.'

Douglas laughed. 'Sit down and I'll see about another bottle.'

'Wait a bit!'

They began to argue, but it was Douglas who brought the bottle.

Maitland's sharp intellectual face and bland polished manner produced in Iain a feeling of uneasiness, a consciousness of his country origin which made even the movements of his arms seem heavy, awkward, and slow. Maitland's voice, too, was very 'English', that is, it had those inflections which gillies were accustomed to in shooting tenants. It was the voice which Hee-haw tried to emulate but without complete success, for every now and then Edinburgh would give its native tilt to his flattening of a phrase. Iain knew that Maitland had deliberately, in that first steady look, tried to read him to his social origins, using the elevated eyebrows, the momentary interest in the wine, as polite cover. And when Douglas tried to get Maitland drawn into talk on sheep, there was a smile, an amusing evasion, and in no time the two men were lost in personal talk and laughter over a recent meeting.

Maitland now seemed a charming fellow, full of witty sallies. As the talk went on, Iain gathered that there was a group of them, a group of 'Bloods', who had a weekly meeting-place somewhere in these regions, but clearly not in this pub, though one Sandy (presumably the landlord of the pub) supplied the perfect vintage for them by arrangement.

This lull in the drinking for Iain – though the other two saluted expressive moments in wine and Maitland continued to use his glass for gesture – taught him one thing more, namely, that though the wine seemed thin and almost bitter in its weakness, it contained an equally thin but yet insidious potency, as if it had long eel-like arms or flavours that curled not only about his body but upward over his brain. Very faint all this was, and not unpleasant, but his country caution told him to beware and go easy.

Two others came in, also of the group. There was hushed talk of police, of three women, and then bursts of laughter. For a long time Iain was forgotten.

The group separated at last, and Iain found himself alone with Douglas. His feet hit the pavement softly; he knew he was a bit drunk, felt immensely lonely, and, far inwardly, strangely exhilarated. Now that he was on his way home and knew he could carry himself, something of his rising manhood, which had been denied that evening, wanted to assert itself.

Douglas, on the top of his form, was talking, not asking Iain how he had enjoyed himself but bringing him into the full rush of his discourse as if he were apostrophizing Maitland. He was improvising on the word *Lands*, which had been esoterically cried in a parting phrase outside the pub, and which was the word actually in use for these tall dark buildings, 'the world's first sky-scrapers'. Douglas repeated the word, savouring the sound of it, its unfathomably ironic connotations, tilting his face at the great darkstone buildings and murmuring 'The lands' in a voice of incantation, before he shook with the unspeakable and strode on in a wild and splendid humour.

It was at this point that Iain had his first strange movement of the imagination, so clearly defined that it bore a resemblance to hallucination. He saw the earth, the flat lands, being deeply skinned and slowly swung up like massive doors, to stand erect, with the causey stones which they trod as the ravines between. And in these great upright lands people contrived to dwell as they had once dwelt on the flat lands.

'*Land. Land,*' Douglas was intoning. 'What a lovely word!

Such beauty in Man's mouth! And what fantastic perversion achieved in the act!'

The windows in the dark lands were suddenly cave holes to Douglas's new fancy, and man was completing his evolutionary cycle by assuming once more the general habitat and condition of certain monkeys. The fancy staggered him with delight. Such was man's tale! 'Do you know,' he boomed, 'the length of Edinburgh's tale? One mile from the arsenal of the Castle to the tip of the Holy Rood!'

Did Cattanach know the history of this immortal tale? No? Then, by God, it was time he did, and, turning, Douglas made for Holyrood Palace. 'Do you want to know?' he cried, pausing, 'or do you want to go home and sleep in sloth?'

Cattanach wanted to know.

Douglas came closer to him in drunken intimacy, his breath warm, then leaned back and, lifting his eyes to the sky, chanted: 'Ah, Holy Inquisitor, in our evolutionary ambitions we do but the more surely exhibit the lash of that tail which thou didst first stick, in thine inscrutable wit, to our unchanging and eternal behinds.' Then he rolled on.

He had many mimicries that long wild night, as though everything was being played on a stage in his mind and he was the poet or the pageant. Indeed often he must have been repeating what had long sat in his thought, nursed with jealous care, and now given the crown of the causey.

Down there before Holyrood Palace, Mary Queen of Scots and the Young Chevalier, all the dressed figures of romance and action, of the school history books and the novels, were torn from before Iain's sight as a painted page might be torn, and turret-stairs and bedroom, footsteps in corridors, the catch of a breath, a cry – the Palace itself came alive to its inmost recesses in hand and eye and the flush of blood. Yet with meaning behind movement, mind behind the act, until the dagger that slew Rizzio gathered a dreadful symbolism of its own, and the number of its thrusts in that unfortunate Italian's body became a cabalistic number, revealing the Scots nobility in a dark self-seeking of violence and treachery without example, declared Douglas, among the kingdoms of the earth. More than that, and higher, until Rizzio's body became Mary the Queen's, and Mary's body, gathering for the moment all loveliness and gallantry, became the slain body of her country.

One flashing picture stuck in Iain's mind. James I and his court are assembled in the Palace to celebrate a great festival of the Church. Upon the pomp and the brilliance enters dramatically a knight in full armour who, taking his sword by the tip, offers it to his King. It is the Lord of the Isles, asking a rebel's pardon. The Queen intercedes for his life. And Iain, for one long moment, has an absolute understanding of the Isleman's feelings as, saved from hanging, he cools his heels in the fortress of Tantallon. The wild hope, the Highland gamble with chance, the chance chosen for its boldness and drama, its style, 'to win or lose it all', – and the Gaelic blood cooling behind the prison wall, and the long thoughts.

Iain stared at Holyrood Palace under the moon, and his eyes lifted to a darkness of crags, like a fortress against the sky.

'Six years after, his nobles murdered that First James at Perth. The Second James was killed at Roxburgh Castle, the Third was killed at Sauchieburn, and the Fourth and greatest of them all was slain on Flodden Field . . .'

But Iain has no very clear memory of Douglas's words or tales from this point. The wine had had so much time to work in him that he might well have been weary to sickness. But actually the subtle chemistry of excitement and strangeness so refined mind and flesh that his vision gathered the penetrative force of a 'Second Sight'. His body felt not unlike that sword which the Islesman had proffered by the tip, and up the Canongate it went with the men from the hills and the glens, and from the Isles, and from the broad lands of France, past wynds and closes of historic name, and haunted walls, and deeds that still moaned from the street, and ghosts that walked from Europe's history.

There was one long pause opposite Moray House which did work its illusive effect. Montrose is being drawn on a

one-horse cart to his execution at the Mercat Cross and for
some unknown reason at this spot the horse stops. Montrose
looks up at Argyll and his wife on the balcony, and Argyll's
eyes cannot hold the calm eyes of Montrose and turn from
them; but Argyll's wife leans over the balcony and spits.

Iain remembered the incident from his history readings,
but now it got mixed up in a fantastic way with Dan-the-
trapper's booming voice on a New Year's morning and he
hears his own voice solemnly chanting:

> *And then uprose*
> *The great Montrose*
> *In the middle of the room.*

And though the words have no bearing on the tragic incident of the moment, yet Douglas looks at Iain in a sort of
wild amaze, as if the idiotic words had a hidden power
whereby the great Montrose was there and then evoked
calmly, and vastly greater than life-size. It lifted Douglas's
spirit and drove him with ironic power and strange oaths to
describe how the nobles in the very garden of that Moray
House bargained for their signatures to the instrument which
was to demolish Scotland's Parliament, to sell their country's
freedom. He mentioned noble names and the paltry sums
they had been willing to receive, and decided, on a financial basis, that, in comparison, Judas had been overpaid.

Until at long last the Mercat Cross was reached, and as
in the completion of some inscrutable circle Flodden cried
its name once more.

Extraordinary the picture that Douglas drew now of a
city lying under the plague; all shops closed, doors and
windows tight shut, the hour of midnight, and the English
army coming, that army which always came 'to slake its
thirst and glut its bloody maw, for, like a beast, learn it could
not that its thirst was insatiable and its maw without bottom.'
Here, then, in the dead of night, a solitary man passed the
Mercat Cross, and as he passed there sounded a great fanfare
of trumpets, and when the fanfare had died, leaving him stiff

on his feet, he heard a ghostly voice reciting the names of all those who would die in the forthcoming battle, starting with the name of the King. And when the voice had reached the man's own name, which was Richard Lawson, he cried aloud: *I appeal from that summons and sentence, and take me to the mercy of God and Christ Jesus His son.* But the man went to battle none the less, and of all those whose names he had heard proclaimed that night from the Cross, only he alone returned from Flodden Field.

The street was deserted and Iain's eyes roamed and lifted. It must have been midnight now, and Douglas was silent, the forest flowers of his rhetoric a' wede awa'.

But not for long. And his resurrected vigour, finding naught to lay into, slung phrases at the night, forceful and ribald, as they stood upon 'this navel hole of Scotland', where the great had been damned and reviled and beheaded, Montrose and Atholl – 'that Atholl whom, on three days running, they crowned with a red-hot crown of iron', in mockery of his bastard ambitions.

The Mercat Cross, where that death-defying Solemn League and Covenant was burned by the hangman; where a triumphant Prince Charles Edward Stuart was proclaimed and where his standards, captured at Culloden, were destroyed; where kings feasted with the city's Council; where the trade of a capital had its tongue; and always where a voice was heard proclaiming what boded ill or good for a nation. But the voice is silent at last, and wanderers passing by, however their blood hearkens, catch on the midnight air no ghostliest echo.

Massive, before them, arose St Giles Cathedral, with its thousand years of Christian history, ringing all the changes of worship in the heart of Western man; and there had stood the Tolbooth, the dread prison, and here behold Parliament House.

Parliament House – ghostliest of all buildings in Europe.

Many, said Douglas's voice, itself at last growing ghostly among the stark moon-shadows, thought, and think still, that Flodden was Scotland's dule, her greatest defeat, her major disaster, but, as always with the many, they are wrong. In all her gallant history – gallant because fought for ever against murderous odds – Scotland suffered only one irreparable defeat, one conclusive disaster, and that was when her nobility – God save the word! – when her nobles sold her Parliament for cash, for cash bribes of the hungry enemy, the devouring monster that could never leave her in peace. With that sale they as certainly brought her head to the block as did Elizabeth the head of Mary to the block in Fotheringay Castle.

But Mary went with dignity and gallantry. Wanton on occasion she may have been, as the preachers said who hated her lovely body, wanton with that woman's dower which has inspired the greatest poets to their loveliest lines, but bitched she certainly was by that same self-seeking rabble of nobility. For at the end, rid of them and alone, she went with dignity and calm, dressed not in the black gown with which she had wed Darnley and Bothwell, with which, as by a preternatural intuition of her act, she had married the black nobility of Scotland, but clothed at last in red velvet for her marriage with death. And the wizened hag of England, surrounded by her crafty courtiers and their money-bags, remained at a distance, tortured in her withered virginity, while the rites of this final marriage were consummated.

Mary went with dignity and gallantry. But Scotland, her mother, was sold. And so great was the wrath of her children that they besieged this Parliament House before the rites of sale were completed, and the noble sellers had to fly from their wrath, and they did fly – into a cellar – and there in haste and stealth they subscribed the last signature of dishonour, and concluded the final act of sale. And once more, from a distance, the greedy courtiers who had moved the pieces, rubbed their sly hands, for at long last they had achieved a checkmate and won the age-old game. The same courtiers as Elizabeth's courtiers, though Elizabeth herself had been dead and rotten for a century. The same courtiers as Edward the First's courtiers. Always the same courtiers, the same king or queen, in the same game – which at last, not on the field of battle, not at Flodden, never face to face, but by an accursed bribery, they won.

That, then, was Parliament House, the headless body, the national corpse, which the maggots of a dwindling Scots legality still contrived to inhabit, worming for what pickings may be left on the rotting bones.

Douglas's laughter had long left him, his wild improvisations, his exhilarating gaiety. A bitterness was upon him, whether from the waning of the wine's effect – for Iain himself was now conscious of a coldness on his forehead – or from some secret preoccupation with his theme of Parliament House and that very legality which was his own profession, some personal bitterness deep hidden and now stirring in him, Iain had no way of knowing.

After he had stood for some little time, brooding in silence, he turned to Iain and said, 'Perhaps that will do for a first lesson.' His dark eyes were inscrutable socket-holes. 'You live? . . .'

'Round beyond the Castle.'

'Then our ways divide. Good night.'

'Good night,' replied Iain and found himself walking alone, his flesh contracting in quick self-conscious spasms, smiling, bitterly stirred, for he knew he had at the end failed Douglas utterly.

ELEVEN

In the office the following morning, Iain did not lift his head as Douglas passed. He had the feeling that Douglas would not wish him to show by the slightest sign how they had spent the evening. The secrecies and sensitiveness of his hill blood helped him here, and once when Douglas had to consult a Letter Book, Iain, asking calmly 'About what date?' in no time had the appropriate impression displayed. They might never have met outside the office door. Iain was glad after this had happened, and felt relieved a little.

He felt, too, that he was growing up, and when, later in the day, opportunity offered and Corbet suggested they might have one, Iain shook his head, smiling.

'You looked a bit white about the gills this morning,' said Corbet suspiciously.

'Did I?'

'You did.'

'You hadn't your glasses on,' said Iain.

'You don't need glasses for that,' answered Corbet, 'any more than for a verbal agreement.'

Iain laughed and Corbet made a genuinely solicitous inquiry about his bowels.

But it was when Angus arrived for his University classes that Iain realized how far in these last two months he had advanced in knowledge of the city and of himself. To his eyes, Angus was so palpably the country boy, with the country's fond soft ways and quick-eyed bewilderment, that he smiled, feeling hardened in self-reliance.

'Hungry? What about a cup of tea?'

'No,' answered Angus. 'They'll be waiting for me. I told them you would be meeting me.'

He was staying with some 'far-out relations on his mother's

side'. This had earlier been a subject of regret between the lads, but the matter had been arranged by Angus's mother.

While they lugged the large bag up to a tram-stop, Iain kept asking questions about the folk at home. 'And how is Ewan doing?'

'Oh, the same old Ewan. He was working late last night, making a coffin for Widow Ross.'

'Ah, is she dead? I'm sorry to hear that.'

It was dark and Angus was excited, for the traffic seemed to be going all ways at once, but Iain got him onto the right tram and off it, and at last brought him to the proper street number in a district just beyond the Meadows. There he delivered him to his relations, and, refusing to go in, saying he had had his supper, made an appointment for the following evening.

As he walked away, he muttered to himself, 'He might have mentioned Mary.' He kept thinking about it all the way to his lodging. Somehow he hadn't liked to ask about Mary point blank, lest he embarrass Angus, but he had given him three opportunities of mentioning her himself.

The very smell and sound of the country had been about Angus, the people he knew, the hills, and this excited Iain, made him restless. He took out his fiddle and began playing. Fingers and bow found their own troubling melody, and at once the world behind the music came through. And now there was no doubt of that vague traditional face which haunted the music. The voice that sang was not the disembodied voice of the past. The mouth and the eyes were Mary's, although it was not Mary singing to him, but Mary as the instrument of the song, through whom the song came as it came through the fiddle. In the profoundest sense they were both caught by the song, listening to it. But now he could see her face, calm and almost child-like, recording the song.

It was not Mary he wanted, but Mary and her song. He played so deeply, with such emotion in him, that he was carried away from Mary. But he could not reach to the end of where he was going. He had never been able to do that, for always the music lifted a final wave that drowned him.

As he laid the fiddle on the bed, he was more restless than ever and kept walking about the room. The excitement did not ebb from the final wave, as it usually did. His brain itself caught at meanings to give him steadiness. For there was no doubt about one thing: this effect upon him from playing his own traditional music was more positive, literally more potent, than any other emotional effect from any other kind of experience. It had always been like that. This might be a weakness in him, a personal weakness, but it was true. He could forget about it, did not easily want to remember it, but when it came again it came with surprise, with an overpowering assurance; a door opened and he walked through to where emotion, even in an ultimate suffering (and particularly then) was pure, where beauty could no more be fined away, and death was an ultimate head with invisible face bowed in acceptance.

But that world to which the door led was his own world which his blood knew, and when the girl danced to *Mairi Bhan*, the movements of arms and body, of light toes and glancing eyes, called to him and he danced before them, at once anticipating and creating every step, in a perfection of form and delight.

Suddenly he remembered Douglas's remark on first drinking the claret, 'My God, it always surprises me!'

And at once a touch of wild silent laughter went through him. He appreciated now what Douglas had experienced, not so much drinking the claret as in that mad jaunt up the Royal Mile. For one instant he seemed to touch Douglas's own spirit, to understand it. There were no words for his understanding, but somewhere behind the trappings of history, Douglas had come alive and something had cried out of him in an authentic voice.

The ghostly voice at the Mercat Cross. The voice crying in the wilderness. Not music for Douglas, but a voice.

The following evening, Iain met Angus and took him up to his room. Even to their senses, this room, the street outside, was different from Angus's new quarters, not only in material appearance but in its smell of poverty and decay. Where

Angus lived there was the aspiration to genteel decency; here it was lost.

Angus, however, just because he came from the country, felt the freedom in this loss, and said something about envying Iain his own room. Iain wanted more news of home. When had Angus seen his father last? And Hamish? What had Widow Ross died of?

'Ewan said the old clock had run down.'

Iain could hear the way Ewan would say it, and smiled. 'And how's Mary?'

'Fine,' replied Angus in what sounded a natural tone, and stopped there.

'Had you a bit of a do the night you left?'

'Not much. You and your fiddle were missed. What about it – what about a tune?'

'Oh, I don't know,' replied Iain, but he took out his fiddle and played a reel. When he had finished, he abruptly put the instrument away. 'Come on, let me show you this famous city.'

'Do you like it?'

'Not too bad.'

In a few moments they were on the street.

'How are you getting on in your office?' Angus asked.

'Right enough.' Iain gave a chuckle. 'A bit strange to begin with, but you get used to it. A country fellow has to keep his end up.'

'I suppose so.'

'Yes.' Iain's voice, his manner, held a sarcastic assurance. He strode on with a reckless confidence to cover a queer bitterness that was stirring in him over the way Angus had defeated him about Mary. 'We get the wrong ideas about city life in the country.'

'How that?'

'We think they're so important here. All in my eye! Hang it, you get *men* in the country: here you get super-clerks. In the country we think a man a great fellow because he comes back from the city with a collar on him and because he never dirties his hands, back for a few days' holiday "to see the old folks"!' He laughed.

'You seem to be getting notions.'

'Oh, you get notions here all right. That's one thing the city can do: it can show you what a damn fool you are.'

'Are you sorry you came?'

'No. We've all got to learn.'

They walked on in silence for some distance.

'Do you mean', asked Angus, without emphasis, 'that you're not too sure about – about becoming a lawyer?'

'What does it matter what we're sure about? Here we are; we'll have to go on with it. All I know is that this sort of thing was never meant for me. However, as they say at home, we'll have to "stick in"!'

'It's the last advice I got,' said Angus.

The touch of dry humour set Iain going. 'Funny thing,' he said, 'that they never thought of telling us to "stick in" to the job at home. No-one ever thought of telling us that raising sheep and crops was at least as important as being office boys and copying letters and writing out deeds *about* sheep and crops and houses and steadings and all the rest of it. But did they? Not they!'

'Yes. But—'

'But what?'

'You know as well as I do that there's nothing but hard work and little for it beyond a grim living at home. At least our folk are trying to do their best for us.'

'Do you think I don't know that?'

'I said you did.'

'I know. It's just that it makes me feel a bit savage when I begin thinking about it. I mean I don't see why it should be a grim living. The fellows who run the law offices I know make more than a grim living, and the fellows in all the other offices, Government offices, Register Houses and all the rest, not to mention the big shops and other businesses. Hang it all, man, the head porter in one of the big hotels here makes more than your father and my father and four or five other fathers in the glen at home put together.'

'All the more reason for leaving home,' said Angus.

Iain laughed. 'We cross here.' But when they had crossed

he did not renew the argument, he began naming streets and places. 'This is the West End.' Soon they were on Princes Street. Iain was about to draw attention to the Castle on its rock when suddenly, in the small crush of people from a tram, a voice said, 'Good evening, Mr Cattanach.' It was Morna Galloway.

With her was Joan Dowie. Iain shook hands with them. No happening could have better suited his mood of the moment, for the underlying bitterness might have done something irreparable to the old schoolboy friendship. Now he introduced Angus as Mr Gordon, so it was Mister and Miss all round, and smiles and politeness. As master of ceremonies Iain extravagantly rose to the occasion, explaining that Mr Gordon was a fellow countryman come to study Arts in the halls of learning. To the girls, this blossoming of the shy country youth into ready and amusing talk, into a sort of exaggerated ease, was as pleasant as it was unexpected. To Angus, Iain was behaving as he would behave in similar circumstances at home, if now with an added something of city manners.

'And where are you going?' asked Iain.

'We had thought of going to the pictures,' answered Morna.

'To see "The Master Mind",' explained Joan. 'They say it's a marvellous film. Have you seen it?'

'No,' answered Iain. 'Miss Galloway and I see so many of them.'

'What? Films?'

'No. Master minds in the office.'

The girls swayed with laughter, for Joan had had her dramatic moment of uncertainty.

'Are you really going?' asked Iain. 'It's such a lovely night.'

The girls looked at each other.

'Well—' began Joan. They both laughed. 'No, but, seriously, we said—' Joan stopped.

'Look!' said Iain. 'There's a Marchmont tram. Come on!' And he led the way in a rush for the tram.

Breathless, laughing, they got on top, and Joan cried with

that serious air she could so readily assume, 'What on earth am I to say to Elizabeth when she questions me about "The Master Mind"?'

'Tell her he was so overpowering he put you to sleep,' said Iain.

'Even mother would hardly believe that.'

'Your father might,' suggested Iain helpfully.

'You're quite hopeless,' said Joan, her round eyes upon him. 'You don't understand how serious this is for us.'

'It's not serious yet,' said Iain. 'But the night's young.'

'I was quite certain you had a tongue. Where *do* you hide it?'

'I always swallow it when I'm hungry.'

Morna swayed with laughter.

'If you don't believe me,' added Iain, 'ask Angus here.'

'He doesn't really, does he?' asked Joan, taking the opportunity to have a good look at Angus. She thought Angus an adorable name, and was thrilled by her manipulation of the talk.

'Yes,' answered Angus, 'regularly.'

'How awful! It must have a horrid taste. Don't you think so?'

'I should think it would,' agreed Angus. 'Especially as he chews it.'

In what seemed no time the tram had stopped at the top of Marchmont Road and they were on the street.

'Where *are* we going?' cried Joan.

'Actually it's like this,' explained Iain. 'Angus here is taking astronomy as one of his subjects. He has only just arrived and I promised to show him the way to the Observatory on the Blackford Hill.'

'Is that true, Mr Gordon?' asked Joan.

'You don't mean to suggest you doubt what he says?' asked Angus.

Joan turned to Morna, who had enjoyed everything but said little.

'We mightn't have been able to get in anyway,' said Morna. 'Bessie told me there was a tremendous queue last night.'

'So we went for a walk.' Joan sighed. 'How disappointing!'

Iain paired off with Morna and soon they were passing through the small iron gate and taking the steep path up to the left towards the Observatory. The occasional lovers' sounds from a whin bush or the sight of an embracing couple intensified his reckless mood He made it a game with Morna to give the slip to Angus and Joan who were coming behind. Morna said they perhaps shouldn't, but when at last they were below the Observatory, Iain caught her hand and at once she ran. Flat in the black hadow of a whin bush, they watched the other two solemnly pass. In the midst of their warm suppressed humour, Iain caught Morna and kissed her firmly and long.

Presently Morna said, 'We must go.'

'Why?'

'Because we must.'

'You think so?'

'Please . . .'

When this interrupted talk had gone on for a little while, Morna asked, 'Are all Highlanders as wild as you?'

'Oh, no,' replied Iain, 'many of them are much wilder.'

'How could they?'

'Easily,' began Iain.

But she quickly sat up. 'No, please. Let us go.'

Iain did not let her go. As he had had no intention of harming her, her air of uncertainty and half-fear now provoked him. She sensed, however, the reckless element in him and was very soon on her feet, saying, 'They'll wonder where we've gone.'

'Very well,' said Iain coolly. Putting his fingers in his mouth, he let out a piercing shepherd's whistle. It startled Morna and, turning to him, she caught his head against the sky.

Soon the others came drifting into view and there was much talk again. Iain noticed that Angus was almost silent. So this time they kept within shouting distance, made the complete circuit of the Hill, and parted at the top of Marchmont Road.

As the lads went down the street, Iain, to defeat the self-consciousness between them, began telling who the girls were. He described his first – and last – visit to Dowie's home. 'Two or three weeks ago, the old boy asked me out again, but I told him I couldn't come because I had promised to meet some people and would probably be going to church with them.' He laughed.

'You made that up?'

'On the spot,' said Iain. 'She's a nice girl, Joan, though, don't you think?'

'Yes, very nice.'

'The other one, Morna – something about her like a dark puppy.'

'She's all there,' said Angus.

'Do you think so?' asked Iain. 'What makes you think that?'

'Have you known her long?'

'See her occasionally in the office. But this is the first time I've ever been with her alone.'

'You're a fast worker.'

Iain laughed. 'Perhaps they expected us to make a date. But I steered clear – though if you feel like it? . . .'

'I think I better find my bearings at the University first.'

'Might be as well,' agreed Iain and he chuckled. 'Nice girls, though.'

'Yes, very nice.'

Soon they were at the corner of Angus's street.

'I'll look round to-morrow night to see how you have got on,' said Iain. 'You'll soon find your way about. Edinburgh is very easy. That old Castle sticks up in the middle of it.'

'Righto. See you to-morrow night, then.'

As Iain went on by himself the bitterness came to the surface through the grin on his face. At last it was clear to him beyond a doubt that something had gone wrong between Angus and Mary and that he was to blame. The scene in the Dell came back with a desperate clarity.

As he sat in his chair and unlaced his shoes, he looked about his room, at its arid furniture, the glass of blue milk on the table, the two dry biscuits on the plate. Bare and mean! Like himself! He jerked the shoes off his feet.

When he had suddenly asked about Mary, the very way Angus had said 'Fine,' and then, 'You and your fiddle were missed,' in that natural voice – how it had revealed the unspoken! The natural voice, that was Angus's sensitive mask, before he switched the talk.

In that same natural voice Mary would have been cool to him – no, not cool, but friendly. Or had Angus spoken? Had there been a quarrel?

If only there had been a quarrel, they might get over it. But now, after being all night with Angus, he felt there had not been a quarrel, but something much less definite – and more fatal. Angus had not wanted to come with these girls. So Iain had forced the outing upon them all! Driven by this feeling of having been disloyal to Angus. Disloyal. Hellish!

He worked himself into a state of angry misery. For it was beyond him to make any contrast between his actions that evening and his behaviour at home. It could not occur to him that girls were girls whether on the Blackford Hill or in the Dell.

What had touched Angus and Mary and, by repercussion, himself, touched the profoundest elements in life. It was real and everything that derived from it held significance and meaning. In that home world he was responsible, and because he had never consciously loved Mary, he felt his disloyalty as treacherous. What happened in the city bore about as much relation to that reality as one of his copied letters to the actual property it described.

TWELVE

This aspect of the city as a place of study and preparation, as a sort of vast barracks and training ground, was never quite lost by Iain. The university classes, the lecture notes, the study at night, all emphasised it. When he took an hour or two off and wandered about, he beheld things with a traveller's eyes, with the temporary gaiety of a recruit freed from restriction. At times he knew an irresponsible pleasure in this. Once, when he had taken Angus to the Mound, he asked the orator on Scottish affairs, 'Are you just going to go on *talking* about it?' There had followed a lively five minutes, but the incident did help relations between Angus and himself, did help to dissipate the dumbness that could so readily and heavily fall between them. Talking of socialism and Scotland, Iain could let himself go, and all the more extravagantly because of the underlying personal problems and difficulties. At such times he was like one going on a poaching foray: to blazes with privilege and the law, let us take a chance!

But this required for its more triumphant expression a certain basic knowledge, particularly of the law. Iain was not by inclination a student, but when something came his way which was not only part of his life's job but in which he was naturally also interested, like the Crofting Acts, he could devote himself to it with the enthusiasm of a debater hunting 'telling points'.

Smeaton worked in the conveyancing department of the business, or at least in that section of it which dealt with country estates. On the matter of leases for shooting and fishing tenants he considered himself an expert, and indeed his knowledge here was extensive not merely on the legal side but also and more particularly on the social or personal side. Even when a prospective tenant was an American or foreigner, Smeaton knew all about him, or could tell of him at least in connection with recent distinguished sporting parties at home or abroad. Had he ever entertained even minor royalty, Smeaton knew the date.

But this estate work necessarily included more troublesome if less exciting detail, such as agricultural accounts, saw-milling, and the eternal crofters with their eternal complaints which, because of the existence of an impartial tribunal called The Land Court, could be very tricky and exacting.

'I think these crofters are too molly-coddled. As a onetime sheep farmer, don't you think so, Cattanach?'

'No,' said Iain.

'No?' Smeaton smiled. 'You will one day – if you really intend to do your job.'

Iain was silent. But Smeaton could not leave him alone, for Iain, though still 'at the counter', had been directed 'to assist' in the estate department.

'They're always wanting something for nothing,' added Smeaton. 'If it isn't a reduced rent, it's compensation. If it isn't more sheep ground, it's a deer fence. A complaining, thriftless, grabbing lot, if you ask me, who can never do anything for themselves.'

'They have done things for themselves,' said Iain.

'What?' Smeaton turned on him. 'Mention one thing.'

'They got the first Crofting Act through Parliament in 1886.'

There was a quiet chuckle from a near desk.

'Again in their own interests! Again something for nothing!'

'Whose interests would you expect them to fight for?'

'Fight!' echoed Smeaton sarcastically. 'Who fought?'

'They did – the Highland crofters. They formed a Land League, put up their own men for Parliament, and against terrific opposition fought the landlords to a standstill and got their Act. It was the first thing of its kind in the world.'

'Really!'

'Yes, really,' said Iain.

There was a chuckle now from here and there.

Smeaton coloured. 'In the world! Marvellous!' He gave his own quick laugh, as if thereby adding to the office laughter against Iain.

Lindsay, who was bending over a flat desk, turned his head to look at Iain and saw that, though holding himself in, he was none the less quivering slightly.

'It *was* marvellous,' remarked Iain, his voice dropping as he turned to his work.

'As an authority on systems of land tenure throughout the world, perhaps you can tell us what was so marvellous about it?'

'It was marvellous that at that time of day crofters could win for themselves security of tenure so that landlords could no longer burn them out, compensation for improvements, and also the right to pass on their holdings to their own successors. If you know of any system of land tenure in this country or in Europe, or the world, that gave tenants such rights, I'd be glad to hear about it.'

'Up the Highlands!' said old Mr Macready, his watery eyes smiling over their spectacles.

'Up my foot!' retorted Smeaton. 'The British Parliament let them have it to keep them quiet.'

'Whatever the motive, it doesn't alter the fact – or at least Mr Cattanach's world challenge,' said Mr Macready, with dry humour.

'If a few Highland crofters intimidated a British Government, mostly landowners, they were tough guys,' suggested another voice.

'Sentimentalists, shouting about their wrongs – when tenants elsewhere in the world kept their mouths shut and got on with their work,' declared Smeaton.

'What wrongs?' asked Iain, now with better control, for the other voices had helped to still the inner quivering which tended, at such a moment, to show in his voice.

'Well, what wrongs?' countered Smeaton with heat. 'The land didn't belong to them. Yet when they had been served with proper notice to quit, they refused to go, they began to squeal, and so you had your famous Highland clearances.'

'The infamous Highland clearances,' corrected Iain, 'when the people were burned out of their own Highland homes in a way that would have made cannibal islanders blush.'

'Own Highland homes! Rubbish! Sentimental tosh!'

'But they were their own homes,' said Iain. 'They built them.'

For a moment Smeaton was clearly taken aback. Then he waved an impatient arm. 'If you mean the mud hovels they put up – you can call them homes if you like, the point at issue – the only legal issue – was the land, and the land wasn't theirs.'

'But the land was theirs. That was the point on which they based their fight. The land had always belonged to the clan, they said.'

'Belonged to your grandmother! Had the clan any legal entitlement to the land?'

'They had no written—'

'Exactly! The chief or landlord had his charter or legal entitlement to the land. He could produce his deeds of ownership. The clan or any member of it couldn't. That was the fact. It is still the fact. We run this office on that fact, and the sooner you learn it the better for you.'

As Smeaton turned away with a flourish, Iain remarked to his ledger, 'The British Government didn't seem to learn it.'

There was a general laugh and Smeaton swung round again. 'I was discussing law: not trying to be funny.' He was now clearly losing his temper.

'I didn't say you were being funny,' admitted Iain. 'All I said was that on a claim that the land had once belonged to the members of the clan, the Highland crofters put up a fight against being driven off that land. They did not fight for ownership of the land, but for security of tenure and the other rights in the Act. And they won their fight. That's all.'

'And I say that in their whole fight they didn't have a legal leg to stand on.'

Then Iain, just because he was now sure of himself and did not really want to offend Smeaton, was struck by one of those characteristic touches of country humour which came from him before he could stop it. 'Well,' he said, with a smile, 'if you ever win a fight when you haven't a leg to stand on, I'll pay to see it.'

And it needed that stroke to make John Lindsay add his cool laugh to the office guffaw.

But such passages did not help Iain to like the office any better. He realized that Smeaton and himself were really being made butts for the office humour. They provided relief, entertainment, and in a solemn voice anyone could ask an apparently innocent legal question on land tenure and have faces brighten in expectancy.

Moreover he sensed in Smeaton a growing dislike for him that at moments became acute, so that he could hardly repress it. When alone and thinking over it, this made Iain uncomfortable, even miserable. By his very nature, he hated nagging relations in human affairs. His whole instinct, with the blood roused, was to fight a thing on the spot and be done with it. But in Smeaton he sensed that cruelty of the snob which is insatiable. He could have borne with this, by paying no attention to it, ignoring it in silence, if only Smeaton had kept his tongue off the crofters, the sheep men, his own people. Here he would not let a challenge pass whatever happened. And the office knew that he was entitled to meet such challenge, irrespective of age, seniority, or other consideration of etiquette or discipline.

Apart from Smeaton and Wilson (whom Iain had disliked from the beginning), he realized that the office was on his side. For principal clerks like Mr Dowie and Mr Macready, he had a natural respect, and from his first talk with the cashier, he had liked the friendly blue eyes behind the spectacles, the untidy grey hair, and the Lowland voice with its ready use of the old Scots tongue. But the subtle way they egged him on to controversy, or exclaimed with mock solemnity 'Ah, here comes the Highland Champion!' made him shy and uncomfortable.

But mostly his days were uneventful, and he went home at night to study, never stirring from his chair until he tumbled into bed. Angus was finding his own friends, and if, occasionally, a few whistled notes called him from the street, he would, more often than not, find that Angus had a fellow-student with him. The first time this happened and they came up to his room Iain refused to play his violin, remarking banteringly, 'It's all right for you fellows, but I have done a day's work.'

Once after that Angus asked him to play, but never again.

Then one afternoon, Iain was called to Mr Hutcheson's room. He knocked and a girl's voice called, 'Come in.' He entered and found Morna sitting alone. She looked at him for a long moment out of her dark eyes. 'Hullo, stranger!'

'Hullo!' he answered, confused by the warm uprush of his blood.

'Have you been away?' Her soft voice was mocking him.

'No. I – I have been hard at it, studying, you know.'

'Have you?'

'Yes. I really have. Trying to get a grip of things.'

'No time to yourself at all? How dreadful!'

'It is. But then – what can a poor fellow do? I mean, there's not much – nowhere to go much – alone, I mean.'

'You like being alone?'

'I wouldn't say that. But what can I do about it?'

'If you don't know, how should I?'

'Do you mean – you—'

'Hsh! Later!' whispered Morna quickly.

The door opened and Mr Hutcheson came in. 'Ah, Cattanach, I wanted to see you about sheep diseases. You needn't wait, Miss Galloway.'

Morna lifted her notebook and withdrew.

'Do you know anything about sheep diseases?'

'No. Not much. I have sometimes been with my father and others.'

'It's all really damned complicated, especially when questions of excessive loss of stock arise. Scab and maggot and the dipping regulations, with the police doing their stuff. But this particular case does throw a definite suspicion on the estate shepherd. I don't like it. What do you think of shepherds as a body?'

'You can get good shepherds and shepherds not so good, but I never heard of a really dishonest one.'

'Good! That's my own opinion. What I want to know is this, for there's a point where the evidence hinges on the killing and eating of mutton. Do you know anything about *braxy* mutton?'

Ten minutes later, Mr Hutcheson remarked, 'And you said you didn't know much about it!'

This interview, which lasted a long time, for Mr Hutcheson had to indulge his private nostalgia for 'life in the open', had a bright, uplifting effect on Iain. His father had spoken through him, the sheep and the dogs had come alive, men moved on the hills, real men on real hills with wind and rain or sunlight in the eyes.

'You've been a long time,' said Smeaton, obviously fishing for news, but all Iain replied, negligently, was, 'Oh, he was wanting to find out about sheep.'

But the interview made him restless and very conscious of how he had avoided Morna. Now he suddenly wanted to see her, to go out with her. He felt starved of movement and life. She had been sitting in the room – what a confused fool he had been! – like that queer vision of her he had once had. But not the same, for she was dark and soft – and deep. Like a pool. Soft as a dark puppy bitch. Very attractive and friendly, drawing him with her eyes.

The Rock Pool on a summer's day, and taking a header into it. That's what he needed, and to blazes with all else.

As the office was emptying, he left the letter-press on the off chance that he might meet Morna and whisper quickly an hour and a meeting place for that night. But though he climbed the stairs and returned, and hesitated, as though he had dropped something, he did not see her. As he was coming out of the lavatory, Douglas met him.

'Doing anything to-night?'

'No,' answered Iain.

'I'll be round about the Mound at eight.'

Iain nodded. 'All right.'

He spun the handle of the press with such healthy vigour that Corbet cried, 'Here, mind the office property!'

Iain laughed.

THIRTEEN

Iain could feel the wine going to his head in a subtle, enlivening way, as he listened to the talk. They were in the same pub as before, but Douglas had brought the speaker on Scottish Nationalism along with him. His name was Davidson, and he clearly knew Douglas well, and as clearly was a University man. He was now full of fun, of humour, and Iain could see that he did not want to become seriously committed to any fundamental arguments. This was his time off, when he could relax, expand, in so unusual a place, among his peers. And he was certainly not over thirty.

He had shaken his head at Douglas's offer of claret. 'No thanks. It makes me bilious. I'll have a small spot of the wine of the country.'

They had wrangled cheerfully and traversed the traditional drinking habits of the Scots.

'Claret may have been the classic drink of the nobility,' Davidson allowed, 'but the Scots didn't grow grapes, they grew barley, and out of their barley they distilled *uisgebeatha*, which means "the water of life", and in the English tongue is "whisky". For better or for worse, they gave it to the world. Slainte!' And he drank his whisky.

'Do you mean your nationalism is of so narrow a brand,' said Douglas, 'that you would repudiate what the world's finest palates have agreed is superb, in favour of a native brew, distinguished mostly for its alcoholic content?'

'No,' replied Davidson.

'So what?'

'So presumably you will have to exclude my palate from the world's finest,' said Davidson, with an effort at solemnity which his smile defeated.

'You make a joke of it, but it is symptomatic.'

'Of what?'

'Of much of your propaganda.'

'You mean?'

'I mean you make too much of the commercial, the economic. If your whole case for Scottish self-government is based only on economic considerations, only on our economic decline, then a mere change for the better in the economic system could wipe your case away, and there would remain no *fundamental* need for self-government.'

'You mean man cannot live by bread alone?'

'I am aware it is not an original observation. It is, however, none the less true.'

'For a psychologist, or religious, or even for an historian, the observation has its interest, I admit. What is *fundamentally* certain is that without bread man cannot live at all.'

'You evade the point, which is: assuming the solution of the bread problem, what then remains?'

'Assuming the moon is made of green cheese, what then of the cheese problem? I see your point. A picturesque assumption.'

'That's the devil of becoming a public speaker, Davidson. What you cannot meet, you must evade. If you don't look out you'll be the professional politician one of these days.'

'If I thought our cause was wealthy enough, strong enough, to pay me, how happy I should be – and how much more I should be able to do!' He leaned back, laughing. 'I work all day – a bit harder than you, perhaps. When *you* come and do your stuff at the Mound instead of sitting, a sea-green incorruptible in your history tower, I'll then be glad to entertain your assumptions about bread and cheese – or even claret.' He finished his whisky.

Iain could see Davidson was evading Douglas, but also, deep in him, Iain realised why he was doing this. Davidson could not readily, now, in this place, begin arguing fundamental things. There was something so kin to his own spirit, even to his own office experience, in this that Iain was fascinated and felt curiously freed. He had just about worked himself up to saying that the earning of bread and butter was so fundamental in his own experience of life that he appreciated Mr Davidson's point, when the door opened and Maitland and another came in.

Laughter, banter, more drinks, and soon Douglas had them all involved. Things were lively for a time and Davidson found himself cornered.

'All right. If you want to talk of the mighty things of the mind, we will. Let me start like this. When the normal man is down and out, he not only loses respect for the existing economic dispensation, he loses respect for himself. Once get him into that condition and his creative faculties are affected. Others must do things for him now. He has lost initiative for he has lost two fundamental things: first, belief in himself; second, belief in that traditional pattern of life which being his could alone help him. If that is true of the individual, it is true of the group, and so finally of the nation.'

'I should say,' suggested the newcomer, MacGeorge, 'that loss of self-respect, of belief in oneself, does not come first. It is an effect—'

'As you like,' agreed Davidson. 'It derives from the loss of the traditional pattern; in this case, the loss of that control of our affairs which had to do with the economic and administrative factors involved in the condition of being down-and-out. I agree. I was looking at it from the point of view of the man who finds himself in that unhappy condition. To him, his condition comes first. He then searches his own country for that directing help – which isn't there.'

'But that argument could apply equally to socialism,' said Maitland.

'Or to communism, fascism, as you like. Agreed.'

'Where, then, is your self-governing point?'

'I should have thought obviously in this: that no communist, fascist, Tory, or what you will, ever thinks of realising his system except through existing national governments. That's the machinery he must capture and then remould nearer to his heart's desire. There is no other way. In Scotland we have no such machinery. Therefore, whatever system we may want for ourselves we absolutely have no way of realizing it.'

'Are you forgetting the Board?' asked Maitland blandly. Davidson gave a roar of laughter. 'Weren't you "borrowed" from the English Ministry of Agriculture?'

'You are still evading the point,' said Douglas. 'You are still founding your case on economics.'

'You are founding your life on it,' retorted Davidson. 'If you hadn't been able to put food in your stomach – not to mention claret – you wouldn't be here now expounding your mind. Your assumption that the bread-and-butter problem may be solved also assumes that someone else, some other people, will solve it for us, because manifestly, as I have shown, having no governmental machinery, we cannot solve it for ourselves. If you are the sort of fellow who is prepared to accept that dependent position, to wait like a dog for a bone – and then in the hope that it may be the bone he likes – all right. But don't expect me to be impressed when you talk of government.'

'There's never any bloody end to this argument,' said MacGeorge. 'Besides—'

'There is an end,' interrupted Davidson. 'But it requires some courage to face it.'

This started the same argument all over again but pitched on a higher key. Davidson kept his head better than the others and smiled when two spoke at once. Then suddenly, instead of replying himself, he turned his face to Iain and asked in a perfectly natural way, 'What do you think of all this? You're not saying much.'

'I agree with you,' replied Iain. He wanted to say more but his heart began beating strongly.

'Good!' Davidson laughed. 'Glad to have someone on my side.'

'What do you agree with him on?' asked Maitland, and Iain felt his assessing eyes. Douglas and MacGeorge were also looking at him.

'If a fellow can't get bread and butter, there's not much good talking to him about – about his soul.'

Davidson threw his head up, at the same time giving the table one firm bang with his fist.

'Do you think he has a soul?' asked Maitland.

'Perhaps he has,' replied Iain. 'But, if so, he can't do much with it on an empty stomach.'

'Precisely,' said Davidson. 'Physical control of the body before the mind can function. The thing is physiological. In the same way, co-ordination of the body politic precedes any cultural expression of that body. You can't have culture in a vacuum. And to prove my point – what is the present cultural position of Scotland? Her creative position in the arts on the world level?'

'Granted, it may not amount to much,' said MacGeorge. 'But this argument is getting us nowhere. I am a psychologist to trade and, as I understand it, Douglas's position is this. He does not see why you should concentrate so much on economics, on the physical expression of self-government, when what is primarily important is that which should be expressed through your economics and self-government as the—' and he nodded towards Iain – 'soul is expressed through the body. Is that clear?'

'Go on,' said Douglas.

'Now do you, Davidson, accept a distinctive Scottish soul – or rather, a distinctive Scottish capacity for creativity in the arts?' asked MacGeorge.

'I do.'

'On what grounds?'

'Two grounds, historical and psychological. And they apply not merely to Scotland, but to every other country in the world, Czechoslovakia, America, Russia, France, England, and so on. This is not a case of a little nationalism, or a perverted nationalism. It has to do with the expression of the human spirit. You can murder that spirit, or you can free it for expression. But before I go on, I must again – and I offer no apology for my insistence – make it clear that before you can do anything about a country's creativity on the world level, that country must first of all be in a position to control her own affairs. Do you agree?'

'For the sake of argument, let me say Yes.'

'Nothing doing!' Davidson pushed himself back from the

table. 'If you don't know your own mind on a matter so potentially vital to Europe, and therefore to civilization, then argument is valueless. This is too deep a thing for a swithering intellectual's amusement, Mr MacGeorge, and you, as a psychologist, ought to know it.'

'Swithering intellectual!—'

'I agree,' said Douglas, cutting MacGeorge short.

'But analysis—' began MacGeorge sharply.

'Oh, hell, never mind,' interrupted Douglas again, his elbows on the table, the dark eyes in his lumpy face staring at Davidson. 'Let us hear what he has to say about it.'

Davidson met Douglas's eyes directly. 'Historical means that we have had a history; that we cohered as a people over a vast stretch of time, fought our battles for our country, were moulded by our environment, created our own distinctive kinds of institutions (church and law, for example) expressed ourselves in distinct lingual forms, in music, even in architecture as these very streets show. But I needn't go into all that. I am prepared to leave it to you as umpire. Very well, then. I submit that we have a history, with everything that history connotes in the make-up of a people's mentality, as old and as distinctive as that of any country in Europe. Do you agree?'

'Absolutely,' answered Douglas, 'if with this proviso, historically incontrovertible, that as a fully self-functioning community, *communitas*, it's a damned sight older than most.'

Laughter and more drinks. Iain sipped his claret, finding, for an elusive moment, something subtly attractive about it, as about an argument that he could not grasp in its fullness but that yet he apprehended intuitively with a mounting feeling of exhilaration.

'Psychologically, the matter may not appear so susceptible of demonstration,' continued Davidson, 'but to me, it is equally clear.' He eyed MacGeorge. 'Just as a country has a history, so it has a psychological pattern. History – in the sense of a social life and given environment, with institutions, customs, habits – conditions that psychological pattern. Let us take literature as an instance of the expression of that pattern in one form. And let me ask Maitland, who knows something of European literature, whether he finds a recognizable difference in spirit between, say, French literature and German literature – two countries which have shared a common boundary for centuries.'

'A clever manœuvre, seeing you have heard me hold forth on the difference,' said Maitland, with a French gesture.

Douglas laughed. 'The Auld Alliance is coming home to roost!'

'Why use the word manœuvre if you believed what you said?' asked Davidson without a smile.

'Merely as tribute to your Socratic quality. Proceed, my dear fellow.' Maitland delicately sniffed his wine.

'Need I go any further?' Davidson asked MacGeorge.

'I see the implications, but they do not impress me, apart from what has happened in the past. If you are arguing for a modern literature in Scotland, then I see no reason why it should not be produced in the existing circumstances.'

'Without reference to the past?'

'Without any direct reference.'

'Then by indirect reference?'

'What do you mean by indirect?'

'I am merely trying, politely, to keep you from denying your own psychological gods,' suggested Davidson. 'Literature, as indeed all the arts, is in its highest form held to be an expression of what you call the unconscious. Its expression is made, of course, through the intellect, but its power derives directly from the unconscious. And the unconscious, I understand, is the sum of our past.'

'But we have had our past.'

'Precisely. That is my point and we can deny it in this instance only at our literary peril. The psychological pattern produced by our past is part of our mental inheritance. To deny that pattern is to cut ourselves from our roots. Once cut from our roots, we cannot flower.'

'I don't know what you mean by "psychological pattern". If you are saying that we inherit a national psychological pattern, then you are talking nonsense.'

'Don't put words in my mouth which I didn't use. Let us stick to your psychologists. Freud says that we inherit what he calls an "archaic heritage". Jung calls it the "collective unconscious". I might call it here an essence of our total past history as human beings—'

'Do you mean that we inherit specific memories from the past?'

'No,' replied Davidson, 'and you know I don't. We inherit an aptitude for a certain pattern, just as a chemical solution may be said to hold an aptitude for a certain pattern in the sense that in given conditions it will precipitate crystals of a known form. It is, I understand, the accepted illustration.'

'Yes, but that refers to humanity at large. It isn't a national matter. So far as I know, Jung does not say that you precipitate *national* mental crystals.'

'Before we go on to consider the implications of Jung's concept of the collective unconscious, let me ask you this. If great literature and art derive from the unconscious; if they are, as it were, the crystals which genius precipitates; how comes it that Maitland here can distinguish clearly between French literature and art and German literature and art, if there is no difference between the French collective unconscious and the German collective unconscious?'

While Maitland was drawing his mental wind, Douglas said in his forthright way, 'For French and German substitute Scottish and English, the history and the psychological pattern being already in each case, whether we like it or not, determined by the past?'

'Exactly. Accordingly a Scot or an Englishman is most highly creative when he is flowering from his own unconscious root. To cut the root is fatal to the flower. So to destroy the flower is to lessen the world's wealth of blossom. In the mental sense, it is murder. In the international sense, it is loss. As a concept of growth, progress, human enrichment, it is unscientific.'

Then MacGeorge got going again, and broad generalizations were narrowed to highly contentious instances or 'points'. Davidson was now smoking cigarette after cigarette,

and Douglas so far forgot the normal courtesy he extended
to his claret as to smoke also. The cubicle was thick, with
smoke and the flashing of voices and faces. Iain was beholding
all this in the kind of entrancement which made its ultimate
meaning if not intellectually clear, at least intuitively or
emotionally apprehensible.

And then something extraordinary happened whereby he
did, in a fantastic way, unconsciously crystallize much of the
endless talk.

He had heard, at a distance, a street musician scraping
Scots melodies from a violin. This must, in some way, have
penetrated Davidson's mind for he began instancing Highland
folk music as so much part of an inherited pattern in the
realm of sound, that no Highlander from any other kind of
folk music could ever get the same utterly unconditional thrill.

This suddenly affected Iain like pure revelation. He knew,
in his secret places, that for him it was absolute truth. For,
of course, from his earliest tackling of *Home Sweet Home*
to the latest imported dance music, he had tried many things
on his fiddle.

Maitland was coming in strong on this musical argument,
was pinning Davidson, for a start, to the 'logical conclusion'
that therefore a Highlander – 'such as Cattanach here' –
would find his highest musical deliverance only in an evolved
or symphonic form with Highland thematic roots, when
suddenly the street musician, who had been silent for a while,
started sawing dolefully on his fiddle, right by the window,
in their ears, the melody called 'Highland Laddie', at one
time the 'march past' of nearly every Highland regiment.

The effect was so utterly incongruous, so vastly ludicrous
a comment on their elevated discussion, that all, except
Maitland, collapsed in laughter.

'Oh hell! Tell him to clear off!' cried Maitland, his ears
and his argument alike assaulted, and, taking a shilling from
his pocket, he handed it to Iain.

Iain took it automatically, but inwardly a hot flush went
through him as from a knife edge. It was not altogether
Maitland's unconscious acceptance of him as the office boy

of the group. It was something more than reaction to Maitland's intellectual self-conceit, his social assessing eyes. The melody was in it; personal pride that springs from the root. He sat for a moment, looking at the shilling. The laughter covered him and, smiling awkwardly, he slowly got up and went out.

Standing in the gutter was a little old man, sawing away mechanically at a fiddle whose broad end was shrouded in a grey beard. There was a droop to his shoulders, to his arms, to the fiddle, and he looked like a figure that had wandered from very far away, and had come here under a strange compulsion of misery, not to expect anything, but to be by himself.

His cap was on the kerb and Iain's blind instinct was to drop the shilling in the cap and walk away. To tell this poor old man that his playing was so offensive that he would get a shilling if he moved on was utterly beyond him. He stood uncertain with the horrible feeling of being caught in shame in a public place. Two or three, passing, glanced at him. Some children who had been playing about, stood still, looking. From their arrested attitudes, Iain knew they had been teasing the old man, just as he and other children at home used to tease Mad Mairag. Then in a moment he became aware of two eyes looking up from under the grey hair that fell over the deeply scored forehead. In the street-light, the eyes glittered narrowly. The music stopped and Iain, as if he had not seen the cap, took a step forward and handed the old man Maitland's shilling.

'God bless you, sir.'

It was a country voice and Iain, as though on a country road, said heartily, 'What's gone wrong with your fiddle, man? Your bow is too slack.'

'Och, yes. Like myself, it's getting done.' There was a weary humour in the low, husky voice.

'Let me see it.' Iain took the bow and tried to screw it up. At first it would not move as though the screw were frozen solid, but at last there was a twist and a jerk. 'That's better, now! Your fiddle has a good tone.'

'It's an old, old fiddle. I have heard it sing in its day, but—'

'Show me.' Iain handled the fiddle. He now had the fine, reckless feeling of one who has taken the plunge. The wine was no longer in his flesh but in his spirit. Who looked or heard did not matter. To blazes with them all!

'Watch the strings!' wheezed the old man anxiously as he heard the keys creak.

'You can't play on slack strings,' answered Iain cheerfully. Soon he had the fifths in perfect harmony. 'Have you a bit of resin on you? The old hair is tired.'

'I have a bittie somewhere.' He doubled over as he plumbed the pouches of the long ragged tweed coat that covered him. In the end he brought forth a dark lump not much bigger than a hazel nut. Iain scraped the grease off it with his knife before treating the bow. Then he tucked the fiddle under his chin and began playing 'Highland Laddie'.

It was exactly as if the dying and the dead of the old man's playing came to life and went marching on the street, marching on their own independent feet, proud and sprightly, full of the gaiety of life, with a cheer ready in the throat. No slurring now. Every note alive, and every foot coming down on the beat and advancing. The swift notes, each with a fraction of bow to itself, rippled like the tartan ribbons from the pipes, ran about the advancing men of the Highland regiments like laughter.

And what distinguished Iain's playing was not its clear note-production, not even a certain wildness of the blood, but something of body and dignity, of power, so that he seemed to hold the fastest movement within his own easy mastery of time. Proud men marched to this time, and the children, in order to keep up with them, ran. It was when the children began to shout that Iain, remembering where he was, but still playing, started marching up the pavement. It was a corner pub and at the entrance to the side street, he stopped and switched to a fast reel.

Girls and fellows paused. Men on the move after a last drink drew near. It was a narrow street and the tall buildings caught the ringing notes and sent them echoing along the walls into darkness. More children came running and pushed their way through the thickening ring. Shouts went up beyond the ring. Two young men began swinging their girls, whose high voices screamed their mirth. Becoming aware of the growing crowd, Iain stopped. But the old fellow had vanished. He had, in fact, gone for his cap, which he had forgotten. But now a big, swaying man – he must have been forty – cried to Iain, 'B' Jasus, mister, give us a jig!'

'Right!' called Iain and at once struck up an Irish jig. The Irishman took in a hole on his leather belt and Iain, finishing a phrase, began again and the Irishman began to dance.

On the causey stones the Irishman's boots clicked like massive castanets. From the hips upwards, he kept his body ramrod stiff, arms by his sides. The blue eyes in his great fair face became round and earnest as a child's. The light from a side window shone on him. But from the hips down he danced.

Iain, who knew only the graceful body-swinging and upward-curved arm of the Highland dance, knew also and in a moment that here was the classic way of the Irish dance. Within a couple of bars of the music, he had the dancer's own time, and, unison being complete, he could emphasize with an extra sweep of the bow those notes or beats which only the blood knows, and the Irishman, responding, was lifted off his feet to a clearer grace, a finer accuracy, and toes tapped and kicked the air, side-stepped and came together again, with the lightness of a youth in his twenties. Only once did he permit himself a gesture and that was when he caught his cap, which was slipping from his head, and with a sweeping forcefulness, in perfect time to a descending rhythm of the jig, threw it flat on the street. And the crowd, caught by a nameless grace and strength in this act, by its wild, solemn humour, laughed and cheered. Whereupon the Irishman was driven to excel himself, and finally brought his dance to an end with a foot that hit the street with the sharpness of a gun-crack. Iain had seen the end coming and finished on the explosive crack.

Swaying from his slim hips and breathing heavily, he approached Iain. He was probably a lorry driver or slinger of beer barrels from one of the neighbouring breweries.

'Begod, mister, you can play!'

'Begod, mister, you can dance!' promptly replied Iain.

'Eh?' said the Irishman, coming close. A boy handed him his cap. He looked at it as if he hadn't seen it before, then stuck it on his head. He saw the old man. 'Old Father Christmas, is it?' He laughed, thrusting his hands into his trousers pockets. 'Is this your long-lost son, Father?'

The old man did not answer, but stood there, the drooping cap in his hand, dumb and witless. A trickle of pennies ran into the cap from the Irishman's fist.

'Go on, now! Put it round! Sure it's not every day they get such an exhibition of dancing.'

But the old man mumbled and stood.

'Here, Johnnie, round with it; and if you pinch a penny out of it I'll tear the gizzard out of you.'

Before the cap came back, heavy with copper, Iain was playing again, egged on by a crowd freed from the feeling of getting something for nothing by having contributed their pennies.

Instinct told him to play a slow measure, a song, for a change. His bow and fingers found a phrase of one of Mary's songs, then found another. But he could not go on with either song. It went too deep, too deep. They would not know. Prompted by an earlier echo from the street musician, he began playing 'Loch Lomond'. A shrill, female voice rose here and there and fell away in giggles. He changed his key. Men with some drink in them began bawling a few phrases and waving their arms in careless pride. Soon the street was a mass of ragged singing and laughter. At the end of a verse, Iain switched to an eightsome reel and now he let himself go. The sudden transition set the crowd cheering and dancing-wild. Two policemen appeared, forcing their way through to the player. It was closing time.

'Here!' said one of the policemen abruptly to Iain, 'you'll have to move on.'

As the fiddle dropped from his chin, he stared at the policeman, his eyebrows gathering for a moment in a fighting, hawk-like concentration.

'Sure an' what the hell harm are we doing?' demanded the Irishman, squaring up.

'You're blocking the traffic,' said the same policeman to Iain. 'Come on! Move on!'

'All right,' said Iain, with a wry smile. He turned to the old man but found him at his feet, sitting on the kerb. He bent down. 'You'll have to move on. Here's your fiddle.'

The old face looked up at him with an expression which Iain was to remember afterwards. 'I once had a son—' mumbled the pitiful voice. But, at the moment, Iain merely helped him to his feet and put the fiddle and bow in his hands. Without a word, the old man shuffled away.

Iain turned round and found Douglas, Maitland, MacGeorge and Davidson looking at him.

FOURTEEN

Christmas was at hand and Angus, who had a fortnight's vacation, was going home. After Iain had seen him to his lodgings, Angus had insisted on walking back half-way. Then that last cry of Iain's in the street: 'Well, remember me to them all at home!'

Remember me to them all at home. And in that moment home had receded suddenly in some distant and fatal way, and the street along which he returned alone was an echoing street into immeasurable farness from his home.

At last he was committed to this street and his new life, and he realized it in a curious suspension of the mind, wherein sound became echo and the ear finally caught the silence beyond and around life and the waiting things of the world. There was a relief in the parting with Angus, in the knowledge that he was leaving the city. Now Iain was alone in it and he had no responsibility. The tie with his home was severed. He would never go back there to work and live. That phase of his life was over, and the landscapes of home and the figures moving over them became diminished and, emotionally, could hardly touch him at all. He was at last freed from them, and from everything that could happen to them.

But he found he could not play his fiddle. It lay dead in its box. If he thought of it at all, he did so indifferently.

For one thing, he hadn't the energy to play it. He realized he was underfed. Once or twice, having rushed too quickly from his lodgings, he had had to lean against railings until a lightheadedness had passed. He was worried about money and had put off writing to his father. For a fortnight now he had had nothing but either a glass of milk or a couple of penny buns for lunch. Lunch must stop altogether.

He was himself to blame for this. He knew that. In the three letters he had written his grandmother, he had been cheerful and said he was getting along fine. In the second letter he had made a joke about town eggs, as something amusing to say, and since then a two-dozen box had arrived three times. They had saved his landlady the cost of a few high teas, but not added much to the amount of his food.

He had spent too much on drink and cigarettes. Somehow he had accepted Douglas's hospitality without thinking about it. Then one night he had overheard Douglas and Maitland in argument, and he perceived that the general practice among the group, when it was more than a matter of a drink or two, was to divide the night's bill equally among them. Douglas was wanting to pay the lot but Maitland would not have it. Iain listened, and Maitland, turning his head, saw him listening. At once Iain got up, went to them, and said he would like to pay.

'Not at all,' replied Douglas, impatiently, 'you are my guest.'

'I would rather pay, if you don't mind,' said Iain, smiling in a shy but dogged way, taking money from his pocket. 'How much?' and he looked at Maitland.

'Well – it's not for me—' Maitland shrugged, with a glance at Douglas.

'Next time,' said Douglas shortly. 'You can pay for me next time.' Iain could see that Douglas was furious with Maitland.

Next time, Iain quietly insisted on paying for both. It had cost him fifteen shillings. Nor could pride permit him to let that occasion be the last.

But the time came when he felt he had squared his account and could refuse. He did refuse. Douglas pressed him, saying he was genuinely inviting him on this occasion as a guest, not to the pub, but to the place where the group met once a week. 'I want you to take your fiddle with you.'

Iain replied flatly that he wouldn't play.

'In that case, that's that. I was asking you as a personal favour. Incidentally, you would have saved us some cash.

And the girls who are coming are real dancers. They would have shown you how to dance an eightsome to your own playing.'

In the end Iain went with his fiddle. The girls were Scots chorus girls from one of the pantomimes, and among other accomplishments, they certainly could dance.

An interesting, revealing night it had been. The girls brought green and red streamers which, on the stage, they used for one of their pantomime dances. Christmas crackers, cold grouse, plenty of wine and hot coffee. Though at first embarrassed a bit by the free and easy manners, the terms of endearment thrown so lightly, the unceasing chatter and laughter, he had liked it, had felt incomparably more at home than in Mr Dowie's Sunday parlour. One girl had singled him out after he had played them a warming eightsome reel. And within a minute, the shell of his reserve was broken.

She had endearing ways, tugged the lapel of his coat, straightened his tie, looked into his eyes with a wondering innocence.

But it was not until after she had danced on the table that he got to know her to the last cunning thought in her mind. She danced the Highland Fling in tartan kilt and velvet jacket, her pantomime dress. She wore diminutive white pants, and her legs, bare downwards to just below the knee, were firm and cool and beautifully shaped. He saw at once that she was not only a born dancer, but danced the Highland Fling with professional accuracy, with that subtle command of abandon which won awards at Highland Games.

He had never played for any dancer like this, and his playing and her dancing lifted him out of himself, sent fire over his body in cold shivers of exaltation. She smiled to him as she danced, used correct gesture as a subtle communication, and, between them, they held their audience in what was clearly felt as the summit of this particular art's perfection.

As they talked together afterwards, he pointed to some medals she wore on her tunic. 'Does the theatre provide these?'

She looked at him as she drank her wine. 'Of course. What did you think?'

He smiled back. 'Where did you learn to dance?'

'Where do you think?' She kept the rim of her glass at her lips, looking under her brows at him with grey, intelligent eyes.

'You have danced at Highland Games.'

She hesitated for a fraction of a second. 'How do you know?'

'You dance very, very well.'

She laughed and looked around. Then she nodded to him. He thought of the troupes of little girls who went round the Highlands dancing at the annual games.

'As a little girl?'

She nodded and watched the effect. 'Where do you come from?'

He told her.

'A poor student from the poor Highlands?'

That was rather disconcerting, but he laughed. 'Dead right!'

'I thought so.'

'How?'

She regarded him for a moment with her wide-spaced eyes. 'Because you play very, very well.' She had mimicked his utterance to perfection. 'I only had my mother. She was poor.'

In a flash he realized that in her eyes they were of no use to each other, both of them being poor, and thus, relieved of any need to play the love business, they could talk and tell. Deep down her intelligence was cool and calculating. He saw she was greedy; she would play deliberately for what she wanted; in a final moment she would be relentless, tough as nails. But she was good at the game!

Even now, he became aware, she was playing him off against Maitland. She was using her arts on him – exhibiting a different aspect of herself – for Maitland's benefit.

He played up; appeared to be carried away by her. They both knew what was happening and began to enjoy the fun with a certain cool affection. He liked her. They were artists now, not in the interpreting of a dance, but in the far more intricate measures and compulsions of the moneyless pocket. Only her life experience here was so very much profounder than his, that he got an understanding – like a vision – of the awful terror of poverty to a girl.

Douglas was insisting on a dance called 'The Flowers of Edinburgh'. Maitland came for her. She flashed him an intimate glance, at once sweeping away his suspicion. Douglas, who insisted on every movement of the dance being performed properly, was netted in thrown streamers, green and red.

As she was going away with Maitland, she cast a look behind her, smiled to Iain and winked. Being the musician, odd man out, Iain went home alone. Besides, he had no money. But he felt cool. Cool as the grey, managing eyes which Maitland had never seen. Life's skeletal bone was pretty hard and grey!

He would have to write his father. But he knew that his reluctance to write came from a deeper source than any pricking of conscience over the matter of drinks. There was a pride in his father that would like his son to keep his own end up in any company. Like most normal boys at college, Iain could have his shot at explaining to himself that this sort of thing must be done. And even if this could not altogether take the sting out of the conscience-prick, it could in a few days dismiss it. One had to go on living.

But it really had been humiliating to have to think of the cost of tram fares the other night when taking Morna to the Blackford Hill. That he had not offered to take her to a picture house did not trouble him, because he knew she preferred the Hill.

Four days before Christmas, Corbet regarded him critically and referred to his gills. Iain said something about a bit of a chill, but refused to 'have one', though, for the first time, he felt the real need for a drink. The following morning he swallowed his porridge with difficulty. As he went to the office, his body felt light, with shivers running over it. Usually when he caught a chill or a cold, he was troubled with a stuffy head and running nostrils. Now his head was abnormally clear and his nostrils were so drily sensitive to the wintry air that he decided snow was not far off. When he happened to touch the cold iron handle of the letter-press, his hand leapt away as if it had been stung. He did not go out for lunch, and by the end of the day he knew he was about all in.

'What you need is a hot rum and a pile of blankets,' said Corbet. 'I've seen it coming on you. You're not half the fellow you was when you came here first.'

He managed to joke with Corbet and set out on fairly steady legs for his lodging.

It was altogether a remarkable walk, and one which would have been not unpleasant but for the fear of collapse. When he staggered he smiled. It was a new kind of drunkenness, with his head light and airy. Half way, his body grew very light, like cotton wool or thistledown. How it kept on its legs was a mystery. It was the first time he had ever felt incorporeal, without real weight. The pavement was rubber, the impact of his feet soft and distant.

Then he began to feel a spot in his lungs or his heart as hotly solid, and when it radiated treacherous flushes his brain dizzied and his eyes darkened. But he knew the trick for combating this. He hadn't, as a lad, struggled against a snowstorm for nothing. The trick is to draw inward and leave everything to the will. Leave the will in command and struggle on blindly. Get past people; round corners. Ignore all voices, all eyes. The slightest touch upon the will, and it will collapse.

The great difficulty is the key-hole. Time now takes on a terrifying arrestment. Patience, patience. May God shut the landlady in the kitchen. The door swings inward. The miracle of this relief is so perfect that it leaves the key forgotten in the lock. The room. The bed. The bed comes up and meets the body and both fade out in divine consummation.

FIFTEEN

From the high rock, he looked over the city. Douglas showed him all the important places, and each spire lifted (as it was named) its pointing finger to the sky, and each roof, like a dark-blue back, remained immobile, covering the deeds of its body. The names that rang out of history went in procession down the Royal Mile.

Tilting over, like a bird in flight, his mind suddenly saw Princes Street. It was away below him, flat and wide; tram-cars moved along it like automatic beetles and the people were dark points like black ants hurrying away but never leaving; yet the street itself was wide and full of air and princely. Behind the street were other streets, which, in the act of coming among them, he knew intimately with the momentary pleasure of surprise. Entrances to legal offices, insurance offices, brass plates, names, doors. Law and finance, banking and accountancy. First floors and second floors and third floors. Lifts. Public Enquiries. Private inner doors and swing-door lavatories. Along Rose Street, round the art shop at the corner of Hanover Street and there, in its narrow gilt frame – the portrait of his mother.

Douglas was all at once coming along the lane, so he went to meet him, as he did not want him to see the portrait. It was broad daylight and he said 'Hallo!', smiling. Douglas looked at him with an ironic expression, much as to say: Studying art now! But he did not speak, only glanced sharply at the window; then stopped, with a piercing fire in his eyes directed at the picture.

Iain kept his back to the picture, taking a step or two onward, enticing Douglas away. But Douglas went to the window, and when Iain looked over his shoulder, he saw him peering about the edges of the canvas. Iain felt with a shattering embarrassment that in another moment Douglas would know who she was. His body twisted away, a step and half a step. Douglas came on. 'Queer. It has no name,' Douglas said aloud to himself. And the two terrible words NO NAME held for Iain the dark suffering of the world and a sense of eternal loss.

So much did this affect him, that he did not notice how they had come to the darkened stairs which they were now ascending. But there was more light on the landing, for the top half of a door facing them was all frosted glass and the light shone through it, bringing into sharp relief the black lettering of the word PRIVATE printed across it. Douglas, without hesitation, caught the knob of the door and swung it open, inviting Iain to enter before him.

But Iain did not enter a room, he entered a new city. From a balcony, where they paused for a moment, he saw the fine ordered streets below him, and beyond them the sea, and away inland the low curves of remote hills and mountains. All was clear and peaceful and waiting, in this new city and new land. There were gardens before the houses, flowering shrubs and trees. And the light was finer than the light of broad daylight.

But Douglas was walking on, darkly concentrated on his destination or his hidden purpose. Iain now knew the streets, realised he had been here before, though when or for what purpose he could not remember.

Actually, Douglas had taken him here one night under a clear moon, to show him the architecture of the New Town, and had praised the architecture as the noble beginnings of 'what might have been'.

The straight streets and the lovely curving crescents, the ascending terraces, the breadth and fineness of conception.

But Iain had forgotten that, because he saw everything now not through Douglas's talk but through his own eyes in this fine light. No-one moved on the streets except themselves. It might have been a city of the dead. But Iain did not feel the city was untenanted. The inhabitants were withdrawn behind the walls, but they were there, following their own rites and practices. He suddenly remembered a car which had driven up to a door in the darkness. The door had opened and against the beam of light a young woman had entered, stooping slightly as she took the step and lifting a silken dress from her ankles. Under her fur coat the dress had seemed very flimsy and her ankles fine and graceful. A young man, with a dark overcoat over his evening clothes, followed with a quick, springing step. The door closed, the car was driven away, and the house again became as quiet – as it was now. An end house. He recognized it, and his eyes were drawn, under an irresistible compulsion, to a particular window on the first floor. Looking down at him through the glass, not curiously but with an inscrutable reserve, was the pale face of John Lindsay.

So profound a shock did this give him that he could not speak of it to Douglas. Indeed for a little while he forgot Douglas altogether and only remembered him when he saw him in front and now going fast. He was climbing up a narrow street or lane, not unlike Rose Street, a Rose Street that had been swung round and twisted slightly. Though now and then – when he lifted his eyes and realized he would have to run if he were going to overtake Douglas and for some reason he refused to run – he saw it as a narrow street of ascent in a foreign city, yet somehow not a wholly unfamiliar city, as if someone had gone up that way with a cross.

He began to walk as quickly as he could in order to overtake Douglas. His heart started pumping at so tremendous a rate that the actual thuds were suffocating. Then his breath began to catch him in a short, sharp pain, a stabbing constriction, which he could not and dare not ignore. Little by little Douglas gained on him, and when he disappeared round the next curve, Iain stood gasping in terrible stress and anxiety which passed, however, into the deep unconsciousness of defeat.

Then suddenly he was behind Douglas again and he smiled, for Douglas had plainly been toiling all the time upward, while Iain, by a mysterious short-cut, was reaching the end of the narrow street quite fresh.

As they entered upon a broad, straight thoroughfare, Douglas paused. Iain recognized the street. It was George Street. But Douglas had stopped at a little distance from some broken columns which had the familiar shape of those on the Calton Hill. The broken columns were very historic looking, like a piece of ancient Rome. But Douglas was staring at them with a fierce fire in his eyes, and when Iain looked at the ruins again, he saw a man standing on a plinth, making a public speech, but no-one was listening to him. It was Davidson, and Iain smiled as he stole a look at Douglas. Then he shifted his eyes and saw men coming discreetly out of a hole in the base of the Calton Hill and, knowing the public latrine, his friendly humour increased. It was so like humanity in a city to crowd into one hole that he turned his back to Douglas in order not to offend him with the soft mirth that was rippling through his body. His eyes lifted from the street which crossed George Street at the point where they had stopped, and he recognized that all thoroughfares came to this point, from the farthest Highlands and from the sea, and not only the visible ones, but also the invisible. The invisible, the hidden ones were like veins, quietly coming back, sheep-tracks, paths, side-roads, through the vast body of Scotland, lying prostrate on its back.

Iain could see it was a holiday, a day of celebration. And then he heard music, a slow, solemn band music, which seemed to grow out of the fine light. The men were coming up now in a stream from the latrine in the base of the hill and soon George Street, which had been quite empty, began to flow with a soundless life.

The music quickened in a mounting, dramatic way. Expectation everywhere increased; tension was drawn to bursting point. Then within a nearby office there was a sharp explosion, as if an immense Christmas cracker had been pulled, and from its roof a grey, curving streamer shot over the city. As though at a signal, all the other offices around began to go off like Christmas crackers, and streamers curved in the loveliest arcs over every part of the city.

It was a remarkable and strangely thrilling sight. Iain

found himself up on a broken column, watching where they
fell. The Castle and the church spires were caught by the
grey ribbons – they were all grey – in a gay, festooning effect.
But down on his left the ever-diminishing ribbon balls
vanished in a mile-long black chasm, which Iain recognized,
in the moment of surprise that is also revelation, was the
Royal Mile.

So disturbed was he by this feeling of the Royal Mile as
an abyss that he jumped when a ribbon struck him. Realizing
it was only a ribbon, he laughed, holding it in his hand.
Then he saw that it was not an ordinary ribbon. His fingers
felt its texture. It was tough like a thin strip of fine vellum.
It was the colour of his violin strings. Then indeed he saw
that it was gut, as thin, as broad, and nearly as pliable as
the red tape with which he had tied bundles of legal documents. But not sheep gut. What kind of gut? His country
mind, curious over so natural a point, began to feel the
answer coming. He tried to choke it, with a profound and
sickening sense of horror. But he could not. For already the
answer had been spoken within him. It was human gut.

His eyes lifted and roved slowly over the city, and he saw
it netted in the ribbons everywhere, church spire and Castle,
Parliament House and chimney stack, shops and dwelling
houses. And in a moment of arid and dreadful understanding,
his eyes closed. He was on a hillside at home and he was
standing by his father who was looking fixedly at a dead
sheep upon whose black skin, where the wool had been
stripped away, the grey maggots were crawling.

The music brought him back, and as his eyes opened
George Street was gone; in place of the broken columns was
the round bandstand of Princes Street Gardens. They were
far below the height now, and out of the bandstand, as out
of a navel hole, shot grey streamers over the dancers, who
wove in and out round the bandstand as round a maypole.

They danced, however, not singly but in couples, 'walking'
the dance in a curious staccato movement like life-size toys,
and when they turned, so that the man for a few steps might
go by the back instead of the woman, it was as if part of

their hidden clockwork produced this automatic and quite flawless reversal.

Then Iain saw their faces. They had the solemnity of those walking in their sleep, and suddenly Maitland's face swam up to him, like a drowned face from water – and went on.

Something spent or satiated in the strangely fixed features so affected Iain that when a small disturbance occurred among the dancers, as if part of the clockwork had jammed, he knew a moment of intense suspense. Then a girl started from among the dancers towards him, running in short, eager steps, and he recognized her at once as the chorus girl who had danced the Highland Fling on the table to his playing and had danced it superbly.

Now she was coming, running through the standing spectators, the paint on her face no more than an extra-vivid blood. She put up her hand and caught the lapel of his jacket. Blood swam to his head and dizzied him.

Through the blood-darkness he became aware of a face peering at him. Though the face did not become completely distinct, he knew it was his mother's. Beset by a whelming burden of dumbness, he tried to turn his own face away.

But the watching face persisted and cleared a little. With a feeling of appalling bewilderment he saw it was not his mother's face. Now he was finally lost, with that dreadful spirit face, hag-like and whimpering, coming up out of the shades; growing clearer, coming towards him.

But there was no escape. He was caught. His head rolled from side to side, staring everywhere, at everything. Then memory came over him in a wash and he looked into his landlady's face and said, 'No, I don't want a doctor.'

Must he carry on this conversation for ever? Hadn't he told her already? Money, money, he had no money for doctors. Must he shout that at her and be done with it?

But now a man moved from behind her. It was not a doctor, it was Douglas.

SIXTEEN

By the time Douglas fetched a doctor, Iain was past the crisis. The doctor called every day for a time and chatted away to Iain while he sat on the bed. Grapes and oranges arrived from Douglas, whose offer one evening to 'write anyone at home', Iain politely refused, saying he would rather write himself.

Douglas gave him the news of the office, related amusing little incidents, but did not stay long.

'Anyone you would like to see?' asked Douglas from the door.

'No.'

'All right.' Douglas smiled cheerfully. 'Lindsay was asking particularly for you.'

'Thanks. No. I – don't want anyone.'

'Not even Mr Dowie and the minister?'

Iain's instant alarm passed into a smile as Douglas laughed and withdrew.

When he had his room to himself he felt immensely relieved, for he had had a terror of people calling on him from the office. He had felt certain that Mr Dowie would come, with his 'What's all this, young man?' and then begin ordering things for the better. That would have drained his last drop of energy, and he hadn't much. The thought of it once or twice had so exhausted him that he had seemed to sink through the bed into unconsciousness. He had also had a premonition that Lindsay would like to come. Not altogether out of curiosity, but out of the native streak of reality in him. He would either have taken the room for granted or have said calmly, 'This is a hell of a hole.' In either case, there would have been no condescension. But Iain would have had to be very much tougher than he was to meet it.

He was anything but tough at the moment. From the small table which the landlady had placed by his bedside, he lifted the Christmas card. Its coloured picture was of a little country scene in snow with a robin singing from a field gate. Inside, (beneath the printed greetings in rhyme) was written 'From Father and Mary'. He knew Mary's handwriting well, but now it had a detached life of its own which translations from the Latin in school exercise books had never achieved. These words were not translated from anything. They came straight from the kitchen table in Ewan's house.

Young fellows had always looked upon Christmas cards as a bit silly or amusing. And Mary would have smiled when she was posting it, but yet, he knew, there would have been that irrational eagerness which had its own gaiety. Ewan would have smiled at the little chap on the gate, admiring the way he was getting the song out of his puffed-out red breast. For, of course, what mattered was sending it to Iain as a thought from his old friends in the country.

At the knock on his door, he immediately turned the card face down on the table. His landlady came in with a bowl of chicken soup and half-a-slice of toast. She was very attentive. There was, however, an air of long-suffering and misery about her which he dared not acknowledge or encourage, lest in some way it should suffocate him; and, of course, he had no idea of the poor old woman's terror and fear of death in the hours when he had been raving.

Douglas had probably been doing things behind the scenes, and his debts were growing, but he did not want to think about them, he wanted to escape into the Christmas card.

And never could escape be more perfect than into that snow scene. Not in his true dreams, but in those half-dreams, when he was still semi-conscious and could guide his desires in some measure, did he walk confidently, exploring and recognizing old places with an exquisite surprise and freedom. He did not recall old memories so much as walk through them freshly in a new experience. The brightness of the snow, the hiss-hiss of his feet, the rabbit tracks, the occasional track of a hare, and the coolness of the air, that divine coolness turning to sharp coldness. His lungs, his body, the movement of his feet, his quickened senses, all craved it. The doubt about bird tracks in the snow – partridge or grouse? The deer coming down under the stars or a half-moon to eat the turnips.

Sometimes the scene would bring him fully awake, his heart beating with excitement. Hamish or Hughie and himself, behind the dyke, waiting for the deer. The destruction of the precious feed by these aristocratic, leaping brutes.

For that was the real problem in hill farming: how to increase the winter feed, the hardiest kind of turnip, the right grasses for the given soil, for feeding value . . .

He had read everything he could find about it in the last three months, particularly the latest accounts of actual experiments and research. Maitland had quite unexpectedly been able to help him here by loaning one or two stereotyped reports by officially recognized experts. They were not yet in print. Douglas had really arranged this, for he always called Iain the firm's agricultural expert. 'You may be a marvellous researcher, Maitland, but Cattanach was born on the land and among sheep. He handled the actual stuff from birth. That kind of thing, which always embarrassed Iain.

At first he had read, much as a boy reads his school lessons. The sentences, with their long words and technical phrases, had appeared tremendously important but somehow quite alien to the simple things his father did so naturally. And he would almost certainly have thrown the stuff aside, were it not for the two talks he had had with Mr Hutcheson. He knew these would be renewed, and his pride was not going to let him appear stupid on the one subject which he should know a little about, and which might be necessary for future work. Moreover, he had so far done fairly well with Mr Hutcheson.

Then one day he had found himself interested in a short paper dealing with sheep diseases, so interested that his eyes glimmered and once or twice he laughed. From the humour in his face, he might have found some good jokes to tell Ewan and Andrew.

Braxy, for example, to the old sheepmen at home was produced by a change of feed which caused some sort of constipation; it happened in the same mysterious way as a man got 'inflammation of the bowels'. It just happened and there it was.

Now he learned that it was caused by an organism. This organism belonged to the gas-gangrene group. (He would have to find out more about that group, though 'gangrene' seemed familiar enough.) The condition produced was called a toxaemia; and his dictionary had told him that toxaemia was blood-poisoning. His father's story about the shepherd who hoped to find the dead sheep warm so that the blood could be drained easily away and who, in any case, left the pressed braxy mutton in the running burn to be cleansed of blood, had its basis in practical reality!

Then again there was that mysterious sheep they called the 'piner', who left the flock and went away to a lonely place to die. Very mysterious, almost as if some strange power or spirit had afflicted him; nearly human.

And Iain learned that the affliction was brought about by no more than a deficiency in the feed. A certain mineral lick spread about would prevent it. He had to laugh.

The life history of the liver fluke, which made use of fresh water snails and sheep, was a marvellous short story. Iain had a sense of wonder before the patient and exquisite research which must have gone to the discovery of the full life cycle.

Louping-ill, sheep scab, tick – all the home names were here, the old familiar names, heading paragraphs written by research men. Somehow they brought his father and the research men onto common ground. His father was doing the producing and the scientists were helping him by defining his traditional knowledge and adding new, precise, and immensely helpful knowledge to it.

He had come to see Maitland in another light, not so much personally as in his official work . . . This new-found knowledge took on a life of its own, began to haunt him as he lay in bed.

*   *   *

One afternoon it began to snow and from his bed Iain watched the flakes coming about the window like lazy bees. The glass of the window was dark and the atmosphere heavy and dull. This darkness of the protecting glass spread outward into an immense desolation. The flakes lifted and fell, drifted away, silently. The street was silent and he held his breath so that his ears might catch the least sound. But there was no sound.

This was the loneliness, not of death, of fear, but of the desolation beyond them. At first he could not close his staring eyes, but at last, and with a tremendous effort, like an effort at self-annihilation, he did, and slowly the desolation, which had hitherto been outside and beyond him, now began to swell inwardly into distances even more vast.

As this could not be borne he searched for his own weakness, the weakness that was himself, and that he could weep over. But he was too tired, and something in his nature could not, anyhow, let him quite find it. So he let go, let himself sink and drown.

He awoke to the shadowed features of the woman between him and the light, and he thought his mother had brought in the lamp. He stared at her and saw that it was not his mother; it was the landlady.

'You've had a sleep?'

'Yes.'

'It's snowing outside.' She said something more about bringing in the tea, but he hardly heard her. It was snowing outside.

When she had carried away the tray, he looked at the light. It was too far from his bed for even his keen eyes to read comfortably. So he began thinking of the snow, the white hilltops and the whitening valley at home, his father and the sheep.

His short sleep had refreshed him and he began helping his father as the snow deepened. This action was a tremendous unconscious relief. He started telling his father some of the new knowledge he had acquired, not with the manner of one possessing positive knowledge but rather with the air of passing on what he himself had heard. 'They say that braxy occurs most often in hoar frost. That's what they say.' And he would wait for his father to think this over in his slow way and answer. The quiet easy conversation grew very interesting in the long hours on the hillside.

But soon Iain's thought was spreading from his father all over the valley. Gradually it became a complete and exciting fantasy. All that he had learned, the new facts about soil and growth, varieties of grasses, the scourge of bracken not merely as a destroyer of pasture but as a breeding place of green-bottles, of the flies that 'struck' the sheep, infesting them with the deadly maggot, all began to fit into actual places, actual farms and crofts.

But, of course, the older folk – he thought of them individually, saw each characteristic reaction – would smile. They knew the unchanging nature of hills and landlords. And though he could smile with their country humour, in his mind he knew he was right and would have to go beyond them. And 'beyond them' meant going, as for a discussion of a poaching foray, to fellows like Hamish and Hughie. These and others like them were the lads who would do it, once he got them roused up, once he got the knowledge in their minds and the light in their eyes.

He was leading them now. It was exciting, for by heavens there were intricate questions of land tenure, of market prices of capital loans for stock, for hardy cattle that would enrich the ground, which the sheep exhausted, and tread down the young bracken, of fencing, of scarifying the heath and broadcasting seed, of all the things before which they were surely impotent.

But why? Had the crofters who fought for their Act of 1886 been impotent? And what they, their forefathers, had done – couldn't we, the men of this generation, do?

Are we as sheep in a snowstorm waiting to be smothered? It would be worth it for the fun, if nothing else! It would bring back life. At their nightly gatherings, their ceilidhs, they would have something to talk about! And the girls, the women, would be as keen as the men. For the one thing girls wanted was life and the gaiety that came out of it. Iain heard them laughing, saw them dancing to his fiddle. It was not a simple standard of living that killed life; it was dullness. Dullness that was like the mud about the door, the mud, the ooze, the decay; the inner knowledge of decay, and the children. Dullness, a slow-eating despair, like a cancer.

His thought darkened and deepened, and he turned his eyes from his mother's face. But he was not giving in. With a passionate surge, his thought rose, fighting, fighting that which had defeated her. The sweat ran into his eyebrows.

Political action as the crofters of old had fought and got their Act, got the right to sit by their own hearth-stones. But now they had to take the fight a step farther. Security was not enough. They must begin to develop, to create. Not merely to be better off, but to have the thrill, the fun, of doing things and guiding events, of knowing in themselves that their labours were fruitful and at least as important as any other kind of work in the country.

And suddenly, in a further twist of his fantasy, he seemed to see the inner meaning of Davidson's politics. To do things themselves in their own land and to be allowed to do them. Not to be frustrated from outside but to be inspired from within. For they knew their own land as no others could know it. And it was what folk knew, what they knew in their blood, as he knew his own music, that excited and interested them.

Douglas went along his Royal Mile, crying out for this, but he did not know he was crying for it. Drinking his own dark blood out of the old history bottles. Getting drunk in the past, because there was no moving glory, no excitement of present or future, to get drunk in. No new creation, no inspired doing or making of things. Cursing a treacherous nobility – as if they had sold the pass for ever! To blazes with *for ever*! Let the nobles rot in their own dark ditch – as a horrible warning!

And the socialist orator, what was he getting at? Finally, that the folk should be free to cultivate their own valley. He was for the future. But Davidson saw that we grew out of our past, that a country grows out of its past as a man out of his childhood. His was the complete picture. Not the growth only, but also the root. Not only the plan in the head but also the blood in the heart.

The words hardly formed in Iain's mind. Therefore precise thought might hardly be said to have formed either. But this is not what really happened. It was mostly an intuitive process, but it had at times an extraordinary clarity, so that he saw his thoughts happening. And this clarity moved him, lifted him, profoundly excited him, as at times his own music did.

When the knock came on the door, he could not speak. His landlady entered and stood.

'There's a young lady asking for you.'

His flesh was trembling and with the back of a hand he wiped his wet eyebrows.

'Miss Galloway,' she said.

'No, no,' he whispered quickly. 'I – I'm not seeing anyone.'

'I'll tell her.'

'No, wait.' He felt sick with excitement. 'Tell her – thank her – say I hope to be about in a few days. I'll – I'll let her know.'

'Very well.' She stood for a moment, looking at him. As she turned away, she said in her ordinary, mournful voice, 'It's still snowing.'

His whole being strained towards the low, indistinct murmur at the door of the flat. It seemed to go on a long time. His landlady would be gossiping, damn her! The door shut and he fell back.

SEVENTEEN

'You've fairly got a shake,' said Angus, returned from his Christmas vacation.

'Och, I'm fine now. I've been having a holiday, too, but it's work again next week.' Iain smiled.

'You never told them at home?'

'No. What was the use! Had a good time?'

'Not bad. Sort of dull a bit. And the weather wasn't up to much.'

'Wasn't it?'

'No.' Angus stretched his legs. 'Not much doing.'

Iain looked at him, the smile in his eyes. 'Glad to get back here, in fact?'

'Well, I was so looking forward to going home, and then – I don't know – there was so little to do. You weren't there and – now and then time hung a bit heavy.'

'You wouldn't like to live there all your life?'

'Honestly, I don't think I could stand it.' Angus smiled, as if amused. 'The whole place seemed changed. Queer, wasn't it?'

'It is a bit dull, I suppose,' said Iain, looking into the glimmer of his small coal fire.

'Yes. No *go* in it. Everyone was very kind, of course. I don't know what it was. I felt annoyed at myself for being disappointed.' He laughed.

Iain had a sudden temptation to talk at length, but resisted it. 'Dead as a door nail,' he remarked cheerfully. 'Hadn't you a dance itself?'

'Yes. Oh, a proper dance.'

'Did Mary sing?'

'No. It was the real thing. Band from Kinmore – the whole three of them.'

Iain laughed and named the three players, whom he knew.

Angus nodded. 'Yes. All the latest dances, ladies and gentlemen. You should have seen Alan! He's the big boy now. Assistant to Major Grant an' all.'

'Not his office boy?'

'Oh dear no.'

'And Anne would be doing her stuff with him?'

'No,' answered Angus, 'she wasn't there. You know she's at Aberdeen University? Apparently she stayed on there with her rich aunt – for the festive season, the high social life.'

'And who is Alan running now?'

'Seems to be Mary. Anyway, he saw her home.'

'Did he?' Iain smiled – and took the plunge. 'Did you in the eye, did he?'

'Oh properly,' answered Angus in the same light tone. 'Not that I competed.'

'Why not? I'm dashed if I would have let him off with it.'

'But that's you.'

'All the same, I'd have had a shot at putting his bike in the ditch.' Iain's eyes glimmered thoughtfully, but inwardly he was dismayed, felt his heart beating uncomfortably.

'I had a long talk with your father. I was giving him all the news about you.'

'How's he looking?'

'Fine. But the autumn sales were really bad. It's a blue outlook for sheep. Hamish says the whole bloody place is done.'

Angus's tongue seemed now to be set free and he gave Iain all the home news. Mad Mairag hadn't been seen for a fort-night, so a few fellows set off on New Year's day, in the afternoon, for Achmore. Took their whisky bottles with them – and didn't come back till next day. What yarns! 'They seemed miraculous, but probably they just got tight. They say Dan-the-trapper slept with the goat! You should hear Dan on that!'

As they probed the story, their laughter grew.

'The minister was going to speak about it from the pulpit.

Hush-hush talk of bewitchment and calling up the dead. "Mad Mairag's brotherhood" – that's what Geordie has called them; and certainly they had a night of it!'

'A good night,' said Iain. 'I wish I had been there.'

'So do I. It was the one and only bright spot,' declared Angus.

When Angus had at last gone, Iain was still smiling to himself. Mad Mairag and her cottage came back to him in a still, clear light, like the light in a dream. *You must love the land.* The curving breasts of the land about her cottage and the white goat. The little path that went to the drinking well . . .

And suddenly he remembered he had had a dream about that well. He had completely forgotten it until that moment, but now it came back with an astonishing clarity. It must have been at the height of his illness, when he had wandered in so many queer places. How he had got to the well, he could not remember, but the well itself had all the vivid detail of reality, even a heightened reality, so that the very texture of the flat stone, before it, had been observed, not to mention the tufts of grass, the gravelly bottom, the four bubbles of water that had ascended one after another and vanished on the surface. When, however, he had stooped and drunk, the water had moved in crystal waves that broke on his face . . .

He hadn't mentioned his Achmore experience to Angus because he didn't want to mention Mary again. It was so difficult to know what Angus was feeling. Impossible to be sure. That the whole affair had cut him to the marrow was, of course, certain. But we all get cut. The point was: could he forget Mary? Get rid of her from his blood? Murder the longing? Iain remembered that moment in the Dell, when Angus had seen them embrace. A small white flame had hit Angus's face, as if actually he had been knifed inside; a curious quirk of the eyebrows and a straining of the eyes. Only a moment – but it had become a haunting moment.

Pretty cool of Mary, going home with Alan! Even if she didn't want to go home with Angus, at least she could have steered clear of Alan. She needn't have hit Angus with him in the face. Unless, of course, she wanted Alan to see her home. Why not? Most girls, it was said, would like Alan to see them home.

Iain took a turn about the floor, laughing softly, sarcastically. There was a glisten in his eyes, however, a hawk-like gathering of the eyebrows. Had Mary tried on any nonsense like that with him, he would have given her what-ho! And he would give it to her yet, for treating Angus like that. There was a limit!

But that was the devil of it, when a fellow fell in love with a girl and so on. He lost all his ordinary fight. He withdrew, like a sick sheep, like a 'piner'! Angus did not 'compete'! Extraordinary. Really extraordinary.

Iain became so extravagantly amused about this that he was astonished to find himself angry. He had now forgotten all about Alan. Indeed Alan in no way worried him, for he could always coup him in the ditch. But he was sorry for Angus. He was really.

Suddenly he realized it was his own conscience that was making him angry. So he had a swift open-eyed slash at it: Well, what if a fellow does kiss a girl? Hang it, what are girls for?

He dismissed Angus and Mary and deliberately began to think of Morna Galloway. Since he had become convalescent, he had in fact thought of her a lot. She certainly had moved in his blood! What a fool he had been, turning her away, not letting her in! It could all have been arranged so easily, and his landlady would have got used to her coming. What times they might have had! Once or twice, when pictures of love-making had become too distinct, he got pen and paper and, shaking a little from excitement, prepared to write her, saying how sorry he was that he had been unable to see her when she called, but that now . . . He could send the letter to her at the office. She would come at once. Had she not come through the snow? She was dark and soft and warm. Then his hand would tremble and he would get up and walk about. If only she would come again on her own! Perhaps she would; that very night. And he would wait for the bell to ring, for his landlady's shuffling feet, for the knock on his door.

But Morna did not come again.

When he got back to the office, he received quite a welcome. 'Ha! ha! young man, and what have you been trying to do with yourself?' demanded Mr Dowie. 'Had a jolt?' said Lindsay, looking at him critically. 'Feeling better?' asked Smeaton, pausing for a moment, documents in his hands. Corbet had a searching look at his gills.

For the first time, Iain felt at home in the office. He knew all its sounds, what the ringing bells meant, when important clients were with the partners and the personal repercussions upon the clerks who did the real legal work. For the partners were considered little more than the 'big noises' who confidently talked to clients and signed documents. The capacity of each was intimately known to the responsible clerk who did the actual work and upon whose knowledge and judgment the partner relied.

As a glorified office boy, Iain had merely to do what he was told. The tasks were simple and his only real struggle was with his handwriting. It was inclined to be a bit unruly, and often he became quite absorbed in trying to produce a round, smooth hand. The copperplate writing of the old men always astonished him. He had settled on a particular penholder and nib which, he believed, suited him, and sometimes he nearly astonished himself. But he knew he hadn't it in him ever to produce the distinction, the perfect fluency, of the old hands.

However, he could only do his best, and now that he had come back to the familiar routine, it felt easy and safe. There was nothing really to worry about, not even the classes at the university, for he was used to classes and the slow grind of acquiring facts and reproducing them. The office itself was no doubt huge and complicated, but his niche in it was circumscribed and safe. Everyone got paid with certainty. On that first day in the office, it was very pleasant to feel safe. Then to wander out for lunch (he was in arrears with his landlady, but she knew that he had his pay to lift from the office), see the old streets, have his glass of milk and buns, observe that the art shop had not yet found a buyer for the Christ, was all amusing in a familiar way. Many faces he knew, and a couple of lads in the café spoke to him for the first time. They were soon chatting away like old friends. They said they had missed him.

Wandering along, he remembered his fantasy about his leading the men of the valley towards better things in sheep-farming, and that, too, seemed youthfully amusing and very distant. Then at the street corner, where he turned along to the office, he saw Morna Galloway standing alone.

'Hullo, stranger!' she greeted him.

'Hullo!' He saw her dark eyes run over his face, at once searching and reserved. His heart began to beat heavily.

'Feeling quite better?'

'Yes, thanks.' He was smiling, trying to laugh lightly. He could hardly speak.

'It was kind of you not to tell your friends, wasn't it?'

'It was,' he said. 'Didn't want to bother them.'

'Is that all you think of them?' Her dark eyes were deep and though smiling with reserve yet seemed to melt inwards, drawing him, as it were, against their own intention.

'It was good of you to call. I wish—' He looked away, feeling the blood mounting to his face.

'What?' she asked.

'I wish you could have come in.'

They were both silent.

'What are you doing to-night?' he asked and swallowed.

'To-night?' She thought for a moment. 'I don't think I'm doing anything.'

'Could you – could you meet me at the old place?'

'I'll think over it,' she said, but now with a quick, teasing light in her eyes. 'Here's Ethel. Good-bye.'

During the afternoon, the office became so safe that he never thought about it. At home a registered letter was waiting for him. He had written his father at the beginning of his convalescence, using his illness, with the special expense it entailed, as the reason for asking 'a little money'. Inside the tough envelope were ten single pound notes and a short letter. They were sorry, said his father, to hear of his illness and hoped the enclosed would be enough for the time being. But Iain must let him know whenever he was short. He would send him a little more later on. 'It's been a very open winter. A little snow fell but it soon went off. We are hoping it's not keeping back for the lambing.'

A hot, melting sensation went through Iain and he sat down. He realized he was still in pretty poor condition. No word, he thought, from his father of the bad autumn sales. Only that reference, earnest yet with a country humour in it, to the weather they might expect for the lambing.

Hang it, he felt weak, and his head fell on his arms as they slumped upon the table.

EIGHTEEN

That early refreshment and ease of convalescence soon passed, and when towards the middle of February the weather, even in Edinburgh, turned mild and sunny, with hints of spring everywhere, from the full-blown snowdrops in the gardens to the ringing songs of thrush and blackbird from trees that seemed to rise before him for the first time, he was struck by a heavy malaise, a bodily weakness that during an ordinary walk could bathe him in sweat.

An inner country cunning warned him to be very careful lest a chill should lay him out again. A second bout of the same illness would almost certainly finish him off. So he wore his overcoat and scarf, though he longed to throw them from him, and sweated all the more.

He knew the value of food, had seen its effect on sheep and cattle, on grass, on birds, on deer in the winter time. But the deuce of it was that though now, having money, he dropped the milk and buns, he found it difficult to eat meat at lunch. He did not want it; it went against his palate. He found the pastry in a helping of steak and kidney pie soggy and repellent. The dry flakes tickled his throat so that on one occasion there had been a dreadful moment when he wondered if what had gone down was coming up. The restaurant had slowly heaved – and settled again. Had he been sick, he would have been sick there and then. There could have been no rushing for the door marked GENTLEMEN. The one thing he could take was the gravy of such a pie with the potatoes mashed in it. So he ate small mouthfuls, with care, and took a long time over the food, until something warned him to swallow no more.

This weakness annoyed him, made his work in the office a tiresome drudgery. Small things angered him, and he became unusually sensitive to criticism, imagining personal slights where he knew none was intended. That study was almost impossible because the edge had gone off his will and left his memory woolly, he didn't mind. Students could ignore lecture notes and text-books for a while and then make up time by an intense burst of swotting. But the office was different. One could not say, with any conviction, 'I forgot.' And when a document was returned from a legal firm, who were representing the defenders in an action which his own firm was raising, with the dry covering remark, 'Presumably this was not intended for us', and when the mistake was traced to Iain, he was rendered hot and silent. Nor was that the end of it. He had been given two urgent letters to copy and deliver personally, and had, of course, put them in the wrong envelopes. The second mistake came to light with repercussions which annoyed Mr Dowie very much. No real harm had been done, though time had been lost, but Mr Dowie had shown, in his bearing even more than in the few unsmiling words with which he had told Iain to be more careful in future, that the dignity of the office had been assailed.

Mr Dowie had been temperate, even considerate, and Iain realized it, but somehow that did not help him. For several days the whole thing gnawed at him, exaggeratedly, foolishly, and he had one glimpse of the office, embodied in Mr Dowie's upright, bulky figure, in the glance of his eyes, that was terrible and forbidding, of an unassailable power and dignity solid and everlasting as the Castle Rock. And suddenly, in his bowels, with an encroaching feeling of dread, he hated it, hated it and cursed it, in a dew of sweat.

Then, to complicate his difficulties, Smeaton had on hand a crofting compensation case from the estate at home. He had asked Iain if he knew a place called Balrain. It was a small crofting area some five miles from Iain's home, and though Iain had been through it once he did not know the people who lived there. Indeed the name was familiar only as the place where Ewan had been born.

But now Smeaton showed astonishment that Iain should

not know 'this hamlet' on his own estate. Suddenly angered at Smeaton's lifted eyebrows, he had replied shortly that it wasn't his estate.

'I am aware of that,' said Smeaton. 'But it should not preclude you, in business hours, from answering questions of fact normally.' He spoke with an apparent smile, not unamused that he was getting Iain on the raw, but also with the dignity of the office behind him. One could forgive Iain's country manners, but there was a limit to forbearance.

Wilson had smiled at Iain's expense, turning his face away.

Smeaton did not stop there. He went on. This was a case, he explained, of an old crofter, named Donald Cameron, who had died in Balrain, and the question arose as to whether the buildings on the croft had been erected by the said Donald Cameron's father or by the estate. If by the said Donald Cameron's father, then compensation was due to his next of kin under the 1886 Act; if not, not.

Iain hardly listened for he knew that Smeaton's elaborate statement of the case, though justified in the circumstances inasmuch as Iain might conceivably be able to offer a helpful opinion from local knowledge, was designed to annoy him, to draw out his ignorance on matters touching, so to speak, his native doorstep.

'There are no documents showing title, of course, not even a scrap of holograph,' Smeaton made clear, 'but then, in these remote places, I take it, we must assume that they are – or at least were – illiterate, that they could not write. Do you agree?'

'I don't know,' answered Iain tonelessly.

'Pity,' said Smeaton. 'However, their illiteracy is assumed, so we generously go on that assumption, and accordingly we are prepared to consider evidence by hearsay from old inhabitants. You understand?'

'Yes,' said Iain. 'But what about the estate's agents? Are they also assumed to have been illiterate?'

'Onus of proof of ownership surely rests on the person who says he owns. I should have thought, in law, that that was elementary. It is not customary for the defender to hold the claimant's title, and then to produce it in order to prove the claimant's case against himself. Or would you say it is?'

Iain was holding himself well in hand, but now, his eyebrows gathering slightly, he said, 'In those days people trusted in a man's word.'

It was the perfect opening for Smeaton's stroke: 'You mean, I presume, everything was done by verbal agreement?'

The office appreciated the stroke, but Iain turned away, silent. His sight had darkened and he knew he could not trust himself. His muscles were trembling, defeated in their surge to smash Smeaton where he stood.

He realized he was weak not only in body but in mind. Memories of office incidents like these would torture him in bed, keeping him awake, making him grip the sheets in spasms of blinding rage, rage also against himself, against some ultimate dark essence of appalling futility.

And this condition of weakness bred its own unexpected and sometimes shameful little treacheries.

One night on the Blackford Hill with Morna, he was made the sport of one of these treacheries but this time with searching after-effects.

Morna was very fond of love-making. She was an adept at it, yielding and warm, dark as the whin bush in whose shadow they lay and as remote from the world of offices and legal work. In that everyday sense, she was the complete escape for him. And just because at the back of his mind he could not help being conscious of this, it only made him the more tender towards her. It bred in him a certain loyalty to her, made him overcome an occasional vague reluctance to meet her, a reluctance that vanished when they did meet. She was always somehow more attractive than he had remembered, more real as a person.

But her capacity for love-making, for drawing all his energies upon herself did sometimes, in his indifferent bodily condition, weary him a little.

On this night he had, after a time, stretched himself out, his head on her lap. Sitting up, she bent a little over him and began gently combing the hair back from his brows with her fingers. It was a soothing action and he decided, quite consciously, to forget her, to take advantage of the moment and sink away into peace. That he wanted to forget her hardly troubled him because he knew that complete forgetfulness of everything would refresh him, and presently, with luck, make him a better or more lively companion. There may have been the lurking feeling, too, that it would help to put in the time but, after all, an occasional weariness was natural! And she did, just a little too much, want to absorb him.

Anyway he forgot her. But the next thing he knew, the next thing of which he was conscious, was the presence of Mary. He began thinking about her quite naturally, as if he had wakened out of sleep, yet not quite out of it, so that he could go on thinking about her, seeing her, without any relation to where he was or to the world of reality. It just happened like that and there she was, as if they were together at home, with no sense of stress between them, and it gave him a sensation of exquisite peace and liberation. Her face looked as if it had been washed in the burn and retained still in the skin a brown, cool freshness. The blue of her eyes had never been light in tone and noticeable, but now he saw the blue, saw that it held a dewy darkness, with something in it of the violet. Then he became conscious of the eyes directly upon him and in the same instant became aware of the hand on his brow. He did not want to recognize the hand, did not want to come back to it, but Mary's eyes troubled and darkened, as a pool darkens under the wind's breath, and the face, Mary herself, faded away.

He lay quite still, holding his breath, but Morna had felt the slight stiffening of his body.

'You were asleep,' she murmured, playfully accusing him.

He could not answer.

'Weren't you?'

'Was I?' He sat up and shivered. 'Foo! I'm cold.'

'No wonder!'

'Come on. Let us walk. I *am* cold.'

She hesitated. 'Such energy all of a sudden!'

Shame was in him, bitterness and anger. He choked them
down, ashamed of his impatience, too, with Morna. At least
one kiss before they started: it was her ritual. But he leapt
to his feet and, bending, caught her hands. With all his
strength, he heaved her up, and, her body coming against
his, embraced her only – but she would have her kiss.

Later, in his room, he decided if it wasn't Judas's kind of
kiss it had, in that moment, been near enough not to matter.
He joked about it to himself as he moved restlessly around
his room, handling and laying things down, opening books
and shutting them with a slap.

All at once, as for a drug, a craving came over him for
his violin. In the light, its brown body gleamed, resurrected,
alive. It was so badly out of tune that his fingers came alive,
eager and cautiously hurrying. He held his face away, lest a
string should snap. The E was getting slightly ragged, he
observed. As he twisted the creaking pegs, his mouth twisted
in a glisten of teeth. Nearer and nearer drew the strings to
their perfect fifths, and then, O divine perfection, they arrived
and sang.

His flesh sang with them, his blood, as if every atom in
his body were polarized by the ascending fifths. This lovely
sound, this familiar absolute, lighter than air, rising through
the lightness in his head, yet sure as a springing steel bridge,
ever-lastingly strong. It gave a man life, and confidence; it
brought him together in himself. Oh, it was delight.

He began to play and at once the slow, traditional music
was flowing through him, the elemental emotions, that had
seas and mountains for background and immense reaches of
human time. Faces came and went, the heads, the dark
bodies, not seen so much as apprehended, in a swaying and
movement onward of time that was space itself in motion.
And in this flux, in this rising and falling of onflowing sound,
of vast waves that darkened and cleared, Mary's face alone
remained in its own place, singing, with the innocence of
song upon it, cleansed as a face in sleep, living its immortal
dream. But he strove beyond it, to darken it, and suddenly
under his hands, as if creation itself were in them, the simple

melody, the Eriskay melody he knew so well, drew away
from its human sentiments and story and became the wind,
immense wave-movements of wind while mountain and sea
were yet in the darkness. Now he knew how to play it, in
a miracle of understanding, and in this new conception of
its time, held it to its crest and sank with it, in storm-waves
of elemental power.

He tried to lay the violin gently on the table but it clat-
tered. Exhausted to the point of fainting, he stretched himself
face down on his bed. He was weak. There was a fluttering
in his chest, a closing of suffocating wings. His throat and
eyes stung. Tears wet his face. His mouth closed on the
knuckle of his wrist, his gnawing teeth searching for a hold.
He began to sob. But he fought still, muttering 'God, I'm
weak!'

Iain was reading over his Indenture, his personal contract with the firm, which he had belatedly prepared in his nearest possible approach to copperplate. The law had its own subtle humours, he was discovering. He had been warned that when he presented the document for signature, the partner might look up and inquire solemnly 'How do I know this is not a bond for fifty thousand pounds?' Now, in the body of the document itself, he found a long sentence, about the obligation on the firm to instruct their apprentice, that he thought was the legal smile at its driest . . . 'cause their said apprentice to learn and conceive the same as they know and practise themselves and the capacity of their said apprentice will admit . . .'

When the summons suddenly came to attend in Mr Cunningham's room, he was obviously startled. Smeaton gave him a peculiar look and Wilson, turning his face away, smiled.

So it has come at last, Iain thought as he climbed the stairs, taking his time, like one who had been hit under the heart.

For some time there had been occasional remarks in the office about wild Highland music and violin playing, always with an ambiguous humour. Smeaton had seemed to be particularly interested, and Iain knew, from the very smirk on his face, that the hidden joke gave him some power. He suspected that they had found out he played Highland dance music and were making the most of it, but when he was nearly trapped into going to the Macaw's room for certain documents in a cleverly trumped-up case of 'an Italian ice-cream vendor named Verdi', he decided to tackle Corbet when he got him alone. And this he had done.

'Don't you know?' Corbet asked, with unusual reserve, as he blew froth from the edge of his pint.

'No.' Iain eyed him.

'Well—' He made a reluctant gesture, then threw a glance at Iain. 'You were playing on the streets, weren't you?'

Iain's lips parted as he remembered the playing outside the pub. His eyes concentrated on Corbet. 'Well?'

'Well, it's none of my business how you make a bit of extra cash. That's what I said. Dammit, I said, a fellow who can do a thing like that to carry on has guts. Only – in an office like Cunningham, Cunningham and Scott – it's not done, you know.'

Iain slowly filled his chest with air, but he did not speak.

'That's the way they look at it,' continued Corbet. 'Letting the office down. And – I'll be honest – I didn't like it myself. It's the sort of thing we can't afford. Hell, when old Jock Howieson at Duncan and Roberts began taking a rise out of me, asking if it was high-tie-tiddly-ities we were raising—'

'Who told you?' asked Iain, his face cold as stone.

Corbet looked at him. 'It's true, isn't it?'

'Who told you?'

Corbet, about to question Iain's tone, thought better of it. 'Who told me? Who hasn't? But the first I heard of it was from the policeman on the beat here. One night him and Jimmy and me were having a quiet one when he asked me what sort of fellows we were now taking into the office. I thought first he was just taking a rise out of me. But then I saw there was something in it. It seems it was his pal, on beat in that low part of the town, who cleared you off and told you to get a move on, and the thing stuck in his mind because he was in such a hell of a stew when he was doing it because there was an Irishman at his ear, a bloody fellow with a fist like a pole-axe, who hits first and takes his prison gruel afterwards. He says this Irishman was dancing before you and the whole bloody street was blocked with the crowd. I don't know, but that's what he said.' Corbet drank.

'So you told them in the office!'

'What the hell do you take me for?' Corbet's pint hit the table.

'How then did they get to know?'

'How the hell should I know? But if the police didn't speak to you afterwards, you can thank your friend Mr Douglas, who came on the scene and took you off. They know him. So I'd advise you to put your question to him.' Corbet, offended, deliberately finished his pint.

Iain sat unmoving and silent. Douglas could never have told the story in the office? The thing was impossible, even as a joke.

'Some of the ongoings of your fine friends is getting known. That's all I'd warn you about.' Corbet pushed his glass from him and prepared to get up.

'Have another?'

'No, thanks. I must get round.'

Iain finished his port in a gulp and got up also. At the door, Corbet glanced along Rose Street both ways then set off, to find Iain walking by his side. He stopped, again glancing about him. 'You'd better beat it your own way.'

'Why? Think I'm not good enough company for you?'

Corbet's heavy eyebrows, lowering, concentrated a greenish glint upon Iain. Something hard and battling came out of him, a cold bayonet gleam, then in a moment his eyes lifted, hazed, and the commissionaire prepared to move on.

'So I took my share of the old man's pennies?'

'That's the idea,' said Corbet.

'I see,' said Iain. 'It happens to be a lie. However – so long!' And he turned and walked away.

He had there and then made up his mind to tackle Douglas the following day. But Douglas had always kept his distance in the office, though not more so from Iain than from anyone else. He was made that way, and Iain had always thought he was the only one who understood him. Yet it was surely an extraordinary thing that Douglas would keep silent, knowing the story that was going around? Was there something in him – that could do this?

Apparently there must be. So Iain, by the following day, decided to keep silent. If Douglas was that sort of fellow, then pride could not permit Iain to speak, nor should his life depend on it. They could all believe what they damn well liked. But he had been pierced more than once by an intense desire to tell Douglas just what he thought about it all, so that Douglas might work out what he, Iain, thought about him.

Sometime the whole thing was bound to come to a head, and now, as he walked along to Mr Cunningham's room, he had a horrible premonition, roused or strengthened by Smeaton's parting glance, that the first step in the process was about to be taken. As he entered and found both Mr Cunningham and Mr Hutcheson seated, he decided the court was in session.

'Take a chair,' said Mr Cunningham, in his normal polite way. Iain thanked him and sat down. There was a quivering inside his breast, but he was prepared for battle. There was only one thing he had to do – keep his head, tell what happened, and let them think what they liked.

'We want', began Mr Cunningham, 'to have a personal talk with you. Mr Hutcheson thinks your knowledge of the conditions in sheep farming is fairly wide. You are a young man and may have ideas. It's these ideas we want to get. Don't hesitate to say exactly what you think. We are not experts. We want to get the human point of view of a young man who threw up sheep farming to come to an office. You follow?'

'Yes, sir.'

'Good. Well, you know Mr David Henderson, your land-lord at home. In addition to being our client, he is also a friend of mine. He has had a very varied life and at one time was farming in a big way in the Colonies. When Mrs Henderson died, he turned to his old interest in farming. When he bought Balmore, it was as a sporting estate. But in the last few years, as you know, there has been a lot of public discussion about the condition of agriculture gener-ally in this country and in particular about the degenerating prospects in hill sheep farming. He has got very interested in this, so interested that he may have political ambitions. However, the point is that he is coming here to-morrow to go into the whole facts, on the agricultural side, concerning

Balmore – rents, extent of holdings, stock carried, what the
estate has spent in recent years on improvements, and so on.
Mr Hutcheson has been getting detail from Major Grant,
and we are ready for him, but he is the sort of man who
asks human questions. He thinks, for example, no doubt out
of his experience in the Colonies, that – well, the people on
Balmore, for instance, haven't enough spirit, aren't go-ahead
enough. He thinks they could do a lot more for themselves,
just as he thinks the landlord should have done a lot more
all round. And he wants, as he says himself, to open out on
that.'

Mr Cunningham leaned back. Iain looked so like a student
up for his oral, sitting there on the edge of his chair, keeping
his nervousness in hand, that clearly Mr Cunningham hardly
expected the destinies of sheep farming in general, and on
Balmore in particular, to be affected by what might proceed
from these young lips. So to cover his smile he turned to Mr
Hutcheson, and said, 'I think that's about it?'

'Yes.' Mr Hutcheson nodded and looked at Iain in his
friendly way, and in that instant Iain knew that his appearance here was due to Mr Hutcheson. He decided, as swiftly,
not to let him down. The fighting spirit, invoked outside,
rose into a cleaner air.

'Tell us,' said Mr Hutcheson: 'did you care for sheep
farming? Would you have liked to carry on your father's
place, for example, assuming there had been prospects of a
good living in it?'

'Yes, I – would have.'

'Your father has been a long time sheep farming?'

'All his life. And his father before him.'

'He should know about it in that case! Yet he wanted you
to get out, into something else?'

Iain remained silent.

'Did he – or am I being too personal?' asked Mr
Hutcheson.

'He didn't say much,' replied Iain. 'My mother—' He
stopped. 'She didn't care much for it.'

They both regarded his embarrassment and reserve.

'Major Grant,' said Mr Cunningham in a friendly voice, 'has the idea that until the women are satisfied the men won't stay. You think there's something in that?'

'Mothers want to give their families a chance. They don't want them – to stick in the mud.'

Mr Hutcheson laughed. 'That's clear enough – even for Mr Henderson! In your opinion, is it mud? Is the industry going down hill?'

'Yes, it's dying.'

'From your own knowledge, you say that?'

'It's happening at home.'

'You mean by *dying* that it's not paying and therefore people are leaving it, especially young fellows like yourself?'

'Yes. But it's more than that. The land itself is dying.'

'How do you mean?'

'For a long time the heart has slowly been taken out of it and nothing put back.'

'The soil has been impoverished?'

'Yes. And neglected in other ways; not drained and fenced. It's been a slow process. Old people have pointed out land to me, pieces here and there, that once bore heavy crops. Now it's sodden, with rushes growing. I sometimes thought it was just old talk. But now I know the land there has gone sour. It needs draining and liming.'

'Do you mean they have neglected it?'

'It's – it's more than that. The land has been neglected, but – it's not the tenants' land. When you can barely make a living and pay your rent, you haven't much left over for improvements. You may be working on a lease or from year to year. The crofter has security of tenure. But then his holding mustn't be more than fifty acres. And very, very few crofts are anywhere near that. But anyone who is running his own flock of sheep, say about five hundred ewes, his acreage is large, he's not a crofter, he's a farmer, and so hasn't security of tenure and wouldn't get compensation for sinking his money in land improvement and so on, if he had to clear out, or was told to clear out.' Iain swallowed, for it had sounded a long speech.

'I see. You think security of tenure important?'

'It's only one thing. At the moment, it doesn't seem to matter much. I mean farmers who once took leases – my own father had a fourteen-year lease – are tending to carry on from year to year. It's going that way.'

'So the trouble is much more deep-seated than that?' said Mr Cunningham. 'Could you say shortly what it is?'

'Just money,' answered Iain with a faint smile. 'The market doesn't give them the money.'

'So you consider the position hopeless?'

'The present position – yes.'

'A nice distinction!' exclaimed Mr Hutcheson, now thoroughly enjoying himself. 'Have you any ideas at all on how the present position came about?'

'Yes,' said Iain. 'But it's a long story.'

'Do you smoke?' asked Mr Cunningham, taking a box of cigarettes from the drawer of his broad mahogany desk. Iain thanked him and found he had to control his fingers as he accepted a light from Mr Hutcheson. But he choked down the excitement that was troubling him. He could not give in now. If only this accursed nervousness would keep out of his voice!

'Well,' said Mr Cunningham, leaning back and blowing smoke, 'this is very interesting.'

But Iain now could not start. There was too much to say. He did not know where to begin. The accursed quivering was coming up into his throat.

'I suppose those early days, the troubles with landlords and evictions, started it,' suggested Mr Hutcheson helpfully.

'Yes,' said Iain at once. 'In the old days, the cultivated land, the in-by land, *and* the hill pastures – they carried both sheep and cattle. The cattle were good for the land. It was a proper balance. But then the landlords found they could get more money – bigger rents – by driving the people off the land and turning it into huge sheep farms. So they did that. And for a long time sheep farming paid. But they did not then realize – what the old folk had always known – that sheep alone eat the heart out of the hill pasture. These sheep farms were thriving at first on the – on the goodness – on the stuff, the – fertility, that the old way, the old economy, had put into it.'

'I see,' said Mr Cunningham, tapping the ash off his cigarette to give Iain time. 'So when the sheep began to eat the heart – I like your phrase – out of the land, then the trouble, the decline began?'

'Yes,' answered Iain, the surge of his nervousness suddenly dying down. 'But then sport came in, grouse and deer, and the landlords found they could get big rents for that. So they didn't mind so much about the sheep farms. It was up to them to build shooting lodges and pony tracks and kennels. In fact, it often paid them to clear the sheep farmers off, as once it had paid them to evict the crofters.'

'You simply mean that they neglected the agricultural or stock-rearing land?' asked Mr Cunningham.

'Yes,' answered Iain, who was far beyond remembering to add 'sir', the use of which, being unknown in the old Gaelic tradition, was still considered in certain circumstances somewhat slavish among his folk at home.

'Could you say exactly how their neglect mattered, what it consisted in?' asked Mr Cunningham. 'We don't want to blame them for what they may not have been responsible for, do we?'

'No.' Iain's expression grew troubled. 'It's difficult to tell you. It's a sort of mounting up of things. And most of it occurred before my time. But I have heard the old folk talk of it. It was something like this. While the landlords depended on their rents from all the crofts and farms on their estate, they looked after things on the estate like side roads and little bridges and river banks. There were ditchers and dykers. I can just remember the old estate mason. There was that kind of labour always about. Now there isn't. Sport changed the – the aspect of things. I mean the estate now went in for gamekeepers and stalkers and the only labour it wanted was a few gillies in the season and a few girls as maid servants for a short while. The gamekeeper became in a way the – the enemy of the man on the land. It was his job to protect the game, and he thought no more in the old days of shooting a crofter's dog than of shooting a hoodie crow, and the crofter daren't say a word or he would be evicted. Many blamed the gamekeeper for this, but, of course, he had to produce the game in order to produce the shooting tenant's rent. The higher the head of game the higher the rent. I know I can't – it's difficult to—'

'Thank you,' said Mr Cunningham. 'That's exactly the kind of picture I wanted to get. I realize there may have been all sorts of variations of it, but roughly – I see.' He nodded.

Mr Hutcheson lit a match and held it towards Iain's cigarette which had gone out. Iain puffed quickly, a flush on his face.

'Now, look,' said Mr Hutcheson in his easy, friendly voice, 'you mentioned sheep *and* cattle on the hill pastures. You said they produced a better balance, kept the land in heart. Have you really any evidence of that?'

'No,' said Iain, after a moment.

'You were just repeating what has been said?'

'It's more than that. I know you want me to be exact. There are two things anyway. In the old days before the evictions, the people did keep sheep and cattle on the hill. That's certain. And they must have done it for hundreds of years. Now if that kind of mixed farming was bad for the land, it would surely have shown?'

'It's an admitted point,' agreed Mr Hutcheson. 'Your next point.'

'It just occurred to me,' said Iain, 'but a sheep and a cow – they eat differently. I mean a cow puts her tongue out like that' – he indicated the curving movement with his open hand – 'and pulls the blades of grass, the rough and the fine, into her mouth. But the sheep eats like this' – his fingers gathered to a point that nibbled a small spot on his knee – 'it selects the tender shoot and nibbles the heart out of it. Perhaps that exaggerates, but on rough grazing—' He stopped for they were both smiling in appreciation of his demonstration.

'Very interesting,' said Mr Cunningham.

'Then there's the manure side,' said Mr Hutcheson. 'And they say the cattle tread down the young bracken. Is bracken becoming a scourge up with you?'

'Very much on some of the hillsides.'

'Now do you think that bracken has become a dominant weed only in recent times – or was its menace always there?'

'Always there,' replied Iain. 'In the old days they went long distances to cut it. When it had dried brown they made it into quoils, just as they do with hay, and then took it home for bedding in the byres and covering potatoes and other things. They needed all the straw they could make then for cattle feed.'

'Bracken in these days was even scarce and valuable?'

'Yes, as far as I know.'

'Tell me this. Assuming you were going back to the land, back home, would you go in for sheep *and* cattle?'

Iain smiled awkwardly.

'Why do you smile?' persisted Mr Hutcheson.

'Well, theoretically, I would have a shot at it,' said Iain.

'But practically there's not an earthly?' Mr Hutcheson laughed.

'It's a matter of money,' said Iain, encouraged. 'You would first of all need to find out what the soil wanted. Then you would have to put it there. You would have to drain and plough up. You would have to build dykes and fences to contain the cattle, because to make a job of cattle you would have to breed them. To breed them you would need winter feed. That might mean certain root crops, though not necessarily, but it would mean the right kind of grass and a better way of drying the grass. With enough grass saved, you might winter your ewe hoggs.' Iain abruptly stopped. 'At present there aren't enough fences to keep the deer from eating the winter feed – such as it is.'

The touch of final sarcasm in his voice made the partners laugh. The telephone rang. 'Yes?' said Mr Cunningham. And then 'Show him up in one minute.' He arose.

'I have been very interested in all this, Mr Cattanach, and am sorry that we are interrupted. Now I'll tell you what I want you to do. Think over all this, think over it in terms of what you know at home, and then to-morrow, when Mr Henderson comes, I'll send for you. You'll talk to him just as you have talked to us. Don't keep anything back. Come out with it. He'll enjoy it. Thank you.'

Opposite his own door, Mr Hutcheson paused. 'You did damn well,' he said. 'Pity we were interrupted.'

Iain went on. At the foot of the stairs he met Douglas who asked, 'Doing anything to-night?'

'Yes. I have some things to do.' He did not look at Douglas. His manner was reserved.

'Something I wanted to tell you,' said Douglas. He gave Iain a penetrating glance. 'However, if you can't come—' He turned his shoulder. 'Anyway, I'll be passing the Mound about eight.' He went on into the lavatory.

As he entered the main office, Iain was aware of inquisitive looks, but he paid no attention. Smeaton certainly got no change out of the way in which he settled down to his interrupted work. A bit of a dark horse, this young fellow from the glens! There was a wink or two, but no-one said anything.

TWENTY

Iain decided he might as well meet Douglas at the Mound. For excuse, there were some papers he had to return to Maitland. Perhaps Douglas might hand them back. It was a cold March night and he tied the top button of his coat over his muffler. Edinburgh's east wind searched for the marrow. For five minutes he stood in the lee of a pillar of the Art Gallery, watching the people hurrying by like fugitives in a beleaguered city.

Then he saw a figure standing, looking around. It was Douglas, and for a few seconds Iain watched him. Douglas came back to the corner of the Gallery and looked up towards the Mound; he sauntered to the outer edge of the pavement and glanced at the clock on the North British Hotel. It was seven minutes past eight.

'You managed to come after all?' he greeted Iain.

'Yes. I managed.'

'Shall we go along and have a drink? It's the weather for it.'

As they bore into the wind, Douglas repeated the 'east windy west endy' description of Edinburgh with an unexpected ironic oath. They walked for some way in silence, then he said, 'Haven't seen much of you lately?'

'I have been doing a bit of work.'

'You like it?'

'It's all right,' replied Iain indifferently.

'Pity you couldn't have gone home for a week or ten days as the doctor suggested. You were hit pretty hard.'

'I'm all right now. Besides—'

'Yes?'

'I haven't the money to throw about on holidays.'

'I suspected that,' said Douglas. 'And you're the sort of damned independent fellow who can't take a loan.'

For the first time Iain, because of his critical detachment, had been able to overcome and hint at his financial position, not so much in connection with a holiday, which didn't matter, as in his personal connection with the group. The forthright way in which Douglas acknowledged the position had a curiously easing effect upon him, though at the same time every step they took brought nearer the moment when he would tell Douglas just what he thought about the office story and Douglas's attitude to it.

They walked on in silence. Presently Douglas said, with that movement or lifting of the spirit which the Old Town always seemed to effect, 'Maitland and the others have been asking about you, wondering why you didn't come along.'

'I have some papers here for Maitland,' replied Iain coolly. 'I thought perhaps you might give them to him, if I don't see him. Or if you gave me his address, I could post them.'

Douglas deliberately glanced at Iain over his shoulder. 'I expect to see him,' he said shortly and did not speak again until he had had the surprise of his claret in the pub. Then, looking directly at Iain, he asked, 'What's it all about?'

'Oh, nothing much,' said Iain.

'Out with it,' demanded Douglas.

'Just this matter of money. Got a bit fed up being told in the office that I played on the streets to pay my way.'

Douglas's expression hardened. 'Who told you that?'

'Everyone has it. All the offices. Corbet, the commissionaire, explained to me privately how it was considered to be letting the office down.'

'By God,' said Douglas, 'aren't they bastards?' He kept looking at Iain. 'So you wondered why I didn't put the thing right? I see.'

Iain sipped the wine.

'Corbet!' exclaimed Douglas. He laughed harshly.

'Corbet is a friend of mine,' said Iain quietly.

'I know,' said Douglas. 'A decent old tough, who usually

would not condescend to drink with an apprentice. I did hear the story or at least suspected it. So, somehow, did Hutcheson. I told him the true yarn. He enjoyed it. Fairly lifted you in his estimation, if that was possible. He said he must tell the chief. Did they mention it to-day?'

'No,' replied Iain.

'I did think of warning you about it, but it seemed so damned silly. And then, the thing itself – I mean your playing and what happened to the crowd – it did hit the fancy. Davidson developed an extraordinary fantasy one night about the magical musician leading his people to the Mercat Cross – to hear the ghost voice telling them of their modern Flodden. It was wild. I wish you had been there. The more we drank, the stronger the fantasy grew. Then we set out. Must have been about midnight, three weeks ago. And Davidson as the ghost spoke from the Mercat Cross. God, it was terrific! No politician's talk, no economic figures, just the pure spirit. My skin ran cold, crawled over bones that had lived a thousand years and would never die.'

Douglas stopped, took a breath or two, and drank.

'So that probably started the yarn going about,' he said. 'The inevitable couple of policemen turned up – and listened. Most of them know me, from court work and what not. Maitland, too – he likes the picturesque. That's what he really likes. The unusual, the bizarre. That, he says, is why he likes researching into the ways of animalcules! Never seen him look at a fellow as a sheep tick? Odd to say that a chap who seems so intellectually cocksure would be even a better fellow if he were sure of himself. He'll have spun a marvellous yarn about it all, in his finished way, with a hint of himself as the deus-ex-machina. Sorry that all this troubled you,' concluded Douglas.

'It did trouble me,' said Iain. 'I just – didn't know. And I admit I wondered why you – why you let them off with it.'

'Naturally. But do you think I could explain *you* to a chap like Smeaton? Which reminds me. I told you I had some-

thing to say to you.' He paused. 'I suppose you thought it
was about this business?'

'Well, I wondered.'

'No. I probably wouldn't have mentioned this at all.
Though I'm glad now you brought it up. No, it was about
something else, perhaps of no special interest to you, but
it annoyed me. I heard him worrying you over the case of
Donald Cameron's valuation. You remember? You made
some retort or other about the estate agent's being illiterate, and he pointed out to you that it was for the claimant
to prove his case, not the estate. There was something in
his tone that made me wonder, and as I have been on that
work, I took a chance to turn up certain old Balmore estate
records. There's an entry by the factor of that time which
makes it quite clear that a Hugh Cameron, doubtless
Donald's father, did as tenant of the land himself erect a
dwelling house, et cetera. I thought that might interest
you.'

Iain remained silent, his brows gathering. 'Must Smeaton
deliberately suppress that information?' he asked at last.

'His point is that, as we are acting for the estate, it's not
our business to pay away estate money except on a legally
substantiated claim. It's up to Donald Cameron's heir to
support his claim in accordance with the statute. If he cannot
do that satisfactorily – well!'

'I see. But it's damned low!' Iain twisted on his seat. 'Do
you think Smeaton really knows of that old entry?'

'Surely. Actually there are the names of seven tenants in
the township at that time, all the same address. And there's
one other Cameron – a John Cameron: in his case, the estate
provided all the wood for the buildings. But Hugh put up
the whole affair himself. It's quite clear.'

'Supposing Mr Hutcheson or the chief knew about that
entry?'

'They would disclose it, of course. After that it's a matter
of the relationship of Hugh, Donald, and the claimant –
about which there appears to be no legal doubt.'

'Why then doesn't Smeaton disclose it?'

'In the first place, he despises crofters and cattle of that sort. They have riled him, so he's damned well going to make them prove their claims. A social superiority is involved. He's fighting for something uncertain in himself. Get the better of him once, cut his vanity to the quick, and he'll never forgive you. From the moment you made the office laugh at him, he was your enemy. It was such a hell of a thing for you, a raw country youth, to outdo him in social wit! Even worse than if a crofter had made a public fool of him. So he must – but what's the good of talking?'

'You think he would let me have it if he could?'

'More precisely – he would like to cut you to the marrow and see you grovel in sections. You can have no conception of the pleasure that would give him.'

'He's not likely to be indulged,' said Iain, 'but, ach, hell, it makes me tired.'

'You look a bit down,' considered Douglas. 'Drink up.' They emptied their glasses. 'How did you get on to-day with the big noise?'

'All right,' replied Iain in the same wearied voice, the voice he would have used to Ewan at home. It was the first time, perhaps, that he had ever been self-forgetful, perfectly natural, with Douglas. 'They were very decent. All about sheep farming.' And, prompted, he gave a rough summary of the talk in the chief's room. 'The whole thing was somehow so unreal. It means nothing.'

'How, unreal?'

'Because – ach, I can't tell you. It was just talk. A new landlord wants to get into politics. It's as far away from the realities as I am from my father working real sheep on real hills.'

'You mean you didn't believe in what you said needed to be done?'

'I did. And a whole lot more that I didn't tell them. All I have read about, too – the need for research, real scientific stuff, and markets, prices, and as for cattle—' He laughed harshly.

'Why couldn't it be done?'

Iain looked at him to see if he meant it. Douglas's face was impassive.

'Money,' said Iain laconically. 'Cash. Sales last autumn were so bad that my father must be finding it difficult to pay for this claret.'

Douglas remained silent.

Iain stirred. 'It sort of annoys me to hear them talking. And now to-morrow, the landlord himself – and more talk! I don't want to talk to him. What have landlords ever done for the Highlands? I mean beyond burning the people out or getting all they can from shooting tenants? Now I suppose they'll be up to some new trick or other – like Smeaton's dodge over Donald Cameron's valuation. And legal offices, your Parliament House, all the money places, offices, this city of offices . . . the *landlord* is our client, *not* Donald Cameron.'

'For one so young,' said Douglas evenly, 'you sound disillusioned. Do I take it that you think the things which need to be done can never be done?'

'They can never be done, or will never be done, by landlords. You can take that as certain. The thing is beyond them now, anyway. Socialism is the only hope.'

'Isn't that just a political theory? Supposing you nationalized the land to-morrow, and so made the State your landlord instead of Mr David Henderson, what better off would your father be? I can see he *might* have security of tenure but, in fact, has your father's tenure ever been insecure?'

'No,' said Iain, 'because the landlord has never been able to let my father's place in a way that would bring in more cash. However, that's not the real point now.'

'What is?'

'Cash is,' said Iain. 'Money for development. Where's the money going to come from to do all that should be done to the land, to the stocks? Who is going to put up the capital? Who is going to do research *and* apply it? Who is doing the research now? Not landlords. Already it is being seen as a national concern. You talk about nationalism, Scottish nationalism. This is what nationalism means to me. If it doesn't mean that we are going to get back our land with means to develop it, and have all the fun of going ahead and making life alive, well – it's not real.'

'That, Davidson says, is what it does mean.'

'And that,' said Iain, with a slow smile, 'is no doubt why he insists on talking economics.'

'That's a sly one at me, I suppose,' said Douglas, filling the glasses.

And then Iain said, 'No, it's not.' His look grew troubled. 'I know what you mean. You talk out of the blood. And – and that's where the music comes from.'

There was complete silence for some seconds. Then Douglas lifted his glass. 'I have never heard it so well put,' he remarked in strangely quietened tones.

As he set down his glass, Iain became aware of a silence beyond the noises in the pub, beyond the sounds in the street; it extended to a great distance and within it everything was harmonized as within an immortal listening ear.

The door opened and Maitland's head appeared. 'Ah here we are,' he said, adding, '*and* the musical magician,' as he glanced at Iain. Behind him came Colin Campbell, with generous ends to his black bow tie, black overcoat and black felt hat. Iain had seen him once before and had thought him an actor, so alive and expressive were his thin face and hands. He was, or had been, Douglas explained, a first fiddle in a B.B.C. orchestra.

'Claret? Charming wine,' murmured Colin to Douglas, 'but – perhaps I'd better not mix them. Shall we say a spot of gin?'

'And where have you been hiding yourself?' Maitland asked Iain, as they settled down.

'Ah, you're the musical magician!' cried Colin Campbell. 'My dear fellow, I'm glad to meet you.' He arose, bowed, and shook hands with Iain. 'I have heard about you. You have been my inspiration. In fact, I hope, if you will permit me so great a privilege, to dedicate the immortal work to you.'

'Where the hell have you fellows been drinking?' demanded Douglas.

'Drinking?' Colin Campbell's eyebrows went up as he sat down and spread his palms abroad. 'There is a crude streak in you, Douglas. It's the crudeness and dark rumbling darkness of the Mile. But I've got even that in my masterpiece. You're the rumble of drums, the growl, from which the pipe theme springs. I haven't written it down yet. But I have it here' – he tapped his brow – 'I mean here' – he tapped his heart. He spread his hands, he swayed, but with a light in his eyes that burned from more than alcohol. 'It's magnificent! Stupendous! It – it chokes me!' He tossed off his gin. 'God, it's terrific!'

Douglas suddenly laughed. Here was the madness that brought him alive. Now began the time of forgetfulness and wild mirth.

And Colin Campbell held them. There can be only one subject at such a time, one theme, and one audience worked upon.

'And what a theme!' declared Colin. 'God, what a theme! What an immortal theme! Starting out of the darkness of time, with the elements in motion, the wind off great swinging seas, whirling round the swing of massive mountains' – he looked at Iain – 'the theme that is ground work, basic, in your simplest authentic Gaelic tune. Have you not heard it? Have you never got beyond the love and the story to hear *that*?'

'I have heard it,' said Iain quite clearly.

'You have heard it? You tell me that!'

'The rhythm of the primeval,' said Iain, remembering something spoken long ago, 'before time was.'

'The rhythm – the *rhythm* of the primeval!' Colin got to his feet, upsetting his empty glass which he ignored. This time he did not bow, but Iain had to take the sustained strength of his handclasp. 'Christ!' said Colin, in an anguished solemnity, and sat down.

Douglas roared his laughter and Maitland's smile, as he glanced at him, was the enigmatic smile of the impresario satisfied with his latest work.

But Colin now had no more to say. He sat with sunken head, like some gloomy raven lost in moulting thought.

'Go on!' probed Douglas.

Colin lifted his head and, turning it slowly, looked at Douglas. 'Do you realize,' he asked levelly, 'that here, for my primeval beginning, my own folk offer me the choice of a dozen themes? Such riches, and what it means, what it implies, what it cries out to me, makes me shiver.'

'But that's only the beginning,' prompted Maitland.

'That's only the beginning,' repeated Colin, looking at Maitland as at a stranger. 'Yes, that's only the beginning.' He looked at nothing. 'We have forgotten how to be moved.' His eyes drifted onto Iain's face and steadied. 'They have forgotten,' he said, as if thinking into distance, 'how to be moved.'

Maitland, by the quiver of an eyelid, would have cautioned Douglas, but Douglas wasn't looking at him, he was looking at Colin, his mirth held by a hair to a wild arrestment.

For a moment it seemed as if Colin, having taken the drink that is one too many, was going to sink into moody deeps and refuse to be stirred. But the silence soon touched him with a need to mould it, to give it form. 'Out of that rhythm before time was,' he said, like one talking in his sleep, 'comes the living theme, the voice of the Rock . . . the voice in the Castle Rock. All composers have searched for the theme of fate, of over-riding destiny, and have announced it each in his fashion. We have yet to announce ours. The dark voice out of the Castle Rock.'

They could wait for him now.

'Do not mistake me. I am not talking in symphonic terms.' His breathing deepened. 'I am talking of this city, this ancient and immortal city, whose curves and bones have come into my bones and blood. It's not a question of beauty, where she has hardly her equal in the world. O God, it transcends beauty, fuses it, until the spirit, the naked spirit, rises, rises through every dimension of human experience, swinging between life and death, swift-changing, knowing the ultimates in a history that for wildness and bloodiness and grandeur is surely without peer among the ancient capitals of the earth.' He stopped, and then in level tones added, 'I am going to compose – and may the gods of our people speak in me – I am going to compose the Ballet of Edinburgh.'

Douglas did not laugh. He drew back, a half-withered smile on his face, and began to probe Colin, and Iain could see that Douglas was so certain Colin would never – and could never – produce such a work, that, out of obscure deeps of perversity and defeat, he had to bait him.

This roused Colin, gave him back his flashing words and gestures. And presently, as they all got caught in the theme of the ballet, some extraordinary pictures did emerge. Occasionally Colin hummed a few notes, conducting them with one hand while with the other he indicated – interpolating a few words swiftly – the choreographer's part, thus bringing, with rapid changes of mood, a whole scene upon the bare table (for they had now removed all glasses beyond his reach).

The voice of the Rock. Then – coming through – the voice of the Holy Rood. The city begins to form along its ridge, its mile-long backbone. And Iain hears, through the solemn chanting notes of the Holy Rood, the far rumble, the beat, the living beat of the drums, and he glimpses a swing of legs and tartan, himself among them, swinging from Holyrood up the Canongate.

The theme of the big pipe (the bagpipe) has an extraordinary uplift. Victory or death, it does not matter, nothing matters but the moment that cries – and lifts the feet – and lifts the spirit – and goes on.

The Castle Rock rears its plumed head and from its dark sides two wings stretch far over the land. Under the one wing, beyond the pipe theme, far into the mountains and the islands, lives the theme that a blind man plucks from a harp, and girls listen to him and youths, and old women and old men, and they are moved to interweave destiny through the threads of their lives. Iain knows the old Gaelic theme, and knows, too, the distant pipe theme that suddenly arrests them, and calls, and calls, and the able men break from the clutching hands of their women, and the youths laugh, sticking a feather in their bonnets, and Iain glimpses the swing of their bodies, up the Canongate, on the way to the Castle Rock.

Under the other wing, far to the Borders, moss-troopers and red lands and beauty stark. The ballad land. Colin is reciting in a slow deep voice:

> *I took his body on my back,*
> *And whiles I gaed and whiles I sat;*
> *I digg'd a grave, and laid him in,*
> *And happ'd him with the sod sae green.*
>
> *But think na ye my heart was sair,*
> *When I laid the moul' on his yellow hair?*
> *Oh, think na ye my heart was wae,*
> *When I turn'd about away to gae?*
>
> *Nae living man I'll love again,*
> *Since that my lovely knight is slain;*
> *With ae lock of his yellow hair*
> *I'll chain my heart for evermair.*

Colin's arms are moving, his long hands drooping and slowly walking. '. . . And whiles I gaed – and whiles I sat . . .' Iain sees the woman carrying the dead body, has a momentary sight of the face uplifted, the empty sky and the bright green grass . . . the anguish in the face, the heavy burden.

The dance of what the women bore when the forays and the follies are over.

Johnnie Armstrang and Johnnie of Bradislee, Kinmont Willie and the Douglas Tragedy. The horses are gone into the night.

And here comes the Black Douglas riding for the black Castle Rock.

There was a long argumentative interlude, when Colin, grown intolerant and sheer in the sweep of his hands, shouted at Maitland who had added something, 'No! Hell, it's not a bourgeois pageant: it's immortal ballet!'

But out of all the subsequent creation and confusion, two pictures remained with a wonderful clarity for Iain. The first was 'The Four Maries', the Ballet of Mary the Queen. The song of the Four Maries had affected him as a boy and now as Colin sang a verse in a low clear voice, to establish a certain mood out of tradition, the words on their long rhythm stole into his heart.

> *Yestreen the Queen had four Maries,*
> *The nicht she'll hae but three . . .*

Colin himself was deeply moved. For him, his arrangement had a passionate restraint and beauty. He spoke with restraint to the end . . . 'The scaffold at last, the headsman's block, after nineteen years in an English prison. It shuts the mouth of clamour. It curls you up, that! And then, the girl in white, interpreting the theme, solitary, to herself, in every movement of her body, in every blood-beat of her sorrow, until tragedy drains her and beauty dies.'

Douglas, who had been leaning forward, elbows on the table, straightened up and looked at Colin with irony. 'Don't you think you're romanticizing the Queen a bit?'

The effect on Colin was instantaneous. He could not have had the blade of his wrath, his scorn, more quickly in action had he been expecting a treacherous assault. He traversed history with flame and riot, he bore Douglas's mind on a pike as a bourgeois exhibit, he drew such a picture of the Good Queen Bess and her courtiers, the canny greedy courtiers 'moving in the ambit of a frustrated virginity with the cruelty that murders from a distance', that he was thanking God for having made all real women bitches, when the door opened and the proprietor's head said, 'Gentlemen! Gentlemen! Not so loud, please!'

The second picture was of the architecture of the New Town. 'The Dance of the Crescents. The Minuet of Charlotte Square . . .' Iain's dream came back to him, and the houses, in curve and straight line, assumed an architectural life of superb grace as they advanced and retired, slowly wheeled and took up their positions again. Here Colin's words were hardly needed. Just a hint, the touching of a secret spring, and imagination was free of the whole wonderful fantasy. The light was the light in his dream. But there was no sinister note now. Beauty, with incomparable grace, came to life in stone. And if sometimes it wasn't so much the houses that moved as the women who danced, yet his mind found no difficulty with the double motion. It was altogether and quite naturally a matter of emphasis, of where imagination's eye momentarily rested.

From that point came the descent into Colin's gloom, for he did not know how to finish his ballet – 'and, hell, I don't want to finish in satire! I don't want to make the descent into the abyss of the Mile, to light up the silent Rock as a peepshow for tourists. We should be done with satire. The best of us have lived on satire too long, that negation of the damned. It's too bloody easy. It's ashes in the mouth. It's death.'

'My dear fellow,' said Maitland, 'Edinburgh is a great modern city, with Lord Provost and Council, and financial houses of vast resources and unimpeachable rectitude.'

Colin gloomed at him, and, looking away, muttered, 'We need to fight. Creation is a fight. The fight of the spirit for birth, for air.' He tugged at his collar.

'Then there are the legal offices,' added Maitland. 'Law and order.'

Colin looked at Douglas.

'Well?' challenged Douglas.

'You'll drive me to it,' muttered Colin. 'Elizabeth's courtiers – as Edinburgh's modern lawyers. Crafty – black silk and wigs. Dancing – dancing—'

'Dancing solemnly round a maypole in Princes Street Gardens,' said Iain, breaking his long silence.

Fire visibly poured into Colin's eyes. He rose slowly and spread his arms, as the Rock had spread its wings, and asked Iain in a wondering, appalled voice: 'What in God's name are we doing here?' Then he collapsed.

TWENTY-ONE

Threading the streets, Iain, remembering bits of the evening's fun, smiled to himself. The wine had not lit him up properly; a dry aftermath was in the mouth; but he felt free, now that he was alone, and his mind had a cool detachment.

All at once he became conscious he was whistling softly, 'Yestreen the Queen had four Maries . . .' He went on whistling, unable, not wanting, to stop himself, until it obsessed him.

As the conception of tragedy, of solitariness, swelled upon the air, he became aware of the streets, the empty darkened by-streets, the wind scurrying round corners and spitting sleet.

> *The nicht she'll hae but three,*
> *There was Marie Seaton and Marie Beaton,*
> *And Marie Carmichael and me.*

Down came the rhythm to its end, down came everything, all action, all life, to that final, solitary 'and me'.

They could quarrel over the music, over the song, over the sentiment or sentimentality, over history, but it was the ultimate feminine 'and me', in the moment of desolation, of realization, that Colin was trying to show. And tradition, as he had said, took centuries to winnow these things pretty fine.

Douglas had been in a queer mood. Colin irritated him in some way. So did Davidson. It was as if Douglas was queerly jealous. Did not want them really to touch his city, his history, his belongings. He would go with them a long wild way – then suddenly, round he turned, ironic, challenging, slashing them back, like an animal defending his hole. By their tongues, Davidson and Colin were not Edinburgh men. Could that affect Douglas? Heavens, it might!

Colin had a flamboyance, the sort of thing Iain himself had often met in the Highlands. He suspected that Colin would never write his ballet and that Douglas knew it. Colin might make the effort, but it wouldn't come through. It would be strangled.

In all these meetings and talks there was that sort of futility. It lacked real satisfaction; left the feeling that all had been froth. Corbet, blowing froth, froth right to the bottom of his pint, would certainly be left with the notion that Jimmy had played a trick on him!

As a trick, a joke, it was good fun. But when a fellow like Colin began to blow the froth off real beer, and yet the beer itself, by some weird trick, never appeared . . . something tragic about it.

The fight of the spirit for birth, for air. And a tugging at the strangling throat.

The nicht she'll hae but three . . .

One less. Then another one less. Then the last one, Colin's last Marie in the dance of death. Not gaunt Death dancing, but a lovely girl, in white, on her toes. In some way, it was terribly ironic. Made Douglas's conception of the same history ordinary, commonplace, like stuff read in history books.

An empty half-dark side street, the east wind searching its backbone for the marrow. The people gone to bed were the marrow in the bone. Extended, inert, their faces marrow-grey.

Iain smiled, pulling tight his muffler and hunching his shoulders. Angus would have turned in. He was moving in that world of country students who never adventured far, who swotted and turned in.

Perhaps he had been out with Joan. How surprised he had been when Morna had told him that Angus was seeing Joan regularly, even going to her home, and not always on

Sunday! It had seemed a good joke. Never a word had Angus said himself, however. Was he drifting away from Mary Cameron, just as he was drifting away from the world at home? The city ways, the college life, the fun of girls and fellows together, cups of tea, societies. The new life.

What had Angus said to him that first night about Morna? 'You watch your step' or something. And he had thought Angus a simple fellow, whom it was necessary to protect!

He would really have to do something about Morna. Hang it, he was beginning to dread the meetings. She was a nice girl, no-one he liked better, but – she was – she was too much—

He climbed the stairs, shut the doors, and struck a match. His glass of milk, with saucer on top, was by the fire, which had gone out. He turned from the gas flare to the table. A letter . . . from Morna.

He turned from it, sat down and began to take off his shoes. His eye fell on a library book on sheep farming in Wales. He had fairly spent the evening thinking out what he was going to tell Mr David Henderson to-morrow! Suddenly his whole nature rose in rebellion. It was too much! The thought of the interview had been dogging him, made him feel nervous and uncertain. His own chief in the office, his father's landlord – as examiners! Had it been class work, he could have stood up to it. But on realities . . . it was asking too much. To find words, while they were looking at him, with that smile on their faces, waiting for his mature wisdom, as old people wait for the prattling of a kid, interested, amused . . . feeling for him when the words choked in his throat . . .

He kicked his shoes aside, shivered, and got up. 'Hell, I'm cold!' he said. Then he turned to the table, picked up the letter, and with a fumbling thumb burst the flap of the envelope.

TWENTY-TWO

About eleven o'clock the following morning, Smeaton left his desk and hurried out. Iain suspected that Smeaton's restlessness, his air of important interviews pending, was due to the awaited visit of Mr David Henderson. Mr Hutcheson would have seen to it that Smeaton, as expert on the Crofting or Smallholders Acts, would be on tap should the wealthy landowner desire specific information. For, of course, the landowner would have to know the crofters' legal rights under the various statutes before he could begin ordering them about or 'improving' them. So much at least would have to be made clear to him. From the signs, too, it appeared certain that Donald Cameron's specific case would be placed before him, both as educative material and as something towards which he, as landlord, could there and then express a personal attitude for the general guidance of his agents.

The firm was certainly leaving nothing to chance in so far as it was necessary to impress an important client! In Smeaton's phrase – 'really good staff work.' And wouldn't Smeaton be important, wouldn't he love the interview! 'Yes, sir,' in his crispest manner. Or 'I doubt if you could do that, sir. Crofters may be ignorant, but they are ticklish fellows for what they call their rights, and under sub-section . . .'

Iain felt nervous and slightly sick. His eyes roved and met the eyes of Douglas. Douglas's eyes switched slowly to a file of papers on Smeaton's desk. Iain knew it was the Donald Cameron file. He looked at it as he might look at a snake. It began to fascinate him. As if impelled, not so much by the snake as by that switch of Douglas's eyes, he got up and sauntered to the file, not intending to handle it, only to glance at it.

The first name his eye landed on was EWAN CAMERON.

In a moment, before he had consciously read a typed line, he realized that the claimant, the next of kin, was his friend Ewan Cameron! It took his breath from him in astonishment, in a swelling light. His eyes, as if they could not quite focus, slid over the lines, the legal phrases, the verbiage ... DUNCAN CATTANACH. His father! The old home, parish, county. Statement by his father ... 'I have often heard my father, James Cattanach, say that the said Hugh Cameron had himself erected the dwelling house, byre ...'

As Iain read his father's handwriting, something moved terribly in him. He turned the pages. More statements by men he knew. Responsible old men, who came alive before him. His own homeland. The men of the glen and the hills, who tilled their land and reared their sheep. That Smeaton, who knew the truth, should be playing with men like them, jeering at them as 'illiterate', prepared to do Ewan out of his money!

O God, it was too much! Everything that had been repressed in him came up. His hatred of Smeaton and all he stood for welled with his blood in a mounting heat of anger.

'Hullo! What are *you* doing?'

Iain turned and looked at Smeaton.

'Thinking of taking over the case?' asked Smeaton, the sarcastic smile licking his face. 'Would like to add its minor detail to your extensive knowledge of sheep?' He could not help himself, for he had only just heard from Mr Hutcheson of the true nature of Iain's talk with the partners yesterday, and of its meaning for to-day. Iain's darkened face, his unanswering dumbness, the damned impertinence of his staring eyes, angered him now beyond reason. 'I would advise you to stick to sheep. And after this you'll remember not to read my files – when my back is turned. Now, get out!'

Iain did not move.

'Will you leave my desk?' Smeaton's thin voice shrilled.

'Your rotten files,' exploded Iain, 'when all the time you knew from the estate records that the buildings were put up by the Camerons.'

'Leave my desk, you sneak!' cried Smeaton. 'I'll report

this at once to Mr Cunningham!' He was shaking, dancing from foot to foot. But he could not turn away from Iain, his dignity could not be defeated, and like a gibbering, hysterical woman he went on, 'This is not the Canongate! We know about you. Skulking – frightened—'

It may have been Smeaton's intention to suggest that Iain was frightened he would be found out in his unmentionable method of filching pennies from the poor, but the office could never be sure, for it was exactly as if the word *frightened* was a trigger which Smeaton pulled. Iain's right fist, released, caught the mouth that had uttered the word a terrific skelp.

Smeaton's head snicked up as he staggered back. His eyes goggled with what seemed intense dismay, as if he were going to weep. Then he screamed and came for Iain. Iain hit him again but didn't stop him. He burrowed into Iain, head down, and blindly clutched him, yelling 'You country muck!' and tugged and pushed at him, perhaps with the high intention of sweeping the muck from the office.

There was little enough room for deployment, only the short passage between two desks and the four paces to the cashier's door, with its upper half of rough opaque glass. Iain couldn't break free, and they staggered from desk to desk. Then Iain gave a sharp yelp as if something had hurt him foully. There was a whirl, a half break, and Iain had Smeaton round the loins, had him up off his wildly kicking feet, but the weight was too much for him, and in the blind instinct to smash the body to the floor, he overbalanced, tried to keep his feet, staggered forward in a small run that the opaque glass of the door could not quite stop. Smeaton's body burst it in a stupendous crash.

If only Smeaton had kept his hold on Iain, he might have escaped much of the damage that was done to his face and hands, but as the splintered glass showered on him he let go and grabbed blindly at the edges of the hole he had made. As the razor-edges cut deep, he screamed and let go, the upper part of his body doubling over into the cashier's room.

Iain stood, straight and still, while Wilson and two others, helped by the cashier and his assistant on the other side, lifted Smeaton's body level and bore it back through the hole. On his feet he was a horrible sight, for the blood was pouring down his face onto his new blue pin-stripe suit, and his bloody hands, in a terribly helpless way, were uplifted. Thin screams were still coming from him.

Mr Dowie's feet came pounding up the floor, followed quickly by the commissionaire, who knew of battlefields and first-aid, at the double.

Iain walked for the door, straight, head up, like some avenging young god who had finished his fell work. As he came to the counter, he saw before him so lovely a young woman that he stared at her out of his rage. His step, however, never faltered. There was a tall man with her but Iain did not look at him. Round the counter he went, and straight for the door, the faces of the young woman and the elderly man following his progress with fascinated attention until he vanished.

Mr David Henderson had arrived for his appointment, accompanied by his niece Evelyn, who acted as his private secretary.

PART THREE

BACK HOME

ONE

'Hallo, Iain! Is that yourself? Home for a holiday! Well, well!'

There was always a little crowd about the post office when the bus arrived with the mail and newspapers from Kinmore, and now everyone there shook hands with him, faces smiling broadly, delighted to see him.

'Making a long holiday?' asked the merchant-postmaster pausing for a moment amid his important duties.

'Oh, home for a bit,' replied Iain, smiling.

'Is that your fiddle you've brought with you?'

'That's the old fiddle,' agreed Iain, forced to take it from the boot, where he had stowed it amid the postal bags.

He was invited to 'give us a tune', and everyone laughed as he pretended to hesitate. Now he was asked how he liked Edinburgh, and one said, 'Saw your father yesterday and he never mentioned you were coming.' But Iain answered someone else. Mercifully the bus was late and the driver in a hurry. Iain got on board and off they went, past Ewan's cottage – Ewan saluted the driver with a chisel – past people on the road, fields he knew, until the driver drew up and Iain got off, with a cry of thanks.

Alone with his bag and his fiddle, he gripped them at once and started off, with a feeling of guilt heavier than any material belongings; so heavy that soon he was hot and sweating behind the cold March air.

Now his home, with the knoll of black pines, was there, at a boyhood's distance. The old place, quiet and waiting. The bag became so heavy that he dropped it and stood, the muscles of his arm trembling. If only he had foreseen this horrible moment as he felt it now, he would never have come. Never! Three heads above the grey dyke ... three bodies coming clear: his father, Andrew McAndrew and Geordie Farquharson. As they saw him they stopped, and for a few moments he could do no more than return their distant stare; then he lifted his bag and went towards them.

'Well, if it isn't Iain himself!' cried Andrew in an astonishment so great that it was grave. 'What!' He shook hands next. 'Home for a holiday, boy?'

'Ay, home for a bit,' replied Iain, carrying it off as he had done at the post office, if now with more warm confusion.

Then he shook hands with his father, but without looking at him.

'Never heard you were coming,' said Andrew.

'No,' replied Iain. 'Suddenly took it into my head.'

They saw there was something wrong. 'You're a bit thinner, boy. Been working too hard?' asked Geordie.

'No,' said Iain, with a slight upward jerk of his head, smiling. 'Had a bad bout for a while but – och, I'm fine.'

'I can see you need your native air,' declared Andrew. 'You need hefting again.' This reference to the acclimatizing of a sheep had an easing humour, and now Iain saw, in a flash, that they assumed he had been sent home to recover from an illness, but that naturally he would not want to talk about it. The cold air on his heated standing body suddenly set him coughing. He had been troubled with a cough, but nothing out of the way, and indeed knew it had almost completely gone. Now as he appeared to choke the cough, it hacked its way through.

'Keeping you standing in the cold! In you go,' said Andrew. 'We'll be seeing you.' In country fashion, he still lingered. 'Brought your fiddle, too! Man, it's been much missed.'

At last they went, and his father, who offered to carry the bag and was refused, carried the fiddle. 'You never said you were coming,' remarked his father companionably.

'No,' said Iain, looking away in front, 'I – there wasn't time.'

'There's – nothing wrong with you, is there, boy?'

'No,' said Iain. 'I – had a shake, and things got – got a

bit too much for me.' The tremble in his flesh showed in his voice.

'Give me that bag,' said his father, taking it from him with a firm kindliness.

Iain felt groggy, slightly dizzy. The thought of using illness as an excuse for his return home could never have occurred to him. Now, with a dreadful sense of personal weakness and shame, he found himself grasping at it. His grandmother was standing in the doorway.

He had to go through it all again, but his weakness at the moment being very real he made for a chair in the kitchen.

'Poor boy!' she cried, flustering about and poking up the fire, 'and you never told us! But it's ill you were, as I knew from your letter, and I told them that. Yes, yes!'

Iain started coughing again, for his throat had gone very dry. His grandmother had seen how thin his face had got, with the cheekbones showing and the line of the jaw all too clear in one so young. The coughing brought a flush to the pale skin.

'No, I'll eat nothing. Just a cup of tea. It was cold travelling.'

'You'll eat what you'll get,' she declared. 'We'll have no nonsense in this house.' Her alarm was steadied by the need for action.

'Just a cup of tea,' he said again.

'You'll get your cup of tea first,' she answered. 'Surely you could have sent a telegram to say you were coming. I'll need to air your bed. I've got nothing ready for you.' She moved nimbly on her aged feet, talking to herself and to Iain.

His father said he had to go out for a minute. Iain wanted to ask him how the sheep were doing, but could not. His grandmother waddled after his father. He heard her calling him; caught the word 'beef'. She would be sending him to the shop. Beef-tea and other things for the invalid come home!

Hurrying back, she infused the tea, and he eased her anxiety by saying; 'A bit of oatcake and real butter.'

'Real butter! Don't you get real butter?'

'It never tastes real.'

'It'll not be that stuff,' she said with an expression of anxious horror, 'that they're calling margarine?' And she stopped and looked at him.

'Some margarine is all right,' he answered, 'but sometimes it has the taste of axle-grease.'

'Ah, poor boy!' she cried, hurrying once more.

When he saw her carrying blankets and sheets and spreading them before the fire, he said nothing. Since he had thrown Smeaton through the glass door yesterday forenoon, he had drunk a cup or two of tea but eaten nothing solid. He had the sensation of having walked immense distances and stayed for endless hours in railway stations where engines hissed and whistled and barrows trundled on cold stone. He had never had his clothes off and slept not at all. The sickliness in his chest was still tainted with the coal fumes of departing trains.

The tea was rich in colour and taste. It was too hot and he blew on it, but it was tea. The taste of the butter went all over his palate.

'Has Jess the cow calved?' he asked.

'Yes, three weeks ago,' she answered. 'And right glad I was. It's a miserable house where the drop milk and the bit butter is missing.'

His father had always arranged for an early calf.

'The hens will be laying too,' he said to keep her talking.

'The open weather', she told him, 'has just put them on the top of their laying. There will be plenty of fresh eggs for you whatever. And you'll have a beat-up egg in milk twice a day – and oftener if you can manage. There's no better food. I remember a doctor once saying that, and indeed the outcome proved him right, for it was a young girl who had been in service in the city, and home she came with the ghost of herself in her face. But the eggs and the milk chased the ghost away – though just to make sure her mother would be boiling a bit of beef now and then until all the good of it was in the bree, and that helped. For there's great virtue in the bittie meat. Now you'll take another cup.'

'Yes. I haven't tasted tea like this since I left home.'

'Ach, what do they know about making tea in yon places?' She smiled, pleased. 'You'll not be having to hurry back, will you?' He felt her eyes on him.

'No,' he answered; then added lightly, 'I'll be staying a few days anyway.'

'You'll be staying more than a few days,' she answered, setting the teapot by the fire. Then she turned to him. 'You will, won't you?' Her voice was pleading with him not to go too soon, but he did not meet her eyes. She probably thought he had consumption!

'I'll see,' he said, dismissing the subject.

'Would you like to lie down – to go to your bed and just have a good lie down?'

He hesitated. Whereupon she got busy, telling him how sensible he was and how one good sleep would be the beginning that would be the making of him. 'I'll bring you in something when I have it ready.' Within twenty minutes, he was flat on his back in his warm bed.

So great was his feeling of defeat that it overcame all thought in a detached and fatal ease, and in no time he was fast asleep.

He awoke from a nightmare of books and study to see the door slowly opening. It was the door of his nightmare, but the head that appeared was his grandmother's.

'Ah, you're awake,' she said softly.

The room was in gloom and as he stared at her, she stood still. 'Did I waken you?'

He looked about the room. 'Yes.' His head fell back.

'You were dreaming,' she said. 'But wait you now, and I'll bring you something.' She brought him a bowl of rich beef-tea and toast. 'I looked in before, but you were sleeping. Now this will keep the heart in you till to-morrow, and then when your tiredness is gone your food will do you good.'

'What time is it?'

'It's getting on for eight o'clock. You've had a nice sleep. Aren't you feeling the better of it?'

'Is that someone—?'

'It's Mary Cameron talking to your father. One or two of them come for milk. They're all asking for you. Now try your beef-tea. And there's the salt.'

He got up on an elbow and she went out, saying, 'I'll bring you in a light.'

'No, I don't want a light.' But she was gone and he fell back and stared about the room, listening at the same time for voices. Presently he began to sup out of the bowl, but after a few spoonfuls, he rested. The nightmare had ebbed, leaving thoughts strewn about.

How on earth had he expected to carry things off? Could he possibly have believed that he would come home, meet his father, tell him what had happened and say, 'I'm not going back to that office; I'm not going to be a lawyer; it doesn't suit me; so I have come home to help you.' Yes, he had! But not quite so simply as that. He had foreseen that there might be trouble, that to some extent he would be misunderstood. It was not going to be easy, but the whole idea was that he was prepared to put up a fight. Not to run away, but to take what was coming to him straight, to fight and endure. Too many of them ran away. He had notions about what could be done in the glen. At least he would earn his own keep.

The argument with himself had been interminable, for his instinct had been to cut clear, even to clear out of the country to Australia or New Zealand (he could work his passage; he wasn't afraid of work) where the immense sheep ranches were and a fellow could ride and have the freedom of the earth about him.

But his own glen drew him. Something, too, was distilled out of all the Edinburgh talk. Douglas's history. Davidson's new vision of Scotland. Some essence of all that, some drop of pure spirit, had bathed an inner tissue of the mind, refreshed it, brought it to life. When in jest he had asked the speaker at the Mound if he was never going to do anything more than *talk*, something had been even then stirring in him.

During the long, miserable self-argument, he had seen

what it was. Each fellow had to act, to work, to build, in his own way. He could work all the better if his mind was refreshed and saw the full design and the meaning. To have that kind of vision or meaning behind him gave his work a greater happiness. It brought gaiety to life, a warmth to fiddle-playing and dancing. It killed dullness at one stroke. Hang it, it was the only thing that could bring the glen to life!

And in that, he could help. That's where his talent lay. Others had talents to be lawyers, public speakers, psychologists, scientists, university lecturers, shopkeepers, engineers.

If everyone stopped talking of the dead past or the ideal future for a time and really got down to action, to work, then a country like Scotland – every country in the world – would rise, each from its own past into its own future, and life everywhere would be rich and warm and full of variety, full of the fun of struggle, of building and making. The world had been choked with talk of perfect ideals since long before Christ. But as they made and built things, the perfect ideals would themselves be surprised into shape.

These youthful thoughts were all the more highly conceived, attained an absolute clarity, because of the figure of Smeaton, streaming blood. So intense was their reaction to that crashing office scene, that their certainty, like a sentence of death, was complete.

Finally he had come to a stand, staring at the white time-table in Waverley Station with its list of trains for the North. His decision – and at that moment it instantly freed him – partook of the same kind of clarity. He would arrive, tell his father he had thrown his job up, give his reasons. If, however much he was prepared to endure, it became finally clear that his father did not want him – right! he was then free to go abroad to a land where men could work and conceive new things. He would at least have done his duty by his father and by his native land. He would have acted.

What a child he had been! What a simpleton!

Suddenly afraid lest his grandmother should come in and find her beef-tea cold, he lifted the bowl and began to drink it, gulping it down. It spilled from the corners of his mouth, but he kept gulping it to the end, like a bowl of medicine, and then, gasping, tried to wipe the drips off the sheets.

When presently he heard her coming, he pretended to be asleep.

TWO

After a cup of tea in bed came breakfast – cream and porridge – and the instruction that he was to return for his egg switched in milk 'in a whilie'. Iain left the house, wandered into the byre to have a look at the cows, talked to them while observing the familiar effects on their hides of the long winter tie-up, scratched the forehead of the butting calf, cast his eyes slowly about the interior which he knew so well, drifted out to the stable, to the barn, and presently found himself standing in the shelter of the group of old pines.

Extraordinary the effect of suggestion, for he felt like an invalid! He smiled slowly, all his movements were slow, except occasionally the glance of his eyes, which could be quick and furtive, as if expecting something to steal upon him.

Not an unpleasant feeling, rather light and airy, and he stood, screened from view, looking abroad upon the world, the ancient line of the hills, the distant group of pines on the skyline which had somehow got mixed in his childhood mind with the idea of prehistoric men – hairy uncouth giants, at the sky itself which was a brilliant dark blue for there had been a touch of frost during the night, and then slowly along all he could see of the glen and the human places.

Into this still peace rose the cackling of two hens and he thought of warm eggs in straw, until he heard the larks overhead and lifted his face. The trees drew his attention and he looked at them individually, remembering climbing feats. He moved over to one tree and all of a sudden started climbing it. The same notches, the same small footholds, until he got on the first real branch. Thus lifted in the air, his boyhood came upon him with the force of revelation, a memory of endless summer days, with a murmuring, a sort of hypnotic singing, from unmoving lips, while his eyes stared far away or at the scaling bark under a poking thumb-nail. Odd that he should have entirely forgotten this experience!

It was from that lower branch that Mary had fallen . . . Angus had gone white and started crying . . . but he had run after Mary and told her to shut up. Perhaps because he was frightened 'the old people' might forbid them to play any more in the secret trees? . . .

Swinging down, he started along the hillside at the same slow pace. The heather, above him, was a dark, dead brown. This was the poorest time of the whole year, the centre of that spring period from February to the end of April when beasts found least growth on the earth. This was the most difficult of all times for hill sheep. He thought of certain patches where cotton grass would now be offering the tender bite of its new leaf – his father would be making the most of these patches, driving the ewes here and there, careful that the young dog did not rush them. In a few days – a week – April would be in and the lambing not far off.

As he looked along the great slopes, he smiled. That fine theory about increasing, year by year, the more fertile patches, scratching, ploughing up, seeding! . . . that one man could think of making any impression on this vast, gaunt, primeval land! . . . those city theorists – who needed gardeners to keep the light, easily-worked soil of their house plots free of weed! . . .

Heavens, how different the reality! And yet, despite himself, he could not forgo the theory. An itch came upon him to order resources and labour, to get things done, not by one man with a hopeless spade, but by many men, ditching, dyking, burying the low, rolling ground with its yellow-green moss under fresh ploughed-up soil . . . He felt the itch in the muscles of his shoulders, and scanned with an amused dryness the beautiful velvety smoothness of the yellow-green moss –

'fog' was the Balmore name for it – under his feet. The creeping, smothering fog.

There was his father, giving the ewes the best bite, herding them along the bottoms which he had so carefully nursed during the summer and autumn plenty on the wide hills.

'Well, boy, you've got out.' The same quiet greeting, the friendly voice. Rarely anything hurried about it, except when it rose in its own peculiar cry to the dogs.

Iain had heard real sheep men compared with seamen. The steady far look, the need for self-reliance, the same kind of independence, often slow in speech, as if experience and thought had never quite got used to a speaking outlet, as if indeed speech at most times didn't help much. A strong urge came upon him to have the uneasiness purged from his breast, but the native silence made it impossible.

'How are they doing?' he asked.

'Not bad. It's been an open winter if a bit wet.' His father looked at the sky. 'We may get it yet.'

'Do you think so?' asked Iain, also looking at the sky.

'We generally get it some time. This morning I thought there was a smell of it in the air.'

Iain knew his father was referring to snow. There generally was one winter snow-storm. If it came early, when the sheep were in condition, it did little harm. To come now, after lean feeding months and with the ewes heavy in lamb, it might be ruinous. One naturally feared the worst, out of age-old experience. Actually it was a lovely spring day, and in the air Iain thought he caught a faint scent of heather-burning. It stirred him profoundly, like a memory of an old tune.

'Is Finlay at the burning?' he asked.

'No, that's not him. He did a bit on the low ground. Not much.'

Iain could not help a small smile. There had been no real complaint in his father's voice, but somehow its judgement, from the shepherd's point of view, of Finlay's insufficient burning of the old heather had been complete. There were sheep men who would have the hills burnt drastically. It was a sore point between estate and tenant, between gamekeeper and shepherd.

'He's a bit of a tyrant,' said Iain.

'It's not better he's getting,' said his father, 'since the new landlord with the money came.' Then with a final look over his flock, he turned for home, and in a few moments Iain had the dogs nosing his hands.

He felt almost light-hearted now and spoke to the dogs in a friendly scoffing way. They so understood him that their eyes shone, and the young one, Mat, getting a trifle excited, lifted his paws against Iain's waist. Heath turned his head away from such youthful exuberance and bad form.

'How are you feeling to-day?'

'Fine,' Iain replied.

'Are you making a long stay?'

'Och, a few days.' Iain tried to speak lightly, but he felt the sudden pounding of his heart and a heat in his face.

His father waited, giving him the chance to say more, but now he could not speak.

His father turned his head and gave him a glance, then looked in front again. 'You'll be staying until April's in?'

'Yes, I think so,' said Iain. And because something had to be added, he murmured, 'Depends on how I feel.'

'You had a bad spell?'

'Yes, pretty bad. The doctor ordered me home just after I was ill – but – I thought I'd try and hang on.'

'There's nothing – nothing badly wrong?'

'No. I'm sound all right. Just – run down a bit.'

'I'm glad to hear that,' said his father and Iain caught the heavy relieved expulsion of breath.

They went on for a little way in silence.

'One of the reasons why I am asking you is about taking home the hoggs. I thought when I went for them maybe you could look after the sheep here.'

'But I could go for them,' said Iain at once, his voice lifting.

'No, no,' said his father. 'It'll take three good days to drive them home. And I would like to see them who have been doing the wintering.'

'But I could go – I would like to go,' said Iain, the eager-ness clear in his voice. Indeed the thought of getting away for a few days, doing useful work, all alone, suddenly obsessed him. To get away!

'It would be too much for you,' said his father. 'You would have a long, long last day coming over the pass. And there's none there to give a hand!'

'But I know the pass. Three years ago, when I went with you—' He stopped, suddenly remembering the quarrel that had smouldered between his parents over that trip.

'I know,' said his father. 'But it would be too much for you alone, and I wouldn't—'

'But it wouldn't,' declared Iain, interrupting his father in his eagerness. 'It's all walking. It's just what I need. I would like to do it very much.'

'Well, well, we'll see. We'll leave it like that. If you feel fit for it – we'll see.'

'I would rather do that,' said Iain, 'and leave you with the ewes – in case any of them needed anything.'

'There's that,' agreed his father, 'I know. And it would let me get on with a bit of ploughing. The earth is fine and dry for it. If the weather was good and you felt strong enough in yourself – we'll see how you do in the next few days.'

They began to talk about the wintering, where Iain would stay each night, the kind of decent men the farmers were, the rising cost of wintering, the tendency for ever more farms to carry sheep stock on their own, the 'changed days' and the uncertain future.

Iain suddenly wanted to tell his father something about the new ideas on hill sheep farming, the experiments which had been carried out in different places, research into grasses and diseases, the interest that real scientific men had in it all, but he felt shy, choked. He realized, however, that he could have come at it, roundabout, were it not for the false position in which he stood. The feeling of guilt, of cheating his father, came upon him in a paralysing way.

They topped the low ridge from which their home was visible and a large part of the valley beyond.

'Is that Ewan's cow getting an airing?' asked his father.

'Yes.'

'Our own would be none the worse of it. Did you hear that Ewan may be getting a bit of a legacy?'

'From old Donald Cameron, Balrain?'

'Ay. He's applying for it whatever, but it seems there's no record that Donald's father built the place. So whether he'll get it or not—'

'I think he'll get it,' said Iain.

'How do you think that?'

'I saw the papers. I saw your letter.'

'Did you indeed?' His father looked at him.

'Yes,' said Iain recklessly – then couldn't add another word.

'That's strange, now! Think of that!' His father was very interested and the small smile came on his face. 'Were you dealing with the case yourself – or did you just see it?'

'I didn't deal with cases. But sometimes my opinion was asked.' He took a deep breath. 'Once one of the bosses asked me about braxy. It seems a shepherd on one of their estates had been up to something. I told him what you had told me yourself about how shepherds used to clean and hang up the braxy mutton. He thought I knew a lot!'

'Did he now? And what had the shepherd been up to?'

'Some question about loss of sheep. I couldn't ask, he had so many questions to put to me about sheep farming.'

'Was that Mr Cunningham himself?'

'No, another partner.'

'There will be more than one?'

'Three altogether.'

'And a few working for them besides?'

'There are nine typists – girls – doing nothing but typing.'

His father's face was full of wonder. 'I have only had a few words twice with Mr Cunningham, but he struck me as being a real gentleman.' He paused, then added, 'I am glad you are getting on well, Iain.'

Iain remained silent. For a little while his father seemed to be thinking over what Iain had said; then he paused, looking at a breach in the sheep fank. Before he might ask any more questions, Iain muttered something about his granny and went on. Despite himself, he stumbled once, his legs were trembling so violently.

THREE

It was an impossible position. He would have to tell his father and be done with it. The longer he put it off, the more difficult it would be. Already it was getting beyond him, and when he found thoughts in his head about leaving a letter for his father and slipping away secretively, his body burned.

It's not that he minded what he had done, he told himself, sitting in the Dell in the afternoon. He would never go back to the office in Edinburgh, to that kind of life, not though they tore him to pieces. But while his thought flared in this wild extravagance, he became aware that one quiet corner of his mind was working out how he might yet be able to return to Edinburgh, without his father or anyone else in Balmore ever learning the real reason for his coming home.

This seemed so ultimate a betrayal of himself that he grovelled where he sat and tore fistfuls of fog from the ground. But presently, like one fatally fascinated, he was working it out. He would have to act swiftly. To stop any possible inquiry from the office – they were bound to give him some days before they moved – he could go and wire now saying he was returning on a certain date. He could follow up the wire with a letter to Mr Cunningham, apologizing for what he had done, and requesting a few days' leave, as he had never felt very well since his illness. Mention of his illness in such a way might be accepted as a sort of natural excuse for his outbreak. It was known in the office that Smeaton had often provoked him. Anyway, it would clear the ground now. It would clear his own mind also, and he could fix the date for his return just after he had brought home the wintered hoggs. It would give him that wonderful excursion, these days all alone with the sheep on the hills, as a last gift from his own land. When he got back to Edinburgh he would face up to the music. For it didn't matter two hoots what actually happened in Edinburgh. Not a tuppenny toss.

His mind slowly drained, and like one in a hypnotic sleep he sat staring at the dull bronze of dead bracken. His breathing was heavy and regular. Then he stirred and his eyes looked unseeingly here and there, his lips apart like one listening. Quite clearly he heard the words, 'I'll never do that.'

They were calm words, but in a moment his throat repeated them, and now they sounded like a curse. 'By God, I'll never do that!' he cried, his young face contorted.

Up above there was a sudden crashing of bushes; a head and horns came through; hind legs, stiffened and thrust forward, ploughed the downslope, as the beast glissaded into the Dell. Her udder swung, her huge eyes flamed, there was a slaver at her mouth, as she got squarely on her legs and tossed her head. Then she saw Iain, stuck out her forelegs in recoil, glared at him, and gave a terrific bellow. Gathering herself, she flung out her hind legs in wild abandon, and danced. Ewan Cameron's old cow was welcoming the spring.

Down into the Dell came Mary, rushing, calling 'Bess! Bess! . . .' in an angry, frightened voice. Her face was flushed, her eyes glowing, her hair tangled by the bushes. The brown jumper had been jerked clear in front from the belt about her tweed skirt.

Catching sight of the cow, she stopped in her tracks like a hind; her body quivered in an anxiety so vivid that Iain heard its silent cry. He never moved, but in an instant, as if she had sensed him, her eyes were on him; they widened and stared.

He got to his feet. 'You shouldn't be running her like that,' he said.

The taut abnormally arrested expression relaxed, and the blood flooded her face. 'I wasn't,' she answered.

'It's dangerous,' he continued in a natural way. The cow had stopped at a little distance and his eyes were on her critically. 'Give her time.'

'I was trying to turn her back.' Her breathing, quickened from running, heightened her voice in a heart-catching way.

'I think she's all right.' Then his expression narrowed. Bess looked as if she were going to lie down. 'When is she due to calf?'

'Not for nearly a month yet.'

He nodded, then his expression relaxed as Bess's rather awkward movements finished in no more than an effort to lick a remote part of her haunch. 'I don't think there's much wrong. But give her time.'

'Father thought she needed an airing. Usually she stands, mooing, wanting back to the byre. But to-day she made off.'

'The spring,' he said, with a small dry smile directed at the cow.

Mary caught sight of her disordered jumper and began tucking it in hurriedly. Iain moved slowly towards the beast. 'Hullo, Bess! What have you been up to, you old fool?' His voice was rough and friendly.

The cow looked at him and with shut mouth emitted a disgruntled moo. The glistening light was still in her eyes. She glanced about her as if searching, under some awakened atavistic instinct, for a secret bed. Then suddenly, as though the instinct had evaporated, she started up the slope, which at this point was not so steep as at the place of her entry. They followed her until they came into the fringe of small birch trees. She was making straight for the byre.

'I think she's all right,' said Iain.

'Oh, I hope so. I'll go and see.' And at once Mary started off.

Iain watched her for a little while, then went down into the heart of the Dell, where she had come upon him, stood for a little while, moved slowly on and out of the Dell, and, swinging round, began to stroll up to Ewan's cottage.

As Mary came out of the byre door she said, 'Here's Iain,' and with a confused smile hurried to the house.

Ewan appeared. 'Hul-lo! if it isn't Iain himself!' He shook hands with Iain heartily, scanning his face. 'And they told me you weren't well! What things people will say!'

'No accounting for it,' agreed Iain.

Ewan laughed. 'Tell me, boy. You're all right? What?'

'Never better,' said Iain.

'That's the lad! And they had you dying of all sorts of diseases! Man, it's grand to see you.'

It was Ewan's way of finding out if there was anything real wrong. Plainly he was yet far from certain, but the country warmth came about Iain's heart.

'I thought you had more sense than to let a cow in calf go dancing about the braes.'

'Just say it!' agreed Ewan. 'I didn't think the old fool had it in her, though there's no fool like an old one as I ought to know. Last spring she came home from the bull and I thought everything was all right, but back she had to go again. That's why she's so late. Enjoying life!'

Mary came with a bucket of warm water and Ewan, making a bran mash, explained the virtues of drink generally. Iain completely forgot his private trouble.

As they left the byre, however, he paused and said he would have to be getting home.

'Whatever for?' demanded Ewan.

'That grandmother of mine,' explained Iain. 'It's time for my beat-up egg!'

Ewan turned to his daughter. 'Mary!'

'No, no!' cried Iain, but Mary was gone.

'Come away into the shop,' said Ewan, 'and don't stand there like a gaping country loon. I thought the city would have taught you better manners.'

Iain was interested in the work in progress in the shop, and Mary found them laughing when she came with the tumbler, yellow-rich and frothed.

Presently she told him that the school had just closed for the Easter holidays, and, to a further question, replied that she thought she had done 'fairly well' in her Higher Leaving Examination. He asked about other scholars and soon she was talking quite naturally, holding her own with the two men. It was like old times. Iain felt he had wandered into a dimension of the past where happiness had always been, and when Ewan asked something about Edinburgh, Iain dismissed it in an airy way that left them laughing.

'Go off home for your fiddle,' urged Ewan suddenly. 'There's not a whole string left on my own, for indeed I haven't touched it since I saw you last. Go on!'

'Did you even hear I brought the fiddle?'

'The fiddle, is it? Wasn't I looking out my hard hat for your funeral!'

But Iain refused to go. 'Later,' he said. 'We'll see.'

'And Mary will give us a song.'

Iain looked at her with a teasing directness. 'Will you?'

'Will you go for your fiddle?' she asked.

'Will you, if I will?'

She took a moment. 'I might.'

'She never had the direct word for me,' Iain said to Ewan sadly.

Ewan recalled an incident of their early school days when she had been direct enough. This set them warmly remembering and laughing. Half-an-hour later Iain left, promising to return the following evening. The thought of sending a telegram to Edinburgh had vanished from his mind.

FOUR

'No, you don't,' replied Iain flatly.

'But I say the estate does,' repeated Alan with a flash from his dark eyes.

'I don't care what you say; you don't know. Neither does the estate.'

'You'll know, I suppose?'

Iain smiled drily. 'I know that much anyhow.'

'You seem to know a lot,' said Alan. 'I didn't know they burnt heather in Edinburgh.'

'They don't,' said Iain. 'But some of them use their brains.'

It was too brutal a retort and Alan went pale. Hamish and Hughie smiled. Big Andrew stretched himself. Mary set some peat on edge and Iain saw the tongs shake slightly in her hands; she had been more than a trifle excited since Alan had come in.

Ewan turned to Andrew with a humoured smile. 'They'll be teaching you how to suck the egg next, Andrew.'

'Oh, I'm hearing them!' said Andrew. 'It's the young dog for the barking.'

Iain laughed.

'It's a matter of fact,' said Alan, trying to smile.

Instantly Iain switched his look on him. 'What fact?'

'Look now,' said Ewan. 'We know about heather burning. We know of the old quarrel between the gamekeeper and the man who has the sheep. You can't tell us anything about that, Iain—'

'How do you know?' asked Iain.

Ewan looked at him. 'Just as I know that you sometimes haven't a great deal of sense.'

Iain knew perfectly well what Ewan meant. It was Ewan's house and Alan must not be provoked beyond courtesy. This, however, merely hardened his own mood. Why specially consider Alan?

'Sense is not the point here,' he said. 'It's a matter of knowledge. Alan hasn't that knowledge; neither, so far as I know, have you or Andrew.' His smiling eyes had a cool hard glint in them.

'What knowledge?' asked Hamish.

'About the heather plant – how it lives, how often it should be burnt, why, and so on. Do you know exactly? Does anyone?'

'We know the old heather should be burnt off so that the sheep may have the young growth to eat. And we know we never get enough of it burnt off,' said Hamish.

'Supposing we owned the estate and wiped out Finlay and the sporting side, what plan would we draw up for burning the hill?'

'This is high science!' declared Andrew.

'You may smile,' said Iain, 'but there it is. If I asked Alan how often on the average Finlay burnt the old heather, I'm prepared to bet he couldn't tell me to within – let me see – ten years.'

There was a moment's silence.

'Could *you*?' asked Ewan and there was a sharpness in his voice.

'No,' replied Iain. 'That's the point.'

'What's the point?'

'That we don't know,' answered Iain coolly. 'I'm prepared to guess at an average of once perhaps every thirty odd years.'

'That's absurd,' said Alan explosively.

'Merely a guess,' replied Iain calmly. 'If you know better – tell us.'

'If you think that Major Grant and Finlay and people who have been carrying on the estate for generations don't know what they're doing! . . .' Alan choked on his own sarcasm.

'I can give you my opinion of what they have been doing in no uncertain terms,' replied Iain in the same even tone. 'But that's not the point.'

'You're as full of points as a thorn bush,' declared Ewan, with a glance that did not veil his annoyance. Mary got up and went into the small back kitchen.

'How often would you burn it?' asked Hughie.

Iain smiled and remained silent.

The discomfort in Ewan's kitchen became palpable.

'Why you didn't bring your fiddle with you instead of all this talk!' Ewan leaned forward and lit a paper spill at the fire.

'That would indeed have been to the point,' agreed Andrew, taking out his own pipe.

Iain knew he was behaving badly, but he couldn't help himself; and Hamish, with a dark glint in his eye, would not now let the subject lie, so he challenged and provoked Iain.

'My own plan,' said Hamish finally, 'would be to set a match to the hill and let it rip.' Talking thus against Alan, against the estate, was like being on a secret poaching foray.

'I've seen you plan better than that,' suggested Iain.

Hamish laughed. And in a moment it was as if Hamish, Hughie and Iain were together. Looking at Hamish and deliberately ignoring the others, Iain said, 'It's just a problem like any other – like stalking or catching a salmon. If you were going to burn all the heather off at once, how were the sheep going to live until the young heather grew? There must be the grown salmon as well as the spawn – or there will be no fish for a while, if you see what I mean?'

'I think I follow,' said Hamish.

'The sheep like the new heather, the young fresh buds. So your problem simply is how to provide them with that kind of heather at the maximum amount without doing damage to the heather plant. Is that clear?'

'Clear as the river water,' said Hamish.

'Those who have studied the thing,' continued Iain, 'as "high science", say that for the first two years or so the young plants live on the strength stored in the base, the roots, of the burnt heather. So if the sheep ate up all that young growth they'd be killing the plant. It takes another four or five years for the plant to become properly established again as a going concern. So for the first three years give it half a chance to get strong. Then burn about every fifteen years or so. In that way you could carry a heavier stock, and that would mean more manure dropped on the ground. It would also mean the burning out of other rough stuff. You'd be making the best of your hill.'

'And where would Finlay come in?' asked Hamish.

'He wouldn't,' said Iain.

Hamish chuckled, delighted.

'Man, that's interesting,' said Andrew slowly, 'about the heather. Where did you find out all that?'

'From fellows who have been studying the subject and making experiments,' replied Iain.

'It's wonderful right enough what they find out nowadays,' continued Andrew. 'You were talking a little while ago about grass, before we got landed in the heather . . .'

Hughie laughed.

But though Andrew told his tale with natural ease, the harmony that always underlay the hottest give-and-take of argument in Ewan's kitchen was not restored. Alan was silent, and looked as if he might get up and go at any minute. And Iain, as though regretting his parade of knowledge, had corrected Andrew on a scientific detail, but shortly and only after having been appealed to. Mary had come back into the kitchen and was quietly knitting.

Presently Iain got up. 'I promised my granny I'd be home early,' he said with an air of innocence.

Hamish began to laugh, and got to his feet still laughing.

Ewan's brows gathered.

Andrew glanced at the clock. 'Lord, it's not that time!'

'What's your hurry?' asked Ewan. 'You're not all invalids.'

Within a few minutes, amid calls of good night, the door closed, and four men walked away, leaving only Alan behind.

FIVE

Major Grant stirred in his office chair. 'What's this?' he said aloud. Alan looked round quickly, but Major Grant had spoken to himself. His expression was concentrated on the letter in his hand. When he had read it to the end, he slowly placed it on the table. Someone is in for trouble! thought Alan, quietly going on with his work. The post had just come in.

'Iain Cattanach is at home?'

Alan swung round on his office stool. 'Yes, he came home last week.'

'Why?'

'They say he's not well.'

'Is that his story?'

'Yes—' Alan overbalanced but caught the tall stool before it fell.

'Have you seen him?'

'Yes, I met him.'

'Is he ill?'

'He doesn't look ill.'

'I mean is he in bed or is he going about?'

'Oh, he's going about.'

Major Grant remained narrowly, vengefully thoughtful, then continued with his post. He dictated three short letters, which Alan scribbled in long hand as swiftly as he could, then got up and went out. At once Alan slipped round and began reading the disturbing letter. Before he had finished he heard his employer's returning footsteps and quickly got onto his stool. Major Grant came in, picked up the letter, and went out again. In a few minutes he drove off in his car. Alan's dark face gleamed with an astonished triumph.

Duncan Cattanach heard the car's siren and went to meet Major Grant.

After the greeting, Major Grant at once asked, 'Is your son Iain about?'

'No, Major. He left this morning for Strathorn – to bring home the hoggs.'

'I thought he wasn't well?'

'He hasn't been well. But – he's getting on.'

Major Grant remained silent.

'I hope there's nothing wrong?' asked Cattanach quietly, his eyes on the Major.

'If he is fit enough to go for the hoggs, don't you think he's fit enough for his work?'

'Yes,' said Cattanach. 'I thought of that.'

'Did he say he wasn't well?'

'He had a bad illness in the beginning of the year, and – the doctor ordered him a few days at home.'

'So that's his story? I am very sorry to tell you, Mr Cattanach, that it is not true. I have just had a letter from Mr Cunningham.'

Cattanach remained quite still, his eyes on the Major.

'He's let me down badly. It's the first time I ever asked that kind of favour from the head office. I did it for his mother's sake. I can't say he has repaid her – or me.'

Cattanach neither moved nor spoke.

'It's an ugly story,' continued the Major. Then he glanced sharply at Cattanach. 'Did he drink, do you know?'

'Not that I know.'

'Well, he ran amok in the office. He shoved one gentleman through a glass door. They had to put nine stitches in him. Fortunately, for your son, it appears he is recovering.'

A bleak wind seemed to pass over Cattanach's face, draining it upon the bone.

'I knew this gentleman. Very polite, clever man, of a good family. He has always been helpful to me, in correspondence and when I call on them in Edinburgh. A real gentleman, with his legal degree. I am very upset about it. I don't know whether he will prosecute your son or not. Mr Cunningham does not say. He asks me if I know where your son is. After his bloody attack, he walked out of the office and they haven't seen or heard from him since.' The Major's anger found increasing outlet as he spoke. Now he glanced at the bleak face before him. 'I am sorry to have to tell you this.'

'Yes,' said the old man, rather stupidly the Major thought.

'When your son comes back, tell him I want to see him.'

'Yes.'

The Major hesitated, then, muttering something, strode away.

He was now very angry. After going about fifty paces, he paused. The old man was still standing where he had left him, but now he turned and began slowly walking away. Behind the bleakness, the silence, there had been a curious sort of deadly power; a slow remorseless gathering of power about the bleakness.

'The bloody young swine,' said the Major, going on again. He was all the angrier because at the end of his letter Mr Cunningham had said that Iain had up to that point behaved in a normal way, was intelligent, and may have been provoked. It was so decent of Mr Cunningham to put it like that, almost as if another chance might be arranged for the boy somewhere, that the Major was furious. Another chance! And Mr Henderson and Miss Henderson seeing the whole shocking business!

This confirmed Finlay. There could be no doubt about it. Finlay had said that Hamish MacPherson had been on the off bank of the river when he, the Major, had been pushed in. When Finlay crossed over he saw a young fellow make off. There must have been two on the Major's side: the fellow he was going to flash his torch on and the fellow who charged him off the rock. Finlay was quite sure that Iain Cattanach was one. Had he not even seen him, after playing for a dance, pat the sleeves of his jacket unthinkingly in the way a man does whose sleeves are wet?

At the time, he had thought Finlay, annoyed at having been foiled, was merely trying to justify himself in a silly way and had charged him rather sharply to say nothing about it. You don't hang a man, he had said sarcastically, because he pats his sleeves.

Nine stitches! Through a glass door! Charging a man into a pool, under cover of darkness, was a simple performance in comparison!

The Major stalked on. This murderous young tough would confess on his knees!

SIX

Iain lay on his back and looked at the sky. The blue was obscured by a smoky haze. The same fine haze as was on the distant hills; like a drift of smoke from heath fires in some other country.

His mind lifted and spread with the haze, so that his body felt inexpressibly lightened. He smiled sensibly at this, with a twinkle of humour, and in a moment was aware of a rare sensation of ease and harmony. He forgot his normal self altogether; or at least he seemed to be everywhere, like an eye in the air, a thought in the distance, light as the haze which had summer in it but also a curious veiled sadness. It was a sadness, however, which did not weigh upon the spirit but invited it. Beyond its dim-blue veil was a coming sunlight; beyond the hills of time were summer days.

Movement was snared in the corner of his eye. Turning his head slightly, he saw the young sheep rearing towards the slender wand of broom. Now it had caught the tip and pulled it down. But immediately it opened its mouth to bite, the wand swung upward. Again the sheep reared on its hind legs, and again the same thing happened. It was an amusing but beautiful picture; the lips moved so quickly, delicately, and the tender wand played its airy game. In the end, the young beast did not open its mouth until it had, after much pulling and nodding, broken off the tip it held. Good for you! thought Iain.

One night more and then he would be home. It had been a fine time. Everything had gone perfectly and in the two farms where he had stayed everyone had been kind, asking questions, of course, but also telling some rare stories about old days, full of dogs and snowstorms and 'characters'. Once you were really interested in a way of life, it was extraordinary how much you could find out about it from others, and how ready they were to tell you. This morning, before he left, the farmer had insisted on showing him the spot where the farmer's own father had made the one and only experiment in pit silage in Strathorn. The slightly hollowed base of a rock, cement, sand . . . the evidence was still there, after more than twenty years. 'For the first two weeks after the pit was opened, it was splendid stuff, rich and satisfying. But then – you couldn't go near it for the smell; rotten wasn't the word! . . .'

Iain smiled to the sky. There were men everywhere who were prepared to experiment. It was a heartening thought. His eyes closed, and now small sounds came upon him that, though near at hand, belonged to space. His mind wandered, following them.

He shivered as he sat up. The air had a wintry nip. Heath, watching him, lifted his head. 'Still there, are you?' Iain got to his feet, shoved the empty bottle, which had been full of creamy milk, into a hole. Heath had had his liberal share of the bread and bannocks with which the farmer's wife had laden him. 'Come on, then, old boy.'

Iain began to observe odd symptoms of weariness among his flock. They were all young ewes, barely a year old and some of them, by nature not too strong, were no doubt growing tired of long days on a hard country road. His concern, however, grew and when at last he could no longer conceal from himself that a beast had staggered for no apparent reason, a throb of alarm went through him.

Within half an hour he was certain that over a dozen sheep had contracted a fatal disease. He collared one of them with his crook. The droop of the ears, the expression of the eyes – there was no doubt about it, the brute was half-stupefied, and when he let it go in dismay it staggered and fell. It got to its feet again in a lunging awkward way, turning in a half-circle as it staggered on. *Sturdy!*

Iain felt the blood drain from him where he stood, unable to move, on the middle of the road. He knew that sturdy was caused by a bladder-worm in the brain, from larvæ which the grazing sheep swallowed. He had been told, or read about, the symptoms. And hadn't Andrew said sometime that Iain's own father could operate – by cutting down into the skull between the ears – and lifting out the watery sac? But it might be some other disease. He didn't know. He hadn't the knowledge. He felt like an inexperienced child confronted by an appalling, an obliterating calamity.

A coldness crinkled over his skin. There were some crofters' hoggs in the flock. His father always arranged for their hoggs, without any charge beyond the basic cost of wintering. Just as he arranged for their dipping in his own dipping trough. In return, they gave labour at shearing, dipping, harvesting. It was a communal effort, with its own give and take, but there was always a final ordering and responsibility upon his father. Andrew McAndrew, Geordie Farquharson . . .

A whole stretch of the glen at home sank under his feet. He felt it giving way, but pulled himself together, pulled the road up. Heath was looking at him out of the corners of his eyes, head lowered; the faithful brute was aware of the calamity, felt the shame, like a fellow criminal.

Now he saw sheep stumbling all along the road-sides. In an instant he was convinced that disease had swept the whole flock. But he was not responsible, if it was disease. A brain cyst couldn't grow in a couple of days! It would be terrible enough to bring home the fatal news; it would be his rotten luck, the curse in his luck that would finish him, but at least he couldn't help it. So acute became the sense of calamity, so intense, overwhelming, his dismay, that he all but wept on his feet.

Then so personal a reaction as weeping – or cursing – withered, shrivelled up, in a new appalling realization. It was not sturdy, they were not staggering round in circles. He watched one here and there. They were stupefied, couldn't control their movements properly. Their blood was poisoned . . . toxaemia . . . *Braxy!*

The disease about which he knew so much!

The coldness crawled along the bone, cooled his brain to an extreme clarity. The disease that affected hoggs in particular. Caused by a change in diet, said his father; by an organism, said the scientist. By feeding anyhow; by something picked up, swallowed. By something they had eaten – under his care!

The disease was quite fatal – fatal within a few hours. Not even the scientists knew any treatment once the symptoms were seen. They would presently fall and die, a dead flock scattered about and the braxy stench would sicken the very air. He saw them lying dead, grey humps here and there.

His eyes lifted and roamed, glittered in the sunless air, but the last farm, Altbreac, was still not in sight. There was no house in sight, no-one.

Automatically he put out an arm, and Heath silently, stealthily, got the sheep going along the road again. He walked slowly, giving them time. The river of heads moved up and down and for a little he wondered if he had been the victim of an illusion. Then here – there – a stoppage, a small commotion. And Heath knew. He did not rush, urging them on. He stopped and looked back at Iain.

There was a rise in the narrow country road in front. The grey backs began to flow up it slowly. Some of the beasts crowded against the bank at one point, to snatch a bite. One of them leapt up, and as Iain shot his arm out, Heath immediately sprang off the road. The sheep stumbled, fell. Iain roared at Heath, but his voice went all high-pitched and ragged; was more a scream than an order.

That sobered him; wildly angered him. He swore at Heath violently, swore at himself. The fighting mood was rising. By the time he topped the gradient several of the sheep were down. Their eyes were glazed. As they struggled to their feet before him, he stopped. Then he saw Altbreac farm house.

'Down! Down!' He pointed at Heath imperiously, his eyes blazing, then began to run for the farm house.

It stood about half-a-mile away on the slope to the right. He cleared ditches and fences, like one being hunted. When he saw the farmer, he eased up at once, controlling his gasping, wiping the spittle from his lips.

Torquil Macfadyen was a big man, without any perceptible neck, so that his chin seemed to lie upon his outjutting barrel chest. He stood, a solid mass of flesh and bone, looking at Iain with narrow eyes.

Iain stopped, smiled uncertainly. 'I'm driving some hoggs home,' he said as casually as he could. 'I think something's gone wrong with them.'

'Wrong?'

'Yes. They're – they're staggering a bit.'

'Are you from Balmore?'

'Yes. My father is Duncan Cattanach.'

'Oh!' The chin lifted. 'So you're Duncan Cattanach's son?' The chin came down in a nod. 'Many a year I've known your father. How is he?'

'Fine.'

'Oh, man, I know your father well. So you're his son? Are you the one who plays the fiddle?'

'Yes.'

'Good enough!' A shrewd smile lightened the dark-blue searching eyes. 'You'll be Iain? Your father was never a man to blow, but I could see he was proud of the way you picked up the fiddle-playing as a nipper! Come away in and see the Mistress.'

'But – I – the sheep—'

'Oh ay. I saw you running. So you're Iain Cattanach? Come in now till I show you to the Mistress.'

Iain had to follow his great back and stumping legs. 'Hey, Bella!'

At the roar, a small middle-aged woman, busked tidily, appeared at the kitchen door. She had the bluest eyes Iain had ever seen; the blue of smoke, the bright roundness of beads, full of merry kindness; and she had the manners to match them.

Ten minutes later he was still in the house, answering questions. 'Hadn't I always to watch her when your father was about!' declared Torquil.

'Be quiet, you great fool,' she said, pretending a shame of her husband's manners that sat on her lightly. 'Wasn't it the other way round indeed, for I was ashamed of the way he would be offering your father dram after dram, thinking decent men were like himself. But many a good night we had here in the years gone by. I will say that. But dear me! here we are at the talking already and you must be starving!' She bounced to her feet.

'I must,' stuttered Iain, 'see about – about the sheep.'

'The sheep!' she cried, 'Never mind the sheep. Well they know how to look after themselves. You'll just wait and have your tea first. Plenty of time for the sheep. But now you'll excuse me?' And off she hurried.

'I can see you're anxious about your sheep. Eh? It's the first time you will ever have had a drove of them on your own?'

'Yes,' said Iain.

'You'll be going to rest them over by in Knockan for the night?'

'Yes. How far is it?'

'Och, not far. A little over the two miles. Plenty of time. That will give you a long day on the mountains to-morrow. And you'd be as well to be over them. There's snow not far off or I'm a Dutchman.'

Iain was turning his cap in his hand. 'Will you come and have a look at them?'

'Surely. Do you think they're more than tired?'

'Yes. I think – there's something far wrong.'

'How that?'

'They're staggering – and falling – like – like braxy.'

'Braxy! Good God, boy, are you off your head? Come on, then, till we see.' Torquil shouted into the kitchen, 'We're going out for a whilie!'

'Dear me! Can't you let the boy rest for a few minutes itself?' She shook her head. 'Oh, that man!'

Torquil was in no hurry. Now and then he glanced at Iain, told about 'wild nights' with his father and glanced again to see the effect, as if he were getting the boy's measure. Iain was aware of all this, and strove for balance; felt like one stepping on slipping stones in a river, but kept his head up, smiled and answered.

But presently Torquil stopped. 'By God, boy, I can see there's a round score and a half of them down!' He now went lunging on. The bulk of the drove was nibbling away, but what had been the odd staggerer a short time ago was over thirty in collapse now. Torquil stood for some time gazing at them; then he approached the nearest one. It tried to get to its feet but he put his arm round its neck. He examined the eyes, the mouth, forced the mouth open, dropped the beast and went on to the next. Five he examined, then he wiped his great hands on his buttocks.

Iain stood still and straight, waiting.

Torquil looked at him solemnly. 'They're bad,' he said. 'You know braxy is deadly? There's no cure.'

'I know,' said Iain clearly. His eyebrows gathered.

Torquil saw the hawk-like look. 'What'll you say to them – when you get home?'

'I'll tell them,' said Iain. But it was as if he had said, 'What do you think I would do – run away?' He turned, under a blind impulse to be alone. A great hand landed on his shoulder with a whack that staggered him.

'By God,' roared Torquil, 'you're the son of your father!' Laughter came bellowing out of him.

Iain swung round, his eyes on fire.

Torquil could not stop laughing, looked like a man who had been drinking.

'Do you know what's wrong with them?' cried Torquil.

Iain waited like a taut whip.

'They're drunk!' roared Torquil. 'Drunk as owls!' And then: 'They've been eating the young broom.'

Five minutes later, Iain sat down on the roadside. He could not hide the trembling of his muscles.

'I thought – they were finished,' he excused himself.

'Damn me, you have spunk!' declared Torquil. 'And you were not to know. Very few do. I have only seen one real drunk of that kind – and then we had to take them home in carts and vans. But yours are not bad. Man,' he said, beginning to laugh again, 'it's the only joke I've had in a long while.'

Iain let him laugh. Any sound was music now. And presently Torquil said, 'That settles it. There's no Knockan for you this night. We'll fold them in my park, and now we must keep them going. That's the cure.' He began to laugh as he heaved a reluctant sheep on. 'By George, I could see you were in a bit of a state!' When he had finished laughing, he said, 'The wife will give you a bed, and you'll give her a tune.'

After supper, a wiry man, with thin close-cropped greying hair, crooked somewhat from labour on the land, came in with a fiddle. His spare clean-shaven face had a shy intelligent smile. Iain instantly warmed to the face, as to an unexpected beauty in a remote place or a distant time. Clearly he was related to Mrs Macfadyen by the light in his eyes. He offered Iain the fiddle.

Iain politely declined it, but Torquil tore through the tissue of courtesies: 'We're tired of hearing Jamie playing. Up with it!' he said to Iain. 'And by George I'll be able then to tell your father if it was blowing he was or not!'

Iain smiled and took the fiddle. He was in the mood to give Torquil the hidden thanks. His heart moved in him. He began tuning the instrument. 'It's got a fine tone. You keep it well,' he said, smiling to Jamie.

A new instrument was always a little strange to Iain, somewhat harsh to his ear, but this instrument, like Jamie's face, was known to him at once, so that it seemed even more intimate than his own fiddle, with an added smoothness and delicacy. In the quiet tuning, it spoke and sang to him. He could hardly start playing, and indeed for a moment or two he could not. Remotely fingers and bow searched for the heart of the instrument, for the melody they did not want to find. He was now on his feet. He should ask them: 'What would you like?' But the bow and his fingers were finding the small clear notes, and now the notes were finding a rhythm, at first with such reluctance that when the pattern of the Irish jig, to which the Irishman had danced on the cobbled street in Edinburgh, became discernible, it was with a curious surprise to listening ears, surprise that there should be so little life in it. Then, as if indeed first heard at a distance, the notes came nearer, growing firm as they came, gathering body, gathering decision, taking power upon them and mastery, until they flew from the instrument with a pride of precision that made the very air dance and leap with man's unconquerable blood. And suddenly Iain found – the rare and lovely power! – that he could take his time, that nothing could go wrong. He had time to see the Irishman, to glimpse at least his decisive movements, to inform them with the swift long sweep of the bow that was courtesy's pause where yet there was no pause, and when he finished it was with the obliterating snap of the living feet.

He took the fiddle from his chin and thumbed the E string. Even Torquil did not speak. In the silence, Iain lifted the fiddle again. He was in love with it. It washed away all the days. Again he did not know what he was going to play. He did not care. He had come home.

The Eriskay song started to play on its own, and at first it was the song, but presently – the delight that this instrument could anticipate his very wish! – it was the wind, the wind round a house at night, round the mountains in a storm, and, ignoring all musical notation, he lifted and sustained the elemental rhythms, sank with them, immense waves of primeval power, the human voice lost in them, yet not altogether lost, haunting them, and at last coming through into the song, but quietened, if with surges still, and finishing with the one long note that imperceptibly died as the bow drew to its tip.

Iain, knowing he had moved them, was shy of looking at their faces.

'By God, you've done it now!' said Torquil with a great breath.

But Bella his wife did not heed him. She wiped her eyes and smiled.

'She'll sing to you next!' cried Torquil, laughing under stress.

And before the night was over she did sing. She hadn't much of a voice; it was small and went a little thin, but it had an intimacy, a naïveté, that was profoundly moving, as simple things in nature are moving, an unexpected primrose in a ditch, the movement of an animal's head at an odd moment, the sight of a burn forever running by the same bank, the same trees, the lie of a landscape, the still line of a hill. The quality of her voice hardly mattered; just as the physical features of Jamie's lean face hardly mattered. Beyond sound and line lay the immortal well, and those who drank knew one another.

SEVEN

About a mile from the house, Torquil stopped. 'It was a great night last night! And you wouldn't be going home this night either, if I didn't smell the snow.' He looked at the distant haze, a darkness now in its blue. 'It's got a root in it like the root in a boil.' He laughed. 'Tell your father from me that he wasn't blowing. So long, and take care of yourself.' But he had only gone a step or two when he let out a roar. 'Will you look at her!' he bellowed derisively.

Iain saw Mrs Macfadyen waving to him. He took off his cap and swung it round his head.

'You're worse than your father with her!' shouted Torquil. Then Iain was going on alone.

Of the nights spent away from home, last night was certainly the 'appex'! thought Iain, his eyes glimmering with good humour, his face warm. The sheep were completely recovered. Indeed the effects of the drunkenness had worn off very quickly and he suspected that Torquil had been glad of an excuse to do Duncan Cattanach's son a good turn and at the same time have him for a night's entertainment. Altbreac was the last, the highest, farm in Strathorn and something of the old native life had lingered about it. Dash it, they're nice folk! he thought. He would like to go back there some time, get Jamie alone and listen to him. At first glance there was a fleshy uncouthness about Torquil, a sort of menacing brutal strength, but inside he was full of a wild humour, with a watchful eye for the effects he wanted. Obviously he doted on his wife.

Iain began to think of his own father and his 'wild nights' with Torquil. What was his father like then? He had wanted to ask Torquil but had felt shy; in truth, the thought of it still made him a trifle uncomfortable, but pleasantly so, for there was something friendly, something right, in the notion of his father's opening out and having a good time. Carrying on the old tradition! Had he known what he knew now, he would certainly have let his father take home the hoggs. Often enough, at the clipping or dipping, he had seen his father's eyes grow merry.

He began to think of his mother – and to wonder. Lifting his eyes, he saw the small homestead of Knockan away on his right at the base of the hill. He was now over the burn and the sheep were beginning the long slanting ascent for the passes, leaving Knockan behind. When he looked again at the house he saw a woman standing clear of the gable-end and saluted her with his stick. She waved, then stood still. She'll be wondering who I am, he thought, smiling to himself. He kept his eye on her. She did not move, and somehow her loneliness, her wonder, touched his heart. He took off his cap and waved it back and fore. She answered with an arm, and he saw that she was not old, perhaps thirty or less. She remained there for quite a while, then went slowly into the house.

He could not help smiling to himself. It was more than a meeting: a meeting and a farewell at the same time. How strange and friendly life was! He thought of the woman as he went on, and little pictures formed in his mind, flashed in movement, in attitudes of greeting. The quickening of human beings meeting in a lonely place. The living mystery in the eyes. The warmth.

As he looked at his flock going patiently on, nibbling when they could, he saw how young they were, saw the delicate bone of the lamb in the lines of the face, saw the lamb-life from which they were bidding farewell, coming through. Very gentle they looked, and innocent, sprightly and shapely, with their black masks, black legs and neat pointed feet, and small pointed horns. They would be shorn for the first time this summer. After that they would be called gimmers. First the lamb, then the hogg, then the gimmer, and finally the breeding ewe. He did not hurry them, even if, by not staying at Knockan, he had lost a couple of hours. Their life cycle was short enough. His own seemed very long. There was no need for haste.

Strathorn fell away and now before him rolled a waste of moor, with hill-lines for distant horizon. The track, with its occasional cart ruts overgrown by long heather, wandered by hags and boggy places. In the old days this had been a highway of communication. Now it was slowly being taken back by the moor. In the softer patches, it had already completely disappeared.

Towards noon, he saw some of the sheep overflow onto marshy ground, and he smiled as one beast stuck her face to the eyes in water. Was this the morning after the night before? But up came her face with a pale-green shoot in her mouth which she consumed with obvious relish. He downed Heath and went nearer the sheep, watched them, examined a plant himself. The famous draw-moss or cotton-grass! It came at a time when most growing things were dead. 'The hill's salvation', he had heard it called. And this time he knew he was making no mistake, for he had seen it before, though he had never, as now, 'come upon it', with the feeling of surprise and discovery. Later it grew coarse and was of no use for feeding.

Only of use for poetry and songs, when with its puffs of cotton, its little white flags dancing in the wind, it was called 'canna' or 'cannach'.

Smiling with a rare delight, he drew Heath off and found a sheltered spot in a hag. The wind was on the move, gently, but very cold. Snow was in the offing beyond doubt. Ever since his father had smelt it, there had been a hanging and hardening in the weather's core. A gripping at the root of the boil! He laughed.

The milk would hardly flow from the bottle, the neck was so choked with cream. And how Bella expected him to wade through this parcel of food, he did not know! Scones and oat-cakes, stuck with butter and crowdie. Two hard boiled eggs. A slice of white home-made cheese, brittle and strong in the smell . . . 'We'll divide it like this,' he told Heath, and having put on one side what he thought they should eat, he parcelled up the rest. Heath had very good manners. He did not snap, did not look unduly anxious. The final scraps disappeared with a quiet celerity, and if he nosed about the heather once it was clearly to ensure that nothing had been left. Iain smiled. 'We're getting to know each other a little, what?' He patted the head in the rough friendly way that showed no undue emotion. Heath wagged his tail once. It was all right. Then Iain found himself looking into the dog's eyes – for a long moment, before he withdrew his own and lit a cigarette.

Across his field of vision, held in a stare, flew a tiny blueish fleck, another, like small wildflower petals. He followed them. Snow!

He got up and shivered. Gosh, it was cold! His mackintosh, which he had hitherto carried round his shoulder like a plaid, he now put on. He told Heath there was going to be a bit of a shower and they had better get a move on. The sheep were still eating. The wind had risen and played on their fleeces. But they hadn't done badly! Their little bags should have a fair cargo of the succulent shoot by this time – if not, it wasn't his fault! By George, it was cold! His arm went out and Heath was off.

As the wind continued to rise, the tiny flakés multiplied innumerably. But his luck was in, for the wind was dead behind them. You cannot drive sheep against a snowstorm. They naturally go before it. And before them lay Balmore and home.

By the end of another hour, there was no sign of a break in the sky behind; it was darkening steadily. The snowflakes were growing bigger. They were white now and whirled on in front like countless maddened bees. When he turned his head over his shoulder, they came at him from the sky, from everywhere, like dark bullets. Peat hags were white. A deathly pallor was spreading over the moor.

The sheep began to wander off the track. But Heath was wise, he was steady, not exhausting himself, not frightening the sheep. How wise his father who insisted that he take the old dog!

Anxiety began to grip Iain, for now he knew that a real storm was upon them. He knew it from the snarl of the wind, from its ravening dark whine. Some of the worst snowstorms, with the greatest loss of sheep, came at the end of March or beginning of April. At the best, he could barely have reached home with the dark. Now it would be dark early, even if he got over the Tulchan pass. The wind would keep the exposed places bare, but the snow had to go somewhere, and every half-sheltered spot would soon be buried.

Early in the morning, he had thought that if he was going to be caught by darkness, he could, beyond the Tulchan pass, turn off towards Achmore. That would save nearly two miles and that meant, with tired sheep, two hours. He could sleep, like Dan-the-trapper, with Mairag's goat!

Soon all thought of reaching Achmore or any other living spot vanished. If only he could make the Tulchan bothy, which lay a good two miles this side of the pass, he would be grateful. In the old days, shepherds slept there when gathering ewes from the hill for shearing or lambing. Once his father and himself had brewed a cup of tea in its rusty iron kettle.

Topping a rise, he found the track had vanished, and the snow with a downward whirl blotted out the sheep. 'Watch them!' he shouted, thrusting out his left arm. Heath disappeared. Then because he did not know where Heath was, what he was doing, he yelled, 'Heath! Heath! Come 'way!' He thrust forward against the sheep, staggered among them, violence in his throat. 'Heath, damn you!' he screamed. He struggled on through the sheep. He caught a glimpse of the dog bunching the leaders together, then returning on the left flank. The sheep stopped; began to move away slowly.

The blinding fear receded. The flock was still intact. There was only one problem for him now: to keep the sheep together. Those that strayed were doomed. The wind tore down on him in a terrific blast, carrying him forward before he could lie back on it. The whirling snow blotted out everything beyond a few yards. He turned his face to curse the elements and was choked and momentarily blinded. But he was fighting.

The ground now sloped perceptibly downward on the left. As they came over the rise the track had borne slightly to the right, bringing the storm more on the right shoulder. If therefore he kept Heath working along the left flank, edging them upward, that would hold them together, for they would not break away upward into the storm, they would by instinct tend to go slanting downward, directly away from the storm.

From this point he entered in a way beyond all rational explanation into the instincts of the sheep, and of the dog. He was not working from experience, from any direct knowledge, of sheep in a snowstorm. He knew in his blood what they would do, knew their follies, their dumbness in going on, could take their fatal mood as his own and go with them. Had they known this ground, he could also have taken that factor into account and calculated its effect, almost without thought.

He put out his left arm, sweeping it slightly up the slope. 'Keep them up, Heath! Up, boy!' There was a firm gentleness in his shouting now, in the up-slope movement of his head. The dog disappeared.

The sheep had strung out, following one another blindly. He went up to the knee in a hole and fell on his face. They were off the track. He realized there was no hope of keeping the sheep to any track now. Only two things to rely on: the direction of the wind and the slope of the ground. The slope of the ground might ultimately be treacherous, but meantime it would keep them from the flat below where the sheep would flounder, from wreaths beyond it where they would stick, turn away, break up, search for tiny hollows of shelter and be smothered. He could see it happening.

He shouted for Heath, and when the dog came back he pointed to the rear and himself went along the flank carried by the wind in a stumbling run; twice he fell, tripped by old heather. But the leading beast was following some old sheep track; anyway, it was going along steadily. He began to count them as they went by, got confused at one point, but was satisfied they were all there. Heath looked at him. 'Good boy!' said Iain, and the old dog went off.

But the time inevitably came when Iain had to decide that they had missed the Tulchan bothy and were lost. For two hours he had been letting a vague hope still haunt him, but the passage of time, the distance covered, had really settled the matter long ago. He could, of course, have passed it within half-a-dozen yards and not have seen it, but he knew that was not what had happened. The treachery lay in the wind, which would follow directly behind him as he bore slowly round a hill-slope, but he could not know he was bearing round because he could see only a few yards ahead. The sheep stopped in front of him, began edging past one another. He went forward and found three of them floundering in a runnel already flushed level with snow. He tried to haul them up the bank, but could not. Jumping down, he got under them one at a time and heaved them up. His heart bursting, he stared about him. The flock was breaking up, going two ways, disappearing at a few yards into the suffocating snow.

Now that hope was lost, he grew cool. He would fight to the end, but sparing himself. His coolness was a bitter anger, the snarl against the wind's relentless snarl, against the white death, the black killing sky. He came out of the ditch on the other side and faced the bunching, dividing sheep and yelled at them. The wind rammed the words back into his throat and ears, the snow bit and blinded his eyes. On his feet, he stumbled up the off bank of the runnel, yelling to Heath. A gasp or two, and he managed to whistle through his fingers. But already the dog, as though anticipating his order, was round them on the up side and driving them back.

Iain guarded the runnel as the sheep came down. He had no memory of this runnel at all; knew in his bones it was strange ground. After a long way it petered out in a flat mound of gravel. From the mound he sent Heath to round up the flock and drive them past him.

Into his sight they came – and out of it they went. Then

Heath appeared. Iain felt some of them were missing. He didn't want any of them missing. Not yet. Not yet the beginning of the breakdown. Heath had obviously been floundering, his tongue spilt over his teeth, but Iain ordered him out again imperiously. The dog made a circling movement of a few yards, gulped awkwardly with a queer sort of embarrassment. Iain controlled a last spirt of anger, then turned his back to the storm again.

The ground began to rise slowly. The wind was getting him almost on the left shoulder. There was only one thing to do, now that he had crossed the moors and come to the hills: he must drive the sheep upward to some exposed place where they would not get smothered. How he could hold them there or live out the night himself, he did not know. But he had to get up first. Again he sent Heath out on the left flank – they were tending to go along the slope, not to climb at all.

It was at this point that he had his vision of death. It came with the first clear consciousness of exhaustion. He just suddenly saw how men and sheep perished. He realized the power of the elements. He heard the tearing whine of the wind, looked at the whirling flakes, and in a moment's curious detachment recognized his absolute impotence. He had got heated rescuing the sheep, and now the wind cut into him. It also slightly choked him with its searching soft fist. He had to gulp now and then. There was a sense of strain on the ribs of his chest. The snow was flattening against the back of his head, behind his ears. To hear the wind's whine was to hear the scream in it and beyond it, the writhing scream of a sweeping invisible blade.

Worn out, a man lay down – and never woke. It was known. The sheep searched for shelter, found it, and then the snow covered them. Sheep had been buried for weeks and been dug out alive. A man, never. But the sheep had to be dug out. Lost here and covered deep, they too would perish. No searchers would find them or him till they found the dead bodies in the wash of the thaw.

Thought and picture intermingled, and curiously calmed

him. Fear and horror he had felt as a lad often enough. The missed foothold, the falling rock, the instinctive clutch with things giving way, deep water ... Here he was lost in the heart of the horror itself and could take his time. The inexorable way in which nature worked was made plain to him.

After a long time it became evident that Heath was driving the sheep up more steeply. The going was heavy. The dog appeared for a few moments, looked at him, and went away again. The sheep began to jump. They were growing tired. Sometimes a beast stood, turning its face to one side, then the other. At last he decided this could not continue. Heath ought to have more sense. A strange reluctance had kept him from ordering the dog in the last hour. Even still he could not shout. Was he already growing weak, fatalistic? He stumbled and fell. The sheep now were bearing more to the left again. The stretch he had fallen on seemed flatter. He scooped the snow from the crack which had tripped him up. The rut of a cart wheel. They were on the track!

He stayed as he was for a moment. Heath came and saw him. He beckoned the dog and with a hand clawed him behind an ear, muttered fondly, felt the sting of emotion behind his eyes. 'Look after them, boy.' Heath went away and he got to his feet.

That access of sudden emotion weakened him, but the weakening passed. The sheep slowed up, stopped. He went forward. Heath was driving them relentlessly through a shallow fold where the snow lay over two feet deep. He was showing his fangs. It was getting near the end of things now, but Iain, with a cry to the dog to keep guard behind, went in to clear the way. Some of them broke away, but he rounded them up. A few of them had gone through. He began to count. Reckoning five as through, he counted two hundred and forty-one. The exact number of his whole flock!

Heath looked up at him. 'They're all there,' said Iain. 'You've managed it.'

The dog's eye softened at Iain's expression, his tail flagged once. Iain put out a hand but gave no order. Heath went on.

If they had to perish, at least they would perish on the right track! That was something. That was one in the teeth of the elements! And he would have kept his flock together, kept it going to the last.

Once again he had to clear a passage. But he realized the end was at hand. The going was getting beyond them. After a little time, he stood. What now? What could be done? What would his father have done? To live in an exposed place all through the night was not possible. He himself would perish – even if he could have kept the sheep together, which was utterly impossible through ten or twelve hours of darkness – through at least three days and nights.

The terrible wind was wearing him down, too. Shelter – even for a little while. The craving had been growing in him. Better to fight the smothering snow than this eternal flailing of the brain, of the body, by the storm.

He went on to find the sheep stopped and Heath waiting for him. For a few seconds he stood. He was suddenly very weary, suspecting an obstruction beyond his powers. But he stumbled on. The sheep were now bunching, spreading out. What looked like a great snow-plastered rock loomed through the swirling flakes. He went nearer, thinking of shelter beyond. He stopped.

It was Tulchan bothy.

EIGHT

His legs weakened and he stood for a little unable to move. The lines of the bothy took on a strangeness. It was small, humped, built of stone and turf; stout fencing wires, weighted with lumps of rock, kept the roof down. The gable-corner nearest him split the wind; the grey weather-worn little door was half-plastered with snow. The wind heaved him forward. He floundered in the snow before the door, put out a hand against it, and turned.

The sheep were pressing in, were being squeezed on. Already the snow was lying on them. They were going round the corners, being split up. 'Heath!' He glimpsed the dog's shape, nursing them, holding them together. The wind carried him past the off corner where already a snow-drift curved like a wave. He went round it, up the swept slope, the wind here, as if funnelled, pushing him solidly.

But he could not find 'the stell', the sheep-shelter, the circular dyke of grey stone. He remembered it so clearly, on the exposed slope beyond and above the bothy. He had asked his father about it, and been told how 'in the old days before sport came in' the enclosure always had its small screw of hay – for just such an occasion as this. There had been the silent surprise – that simple, momentary surprise which is somehow never forgotten – when his father had added that the sheep need not shelter *inside* the stell; they could shelter in the lee of it; their sanctuary, which they made for.

His memory was of a circular dyke covering an area in which his whole flock could be comfortably folded. It could hardly be missed. But now the snow blotted everything out. He could miss it by a few yards. Perhaps he had already missed it. A shout of rage tore out of him. Damn, this was too much! The wind bore him forward, and he turned, half-right, in a maddened spite and bumped into the wall. Old grey-lichened stone, unmortared, still as solid as on the day it had been built. He leaned against it for a little, breathing heavily, then turned and struggled back. His shoulder to the weather, he paused and whistled. But his lips had lost their firmness. Anyway, Heath would never hear. He had to keep his head down, his eyes shut. The sheep were about his legs. They were coming – and going on. He stood, leaning back against the storm. Patient, hump-backed, grey shapes, with the lamb's look in their faces; on and out of sight. Heath was beside him. He could not speak to the dog. His left arm went out in a circling motion, the dog slipped away, and he followed his flock.

By the time he came to the stell, the sheep were crowding into the wall on the lee side, already breaking down the snow-drift under pressure from those on the outside also wanting to reach the wall. When he discovered the narrow opening to the enclosure, he found several of them inside and more coming in. But already banks of snow were forming and he realized that by the morning the whole place would be filled level. The sheep would crowd smotheringly on one another and be covered by a depth of four or five feet. He did not know what to do. It was a terrible temptation to let them in, to have them folded in a known place. But in here they would bunch and smother – bunching under a depth of snow would suffocate, be fatal. He felt the choking in his chest. They must have room to move. What should he do? His father had talked about shelter in the lee of the wall, outside. Keep them out meantime said his own instinct. He began to drive the sheep out. Fortunately the opening was at a point where the wind swept by it and there was only a trickle of sheep coming in. After an exhausting struggle, he got them all out and, shoring up with boulders the rough nailed planking which had served as a gate, he blocked the entrance.

For a moment it was heaven's ease to squat inside in the shelter of the wall and breathe. They might all perish yet, but at least he had beaten the elements so far! The gleam in his eye lifted to the driven snow, hunting the moor in wind-waves of fury. There was a vicious whistling in the dry-stone dyke. And here, wandering in about his feet, gently, softly, with a child-like innocence – snow flakes, landing more lightly than butterflies, covering his out-thrust knees. He watched them till his eyes stared through them. He got up and went over to an oddly shaped mound. He cleaned the snow away with feet and hands. Hay – blackened and rotted. He turned it over; it smelt fusty and rotten. He suddenly thought: the sheep will get the smell! If only it had been sound hay! He kicked it about. Someone had said a stack or screw of hay would keep for ten years because it was weather-proof. This was only a remnant, a rotten heap.

Again he thought of the sheep getting the smell, felt their disappointment within himself, felt it keenly. Restless, they would expect . . . would wonder . . . would *wait!* His body grew still, his lips opened a little, as he waited for the hay, tried to find it, felt the nearness of it beyond the dyke in the dark night.

Awaking to himself, he stirred the hay, threw some wisps of it into the air, then went out.

Standing just beyond the sheep, he saw there was not enough shelter for them. Even as he watched, those on the left were squeezed out into the weather – and walked away. Where the blazes was Heath? At once he whistled and made after the departing sheep. The weather caught him in a whirling movement. He had lost them! Heath was beside him. 'Out!' he yelled. But Heath did not follow his pointing arm more than a yard or two, then he turned, looking along the wall and at his master with an expression that did everything but speak.

It took Iain a little while to understand what actually happened. He had indeed to see it happen two or three times before he could believe it. Then, standing in the driving gale, he made his acknowledgements to his ancestors.

The sheep had not left the wall; they had gone round it and into the flock again at the other side. Arriving there, they pressed forward for shelter and warmth. Together with the pressure from the outside sheep, this squeezed out some more beasts – to make the same circular trip. In this way the sheep were not only kept together, but kept sufficiently on the move to tread down the snow and so defeat smothering!

'Wait with them,' he cried to Heath, and as his words were torn away he turned and made for the bothy. At one spot, though going down hill, he hung on the wind and then was driven back. Blinded and choked, he struggled on, reached the bothy, the door, fought with the snow and the door, got inside, and with the last of his strength, the blood congesting his face, shut the door.

He had heard of shepherds in a snow blizzard who had perished within a hundred yards of home. He had wondered. Now he knew. In a hundred yards a man could get lost, get beaten and suffocated. In that fury, he was impotent as an uprooted scarecrow.

Lying back against the door, he stared into the dark interior. Crossing to a square slot in the back wall, he removed a piece of boarding and light came in. His memory of the interior revived. The pile of old heather in the off corner was still there. The rusty shovel, with the uneven worn edge. The wooden seat or form made of a rough plank resting on a couple of low uprights. The sodden ash on the hearth stone. The kettle! He lifted the kettle; took the lid off, held its bottom against the light and peered into it. No daylight came through. Rusty, but watertight! He set down the kettle carefully and went over to the heather. He was stumbling almost as badly as he had been outside. His head was drumming, too; stupid, drunk. He got down on his knees to feel the heather, and slid over on his left side. Something hard poked into his lower ribs. Up on his knees again, he found it was the neck of the milk bottle. From the wide poacher's pocket of his jacket, he withdrew the bottle and the packet of food. He wasn't hungry, hadn't the least desire to eat, but it was treasure, pure treasure. He put them on the floor, then not trusting the floor, carried them to the hearthstone in the opposite gable and set them there within the direct light from the window-hole. Now he remembered from long ago his boyish notion of leaving the remainder of the tea in the mustard tin as a surprise for some future wanderer. But his father had smiled and said it would only be wasting good tea. At that moment, he had got the old folks' conception of 'waste'. Something austere, something greater than the value of the article itself. He saw his father bending down to light the fire. Slowly he drew off his flopping mackintosh; spread the heather and lay down on it. His mouth opened, he began to breathe heavily as his whole body dissolved into the heather.

He knew he had no more than fallen for a short time into a semi-conscious condition, but when he sat up he was shivering violently. The weather-drunkenness, however, had largely gone. He must have a hot drink. He didn't want that Edinburgh illness again. With the kettle in his hand, he stood by the door. Why hadn't they made the door open outward? By pushing it a few inches he could then have got enough snow to fill the kettle without exposing himself or the interior. There was always a fool! At which sharp thought, he went into the short fight and got his kettle filled and the door shut again. With the shovel, he scraped what snow had come in back against the door.

As the tongues of flame from the crackling heather leapt round the kettle he crouched over them. The colour of flame, the scent of burning heather! They were life, immemorial life. He pushed the heather in between the stone slabs. The new, swift, burning crackling ran over him. The smoke stung his eyes. That twisted him into some warmth. Though still his teeth rattled. But the flame was on his face. He was singeing! He laughed, and took the lid off; thrust a finger into the kettle. Warm! Give it a minute.

He drank the hot water out of the spout. Added some milk to what was left. Opened out the parcel and began munching a piece of broken oatcake smeared with butter and crowdie, aware that he must not take much, careful not to drop a crumb. Then he finished his rusty-flavoured hot drink and drew back the still unburnt stalks from the fire, blowing the last few out.

When he reached the stell, Heath had made a bed for himself in the snow, but he was on guard. The sheep were crowding into the wall. Deliberately he took the decision that he could do nothing more for them now. The light was almost gone; the storm still rising. He could hardly keep his feet and when he found himself on his knees, head down, he yelled to Heath. Then they started back for the bothy.

As he came into the shelter behind the bothy, staggered to the thighs in the great snow-tongue and fell over, he lay for a few moments, writhed slowly, and found himself weeping. The easing animal sounds surprised but did not shame him. Slowly he pushed himself up and brushed the snow away from his neck and breast. Then on hands and knees, fulfilling a task earlier set by his will, he groped around in the snow that fell upon him out of the roaring wind overhead, came on a lip of bank with old heather, and, painfully taking his knife from a trousers' pocket, began cutting the tough stalks near the root. By the time he had an armful, all feeling had left his bare hands, and the serpent of pain twisted sluggishly. Back in the bothy, he dourly crammed the kettle with snow, and got the door shut. Fortunately for him, and for the bothy, the wind was not blowing directly on the door.

Heath went over to the warm hearthstone, sniffed, and looked back over his shoulder. His body seemed to have shrunk and was visibly trembling.

Soon a fire was blazing not only under but around the kettle. On either side of it, Iain stacked the wet heather to dry. Then he slumped by the gable wall and gave himself to the fire. 'You'll burn yourself,' he said to Heath, trying to forget the pain of the cold now uncoiling in his body, working its way out. Old men at home would have said the cold had gone to his heart. Perhaps he had gone out too quickly after being warmed. He fell over on his side and writhed again like a snake in its last death-throe. Heath got up with a small whimper, making room for him. He shut his eyes, let his body blindly have its way, cried out once or twice as the blood forced its way to the extremities, then everything in him receded in a divine exhaustion. Defeating the urge to lie, to go to sleep, he arose and lifted the kettle off the fire.

How to give Heath a hot drink was the first problem. Perhaps there was an old tin about. That set him turning over the pile of heather on which men had rested or slept. Some of it was damp and he started dragging it towards the fire, piling it round in a screen, estimating how long it might last as fuel. But there was no tin, no receptacle of any kind, no candle-end, no luck. He began to think; responsibility touched him with resource. Taking the lid off the kettle, he stuck its knob in the clay floor, poured some water into it, felt its temperature, added a few drops of milk. 'Now, boy!' Heath lapped it up.

How little the quantity of food, when he divided it into three portions! A square inch of oatcake each and one flour scone between them was one portion. A few crumbs of cheese he let dissolve in his own mouth. The bottle with its last half cupful of milk he set against the wall near the door. Better it should freeze than go sour.

The daylight was gone. He brought the wooden form and laid it on its side to act as a shield. Inside it, he made his bed of heather, with a place for Heath. Then he blocked up the little window and lay down, pulling his coat and some heather over him. They were ready for the long night.

He was warm now, and as he sparingly added a twig from time to time to keep the fire going, a seductive ease stole upon him. Once or twice that day he had felt shy of Heath; the dumbness in the dog's intelligence had touched him. Undoubtedly Heath had led the way to the bothy. Of course he had been here many times, had taken hoggs home over and over again. Yet if he had ordered Heath to drive them another way – for example, up the runnel that time the sheep fell in – he would have so driven them. He felt the dog's side warm against his bare feet. His socks were steaming by the fire. A profound unquestioning faithfulness. Yet not unquestioning – not altogether. At least twice, Heath had directed things. He had wanted to fondle the dog in gratitude, but could not. When life went deep as that, it touched strange levels. Before the deep, the very deep, little could be said or done.

He had grown so used to the tearing roar and whine of the wind that he had forgotten it. Now, as the bothy shuddered under a terrific blast, he listened. The edge of the sound was black steel sweeping on, shedding demons in an unearthly whine, bodiless wind-devils . . . a sobbing round the bothy . . . a distant cry . . . and the black edge coming again . . .

He fell asleep and the fire went out.

When he awoke he could still hear the voice singing from his sleep and then above the thresh of his blood he heard the wind carry on the actual rhythm, drawn out to its own time, of the Eriskay song:

The first long note hung on its wind crest with a tremendous intensity, then lifted beyond itself, and slowly fell. But the voice had gone, like a glimmering face sucked into darkness, though he heard it still, not in the actual words now but in the meaning beyond them.

Mary's face . . .

The storm was reaching new heights of ferocity, and he was lifted into regions beyond life . . . presences wandering in the night, lost but searching, seeking but never finding, fugitive spirits thin as air, yet embodied, with dark eyes . . .

He could not still the cold trembling of his body, cold to the bone. He tried to draw the coat and heather closer about him, to relieve the numbness of his haunch bone. His feet had no feeling. Some time he must have thrust Heath away. He caught his feet in his hands and squeezed and rubbed them. For a long time he tried to endure, but at last had to light some of the heather. It was only ten minutes past ten.

NINE

In the morning he decided the bolt had frozen in its catch, for it would not lift from the inside. He kept charging the door with his shoulder. Suddenly the bolt shot up and the door hit him on the forehead like a wooden mallet. For a little while he gaped at the tumbled wall of snow, only half conscious.

With the shovel he started digging himself out. The snow had packed so solidly under the wind pressure that it was tough work cutting into it and throwing it behind him. By the time he got his head above the wreath, he was sweating. The wind had almost died away, and it was snowing, but lightly, lazily. The sky was grey-dark and the air very cold. When he had cut a passage right through the drift, he stood for a time surveying the buried world. Everywhere whiteness, quiet, austere, menacingly still.

The bothy was almost completely covered. Many times during the night he had wondered how the old roof withstood the storm. The snow, of course, had saved it by early filling every crevice, denying the wind's fingers a hold. The long snow lines were flawless in their beauty. He shivered, resisted the impulse to make for the stell, drove Heath back into the bothy and began the laborious business of getting rid of the snow which he had had to shovel behind him. A man can do only one thing at a time; let him do it properly. And it was a good job that the door did open inward or he could never have opened it at all! Actually he was afraid of going to the stell.

At last he got the door closed and set off with the dog. Over on his left, the ground suddenly rose into a rounded hill and again on his right it rose but more slowly. The hollows in the up-slope before him were levelled out and he found he could walk on the snow, so packed was it by the direct force of the wind. His heart began to beat heavily as he saw the high white wave of the stell. Then – sheep! Scraping here and there with their neat, impatient forefeet. Sheep as he had seen them on how many blessed winter mornings at home. Life. His flock. He went among them, casting that first fearful glance. All round the stell he went, counting, estimating swiftly.

At least fifty of his flock were gone. The gate to the enclosure was intact. They had gone with the storm, and, somewhere in the square miles his eyes could cover, were buried deep, were lost. He looked into the stell again. They would have been smothered there anyway, he thought. That gave him a perverse satisfaction, for often he had wondered during the night what a real shepherd would have done.

'Well, what could they expect?' he suddenly cried aloud, in anger, his eyebrows gathering. He was thinking of those at home, those who might accuse him. There was a limit to what a fellow could do – or know! He wasn't responsible for the snowstorm! . . . His disappointment for a little time was very bitter. The snow began to fall more heavily. He faced the sky and a curse rose to his throat. Then he gathered himself.

He must at least have one look around. They might be in a shallow hollow at hand. Heath might scent them. Dare he leave for home to-day, keeping to the high ground? Though the snow was packed in exposed places, it would be soft, impassable, in sheltered ravines. There they would all flounder. Hadn't one little runnel nearly burst his heart? He didn't know the hill well enough, didn't know the tracks. But if the snow hardened, got a crust, an ice-crust . . . as it was bound to – or else thaw . . . one more night must do it, either way . . . But this falling snow? that sky? . . . Another couple of hours should give an indication . . . Midday, and he could tell what to expect.

Having made his decision to spend a couple of hours looking for the lost sheep, he was free to try to enter into what happened, into the mood that set the brutes wandering.

Common sense told him they would have disappeared in driblets, as they left the main body, blown away by sheer force. But he had a feeling somehow that a whole block of them was torn away in some peak of the storm, when the wind shifting a point or two under its own fury and the shape of the land, had come among those on the fringe like an irresistible arm, sweeping them bodily away. For a long time his eyes studied the ground, then he set out.

A little way beyond the stell, the ground sloped downward again and he was soon in difficulties. He searched about here for a long time and often had to help Heath. When he found the snow closing over his head for the first time and the sting of drift in his lungs, he scrambled to his feet quickly. After that, keeping to firmer ground, he worked round towards the base of the hill on the left.

The falling snow had lessened again but not stopped. A silent, deathly world. Fifty yards away rose a long rock-face some twenty feet high. It was just out of the direct path of the storm, and the eddying wind had drifted the snow up against the rock. The sheep, floundering as he had done himself, might also have edged their way in this direction. If so, there was a good chance they might be alive under the snow, against the rock, their own warmth creating a snow-cave in the ample space. Had this actually happened to them in a body they might live many days. It was hope and his heart lifted. For some obscure reason, perhaps to tell the buried sheep that he was at hand, waiting to rescue them, perhaps just to pierce the silence and the whiteness, he put his fingers in his mouth and let out a tearing whistle.

At once his eye leapt to a movement on the brow of the rock. A shooting trickle of rotten gravel and snow, a madly scrambling beast, and clear over the edge hurtled a stag, turning in the air, its feet kicking wildly, its neck twisting, out-thrust, and in an instant it had vanished, swallowed by the deep snow.

Then his eye caught a boulder in mid-air, it was spinning like a wheel, two to three feet across, nearly a foot thick, yellowish in colour, and almost perfectly circular. It seemed to have bounded from the edge, to have far out-leapt the stag, but, still spinning fiercely, it went straight down with terrific force into the hole made by the deer – and the snow fell in. For a long time Iain stood looking at the little depression, where now there was no movement other than the quietly falling snowflakes.

Returning to the bothy, he rested for a little. There was a dull pain in his brow where the smack from the door had raised a broad swelling. When he found he could not help listening to the silence, he put the shovel over his shoulder, went up to the stell, and began clearing away patches of snow here and there to let the sheep eat. The sheep were not inclined to wander. They couldn't – very far. All thought of trying for home had gone. It was two o'clock. The snow was falling again, the wind was stirring, the weather-sky was formless, grey-dark.

He tired very quickly and went down to the bothy, Heath at his heels. He did not speak to the dog. His lassitude induced a weary indifference. Brushing the snow off his breast, he found it was rather wet. Perhaps the thaw was coming? Big flakes swarmed down out of the air, flew on like butterflies, resting everywhere. But the snow did not 'pack' underfoot. It must be freezing as it fell.

In the bothy it was very quiet and he stood for a minute in the dim light. Everything inside had gone a little strange. He experienced the odd feeling of one who comes into a room and knows why those by the fire do not turn their heads. He hearkened, and it seemed to him that he heard outside the soft, noiseless falling of the snow.

This was just weakness from lack of food. But he had already eaten the square inch of oatcake and the bit of scone. The third portion must be kept till to-morrow. Telling himself this wakened him up a little. The truth was he hadn't much stamina. Edinburgh, he thought, took it out of me. All the same, he would have a small fire. He suddenly shivered.

The crackling of the heather stalks was lively. It cheered him up. Heath could not get near enough to the blaze. They would have a hot drink anyway. But the fire died down very quickly. The flame was ravenous ... the night would be long. Last night was already as old as life. The warm water balled in his chest.

The farmer at Sannoch (whose father had made the silage pit) had told him that the deer were coming down from the heights, the hares, the sheep themselves – sure sign, he had said, of a storm. He had been very interesting about the terrible storm in the spring of 1895 when in places the snow was up to the tops of the pine trees. All the sheep were buried. When the storm finished and the wind dropped, men walked on top of the frozen snow, with long handles which they had taken out of hay rakes and sharpened. They walked in lines, in formation, covering the ground methodically, thrusting the poles deep into the snow, trying to feel the sheep. 'They were making little of it,' said the farmer, and Iain was glad to have his voice in the bothy. 'The dogs – they were left at home, for what use are they or their noses in the deep snow? However, there was a dog, and his name was Tweed, and great became his fame in that part of the country. He belonged to a shepherd named Donald Macdonald, a big man with a red whisker. One morning Tweed would not be kept at home. When the wife put down his food and opened the door, he left the food and made off. Donald saw him coming slipping on the snow. The dog started scratching. 'Come here!' yelled Donald. The dog came on – and began scratching again. Then Donald scratched his own whisker and went to the dog. They began digging there – and found sheep ... So it went on, place after place, and gradually the tally of living sheep grew. Many were dead. But out of the fifteen hundred head on that farm, nearly twelve hundred were got out alive ...'

As the voice faded, Iain reached for the vivid picture of the many sheep found against the rock, the snow caverns they had made, the tunnels and caves of discoloured snow as their heat thawed it and their hunger pressed for more ground, more food ...

Tweed was the only dog that had shown this intelligence. ... The intelligence of dogs was over-rated, Iain began to think. Many of them were fools. Mat, at home, would never be a really good sheep dog. He rushed foolishly. His father had suspected this from the beginning. He was getting another pup – one of Heath's own ... If he took a little bit of the cheese and melted it in his mouth ... But Heath would see him. He couldn't eat with Heath looking at him ... He might go up to the stell, leave Heath there, and come back alone ...

Lifting his head, he heard the silence outside. He threw a couple of twigs on the fire and had to blow the embers. The twigs refused to light. He felt dizzy from stooping and slightly sick. Squatting by the hearthstone, he presently counted the matches left in the box. Thirteen. He smiled drily.

Leaning against the wall, he watched the tiny red embers die. Would he be strong enough to do the trip to-morrow – even alone? ...

The deer and the hares came down, down before the black death in the snow ... An old stag ... perhaps driven out of the herd alone ... too late coming down ... sheltering ... hardly caring – pictures formed in Iain's mind. It was an extraordinary thing to have seen ... He began to doze. Intermittently visions entered and left his mind.

He came to himself with the idea complete, a cunning in his pale look. He should have thought of it before. Outside, the snow had taken off, though a flake moved here and there. With the shovel over his shoulder and Heath at heel, he first went to the stell and then slanted away to the rock face. Walking in to the thighs, he began digging.

After nearly an hour, he decided he could never reach the dead stag. The snow kept tumbling in, buffeting and choking him, melting and running down his neck. He could no longer dig it out properly, only try to collapse it in front and tread it down, shovelling where he had to. He staggered out of the cutting to have a look at the depression where the stag had vanished and saw Heath. Some backwash from the story about Tweed must suddenly have got him, for he yelled, 'What the devil are you looking at? Can't you find the sheep?'

And he waved an imperious arm along the cliff. Instantly he turned his face away, eyebrows knitting, the flush of shame dyeing his skin, while the eyes glinted on the depression, unforgiving; then he staggered over the trampled snow into the cutting.

After a time he said deliberately to himself, 'I won't give in. I'll reach the stag or I'll die in the cutting.' His movements became slow, but calm and methodical.

He very nearly died, for when the point of his shovel thudded on the stag's head the snow in front collapsed on him. But he was too tired to lose his head; tired enough indeed to give in. Easing a space for breath, shoving against that into which his fists sank, trying to lift the weight on his back and sinking, pausing, but in the end drawing clear and lying, his breath sobbing. The weight on his back had not been quite enough to finish him; very nearly but not quite enough. He started digging again.

The nostrils, the eyes . . . the stretched neck . . . a gashed shoulder, with the jagged edge of the boulder just showing beyond . . . the haunch. He took out his knife and laboriously cut through the hide, cut out a large chunk of flesh from a hind quarter. Then he stumbled from the cutting, raw flesh in one hand and shovel in the other.

He had heard some sharp yelps from Heath and decided the brute had got snow-bound, had paid no attention. As he went on he saw the dog in near the rock, floundering, hitting out in the direction of the bothy, paws working in a thick sea. If he sank there, he was finished. But his body did not quite sink, and presently, little by little, the snow firmed towards the windswept side, the body rose, and Heath, a little drunk, came down the sloping snow.

Then a curious thing happened, for Heath walked by the lump of bloody meat and did not seem to smell it. Perhaps because he was whining, his eyes on Iain only, until they switched back to the spot where he had nearly perished – and he made a game sally towards it once more. Iain called him off.

There could be no doubt about it: the sheep were there!

Heath was so reluctant to leave the spot that Iain had to speak to him firmly. The darkness was at hand, and Iain plodded slowly on. He felt all in, and when the cold stirring wind caught him on the slope, he started coughing. Once inside, with the door shut, he stretched himself on the heather for a little while, then got up. In Heath's expression, he suddenly saw the wolf. The avid look in the eyes, however, was strangely complicated by a sense of guilt. He did not stretch his head towards the meat; he kept it lowered. Iain had placed it in the window-hole.

'No, you can't have it raw,' Iain explained. Heath moved into a corner.

He must boil the meat. Beef-tea! Heather burnt away in no time. But his mind was made up. Out he went and presently returned with a boulder larger than his head. He rested again. Then, leaning the form against the edge of a projecting foundation stone, he started to smash it with the boulder. It took him a long time and towards the end, so unsteady was he, the boulder rolled sharply against and over his foot. Squirming on the earthen floor, making what noises he liked, saying what he liked, helped.

The meat he cut into thin slices or hacked into small bits. The fire was started and when he had enough water in the kettle from melted snow, he put the meat in. At last he was able to lie down by the fire, to shut his eyes. Heath, flat out, kept his eyes on the kettle. But when his master's breath began to come away in heavy gulps, he glanced at the face, smeared with blood, at the fallen bloodied hands, and with a forward-creeping movement, a faint whine, switched his eyes once more to the kettle.

But Iain was not asleep. In relaxation, his tiredness came upon him in a kind of sickness. His whole arm trembled when he shoved a fresh piece of wood into the blaze. In time the kettle boiled. He drew some of the precious fire away, leaving the kettle to simmer. He was in no hurry for the food, though he knew it was food he needed.

By the time he lifted the kettle away to cool, he was feeling a bit better. 'Not long now,' he said to Heath, and smiled.

Heath's eyes answered, melting darkly.

He was suddenly and deeply moved towards the dog. He loved the brute. 'They can talk about their Tweeds,' he said with sarcastic tenderness. He had wanted no dog to be better than Heath. No dog was or had ever been. With his knife, he sharpened a piece of wood and speared a sliver of meat from the kettle.

'No gulping. Chew it up.'

Heath took it delicately – and instantly it was gone.

'Bad, bad,' said Iain. The next piece he cut and mangled with his knife and fed it to the dog slowly, in morsels. 'No more now. More in a little while.'

When the water had sufficiently cooled, he drank a mouthful from the spout. Its fresh, unsalted flavour was unexpectedly revolting. But he got it down, and it was warm. Another mouthful . . . one more. He felt it working in him – then suddenly, before he could move, it came back out of him in a powerful gush.

An hour later, he warmed the milk in the bottle and sipped a mouthful slowly. It stayed down. Another mouthful. The deathly body-coldness gradually passed. Outside the wind had risen.

TEN

A good lot of snow had fallen in the night, but the icy wind had hardened the crust. He worked slowly and the daylight grew. Often he rested and then Heath sniffed at the wall ahead. Right against the rock it must be fifteen feet deep, he had estimated.

As he approached the rock, he became wary of snowfalls, but could hardly master a weakening excitement. At last his shovel went through – and there was a grey back, a head . . .

They came out, one by one. The first ten – and still they came. A score. The tally went up to thirty. Two score. At forty-eight, the trickle stopped, the last three with ears dropping – but lifting to the light. He sent Heath in. The dog came out alone.

Up to the stell he drove them. His first count gave two hundred and thirty-eight; his second, two hundred and forty-three. He would leave it at that!

In the bothy he kindled what he hoped would be his last fire and put the kettle on. Heath had taken some of the boiled meat, and he had poured the beef-tea into the milk bottle for the journey. By having kept for himself Heath's share of the third portion of oatcake and scone in the early morning, he was now able to have a last few mouthfuls of food. He toasted four thin slices of meat on the end of his wooden spit and wrapped them in the paper which had covered the Altbreac food, put out the fire, tidied the bothy, shut the door, and buried the last of the meat in the snow. He stood for a moment looking about him, then turned for the stell.

ELEVEN

The glen of Balmore lay roughly across the path of the northerly storm and was thus in some measure sheltered from its direct force. But indirectly or by deflection the wind hit it in spots with a funnelled fury that played havoc with outhouse or barn whose roof was not in the best repair. Solid gear was scattered. An old woman's hen-house disappeared. The snow-effects themselves presented amazing spectacles, for drifts gathered in unexpected places, sometimes to great depths, with whorls and cornices of striking beauty. That no man perished while trying to save grazing stock on that first evening and night of the storm was, after experiences were told, considered providential, for when a man was caught in a whirling eddy he stood not only gasping for breath but with a panic knowledge that death had him by the throat. Many had clung blindly to fences, to any anchoring obstacle, until the fury eased and trembling muscles would stagger on.

At the first snow-flake, Cattanach had stopped ploughing. It was his practice to save the low-ground grazing for the lean months and accordingly his sheep had been taken from the heights long ago; but with the opening year and the maternal instinct growing, the ewes tended ever towards the high ground and pockets of feeding they knew. The virtue of the Blackfaces lay in their hardiness and tendency to spread out over poor feeding ground. When he 'smelt' the snow, however, Cattanach had been particularly assiduous in his daily rounds and had his whole flock well in hand. Perhaps his ruinous Torglas experience had always haunted him. Anyway, when the storm broke, he knew exactly what he wanted to do.

Yet the following morning many of his sheep were lost or buried, but as this had happened elsewhere, and as the usual tracks and roads were blocked, no-one came near him. His eye for ground and his knowledge of sheep being expert, he worked steadily and dug out many, but a few were dead. In the best weather a Blackface heavy in-lamb will die in a few hours if thrown on her back. Late in the afternoon, Andrew and Hamish won through to help him and worked until darkness drove them back to the house, where Iain's grandmother had hot food waiting. But Andrew and Hamish would not go in; they had come treacherous ways, they said, the wind was getting up again.

'When were you expecting Iain?' asked Andrew in the pause at leave-taking. It was the first reference to Iain that any of them had made, for the Edinburgh story of his bloody assault was all through the glen. Major Grant's wife, at tea in the manse the very afternoon the letter came, had given its contents to ladies who were so horror-struck that they could not get home fast enough to spread the news. Since then, certain detail had attained such fearsome proportions that the arrival of police in a black van had been expected at any moment. They had never seen 'a black van', but – there was a time for its use, as everyone knew, who knew anything.

Andrew asked his question in the most natural manner, and Cattanach replied, 'He could have been home last night.'

Andrew and Hamish, of course, knew this. They stood silent.

'I told him not to hurry,' added Cattanach in an expressionless voice. 'He may have spent the night at Altbreac.'

'Let us hope he has,' said Andrew.

'His last words to me were that I was not to worry if he took an extra night.'

'That's good news,' said Andrew. Then in casual tones, he added, 'We looked in at the post office on the way here. The telegraph lines are down in many parts. In Strathorn, too, it seems.'

Cattanach turned his face and said, 'Are they?'

'So it seems. But there should be more word in the morning. We'll be over to give you a hand.'

'Very good,' said Cattanach.

As they went on, Andrew asked Hamish, 'What do you think?'

As if a great dammed rage were in Hamish, he burst out, 'What the hell would he stay an extra night for? The weather for driving them was perfect. With snow in the air, Christ! would any farmer keep him?'

'Don't swear like that, boy.'

'I'm not swearing,' said Hamish. 'But by God if I had some of these bloody people I'd smother them under fifty feet.'

'That doesn't help now.'

'You're telling me,' said Hamish and he laughed savagely.

'Why did the old man say he might stay an extra night?'

'Because Iain said it. But why did Iain say it? Because he felt he mightn't have the strength, something might go wrong, he had never done it before. Naturally he would say it – to keep his father from worrying – to keep the rest of us from worrying – not to make a bloody spectacle of him by us going to meet him. But if you think anything would keep Iain back, you don't know him.'

They lost their way for a little, the snow eddying about them, then went on in silence till they parted. Any human being on the hills last night would have perished. In Iain's condition, his fight would have been brief. They knew that with utter certainty.

In the late forenoon of the following day, Andrew found Cattanach still digging one or two sheep out. He looked so grey under the tan and weary that Andrew had not the heart to give him the news at once. He talked of losses, of a good deal of stock still missing, and he wondered if the back of the storm was broken. Cattanach thought there was more weather to come.

Then Andrew said, 'Hamish and two others of them – Hughie and Sandy – have just set out to see if they can see anything.'

Cattanach looked at him, standing quite still.

'News has come through to them at the post office. It

seems that the postman in Upper Strathorn saw Iain making past Knockan. He happened to mention it later to the man who drives the little red post-office van, for the snow was then beginning. This man, it seems, got through to the bottom of Strathorn that night. From there the word seems to have come round about in one way or another.'

Cattanach was still looking at Andrew, then he leaned back against the grey outcrop of rock which he had cleared. Andrew saw he was badly hit, though his expression changed little. He looked into distance in a bleak way.

'What time did the postman see him?'

'About nine o'clock, they say, but that seems a bit late to me.'

Cattanach remained silent for a long time. Then he said, 'Not if he stayed at Altbreac.'

Andrew gave him a glance.

Cattanach's unfocussed eyes fell to the shaft of his spade. His right fist was gripping the handle in small, spasmodic movements. Then he started to dig again.

After a time Andrew said, 'Hamish's idea is to make for the Tulchan bothy. Himself and Hughie will go to the bothy, but Sandy will wait with the glass on the shoulder of the Pap. Hamish will signal to Sandy if he sees anything. It wouldn't take long for Sandy to come back.'

Cattanach seemed to consider this, motionless, staring at the bank. 'We'll clear this spot,' he said. A snow shower came down on them.

A little later, staggering under the weight of a ewe, Cattanach suddenly lost hold and went very grey. Geordie Farquharson and two other men were bearing towards them through the whirling flakes.

'Take it easy,' said Andrew. 'We'll get plenty of help.'

'Is no-one more going?'

'The three that are gone are good lads, none better. They'll spy a lot of ground. The hill will be very treacherous. When Sandy comes back – we'll be waiting for him, ready.'

The others came up and, on the surface, talk was easy and natural, though there was not much of it. Suddenly

Geordie, who was a year older than Cattanach, said in a forthright way: 'Go home, man, and have something to eat. You can't go on doing three men's work.' He sounded impatient. 'The old lady cried to me to send you home for your meat.'

Presently, as Cattanach left them, they kept on working but glanced now and then over their shoulders at the solitary, slow-moving figure disappearing in the snow.

'It's hit him,' said Geordie.

'I saw him working it out,' said Andrew.

'What?'

'The time the boy lost by staying at Altbreac. The storm would have been on him hours before he could have reached the bothy.'

'You had to prepare him,' said Geordie. The air grew lighter as the shower passed.

The afternoon wore on, but Sandy did not come back, and the group of men and youths about Ewan's shop stamped up and down uneasily in the cold, their eyes continuously lifting to the long slopes and distant ridges of the hills, finishing in a stare at the scoop of the pass.

Finlay the keeper was among them, and the clicking of the cylinders of his telescope as he closed them had become a negative and ominous sound. 'Had I known for sure that he wasn't back, I would have tackled the hill on the west side myself,' he muttered.

Again discussion started on the lie of the hills, the glen, the corries, the direction of the storm. When it came to the way in which wind was deflected by the conformation of the hills and passes, Finlay was an expert. They had worked out many theories. Finlay agreed that, assuming Iain had lost his way early and the sheep had gone directly before the storm, then Hamish, by bearing away to the right in his approach to the bothy, would be most likely to come on them. Hamish could still at times command the old road to the pass but he would also be able to cover the northerly slopes of the Pap and, in particular, much of the Black Gully which was the one obstacle that would certainly have stopped

Iain and his sheep – if ever (against reason) they could have got so far.

Why did Sandy never show up? Had the lads got into difficulties? Snow-crusts over gullies – that suddenly broke and engulfed? Allowing for hard going, Hamish should have reached the bothy long before this. The afternoon was wearing on. When the snow shower came it darkened the air like the beginning of night.

In Ewan's kitchen, Cattanach sat quietly by the fire. Ewan and himself had exhausted most of what they could say. Sometimes Ewan left him and went out. Mary was pale and silent, but she kept the kettle on the boil, ready to infuse tea and put it in the two thermos flasks – should they be needed. Two young women with wrapped heads were inclined to speak in whispers. The air of defeat, of death, was thick.

Outside, Alan and some of the younger men were becoming restive. It looked as if soon the night would be down and they would have done nothing. But Finlay silenced them. If the three who had gone were in difficulties, what could others hope to do? 'Hamish knows the hill – and the life on it,' said Finlay, in simple tribute to his poaching enemy.

The minutes passed inexorably. A man or a boy arrived now and then to swell the group. All the glen was waiting for news. Old folk came to their doors in near and distant places. Finlay himself at last grew restive. But he knew the hill, knew what it could do to a man even in mist. Apart from everything else, Iain was now two days without food. To send young men out after the other three was to invite further disaster. That Iain could have survived was beyond earthly hope. He had to admit it to himself in order to keep control of the young fools by his side. Before the next shower started he took his glass once more from its slung leather case. For a long time he squatted on the woodchopper, the glass steadied against his staff. He arose and the cylinders clicked shut. The wind was rising, the flakes whirling everywhere.

The showers were lasting longer, too. It began to look as if it were going to be a night of it. The snow settled on the men and boys. No-one thought of taking shelter. After a time Cattanach came out. Mary stood in the door.

'I was thinking', said Finlay to Cattanach, 'that I'll take two men with me and we'll make for the pass. We'll go as far as the light will let us. We can do no more.'

Cattanach nodded, then stood staring at the pass.

'Mary will fill one of the flasks,' said Ewan.

'She might as well,' said Finlay.

But everyone understood this was merely a diversion. When Finlay had picked his two men, others looked glum and muttered. This started talk, but Andrew silenced it firmly.

The snow fell so thickly that Finlay decided to wait for a little, for it looked indeed as if it were not going to clear, and unless he could use his glass on the way, there was no point in starting. The hopelessness of the diversion was now obvious to everyone.

By another half hour, even thought of the diversion was fading from their minds. Then perceptibly the volume of flakes began to thin, the moaning *whoo-oo* in the wind to die. 'I think we should have a shot at it,' said one of the two whom Finlay had picked, tying a loose jacket button. Others spoke – and then there was a wild cry from the door.

They all turned, struck by the same unnameable fear. It was Mary. She came running out, screaming, 'Look! look!' in a half-mad way, went off the cleared path, fell forward on the snow-bank, but in an instant was up again, pointing and crying.

They followed her arm and there, not from the pass, nor yet from the right of it, but over the breast of the near hillside to the left, half a mile away, came a string of sheep. They were hardly discernible as sheep even to the youngest eyes; vague sinuous movement, rather; but the movement of sheep.

Incredulity held everyone rooted and silent. For as the last of the flakes passed, the hillside came clear; and now there was not only the long slow-moving line but a figure behind, nearly as ghostly grey as the sheep. It was an uncanny sight; a silent and unearthly procession; and when the figure disappeared into the ground, there was an audible catch of human breath – and the clicking of Finlay's spyglass. The figure was up again and coming on. No-one dared move or speak. Mary herself was breathing heavily and quickly through her nostrils, her mouth shut against the emotion that was on the verge of breaking over her in uncontrollable weeping.

'God!' said Finlay on a gasp, but still continuing to spy; 'it's Iain and his sheep!'

Then, but still slowly, they were released. Young voices cried, 'It's Iain!' The cry sharpened and rose. 'Iain! It's Iain!' The boys began to run. Andrew let out a terrible shout after them to stop. Mary burst into tears and, turning blindly, ran into the house. 'Iain!' she cried to herself in the empty kitchen. She grabbed some coats hanging on the door and thrust her face into them. 'Iain!' She did not know what she was doing. Her whole body shook with her sobs. She lifted the teapot, set it down again, and ran out of the house.

Andrew now had the young spirits in hand and the whole group was moving to the base of the slope. Mary made up on them, wiping her face with her hands, stifling her sobs. Andrew stopped; they all stopped; the first sheep was coming, slowly, picking her own way, the others following in unbroken line.

The loss of their hoggs would have been a great hardship to the crofters of Burnside. But they had reconciled themselves to that. Cattanach's loss would have so reduced his stock that, lacking money to replace his hoggs, it would have crippled him beyond any hope of recovery.

The hoggs filed past where Andrew had stopped and waved the others back in order to give the weary brutes an easy passage. Their heads were hanging and hardly quickened at sight of the humans. On they went, stumbling, but going on.

No-one cried or spoke as Iain drew near. They had seen him fall, but now they saw the blood-streaks on his face, for though he had wiped the stag's blood from his hands with snow, he had been unaware of any on his face. He kept himself erect, moving with the conscious care of a drunk man.

'Iain, boy – you've done it!' cried Andrew, his voice gone thick and warm.

Iain stopped before him and smiled back. 'I think,' he said, in a quiet, natural voice, 'they're all there.' Then his will, which had taken him a long way, let go, and though vaguely aware of the pitch of his body, he was unconscious before it hit the snow.

TWELVE

At ten o'clock that same night, a knocking came to Cattanach's door.

'How's Iain?'

'Is it you, Hamish? Come away in.' Cattanach stood back.

'Och, I'll just make a mess of the floor—'

'Come in, man. I'm glad to see you. We were thinking of going to our beds.'

The old lady was waiting for him on her feet and the warmth of her greeting as she shook his hand went through him. 'How glad we are you all got back safe!' she murmured.

'Is he in his bed?'

'Yes. He's sleeping now.'

Their voices were quiet, but also in the atmosphere, in the old lady's greeting, there was a deeper, sadder quietness. Hamish felt it with a touch of horror. They could not help themselves, as though Cattanach's feeling for what his son had done in Edinburgh was behind and overbore everything; was even emphasised by the boy's fight on the hill. It was the quietness in which crime lay asleep.

'When did you get back?' asked Cattanach.

'Some time ago. Not long after the dark. We lost time trying to track him, after we saw he had left the bothy.' Hamish spoke readily, a glitter in his eyes.

'Sandy didn't come back as you arranged?'

'No. The idea was that Sandy would go back for help if we needed it. So we signalled to him as best we could that we had found signs. He wasn't quite sure what we meant, so he tried to keep us in view. In places it was difficult going.'

'It would be,' said Cattanach calmly. 'The surface—'

'It was bearing mostly, but there were bad spots. The showers, too, blotted out the tracks. But here and there we found signs. We don't know yet how he did it. In two places at least, he must have had to handle and lift every beast.'

'He didn't make for the pass?'

'There was a solid face of snow blocked him – and a good job, too, for just this side of the pass it's packed solid and steep as a rock. As it happened, he took the only way that would have got him home.'

There was silence for a minute. 'How he did it all, over that time and without food, beats me,' said Hamish.

'He had food,' said Cattanach quietly.

'Oh?' Hamish's face lifted sharply.

'I was taking the things out of his pockets to dry his clothes,' said the old woman, 'and I found two slices of meat, half raw.' She was smiling in a strange way, as if she were going to weep.

'Meat!' exclaimed Hamish, looking swiftly at Cattanach. Then he added, 'But they told me he brought all the sheep home?'

'So we thought, but I didn't count them myself.' There was no more than statement of simple fact in Cattanach's voice, but Hamish was suddenly, irrationally, angered.

'Well, I'm glad he had so much sense,' he said cheerfully.

'Yes, indeed,' agreed the old lady. 'He must have toasted them at a fire. They're nearly raw.' Tears came into her eyes.

'Nothing will stop that lad!' declared Hamish.

There was silence.

'Many a fool,' said Hamish, 'would never have thought of killing a sheep.' His small laugh went unnatural and harsh.

'That's them,' said Mrs Forsyth, presenting the scorched slices on the wrapping paper which Iain had brought from Altbreac.

Hamish examined one of the slices closely.

'By God!' he said, lifting his face. 'You'll please excuse me, Mrs Forsyth?'

'It's all right.'

'This is not mutton! This is deer meat, an old stag!' He thrust the paper and meat at Cattanach as he got up. 'I'll have to be going.'

'But wait – you'll have a cup of tea,' cried the old woman.

Hamish would not wait and Cattanach, putting the paper and meat aside, accompanied him to the door. 'I can but thank you for all you've done.'

'I did nothing,' said Hamish shortly, and disappeared in the dark.

At one o'clock in the morning, Cattanach was wakened by Mrs Forsyth. 'There is someone at the door,' she said in a queer, frightened voice.

Cattanach pulled on his trousers and went downstairs.

'Who's there?' he called into the dark night.

'Any word of Iain?' asked a low, husky voice.

'Yes, he is in his bed. Who are you?'

There was a pause. Then the voice said, 'Jamie – from Altbreac.'

'Jamie! . . . Come in! Come in! What on earth! . . .'

Jamie stumbled in. 'So he's back?'

'Yes, yes. Wait till I get a light.'

When the light fell on his face, Jamie was sitting swaying on a chair, smiling. 'Is he home long?'

'On the edge of the dark. But wait – wait till I get a drop of whisky for you.'

'No, I'm fine. Man, Torquil will be glad. Bella was in an awful state – we were snow-blocked – Torquil said to tell you you were not blowing about your boy—'

Jamie's mind had clearly lost grip and Cattanach hurried away for the whisky. When he came back, Jamie was stretched senseless on the floor.

THIRTEEN

Iain turned from the window, took a restless step or two; and sat down by the fire. 'What's gone wrong, Granny?'

'How, wrong, Iain?'

'You know fine what I mean. Something's gone wrong.'

She cut two diagonals across the large bannock that covered the girdle, separated the quadrants slightly, and hung the girdle over the fire. Then she stood, with the knife drooping from one hand.

'There's no good hiding it,' he continued in matter-of-fact tones.

'You know what's wrong,' she said sadly.

'Can't you tell me?' he asked with some impatience.

'It's about Edinburgh – what you did in Edinburgh.'

'So that's it! I thought so.' He was silent for a little. 'Who told you?'

'Major Grant told your father. Oh, Iain, why did you do it?' she cried miserably.

'When did he tell him?'

'It was the day you left for Strathorn. Your father – took it very badly.'

'I can see that,' said Iain drily. 'He could have mentioned it to me.'

'Why didn't you mention it yourself – when you came home? Why did you . . . ?' She choked.

'Why did I pretend I was ill? That sort of put the lid on it, hasn't it?'

'How can you speak like that?'

'What did Major Grant tell him? . . . Come on. You may as well give me the whole story.'

'Major Grant had a letter from Mr Cunningham. The gentleman you – you struck—'

'Yes?'

'Iain! How could you do it?'

'Never mind that. What then?'

'There – there were nine stitches put in him – but he was living. That's comforted me, though I have been afraid – I prayed—'

'He would be the better of that.' Iain got up.

'Iain, how can you speak so?'

He stood staring through the window, then turned restlessly. 'It's all right, Granny. You needn't be afraid. This time I'll go away – and never come back.'

She shook her head and blinked against the sting of her eyes. She sniffed and swallowed.

'Anything more?' he asked, sitting down again.

'Major Grant said he didn't know whether the gentleman would – would bring a case against you or not.'

'A case against me?' Iain stared at her then laughed a satiric note or two. 'I don't think you need worry about that.'

She looked at him. 'How do you know?'

'Because—' He paused. Would Hee-haw? . . . Dare he? . . . He might! Iain got up again. He just might! he thought, with an amazed humour. 'Let him!' he said aloud.

This time she did not speak.

'All the same, I don't think it is likely. Anything more?'

'Is it not enough?' There was a mournful fatality in her tone that hardened him against her.

He turned from the window. 'Did Major Grant say anything else?'

'He said he wanted to see you.'

'Did he? What about?'

'What could it be about but the one thing?'

Iain was silent for a time. 'Well, he'll have to go without seeing me. I'm not going to see him.'

'Iain! Surely you'll see him. Surely you'll tell why you did it. I cannot believe the wrong was all on your side. Surely you can tell your old Granny why – why you did such a thing?'

'It's not worth telling. He angered me. That's all.'

'And you lifted your hand against him – you might have killed him – because he angered you?'

'That's about it.'

'I did not think you were a boy like that. Never did I think you would have lifted an unlawful hand against anyone. Never. It's too terrible to believe.' She wiped her eyes with a corner of her apron. 'It's the one thing your father cannot get over. It's brought terrible shame on him.'

'Your scones are burning.'

As she turned to the girdle, he walked out of the kitchen and down to the byre, ignoring his grandmother's cry. It was bitterly cold, the damp in the air freezing on the snow. He had had two nights and most of yesterday in bed, and was feeling light in the step and sore in one or two spots but otherwise almost normal. The temperature hovered around freezing point in raw weather that was plainly going to break into driving sleet. So often, at this time of year, a storm was followed by bright sunshine and a warm wind that ate up the snow in a couple of days. There had been a 'root' to this storm all right! He gave a laugh as he stamped up and down past the rumps of the cows. Granny would now be 'in a state' because he hadn't put on his coat and bonnet!

Unlawful. It was an extraordinary word! 'Lifted an unlawful hand.' He stood and stared into the word, beyond the word. He saw its terrible meaning. He had his vision of the hand raised to kill. The whole arm with the hand lifted up – to slay.

The historic picture – from the time Cain slew Abel!

Men of his own breed, moving solitarily, with dark passion, hunting the fatal moment – to strike.

The murderer, the man shunned, the destroyer of the living blood.

The arm and hand grew dark, hairy.

The men of the glen, the clan – inmost in them, they knew the hand as their own, and outlawed it. From time's beginning they had guarded the sanctity of life against that hand; in ritual trial and death they had destroyed it.

Iain's mind came back to his granny. In some darkening strath, coming out of a pub into the waiting night, on a seashore . . . had she, as a small girl, heard the smash of the male fist? He remembered one night in Kinmore . . . A little girl had screamed . . .

A furtive expression crept about his smile. Lord, it's cold! he thought, stamping about again, smiling.

His father was shamed! But his father himself had the vengeful hand that would strike. Iain felt this in the awful still flow of his father's blood.

He made an effort to joke about it with the cows, but he could not. All at once he felt a heaviness, an extreme lassitude, in his flesh. His body must still be poisoned from excessive effort. The desire to lie down overcame him. He climbed the steep ladder and curled up among the hay in the loft.

Presently he heard her voice below. 'Iain!' It was a whisper more than a cry. A darkness of anger surged to an oath in him. Could they not leave him alone till he was strong enough to go? Must they start hunting him now!

When she had left the byre, he went down the ladder and towards the house. He heard her coming behind him, but did not turn round. Into his own room he went and shut the door. His teeth were chittering. Slowly he dragged off his clothes, sitting on the bed. Stretched out under the bedclothes, he breathed noisily like one who had been mauled.

He awoke to the slowly opening door, to the coming of the yellow light, to the lamp, the face behind it. He turned his own face away.

'Are you awake, Iain?' she asked.

He did not answer.

'Here's some soup for you. Come, now! You need nourishment.'

'Thanks, that's fine, Granny!' he suddenly said. He got up on his elbow. Anyone hearing his voice would think it normal and cheerful. It obviously cheered his granny.

'Take that. And then I'll be in with a little bit of meat.'

As she closed the door and went back into the kitchen, he listened for that other voice, his father's. But it never came. Nothing but silence. Iain's face nodded in bitter understanding. Then he looked at the soup critically, lifting it in the spoon and pouring it back. But it wasn't beef-tea. The trickle of revulsion passed from his throat as the potato soup went down. He was very fond of potato soup.

When she came with the meat, he complimented her on the soup. 'Is Father in?'

'Yes,' she answered, with a quick, scared look.

'How did he get on to-day?'

'Fine. He's got them all now. Just keeping a little hay to them.'

'How many did he lose?'

'Not many. We have been very fortunate – compared with some. Very. They're saying they've lost over two hundred at Knockeera. We have much to be thankful for.'

'Perhaps they'll dig a few out yet,' he said. 'Did Father lose a score?'

'He didn't say,' she answered, shaking her head against him.

'I was only wanting to know,' he added in normal tones.

'Eat the potato. Eat it all. It will put energy in you.'

When she had gone out, he listened again – to the same silence.

FOURTEEN

Two days later, in the afternoon, Iain left the house in a steady driving rain-storm from the sou'-west. The thaw had come with a vengeance. During the night it must have been blowing half-a-gale. Torquil's 'root' was tearing away at last! A distant hillside was striped black and white like some great beast's hide. Dark-rippled pools in fields. The noise of swollen, rushing waters was borne on the wind.

Past the pine planting, sheep sheltering by the park dyke, scattered wisps of hay, on went Iain, his sharp eyes for his father and the dogs. Soon he saw the river as it curved back from the other side of the glen, smoking over boulders in a mighty spate.

Deciding his father must have gone higher up, he took the brae at a slant, following a sheep track, and came on a fairly level stretch, broken with boulders and outcropping rocks. Many of the sheep were sheltering here, as he had expected, and three of them, trapped in small crevices, he rescued. These cracks by the boulders were still snow-filled and treacherous. Then he saw his father's footprints – not very old.

After a time he spotted Heath away down at the fank, but when he got there he could find neither the dogs nor his father. The burn down the hillside that was a trickle of water in the summer was now a roaring torrent. A little farther on, he suddenly came on his father forcibly thrusting a ewe up the steep bank from the pool which the burn made as it flattened out on its course to the river. Bending over the bank he caught the ewe by the horns and hauled her up.

His father's face was impassive and weary. 'I think that's the last of them,' he said, his eyes travelling slowly over the near and far ground. Going on a little way, he paused, took

the slope where it was easy, and came back towards Iain.
He put out a silent arm and Heath began shepherding the
ewe in the direction of the fank. Against a cairn of stones,
he sat down. Iain could see he was exhausted from the continuous heavy work, and sodden. Not knowing what to do or
say, Iain sat down.

'When they lose their heads,' said his father, 'sheep will
rush into water. Especially lambs. You have to watch them.'

It was almost as if he were speaking to himself, as if he
were not bothering about Iain personally any more. Then
he continued to stare away in front of him.

Grassy banks; then broken ground; then the grey stones
of an old water course, bounding on the near side a long
stretch of grass and shrub called 'the Island' beyond which
the river rolled down. Farther on, the trees began that
screened the factor's house and, still farther on, the 'big
house'. Iain thought of Major Grant.

'Major Grant wants to see you,' said his father in the
same voice.

Iain did not answer.

His father turned his face slowly and looked at Iain.
'Didn't you hear me?'

'Yes,' answered Iain, not meeting the face.

'He told me to tell you.' His father, having communicated
the message, looked away again.

'All right,' answered Iain quietly. He was sitting a little
behind his father.

'I suppose,' said his father, breaking the silence, 'you'll
know what you have to say to him?'

'Yes,' answered Iain. Then in his turn he had to break the
silence. 'I'm not going back to that life.'

'Do you think they would take you?' Bitterness hardened
the impassive voice.

'Perhaps not,' said Iain, hardening in response.

His father left it at that.

'I'm going away,' said Iain. 'Perhaps abroad. I'll see.'

'So long as you know your own mind,' said his father,
without moving.

Something of stone-hardness and yet of hopelessness in his father's manner overwhelmed Iain. His eyes lifted and he saw a stream running down the dried watercourse. The river must be rising to a great height to send water over the embankment, he thought. The rising of the river was like the breaking in his own mind. The roar of the river carried his wild thought. Then all at once he saw a ewe move on the Island.

'There's a ewe on the Island,' he said.

'Where?' His father glanced at him and at the Island. He saw the ewe. 'I must have missed her.' Then he saw the old watercourse, now a rushing stream. 'The river's over the embankment!' Astonishment held him for a moment, then he was making in his solid, unhurried way for the Island, pausing only to shout at the young dog, Mat, with an unusual violence, 'Down!' The dog flattened. He waded into the new stream. It came up about his knees, but he kept his footing. Iain followed him, and when he saw his father slanting right to round the sheep up from the down side of the Island, he himself struck up to the left. In this way they could close in on the far side and drive the sheep back before them.

Iain knew, by the way his father came at the sheep, she was one of the old dour brutes that, with the obstinacy of an ass, will not be driven. She had her back to a boulder, but his father worked round between her and the river. Slowly Iain came down the edge of the bank, ready to deflect her should she charge up towards him instead of back across the Island. It was all very innocent and normal enough. His father now had his arms out, stooping slightly, closing in. But she did not charge, she pranced away a few yards and stood glaring, head up – at Mat, who had come straight across the Island and now, with slightly lowered head, was motionless, cunningly watching her. Whether or not there had been an earlier contest between the two, she now hit the ground with her left forefoot, and at the same moment, yelling angrily at Mat to 'Come in!' Cattanach slashed a commanding left arm behind him, for the dog was blocking the sheep's way back. At that, the old ewe wheeled, made for the river, saw it, and swerved in a wild charge. Cattanach lunged at her before she could get speed up, got a grip, lost his balance, was dragged five yards, had her stopped on the very edge of the bank, and then the bank, matted turf undermined by the violent spate, slowly parted, and man, sheep and bank, fell over into the river.

Cattanach had kept his grip and in the raging waters the heavily fleeced sheep was like a buoy. But the current that hit the bank at this point swirled out again past a rocky spit, and on into the main stream. Right across to the far bank, the river, now in its sliding descent to a gorge, was a roaring, seething mass of water, hurtling over great boulders, churning its peaty darkness into froth, and lashed by a wind that tore along its boiling surface in spindrift. To gaze at it was to grow dizzy with its rage and power.

Once his father was caught into the main stream nothing on earth could save him. He would be drowned, smashed, in the gorge. Iain's eye for the river was knowledgeable and swift as lightning. He got to the outer edge of the rocky spit as though on air. But the silly sheep, following her nose, was hitting out into the river. Iain yelled at her in a rage like the river's, but his brain was swift as his eye. When he saw that they would be swept past the spit beyond his reach, he did not wait. Filling his lungs, he kicked off the spit in a flat dive and with an overarm stroke ploughed blindly, with every ounce of his strength. The current had him, swept him down, folded him about the great boulder which he had meant to reach. He clawed his way up and turned his head, spewing water. The sheep was now facing down stream; was even, in some belated gleam of intelligence, tending to turn towards the bank again. His belly anchored on the rough boulder, his knees and heels quiveringly pressing for a hold, Iain let the sheep's head pass him close to the boulder but on the outside, and then leaning over, he gripped his father's clothes at the back of the neck and yelled with all the strength of his lungs, 'Let go!'

Whether his father did actually let go at that moment or not, Iain never could be certain. His arms seemed to be yanked from their sockets, his left hand broke loose, his body scraped over the boulder, he slid down its lower side, but his right fist still had its grip on the fold of jacket behind the neck, and as his feet got bottom in the in-swirl behind the boulder, he came erect, the water lapping to his breast, and drew his father's body up until the head was clear. It was while he was doing this that the most sickening thing happened; for the gravel and stones that his feet needed for purchase gave dissolvingly. Gathered eddyingly from the spate, the gravel had no river-bed anchorage. His father seemed to have lost consciousness and the extra weight was just too much for Iain's foothold. Then, when he felt everything was over and the final engulfing at hand, his right foot held. Inch by inch he edged backward to the boulder and at last got planted, with his shoulders against it.

The river was all melted snow and Iain knew that the reaction from its icy shock would be swift. His father's head gave a small, spasmodic movement of vomit. Iain shouted into his ear. The head lifted vaguely, stupidly. Iain took one of his father's hands and made it hold to his own breast; then he whipped off his jacket; knotted one arm of it to his braces behind, and shouted to his father, 'I want you to grip this. Do you understand?' Iain saw a remote gleam in the eye, as though a dead eye, far inward, still lived. Iain knew it was the will that lived. 'Don't let go!' he shouted imperiously. A wash came over the boulder. The river was rising. Iain pointed to the next boulder. 'There!' When he saw the hands grip, he waded away. 'Take a deep breath!' Feeling the pull on his jacket, he struck out with all his force. His hands only reached the next boulder, but their scraping hold was sufficient to swing him round, and once again he had his father in the in-swirl. Now the water was barely to his waist. But his father gave no response. He tugged and yelled at him. 'Come on!' Gripping him under the armpits and with his back to the current, he started wading sideways for the bank. For one foot that he went forward, he was carried two feet down, yet he managed to keep upright, so carefully, so solidly, did he move. But once they completely disappeared, before at last he dragged his father to the bank and lay there with him for a little time.

His father's body was heavy and inert, sagged as he thrust at it. He opened the shirt band, pushed his shoulder under the belly, up against the chest, tried to get it to roll over onto his shoulder, partly succeeded, made a slow effort to rise, and collapsed. His impotence cried out wildly within him; but he wasn't giving in, not now! Knowing nothing of the process of artificial respiration, he yet stretched the body so that it could vomit, tried to squeeze it, for he knew that somehow water could be squeezed out, the lungs set going.

If only he could carry him to a sheltered spot!

The bitter rain slashed them. To leave his father here while he ran for help would mean with absolute certainty that his father would perish. And he could not admit to himself yet that his father was dead. Not yet!

He lay, shielding his father from the driving wind and rain, and, pushing the body over a little on its side, got his knee under the ribs and began pressing and relaxing, slowly. The head fell forward. There was a yawing movement of the jaws. Dear God! his father was alive! 'Father!' he cried. 'Father! Do you hear me?' But he did not stop what he was doing. Presently, between the slitted lids, he saw a slight, a roving movement of the eyeball. Then that greenish, livid hue of the eye, of the will. His father seemed to be looking at him, looking into his eyes. But Iain knew he was seeing nothing. The face was the face of stone that endures. A shudder went over the body . . . another. It moved slowly like a fatally hit animal stretching to die.

Presently Iain could see his father was dimly conscious. He spoke to him. 'We've got to get out of here!' he cried. 'We'll perish here! Will you make an effort?'

His father never spoke. Twice, though Iain was bearing much of his weight, he sagged and fell. But the tremendous effort stopped Iain's teeth from rattling. They reached the stream in the old watercourse. 'If only we can get to the fank, I'll go for the trap!' he cried encouragingly.

The crossing of that normally dry watercourse was accomplished with only one collapse, near the far bank. But the loss of heat in that last icy plunge quickly took effect on his father, and as he fell over on the grass beyond the stream, he motioned Iain away from him.

But Iain was now remorseless. Letting his father rest, he began chafing his hands, slapping his legs and thighs. He kept on talking, encouraging, asking for one last effort. 'Just a little way more and we're right!'

Slowly his father prepared to make the effort. Bit by bit they went, and always afterwards it seemed to Iain that in some measure it had not been a process of going to the fank so much as drawing the terrible, inexorable fank towards them. The sheltering wall, the hay.

He made a bed of the hay and rolled his father onto it, stripped off his boots and socks, and began chafing the feet. Chafing the hands. Then he got Heath to lie against his father's feet, spoke to the dog, covered the body and the dog with hay, and set out, taking the erratic Mat with him.

He started running and got a stitch in the heart. Something like that would have to curse him! But he eased off to a walk, then began a slow trot, and kept it up, thinking of what he would say to his grandmother, in order not to waste time. She saw him coming and was at the door.

'Father's nearly drowned. Get me the whisky. Quick! Going for him with the horse.' He turned away, running to the stable. There, for a time, he leaned against the stall, and thought he was never going to fill his lungs properly with air. But the dizziness, swimming darkness, cleared. Before he had the mare in the old trap, his grandmother arrived with the whisky bottle and a cup. He had no time to listen to her and said, 'Make your own bed for him downstairs. Yes, he was alive when I left him.' He pulled the last buckle tight, got in, and drove off.

It was a rough road and once he thought the shafts had gone, but there was good stuff in them, good old workmanship. His wet clothes were chilling his body, but his spirit had little time for the body's needs. He knew that the amount of heat between his father and death was not very much.

Very little – if any. When he pulled the covering hay away, the body was alive, but with horrible tremors in it. 'Right, Father! Here you are! Come on, now! Sit up!' Iain's voice cried warmly, gladly, but also with a strong, commanding note in it. When his father paid no attention, Iain began to heave his shoulders up against the wall, at the same time kicking hay behind the back, to support it. Having thus eased the body up, he dashed out for the whisky bottle and cup.

His father's eyes were at last wide open, but when he tried to raise his hand to take the cup, it trembled so uncontrollably that he let it drop. He couldn't do it. 'Never mind!' cried Iain, getting down on one knee and sticking the other under his father's shoulder blades. With a circling arm, he helped the head forward and brought the cup to the lips. His father sucked a few drops, seemed to choke, then began to cough harshly. Iain eased him back. Was the stuff too strong? Drops of rain water were flying from a corner stone of the fank entrance. He caught some of them in the cup, then got his father's head up again. This time, Iain saw that the dram went the right way. Hang it, if only he had thought of dry socks! Dry clothes! However, on the boots must go. His father raised a hand slightly, asking for a few moments, and Iain knew the whisky was searching down the vital ways. He gathered an armful of hay and went out to the trap with it; then backed the trap into the entrance. His father was still shaking as in an ague, but he gave his strength slowly, deliberately. When Iain got him into the trap he made him sit down on the floor, and supported his shoulders with the cushion of hay. He started rubbing his bare feet; got Heath inside. 'Keep your feet on him!' he cried to his father and spread the old leather-and-cloth rug over him. Then he caught up the reins.

They got him into bed, like one stupidly drunk, but with the shivering on him still. He seemed to be infinitely wearied of them, to resent what they were doing.

'I'm off to telephone for the doctor!'

His grandmother swung round on Iain with surprising force. 'You're nothing of the sort until you change every stitch!' She gathered the armful of underclothes from before the fire and shoved him and them into his little bedroom. An ancient thick tweed knicker-bocker suit was spread on the bed.

When he came out, she was waiting with hot tea. It scalded him. She added milk.

'How is he?'

'Fine. Take that.'

'But—'

'Eat it. Go on. It'll get warmth into you.'

'I'll eat it.'

She hurried away.

She caught him at the door. 'Have you no sense at all?' It was his father's best overcoat, heavy and thick, and she got him into it, ordering him – and her voice was sharp – to come straight back without waiting a moment.

Mary came to the door of her cottage as he was driving furiously past and he gave her a salute.

The merchant-postmaster, Adam Robertson, was a strong, stocky man, with a business air, watchful eyes, and, when it came, a quick, amused smile. Iain asked for the doctor's telephone number and then, before the merchant's curious, penetrating look, explained shortly that his father had fallen into the river rescuing a sheep.

'He hasn't collapsed?'

'He's pretty bad.'

Iain got through to the doctor's house in Kinbeg, three miles away, but the doctor was out; had gone to Kinmore; he should be back in an hour. Iain left his urgent message, then stood with knitted brows.

'Kinmore,' repeated the merchant. 'Will I try for you?'

'Please,' said Iain swiftly.

At the second call, the merchant got the doctor.

'He'll be along in no time.'

'Thank you,' said Iain, and turned away.

'Uh—'

Iain stopped and looked back at the waiting merchant. Then his face flushed and he began searching his empty pockets.

The merchant nodded. 'I would do more for your father. It's all right.'

'I'm very sorry,' murmured Iain. In the trap, he cursed himself for a fool. The look the man gave! He knew it meant nothing. Still, it annoyed him. Damn, he was beginning to shake!

Ewan was waiting for him at the roadside.

'Nothing wrong, Iain?'

'Father – he fell in the river trying to save an old ewe. I was 'phoning for the doctor.'

'Is he bad?'

'He was unconscious for a bit, but he came round.'

'Will I come with you?'

'Will you?'

'Surely, boy!'

But when Ewan was beside him, Iain's brows gathered. 'I hadn't money to pay for the telephone,' he said, holding the horse.

Ewan looked sharply at him. 'What does it matter? You'll pay him again.'

'I know. But—'

'He didn't say anything?' Ewan's face opened.

'No. It's not what he said.'

'Drive on, man! I'm getting drenched. Tell me about your father. Were you in the river, too?'

'Yes,' said Iain, with a click of the reins. The horse started.

'It's in your bed you should be. How did it happen?'

'An old devil of a headstrong ewe on the Island. He got a grip of her but the bank gave.'

'And you fished him out?'

Iain remembered the ewe for the first time. 'No, we lost the ewe!' He whipped the mare smartly with the reins. 'She got carried off.'

'What's one ewe more or less? For God's sake, don't think about that now.'

'I know,' said Iain. 'Are you going up the way of the post office to-night by any chance?'

Ewan glanced at him again. 'I might.'

'I had one call to the doctor's house and two to Kinmore. Would you square up with Adam Robertson and I'll pay you later? I mightn't be able to get out to-night.'

Ewan took a moment, but then said heartily, 'Surely! You can absolutely rely on me to do that.'

'Thanks,' said Iain. 'That's fine.'

When they arrived at Torguish, Iain jumped down and surprised himself by nearly falling.

'In you go!' commanded Ewan. 'I'll put up the horse.'

When Ewan entered the house he learned from Mrs Forsyth that she had had great difficulty in getting warmth into her patient, but that now he seemed to have sunk into a sleep. She had hot bottles, wrapped in flannel, round him and a great weight of blankets on top. 'The cold,' she said, 'seems to have got round his heart.'

'Off to your bed!' called Ewan strongly to Iain.

'Will you wait till the doctor comes?'

'Of course I'll wait.'

'All right,' said Iain and went into his room.

'I'm glad there's someone he'll listen to,' said Mrs Forsyth. 'His bed is ready for him.'

Ewan looked at her. 'Keep your eye on him, and when the doctor comes, see that he has a look at him.'

'I'll do that,' she answered, 'you may be sure.'

Under the bedclothes, Iain felt deadly tired. He let his teeth chitter away. 'I know he didn't mean anything,' he said to himself, thinking again of the merchant. 'All the same, damn him, he mightn't have looked like yon.' The story of the Edinburgh criminal would, of course, have gone all over the place. 'As if I would keep his damn pennies!' The surge of his utter weariness came drowning his brain, and he let go.

FIFTEEN

'Ay, he's had a bad shake,' said Andrew, sitting down by the fire. 'Not much pith in him at the moment!'

Mrs Forsyth looked at the clock. Every four hours, to the minute, she administered the two white tablets. 'The doctor is very attentive,' she said. 'That's one thing I'll say about him. He's fought hard for him. Everyone has been very kind.'

'Well, he's worth a fight,' replied Andrew in his slow, jocose way. 'But he needs a bit of heartening to ease his lungs. I think I gave it to him, by telling him we were to do the dipping to-morrow.'

'Good!' said Hamish. 'Look now, Iain, I'll be here in the morning and I'll gather your old headstrong ewes—'

'No,' interrupted Iain, smiling, 'I'll gather them myself all right. If Andrew will take charge of the dip and the dipper – then it's easy. You can have all your ewes in the fank—'

'Am I running this dipping or not, in the absence of your father?' asked Andrew.

Iain's smile coloured and Hamish chuckled.

'Listen,' said Andrew, lighting his pipe, 'to me. We have got a clear ten days before the lambing starts. And that, whatever anyone else says, is to me just right. It may be different in the books and the science – you needn't be winking to him, Hamish. I'm seeing you. Do you know, Mistress, the young fellows nowadays have little of the respect for age that you and me knew in our young days. Isn't that right?'

'Indeed and you're quite right, Andrew. You're a great comfort to me.'

'It looks as if we're not wanted here, Iain,' said Hamish.

'You're only wanted,' began Andrew, but Hamish told him his pipe was out.

Presently Andrew got under way again. 'Now Hamish

will give you a hand to gather, Iain, and yesterday the sheep
went well up, if I know them. So take the top reach, Hamish.
And there's only one thing to remember: drive them canny.
Whatever you do, don't rush them through gates. If a ewe,
only a few days off her time, gets a blow in the passing, it's
not only the lamb you may lose. Leave young Mat at home,
Iain. If you could tell Heath what you want, you could sit
on the fank wall and he'd gather the whole hirsel! We'll take
our own sheep along – and yours, Hamish – and I'll have
every man in his place and the dip mixed. I hope that's clear.'

'Clear as crystal,' said Hamish.

'I'm a great believer,' continued Andrew, 'in giving them
their bath. It will not only keep them over the lambing from
ticks and kebs and other vermin, but it does the skin good
itself. It toughens it up. It refreshes them. And it's certain
we'll have no rain, and that's what gives the dip a chance.'
He paused, then continued on a quieter, more personal note.
'For a while things looked pretty bad for us, but with a good
lambing, we'll make up for a lot. It'll be a longish time before
your father is on his pins again, Iain, and whatever any of
us did to help you now, we'd never make up for what he
was always so willing to do for us. So – you have only to
ask us, boy,' he concluded simply.

'Thanks,' said Iain.

'Och, wait till we do it first!' warned Andrew, passing it
off, for he saw the boy was touched. 'You never really told
us yet how the sheep got him into the river.'

After Iain had explained the position on the Island, with
his father closing in on the old ewe, he said, 'And suddenly
there was Mat, blocking the way back!'

Andrew shook his head. 'And your father had downed
him, too. I'm afraid you'll never make much of him.'

'I've been thinking about it,' said Iain, warmed by this
friendly talk, glad in his heart that he was going to do his
father's work in the coming busy weeks. It would be a small
way of making up to him before he left; something that
would perhaps be worth remembering when he was gone.
He felt all this, and for the moment it gave him a natural

ease. 'You see, it's difficult for Mat sometimes. He really means to do well. His trouble is that he will never be able to do so well as Heath – and that sort of puts him wrong.'

'How can you say that?' asked Andrew. 'Surely a good dog is the best trainer of a young one?'

'Yes, I know. But . . . well, anyhow, this is what I think happened. Heath had been told to drive a sheep towards the fank. When he saw the sheep was on the right way, he turned – and then saw what was going on in the Island. He crossed the old watercourse well up and came in behind me, keeping right out of the way, but ready. Now that was the old dog at his quiet best. But Mat must have seen him cross to the Island. Mat knows that Heath can do no wrong. He also wants to do as well as Heath. I don't mean he's jealous of Heath. But he wants to do as well. So he, too, crosses over – but does it the wrong way.'

After a moment, Hamish said, 'You're dead right!' and smiled as at the solution of a neat problem.

'Yes, I see that, too,' Andrew admitted. 'But that doesn't excuse Mat.'

'Granted,' said Hamish. 'But it explains him.'

Andrew scratched his head, and smiles broke into a soft chuckle.

'You're the two for the explanations!' said Andrew. 'But I never held with taking good out of bad yet.'

'It happens, all the same,' said Hamish.

'It happened in this case at least,' said Iain, 'and with more than the dog.'

Hamish gave him a quick side glance and Andrew stretched himself with exaggerated jocosity. Iain saw in an instant that they hoped he wasn't going to touch the dangerous personal.

'Because of various happenings in my past life,' said Iain solemnly – and paused – and added, 'I know the river fairly well.'

Andrew gave a relieved snort and glanced at him with a roving eye. 'You had a dog as good as Heath to train you there,' he said, elaborately refraining from indicating Hamish.

'When you have been in over the head a few times in the

river, you learn how to hold your breath at least,' suggested Iain.

'Ay, ay,' said Andrew. 'And you lay hold on more than your breath, if you can catch it.'

'And you learn the strength of the current,' and the shape of the river bottom, and how to act swiftly. It's a great education,' declared Hamish with ministerial solemnity.

'But for that education,' agreed Iain, 'I doubt if I would have beaten the old ewe.' He gave Andrew a sudden challenging smile and went on: 'My father had still a grip of her in the water and what with the falling bank an' all, it was pretty rough – and deep. So what should she do but strike out into the spate.'

'Did she, boy?' said Andrew, looking at him now quite simply.

'Just below where the bank gave, there's a rocky spit. You know?' Iain turned to Hamish.

'The Grey Spit. Many a good fish has rested there,' said Hamish, 'shallow though it is when the water is low.'

'There wasn't much of it showing, as it happened,' said Iain, 'but I thought, from the end of it, I might have grabbed them as they came out on the swirl. But the old ewe beat me there! Do you remember a great boulder – it's more a rock really—'

'Down from the spit, but out a good bit? Yes.' Hamish was now looking concentratedly at Iain.

'It was the only chance. So I took a header for it – and reached it. Talk about "snow bree"! Oh, boy, it was cold! The old ewe must have been feeling it by this time, for though well down in the water now, she was trying to come about. My father's hand still had its grip on her back. They came down in great style and I managed to lay hold on his clothes. They scraped me off the boulder, but we came to on the lee side, in the small pool the boulder made. The ewe was gone and my father was – pretty far through. After that it was a bit of a fight, but we got out ultimately. There's one thing I'll always remember. I remember it happening to you once, Hamish. The gravel gives under your feet and you remain upright as you're carried away. How easy it is to remain upright – but it's a nasty feeling.' Iain laughed softly.

There was complete silence and Iain, aware of their eyes and feeling awkward, said, again with a challenging smile at Andrew, 'So perhaps Mat is not altogether to blame. At least there may be times when a little good comes out of the bad?'

Andrew got up. 'We'll be going, Mistress,' he said, 'or they'll be teaching me that much I won't know where I am.' She saw he was moved. She was deeply moved herself. But she smiled and hospitably pressed them to stay. Andrew talked of the early start in the morning and they stood for a little time, the young ones chaffing the old, then Andrew and Hamish left.

Andrew's prophecy of a fine morning was duly fulfilled. First the grey twilight, with the shiver for the skin, the eyes cool and clean as glass, and the ears alert for the crying and singing of invisible birds. From a flat by the river, oyster catchers called sharply. Overhead and passing away, the high cry of a curlew, followed by the sustained, entrancing note that seemed to bubble over golden liquid in a pipe. Then all at once, upon the vision and the ears, peewits, as if thrown in the air, falling – to rise, to swoop, in this fine, mist-beaded dawn. The slow lightening of the cold, disembodied grey. Larks over the fields and broken ground. And then, rising in glory behind the hills – the sun.

'It's a good world, this,' said Iain with a friendly smile.

'You're really feeling none the worse?' Hamish looked at him.

'No. Though I can hardly understand it.'

'It's the mind,' said Hamish. 'When the mind is keen on what it's doing . . . and then, too, you kept on the move. The fatal thing is to sit too long. Once you're in to the neck, keep going.'

'I suppose so.'

'And it's taken it out of you. You know that damn fine. So go easy to-day. Now remember that or I'll be bloody annoyed.'

'All right,' said Iain.

They stood for a little while, looking back over the glen, having reached the spot where Hamish said they must part.

'Anyway, it seems your father has got round the corner.'

'Yes. The nurse said he hadn't a bad night. They're keeping the temperature down.'

'Did you have a word with the doctor last night?'

'Yes. He looked at me and said, "He should pull through, if he sets his mind to it."'

Hamish's eyes narrowed as he stared over the glen. 'He'll pull through all right,' he said abruptly. 'Well, take it easy. I'm off. We're going to have a grand day. So long!'

'So long!' called Iain, looking for a moment after Hamish as he climbed upward.

SIXTEEN

Heath was glad to be with him. Iain could see that. Ever since their experience at the Tulchan bothy, Heath had shown in unobtrusive ways that a silent partnership had been established. Iain never approached him but the eyes looked up, and sometimes the tail moved. Beyond a muttered 'Hullo, boy!' or a smile, Iain took no notice. He was actually shy of showing any affection, and under his father's eyes would certainly never have patted the dog or fondled the ears. The trouble was that when they were alone he found it impossible to break through this reticence, which somehow had its own strength, and which a curiously compelling instinct made him respect.

But it was such a lovely morning, so divine a day with the hill before him, and when he looked at Heath he found him waiting with so alert a patience, that he suddenly smiled and started talking to the dog. 'Well, boy, we're in for a busy day and we've got to take them canny. No rushing to-day.'

Heath looked up, the eyes seeming to soften before the friendliness in Iain's tone, and took a circling step or two, more anxious than ever for the starting order. Iain continued to walk on, stooped and clapped him, the dog's shoulder coming against his knee. 'We'll do it together,' he said, 'and show them a thing or two! What?'

In a curious, sinuous movement, Heath's whole body answered.

'Now!' said Iain, and he put out his right arm.

Head down, with that low movement which had such deceptive speed, as though the dog were thinking cunningly as he ran, Heath was off.

So swift was Iain's access of pleasure that he all but laughed aloud. He would talk to the dog like that sometimes; tell him how things were going on. The dog wouldn't understand, of course, but that didn't matter. A dog could understand only the – the what? The emotion behind the tone? By the pitch of the tone? Anyway, the dog would get the mind of the speaker.

While he thought in this haphazard way, his eyes were alert, his body swinging on. Soon he saw some sheep running together. In a little while, Heath appeared, and stood with head up. He had combed that part. Iain whistled, and as Heath came tearing down, he put out his left arm in a circling sweep, standing still for a little to show there was no particular hurry.

Suddenly Iain thought: That's it! It was not the human mind of the speaker that the dog got but the emotions behind. Anger, satisfaction, the hunting instincts . . . In a clear moment he apprehended how the dog's mind worked and what human sounds meant to it. This clarity passed swiftly, a vision, a glimpse, but it left behind an indefinable gaiety. He could not have put it into words; would not have thought of wanting to; but it was interesting – and friendly. He smiled – and shouted roughly at some ewes. The ewes trotted on, but manifestly not too sure of what the commotion was all about. His eyes narrowed on them. Under the long fleece, around the heaviness of the lamb, the body looked fairly solid, but he knew that, through the scarcity of nourishing feed during these last long months, there had been a big wastage, often nearly one-third in actual body weight. And that, too, at the very time, working up to the lambing, when they most needed nourishment and strength.

It was an enormous problem. He thought: If only I had the means, the money, to experiment! For the next half hour he carried out immense ground reclamation and improvement schemes. And then – the stored winter feed for the brutes, not the tough, fibrous, useless stuff, but the summer grass, full of protein, of nourishment, so that the hardy bodies would be strong and fit for the lambing. What a difference it would make in the hill's death rate! Anyway, hang it, for the brutes' own sake!

A hoodie crow got up in front of him. Another. His mind

quickened. They smelt death, these scavengers! Two ravens rose and he saw the dead ewe. Red flesh showed at the haunch. The eyes were already picked out.

He squatted and felt her body. The belly was swollen but he could see she was terribly thin. He had no idea what had gone wrong. Against the grey fleece, the red was very vivid, life's slain cry. The head was stretched out, as a dead sheep's always seemed to be, with the neck exposed in that strangely sacrificial way. Perhaps all animals dying in the wild, stretched their heads so. A man might do the same. As he went on, he saw that a man might. It was the last dumb question, the blind eyes staring into the silence.

For some obscure reason, this did not repel him. There was fear in it, but there was also the end of life, the universal end. All life was included. No life escaped.

The doctor knew it when he said his father should pull through 'if he sets his mind to it'. He heard the croaks of the black birds behind him and swung round. A raven was flapping down to the dead body. Nature was clearing up her own mess! he thought, with something swiftly vengeful darkening his mind, almost evil, for he was too young for so old a thought.

The blackness of the ravens, too, suggested a funeral to him, and he had the momentary quiet movement of funereal rites far back in his vision, around his own door . . . He saw quite clearly that if his father no longer wanted to live, he would die. That was what the doctor had meant.

Why had the doctor thought that? Curious that he should have thought that, as if he had got some indication . . .

He dismissed the thought in action. Soon he was sweating, his shirt open at the throat, a flush in his skin, his eyes quick for Heath, for the sheep, for a distant glimpse of Hamish. Things were going well. There was airy white cloud against the vast blue of the sky and the dipping would forge ahead in great style.

A couple of hours later, Hamish and himself began to converge, and soon they were squatting, smoking a cigarette, and swopping news of the gathering.

When they reached the fank, Andrew was standing over

the long narrow trough of grey dip, making certain that each sheep got well and truly soused. Two of the crofters were handling the beasts at the fank end of the trough – a grip fore and aft, by horn and rump, and in she went, stern first – and off. There was much yapping and barking from excited crofters' dogs running along the top of the fank walls, leaping down and jumping up again, as men drew the sheep from the fank to the dipper.

'You've managed to make a start at last,' said Hamish to Andrew.

Andrew cleared his eyes with the back of his wrists and turned slowly. 'Have you ever,' he asked, 'gone through the dipper?'

Hamish laughed. 'Isn't it a great day?'

'You would have time to enjoy it strolling about the hill like gentlemen. But some of us have been trying to do a bit of work.'

'That's right, Andrew,' cried one of the two men at the end of the trough as he wrestled with an unwilling ewe.

'Is it yourself, Jock!' called Hamish, in glad astonishment. 'Catch her by the backside, man!' he urged anxiously.

Jock slipped and nearly went in after the ewe. Hamish roared with laughter. 'Iain!' he called. 'Come here and see the fun.'

'If I come up out of here,' said Jock, 'it's not by the backside I'll catch you,' and he wiped the splash of stinging dip from his face.

'What's wrong now?' asked Iain.

'More gentry,' said Jock.

'Jock is giving a public demonstration,' explained Hamish, 'of the way not to dip a sheep. Go on, Jock!'

Jock, a small, tightly built man, launched his next ewe neatly.

'He's shy,' said Hamish.

Jock's beady eyes twinkled. 'You're like the maggot-fly,' he began.

'And like the maggot-fly,' retorted Hamish swiftly, 'I always find a dirty spot to lay an egg.'

'And like the maggot-fly,' continued Jock.

'I strike a defenceless sheep.'

'You fulfil your strange function,' concluded Jock, mouthing the words in so droll a way that Andrew laughed, throwing his head up.

It was warm as a day in high summer and everywhere there was good humour. About the common effort, heavy work, was an elusive air of holiday; and when the women appeared with the food, backs were straightened, hands wiped, and faces smiled in a relieved, leisurely fashion.

Presently Iain, returning from the stream where he had washed his hands and splashed his face, saw Mary and Angus. Angus left her; was shaking hands here and there. He could overhear the words:

'Back from the great city, Angus?'

'Back for a spell.'

'Glad to see you. And how are things?'

'Oh, not too bad.'

They chaffed him about having nothing but holidays. Angus laughed and told them they didn't know what work was. Iain could see they liked him. He looked the student, the young man of learning, preparing himself for higher spheres. Angus knew his people; unobtrusively he missed none of them; he was frank and natural.

'Hul-lo Iain!' cried Angus heartily.

They shook hands, and all eyes looked at the two lads, standing facing each other, smiling.

'Easter holidays?' said Iain.

'Ay, home for a few days. Man, I was sorry to hear about your father.'

'He's getting on. And how are things going with you?'

'The usual round, you know. Same old swotting.'

'Good!' There was silence and Iain looked about for a place to sit down.

'Hey! Will none of you help with this fire?' called a woman's voice.

'That's for me,' said Angus, laughing, and went off.

Iain stretched himself flat out on his back and looked up

at the sky. It was the blue of a dunnock's egg. So lovely was the day, that he smiled drily to himself, aware of what had taken place. There had been no greetings for him! On the contrary, those who hadn't seen him since he came back from Edinburgh took him for granted, thus politely overcoming the social difficulty! But what was in the back of their minds was not obscure! Now they had been able to observe the complete contrast between the fine frank lad who was a credit to his parents and the lad who had failed in so shocking and shameless a way – even lying about it until he was found out! – and who had then come home to sponge on his father! With an exaggerated bitterness in the humour, he added for them: No wonder the old man had fallen in the river!

'What are you smiling at?' asked Mary, a big brown earthenware teapot in one hand and two cups in the other. She looked flushed from the heat of the fire.

'The colour of the sky,' he said, sitting up. Then with a smile he glanced at her face and noticed the colour of her eyes. The violet was there.

She handed him a cup and filled it with tea. Angus had sugar and cream. They passed on and food arrived.

Hamish came, laughing and chewing, carrying his cup carefully. 'Jock's got his own back on me!' When he had settled his cup on the turf, he shook infectiously with laughter. Then he glanced around to make sure the women weren't within hearing, so that he might retail Jock's definition of the word 'function'.

At the end of the day as Andrew, Hamish and himself walked home from the fank, Andrew said, 'Well, that's the finest April dipping I can remember. There's luck on you with the sheep, Iain. Feeling tired?'

'A bit.'

'You can tell your father that everyone was asking for him, and that everything went well.'

Iain smiled, saying nothing.

'Though perhaps,' added Andrew, as if on second thought, 'it would look more neighbourly if I gave him an account of my stewardship myself.'

'I think so,' agreed Hamish. 'It's a lonely job, lying in bed.'

'I'll go to the door whatever.'

As Iain entered the kitchen he heard his grandmother say to Andrew in the passage, 'He's had an easier day. Yes, you can see him for a little while.' Then her voice lowered to a whisper.

He tried to hear what they said but failed, and, pursued by that whispering, went into the back porch to wash.

A grand day! he told himself, but already the day was fading from him. He tried to hang onto it, but had not the energy. He was very tired and sat down while drying himself. Then he dragged his legs into his own room – and saw that it had been changed. He could hear Andrew saying good-bye: 'Don't you worry now. We'll keep an eye on things for you.'

In a few moments, his grandmother appeared. 'Iain, I've put you upstairs. My legs are just not fit for the stairs and I'll hear better here. I hope you don't mind?'

'Not a bit,' said Iain.

'I've put everything of yours up. And oh! there's a letter for you.'

Iain took the letter from her without looking at it and went upstairs to his father's room. She told him not to be long or the food would be spoilt. He glanced at the letter. No, it wasn't from Morna. The handwriting was familiar. He burst the envelope and looked at the signature: John Lindsay.

Dear Cattanach,

It has been suggested to me, as junior member of the staff, that I might convey to you a general feeling of gratitude and goodwill. Hee-haw has not come entirely unscathed out of his crashing encounter, but the facial enhancement of his beauty, a scar on the left cheek, will no doubt in time and fable achieve the duelling blade's distinction of honour. To come to the important matter. Whereas the aforesaid encounter might constitute a slightly embarrassing obstruction to your return here, though not, I fancy, an insuperable one were you willing to make what is called the complete amende, yet this is not the only office in town, and, in fact, after a few words with my old pater (with whom, I suspect, the Cunningham Chief has been in parley), I am in a position to assure you that an application to the firm of Lindsay and Ross would not prove unfruitful in achieving for you a position identical in all respects with the high one you held here. God forbid that I should suggest you follow this course. You have a spirit beyond it. But at least I must inform you that your application would be welcomed on its own merit. Indeed, I had better warn you that you have created a Highland legend of prowess in more than one quarter of this city which you might find it difficult to live up to, much less surpass. It has even been rumoured that the Macaw was heard to macaw (*u.* to chuckle macaw-like). If ever you had any notion of the Bar (legal), we might confer together.

Meantime, pray accept our deep acknowledgements of one memorable high spot amid the tape and toils of office.

Yours,

JOHN LINDSAY.

Iain sat down on the bed and turned his face to the window, to the light. Then he read the letter all through again. So unexpected, so incredible, it was like something fallen from the skies. Warm and yellow as light. Hang it, it was lovely! He got up and walked about. Damn, it was decent of him! O God, it was! The generosity of it stung his eyes.

He sat down again, blinked away the tears till the writing steadied, his face laughing, the skin bringing up the riches of the day's sun. *To chuckle macaw-like.* The high gull-like laughter of the Macaw! Lindsay's manner was himself; what he had done, so clear. Behind the off-hand manner, the dry humour – what he had done.

He started walking again, forgetting altogether where he was, forgetting time.

'Iain!' said a low voice at the door. 'Have you had bad news?'

Suddenly conscious of his wet eyes, he turned his back on his grandmother.

'No,' he said after a moment. 'It's a nice letter from a fellow in the office.'

'Don't hurry,' she said gently. 'Come when you're ready.' And she went quietly away.

SEVENTEEN

The early morning found Iain on his rounds. Lindsay's letter went with him. The heat of the previous day had filled the valley with mist. The damp air was cold but invigorating. He would do the hill in sections, a different bit every morning, gathering the ewes from the high places, herding them down towards the low reaches, where the first flush of new growth would quickly respond to the sun, and where the lambing could be more readily supervised. It was grand having the whole hill to himself!

The sun's battle with the mists was a splendid affair. The grey, pierced by the inexorable spears, went white. The white glowed – and was licked up by a heat that came through and warmed the cheeks, the hands, the grey lichen on the rock. All along the slopes, it routed the ghostly enemy, drove him out of corrie and ravine, throwing him back into the bed of the glen, and breaking him up there into straggling, wispy pockets, until he was utterly consumed. It took time, but the victory was complete.

Iain read the letter sitting on the rock, both dogs flat, with dripping tongues. A strong feeling of confidence flowed through him; a heartening full of laughter. Never had anything happened to him quite like this. He lived again in Edinburgh, in the office; the streets, the pub., the Royal Mile. Reading for the Bar! What a notion! The Law Courts, Inner and Outer Houses, the robed Judges – he had seen it all so often. He glimpsed himself in wig and gown – learned Counsel for the defence – dealing with the evidence as shatteringly in forensic fashion as he had otherwise dealt with Hee-haw. Possibly that was John Lindsay's picture!

The sun was warm on his throat. Where the eyebrows gathered towards each other, as Iain addressed the Jury, the inner hairs seemed to stand out a little, and thus to concentrate the light from the hazel eyes. It was the look that had made Joan think of birds, of a hawk. At such a moment there was a strong delicacy in the bone of the face, a swift strength. In the direct sunlight, these inner hairs had a glisten of brown; indeed all his dark hair pushed back off his brow and caught by the sun, had in individual strands now a suggestion of brown, a warm enrichment. Under the glisten of sweat, the skin was losing its pallor, feeling for the glow of health.

He laughed at the jury of old heather and rock and glanced about him. 'Now, Mat – no rushing. You've got to do it all yourself.' With a quiet gesture, he sent the young dog alone up the hill, kept his eye on him, and downed him with a sharp whistle when he frightened the sheep into a helter-skelter rush. He worked him for an hour, and when he called him in said, 'Good boy!' in tones the young dog could plainly have eaten. Then he kept him to heel and sent Heath out, and Mat watched Heath with an intensity that now and then broke on a small whine.

It was a successful day and he wanted a smoke. But he hadn't any cigarettes and he couldn't afford to buy them. He had, indeed, made up his mind to stop smoking, not to ask his father for any monetary help whatsoever. Apart from his food, all his service would be free. He still had over two pounds left of the ten his father had sent him, but he realized he must keep this money absolutely intact if ever he hoped to reach Glasgow or Liverpool. He had not yet paid Ewan for the telephone calls. But – though it would not be easy doing it – he could ask his grandmother for the pennies. He began to drift along the slopes towards the post office. In case Ewan hadn't paid – it had been a filthy night to expect anyone to go to the post office! how could he have asked Ewan? . . . He began to feel uncomfortable. However, he thought, I have to buy a stamp anyway to reply to Lindsay. Aware of his folly, he sat down and read the letter again.

His path joined the road about a hundred yards from the huddle of five houses, of which the merchant's was one. He had heard the car coming and when he recognized it in the distance as Major Grant's, he deliberately slowed up to let it pass. The car stopped at the point where the path met the road. It was waiting for him.

At once excitement, a paralysing reluctance to go on, got hold of Iain. In Edinburgh, a man of Major Grant's standing would have had no overbearing significance for him. Compared even with Hee-haw, he was pretty small beer in the world of legal affairs. Compared with Mr Cunningham, he was negligible, a minor official of estate business. But time and place, the long years from his childhood, the traditional attitude to the man in authority over the land, culminating in his mother's dealings with him, endowed the Major with even more power and significance than that which the country schoolboy feels for his stern headmaster.

Iain went on, his two dogs at his heels. Major Grant's elbow rested on the edge of the door, his eyes watching Iain as he approached. Alan was sitting beside him.

'Good day!' said Major Grant.

'Good day!'

'How is your father?'

'He's getting on, thank you.'

'Did he tell you I wanted to see you?'

'Yes,' said Iain, 'he – uh – mentioned it, but—' his eyes roved – 'we've been busy.'

'Too busy to come?' The flat, calm voice had an edge.

'Well – I've had a lot to do.' He was losing control of his breathing; felt the blood stinging his face.

'Do you think the rest of us have nothing to do?'

'No,' said Iain.

'Have you written Mr Cunningham?'

'No.'

'Perhaps you think he hasn't much to do either?'

It was the kind of ironic remark that Iain needed to harden him. He did not reply.

The Major looked at his wrist watch. 'I want to see you to-night at eight o'clock.' He withdrew his elbow and gripped the wheel. 'You'll be there?'

Iain stood with his shoulder to the Major, looking over at the houses. Adam Robertson, standing in the door of his small store, was unobtrusively interested. Two men by the shop window frankly stared. Something in their faces, of hard command in the Major's flat voice, gave the moment a sudden inimical arrestment.

'Well, I'm pretty busy,' Iain heard his voice say.

The Major's chin lifted two inches, as if it had been hit; his eyes were on Iain's face again.

'What's that?'

'I don't think there's much to say.'

There was a short silence. 'You mean you refuse to come?'

'Oh, I don't know – but—'

'Well?'

'There's nothing much I can say.'

'Perhaps not. There are, however, a few things I have to say. You may have forgotten that it was I who got you your position, that it is I who have to answer for you. Courtesy is still in use among civilized people. I shall expect you at eight.' The self-starter rumbled; the car shot off.

Against a blinding impulse to turn away, Iain went on towards the faces, the shop. The merchant had now gone into his shed. The two men, whom he knew, asked about his father in a sympathetic way. Iain replied and went into the shop. He gave the same replies to Mrs Robertson, who was behind the counter, bought two stamps and a packet of ten cigarettes, came out, her eyes following him, and went to the shed door.

'Did Ewan Cameron pay the telephone call the other night?' he asked.

'Yes,' answered Adam. 'You were surely in a great hurry about it!' The characteristic smile was searching Iain, in a humoured, watchful way.

'That's all right, then,' said Iain, smiling, as he turned and went along the road, with the dogs at his heels.

That momentary vision of watching, inimical faces now became extraordinarily acute. The road, the little fields, the whole place went quiet and deadly. As in a nightmare, things

were subtly translated. That Balmore, the people, all he had
known and lived with, naturally and frankly, should have
this side, could be seen like this, affected him in a withering
way, more than a little frightening. A place to fly from – for
ever, as one would never fly from an unknown place. He
suddenly saw how grey the old dried grass was.

His fingers fumbled with the packet. He lit a cigarette.
Courtesy is still in use among civilized people. He chuckled.
The Major was dead right, damn him!

He hated having to go to Ewan's, but he had better get
it over. That would be that.

'Hullo!' he called broadly. 'How are things?'

'Grand, boy! Glad to see you. How is your father?'

'Getting on, I think.'

'Fine! Come away into the shop.' Ewan invited him with
a friendly sweep of the head.

'Look!' said Iain. 'I haven't been home since the morning
and the old lady will be getting on to me about food. I was
at the post office and I remembered the telephone. What do
I owe you?'

'Why all the hurry?'

Smiling, Iain drew some change from his pocket.

When he had paid, Ewan asked him, 'Why are you such
a stranger? Surely you can come over of a night and give us
a tune?'

'Yes, I will. There's a bit to do, you know – but I'll be
over some night.'

'Why not to-night? Once the lambing starts you'll be busy
enough.'

But Iain made no definite promise, and though their words
had been warm and friendly, he knew that Ewan was troubled. There had been no sign of Mary, but somehow he had
been aware of her in the kitchen.

He had not been to Ewan's since the night he had argued
with Alan about burning heather. That he had been a bit
brutal to Alan then, did not worry him. After all, it was up
to Alan to defend himself. But Ewan may have felt annoyed
at having to remind Iain of his manners. Courtesy again!

thought Iain, following the winding pathway. A lark swooped to earth, and even let out a few notes after he had landed, as though he had misjudged his distance somewhat. Iain smiled, laughed a note or two. So many things seemed to have been accomplished at once that he had a feeling of liberation. He saw Alan's dark face beside the Major, looking a trifle self-conscious. Alan might have a spot of news for Ewan to-night!

His grandmother scolded him for being so late, vowed she would not let him go to the hill again without some food in his pocket. 'You'll take your piece with you next time,' said she.

'It was grand on the hill to-day,' Iain replied, touched pleasantly by her concern.

'Did you enjoy it?'

'I did. I didn't even see a hoodie.'

'Here's the kettle, and don't take long over your washing. I'm tired of seeing your food go wrong.'

'It's never been wrong yet, Granny,' he said, taking the kettle. 'Always the very best. And I'm hungry as a hawk.'

'Be going,' she said.

As he dried his face, he could not help smiling at the way his few words had touched her. He had always liked his granny. She had always been so old that he could talk to her naturally; or ignore her, because she was old, and not think about her. Now because his heart was lifted up – why, he had no idea – he might give her a few words of flattery, talk away to her, be kind to her. It seemed a good game.

And he played it naturally, telling her about the hill and the way the sun came out. She sat down as though to get the full goodness of this friendly talk, her open hands rubbing back and fore over her knees, or lifting quickly to his needs.

'And what are you doing this evening?' she asked him. 'If you have any writing or anything to do, you'll have a grand fire here and no-one will trouble you.'

He thought for a moment, 'I have a letter or two to write.'

'That's fine.'

He looked at her. 'Well, what is it?'

'You won't be angry with me, Iain?'

'It all depends!' he said.

'Oh, Iain, look!' she said in a rush. 'If only you could go in and say a few words to your father.'

'All right.' He nodded, not giving himself time to think, for he had dreaded this.

'He needs help.'

He got up.

'Do you understand, Iain?' She was on her feet, looking at him, all her being in her eyes.

'I think so, Granny,' he said calmly. Then he turned and walked away quietly into his father's room.

The body was on its back, but the face had fallen over, spent and sagging down. The skin about the temples was grey; the breath was drawn in through the partly open mouth and expelled in abrupt gusts. In the exhaustion, there was something stern and remote, like a sermon about death. He backed quietly away. But his granny, waiting for him beyond the door, shook her head and whispered, 'Speak to him. He's not asleep.'

He went back and up to the bedside. 'How are you feeling, Father?'

His father took a deep breath, like one wearily awakening; the head turned slowly, and Iain saw the livid greenish light between the slitted eyelids.

'Feeling any better?'

The eyes seemed to regard him for a long time, then his father stirred. 'Yes,' said the mouth in a meaningless way.

'I was out on the hill all day. The sheep are looking well.'

'Yes.' Then in a moment but on the same tone, 'That's good.' His breathing had quickened, as if the lungs needed a lot of air.

'Don't worry about anything, Father. I'll see to everything.'

'Very well.'

Iain could see he had made no impression; worse than none.

'I don't want to worry you till you're better, but if you

could help me—' He stopped. 'I was wondering about the ploughing.'

The eyes were wide open now. Iain half turned away.

'I thought I would take a turn every morning on the hill', he continued, 'and then get on with the ploughing for the rest of the day. The weather looks like holding, and there are a few days yet before the lambing. Would that be all right?'

'Can you plough?'

'Hamish Macpherson offered to give me a hand. He's well on with his own work. In fact, they all came to me and said they would do anything for you. They're anxious to help. Everyone keeps asking for you.'

His father did not answer.

'I won't trouble you more just now,' Iain said, 'but I thought I would come and tell you every day about things when I come off the hill, and then maybe you could tell me properly what to do.' He added, 'I'll do my best.'

As his father did not speak, he turned slowly for the door, but his father's husky voice arrested him. He went back to the bed.

'Did you see Major Grant?'

'Yes,' answered Iain.

His father continued to look at him.

'It's all right,' said Iain, then, after waiting a moment, he went out.

His grandmother waddled before him into the kitchen. From a shelf she brought down a packet of twenty cigarettes and put them in his hands. 'My blessings on you,' she said. 'You're a good boy.'

'But, Granny—'

'Be quiet!' she said. 'Haven't I my Old Age Pension and the eggs? And beyond you both, what is there for me in this world? Don't vex me, Iain. Not just now anyway.' She flustered out to the back porch.

He went upstairs and sat down on his bed. Presently he took Lindsay's letter from his pocket and his eye ran over it. Then for a long time he stared through the window at a new and startling thought.

Since he had first read the letter, he had not for a moment contemplated accepting the offer to start in Edinburgh again with Lindsay and Ross. That had never been the letter's real meaning for him.

Now he asked himself: Why not?

It would put everything right at one stroke. Dish all the gossip in the place, dish Major Grant. It would be a pleasant revenge on the inimical faces! He would be through with Balmore for good. And his father – it would be the tonic he needed! Edinburgh again. Douglas and all that talk. What did anyone talk about here? Not a damn thing but the weather! Either that or, 'Oh, he's getting on. He'll have money one day.' That was all.

A clean easy life, too, attending to other people's business on paper. 'It's a gentleman's life,' as the local folk said. No slaving away with sheep and the land. No dirty work, no wettings, no dead and rotting ewes. A nice comfortable job, going to the office in the morning, coming away at night. A house with water and electric light. Baths. The pleasant courtesies of civilized people. Books and music. People who lived on the land were yokels, mugs who could do no better for themselves. Patronized by politicians and others who took damned good care they kept off the land themselves – unless as 'gentleman farmers', pursuing a hobby at the weekends.

They're dead right! thought Iain. They saw the realities. No maggot-flies on them. Life was measured by what it brought in cash and comfort.

How right that was! What other standard was there? None. He suddenly saw this quite clearly. Anything else was just some silly form of youthful longing, like a boy's desire to be an explorer or an engine driver. And the people, well-to-do, who talked about basic work, a noble occupation, who said we all depended on what came off the land – they could be maddening! A chattering of futile 'idealism' beyond bearing!

Well, what about it? Now? A short letter to Mr Cunningham, with a frank apology for what had happened in his office, a word of thanks for kindness and courtesy received, and a final regret that he had not earlier made it clear that he could not return. Then a long letter to Lindsay, in the humorous way he would appreciate, telling of his father's severe illness, asking Lindsay's advice about staying at home here for a month – he could make good fun of the lambing – and generally fixing things up to start with Lindsay and Ross at their convenience.

It could be done, now, with absolutely certain results.

What about it? Think no more. Do it and be done with it. It was really a great chance. He hadn't deserved it.

An extraordinary heaviness came over his body. He knew his right hand could not push the pen. He began to walk about. Another day – two days – would make no difference. Then he would have to write Lindsay in any case.

He went out, past the steading and along to the patch of ground which his father had started ploughing.

EIGHTEEN

For three days Iain struggled with himself. Once he did make an effort to write but found his hand was actually heavy, and when he commanded it, his brain went dull and cloudy.

The reluctance came from some source very deep in him. He realized that, realized that here he just could not come to an off-hand decision. All the reasons for going back to Edinburgh were not enough, not on this level of life where he was trying honestly to fight the issue out. Whatever he did, he must not fool himself. At least he must have no illusions about the road he was to take.

Hour after hour passed, on the hill, in his bed. His mood changed from irritation to anger, from dullness to a dragging despair. He got beyond being able to reason about anything. A sense of stupidity numbed him. There were occasional intense spasms of suffering, followed by extreme listlessness; then the stupid enduring dullness once more. In the house, he behaved normally, but he was only in for a short time, and the amount of work he did was sufficient excuse for a general air of tiredness.

But his vitality was being drained away. He realized this when he staggered and fell on the afternoon of the third day as he turned for home. He lay on his face and told his defeat to the earth. The words came out of him in a bitter cry. He was beyond coming to any decision. He was done . . .

As he wakened fully, he listened; his eyes caught the movement of heath stalks; he saw their tiny, withered, ash-brown blossoms shake in the wind. They were quite close to him, but there was something hearkening and remote about them; as remote as the curlew whistle that arrow-like passed away on its own sound. The heather, the earth, was in his nostrils. He got the ancient disturbing scent strongly, yet finely, a pervasive sustaining strength, coming up out of the ground, bearing himself and all things upon it yet fine as the air that blew past the tiny ash-brown balls in its queerly thoughtful way.

He shivered from a coolness of the refreshed skin. His mind was thin as the cool air. Looking about him, as he sat up, he saw the primeval scene with a newness that had something known in it. This something known was at once ancient and newly minted. The newness was of the instant – and of the next instant, as if, while there, it yet were awaiting its own creation. And it went with the air round the corner into the future.

That same evening, sitting with Angus against the grey dyke watching Hamish ploughing, he listened with a quiver of humour on his eyelids.

'I didn't want to give her your address. In fact, I said I didn't know whether you'd gone home or not, and that was true,' Angus explained. 'I told her I thought she should wait. You would naturally be upset, but the chances were that you would come back.'

'What did she say to that?'

'She said nothing for a time. I promised I'd find out all about you and let her know when I came back.'

'She'll get over it.'

'I don't know. Joan told me she's pretty badly hit.'

'Is she?' Iain smiled as though amused.

'You played a bit fast and loose with her.'

'Fast, possibly; but loose – a difficult word.'

'Anyway I said I'd let her know.'

'What will you tell her?'

'Well – what am I to tell her?'

'Tell her', said Iain, 'that I am a penniless beggar, with no prospects, no job. Tell her I am off to Australia, in the hope that I'll get a job on a sheep farm there, lost in the wilds. Tell her I'll have to work my own passage.'

Angus turned his head and looked at Iain's side face. 'Do you mean you're not going back to Edinburgh?'

'No.'

There was silence for a little.

'I'm sorry about Morna,' Iain said. 'But I don't deceive myself. She'll find someone else. A girl like that always does. You know that. There's a side to this you haven't thought about. What does a girl want a fellow for?'

'Well, she likes him, I suppose, and—'

'And what?'

'Oh, there's no need to be serious as all that.'

'Why the bother about Morna, then?'

Angus did not answer.

'It's very simple really,' said Iain. 'When you're in a job, going ahead, girls and fellows naturally have a bit of fun and things sort themselves out. As you say, no need to be serious about it. You'll take what's coming to you. But I'm not now in that position. That's the almighty difference. I can't have a girl. You can.'

'Hey, young fellow my lad!' called Hamish. 'Come on!'

Iain leapt up and got a grip of the plough-stilts. Hamish watched him for a little. 'He's getting really good at it,' he said to Angus. 'There's not a damn thing but he picks up by instinct.'

On Saturday evening – the last Saturday before the lambing – Iain knew he would have to go to Ewan's. Hamish had been at him twice about it. 'They'll be thinking you're frightened to show your face,' he had said, and been surprised at the intense way Iain had answered.

Hamish had been referring in particular to those who dropped in on Ewan. The shop had long been a natural meeting place, especially on Saturday nights for men wandering home from the merchant's with their tobacco and weekly papers.

Iain stood in the deep shadows of the clump of pines. Darkness was falling in a fine smother. A blackbird sang with great power. He had a very sensitive ear for birdsong, certain notes, turns or twists of song, when pure, giving him a curiously exquisite delight, so that his eyes glimmered not only with admiration but with an incommunicable humour. It was so lovely that he felt the artistry of it in himself, the perfect production of a phrase, the perfect finish. The blackbird was the master singer not merely in the quality of the notes, the song itself, but also in some other added quality that the notes went flashing through. This sort of world or air that the notes created was somehow everywhere in a magical way. It was far off and near. A glisten of silver here, there, on black wings, where wings and silver were invisible. He even found it, if in another way, when a blackbird, in sudden alarm, scolded in a wintry bush. It was something not quite of the world, yet of the inmost heart and quick of the world.

As the blackbird stopped singing, he saw Mary coming round the corner of the dyke. She was running, but began to walk at sight of the house, the small bright milkpail in her hand. She had obviously been away somewhere and was late. He listened to the voices at the door then went down to the corner of the dyke.

As she came hurrying round it, he jumped out. She gave a scream and the milkpail swung and shook so violently that drips ran from under the lid. He laughed.

She stood, breathing heavily, gulping.

'You got a fright!' he taunted her in the old schoolboy manner.

'You cheeky brat,' she said waveringly.

'That's not the way you used to say it.'

'What a fright you gave me!' She was recovering.

'How mad it used to make you!'

'You shouldn't do it. It's horrid.'

'I was listening to a blackbird and it suddenly came over me. Did you hear him singing?'

'Yes.'

'Up in our tree. I'm sorry if I startled you, Mary,' he said contritely. 'It was silly of me. Where are you going?'

'Home. Where did you think?'

'What's the good of going home? Anyone can go home.'

She looked at him, and he smiled in a friendly half-teasing way.

'Do you know what I was thinking?' he asked, the glimmer in his eyes.

'What?'

'I was longing for a song from you. Couldn't we go down this way, by the Dell? It isn't much longer round for you. And then you could give me two songs, quietly. That's all I want in the world this night.'

'Are you quite mad?' she said, turning her face away, looking around.

'No-one will see us. Come on!'

'Iain, I can't. Don't be silly. They're waiting for me.'

'Let them wait. Come on!' He took her arm.

'But, Iain, I can't!' she said, withdrawing her arm.

'Yes, you can. I know Alan or some fellow like that will be waiting for you. But never mind him. This is you and me, Mary. Hang it all, we have known each other a long time. Surely you can spare me one small song – two, I mean. It's all I'll ever ask of you.'

She walked on, silent.

'Have I offended you now?'

After a few seconds, he got his shoulder against her and pushed her off the path in the direction of the Dell.

She swung away. 'You're a brute!' she said.

'I know. They all think that.'

She stopped. 'I didn't mean that,' she muttered on a note of distress.

'But that's nothing. I don't mind really. Won't you come of your own will – or must I force you by brute strength?' His tone was still friendly, companionable.

'I must go home,' she said, in a strange voice, lifted somewhat, startled, like her glance, away from him, in flight. Her colour was vivid as distress.

'All right,' he said. 'It mightn't be much use now anyway.'

She went away on uncertain feet for a few paces, then more quickly, her head up. She's beautifully made! he thought. She went into the deep dusk, past the little bushes.

He lit a cigarette. Pity she should take it like that. This love business and afraid of being seen! Hang it, for old times' sake, she might have given him a couple of songs. Wouldn't have cost her much. That two human beings couldn't meet and have a song without getting cluttered up in all that nonsense! But no! Once a girl got caught she had no use for anyone or anything else. Sex. Damn funny. Even a blackbird could sing for the delight of it before going to his bed.

When he had half-smoked his cigarette, he wandered on towards Ewan's cottage. His entrance would doubtless surprise them!

It did. The stranger, they called him; the man who worked all round the clock. Some overdid their laughing welcome. All kept their eyes on his face.

'Why didn't you bring your fiddle?' asked Ewan.

'I thought it was another argument you wanted,' replied Iain.

'Faith,' said Andrew, 'I gave Finlay your last argument on the heather burning. He didn't think a great deal of it.'

'Perhaps you couldn't make it clear enough for his fine intelligence.'

'That's why I told him to call on you some time. Or, failing you, on Hamish.'

'He's tried to call on me more than once,' said Hamish, 'but I wasn't at home.'

They laughed.

'Talking about argument,' said Jock MacArthur, who had been at the dipper and who revelled in provocative talk, 'Alan here was telling me, Iain, that you're an authority on hill sheep farming.'

'He's quite right,' said Iain.

'I never said any such thing,' declared Alan.

'Didn't you?' said Jock, astonished. 'Then it must have been somebody else. I wonder who it could have been?'

'Now Jock—' began Ewan.

'But it's a fact,' Jock interrupted him. 'If it wasn't Alan, then it was Hamish.'

'I may have said,' replied Hamish, 'that he knew more about it than you and Alan put together, but that's nothing.'

'Speak for yourself,' said Alan.

'That's the boy, Alan!' Jock nodded encouragingly. In no time the banter had passed to challenging statements, and the argument, as Jock liked it, was in full spate. Iain did not want to push Alan, but Alan had clearly made up his mind to have more than his own back on Iain if that were possible. At some length he made the point that the estate already carried more sheep than was good for it, that rents had been declining over a considerable period, and that if any folk thought the landlord was making a profit on the money he had sunk in buying the estate, he, Alan, could assure them they were wrong. 'That's fact,' he concluded, 'not vague talk.'

'And it's fairly put them on their backs,' said Jock, his eyes twinkling in the silence.

'I doubt it,' said Hamish. 'Landlords don't change their spots. I'd need more than Alan's word.'

'If you don't believe me, I can't help it,' said Alan. 'It's the truth, all the same.'

'I believe you,' said Iain simply. 'The only trouble is that what you say has nothing to do with the argument. It's pointless.'

'What do you mean?'

'Simply that a rich man does not buy a sporting estate in the Highlands to make a profit out of it. Shooting gentry expect to pay for their sport, like everyone else.'

'Can you blame them?' asked Jock.

Iain smiled. 'No.'

'You should have heard Colonel Hardcastle when the stray ewe got between him and his royal stag last season,' said Hughie. 'First he blasted all sheep into kingdom come, then he wanted to know what the so-and-so he had been asked up here to crawl a thousand miles on his belly for, and then he used strange language.'

'It would be Hindustani,' said Angus.

They swayed with laughter, and when they learned that the sheep had disturbed the royal and that the Colonel had lost his shot, Andrew sympathized with him. 'It would have been no laughing matter for Finlay,' he added.

'It wasn't Hindustani Finlay used – afterwards,' said Hughie. 'We were frightened to speak to him for three days.

But the Colonel turned out trumps – for Finlay got his tip at the end.'

'Ach, they're fine gentlemen as a rule,' said Jock. 'Many's the good day I've had gillieing myself. Many a welcome pound note has come into the glen from them. And you know that.' Jock looked challengingly at Iain.

'Of course,' said Iain. 'Though if you worked it out per head I doubt if it would make up for the loss of a dead sheep. And they say that sheep die mostly from the bad condition of the hill and lack of nourishment.'

'The landlord didn't make the hill,' said Alan.

'No,' agreed Iain quietly. 'God made it; then handed it over to the landlord for nothing; since when it's gone to rot.'

'That's rot anyway,' said Alan. 'Silly rot.'

'I doubt it,' said Iain. 'But our trouble really is ignorance. Supposing I asked you a simple thing like this: On the Balmore estate, which you help to factor, how many acres go to each breeding ewe?'

Alan was plainly stumped.

'Roughly,' helped Iain.

'That's easily found out. A fellow doesn't carry all the facts and figures in his head,' said Alan impatiently.

'What's your point?' asked Ewan.

'Simply this,' said Iain. 'That if we're going to talk about sheep we should know our facts. We should be able to state the problem and work it out. I am prepared to bet, for example, that the hill grazing all round will work out at four to five acres to a sheep. Could we put more sheep on that land and so increase our profit? If so, how? What are the determining factors involved? How much could we do ourselves? How much must be done for us, because we haven't the capital for initial outlay? What exactly should be done? And so on.' He leaned back with a smile.

'Bless me!' exclaimed Jock. 'Do you think your father, and your father before him, hasn't found out all about that?'

'Never mind his father,' said Andrew. 'God grant he will soon be well and among us. Meantime I would like to hear what Iain has to tell us.'

'It's no good putting it like that, Andrew. You know I haven't any experience. I have been trying to understand things, learning what men are trying to do in other places. I see it as a serious problem. This glen is going down – like the other glens. And we're doing nothing – waiting for the end. Any fellows who have the chance – like Angus, here, or Alan – and the brains, of course! – clear out. That's what's happening. It's no good blinking it.'

'All right,' said Andrew, good-natured but persistent, 'what can be done about it?'

Iain hesitated. He was suddenly tired of the talk, did not want to fight and appear sententious, knew what, deep in their minds, they could not help thinking of him as one who had got his chance and so shockingly failed. He felt their watching faces, and for a perverse moment thought of asking Mary to sing. She was sitting quietly by the dresser, knitting.

'What would you say is the main problem?' asked Hamish, to encourage him.

'Wintering, of course,' answered Iain. 'The number of sheep on your ground depends on the number you can winter. If you could winter more, you could carry more. From May onwards till October you could carry many times more sheep on the hill. But you don't because you can't winter them when the grass dies down. As it is, we have to send the hoggs away.'

'That's not exactly news,' said Jock.

'No,' agreed Iain, 'but it does set the problem. It keeps your mind from being woolly like the sheep's back.'

Hamish smiled at this flash from Iain. He was recovering!

'And how would you set about solving your problem?' asked Andrew.

'There are many ways of looking at it,' Iain said. 'If you could put more sheep on the hill in the summer time, you would not only feed more sheep, but it would be good for the hill. Add cattle and your hill would improve much more still. As it is, at the period of greatest growth the hill is under-stocked, and so the rough stuff is not cropped, is not kept down. Your hill goes back. And when you add that draining is neglected, you increase the rankness.'

'How do you know the rough stuff is not kept down? What rough stuff?' Alan challenged him.

'First, we know that sheep eat the tenderest bite they can get and pass over the rough. They do it because they are not fools. The tender is more palatable and nourishing. If you have comparatively few sheep on a large summer hill, the rough thrives at the expense of the tender. The sheep, like the human being, is always trying to do one thing – to live. But so are the plants. The plants have their enemies in the sheep, and also of course in the deer and hares and rabbits. And the plants find that if they go tough – they survive. So they go tough. The grass turns coarse and fibrous and the small shrub goes woody. This also protects them against the cold weather and against the acid in the soil, lack of drainage. They grow slowly and survive on little. So for the winter and spring months you have the worst kind of plant for the breeding ewe – when you should have the best. In a couple of days the lambing starts – with the ewes underfed and in poor condition.'

'Man,' said Andrew, 'I see your point. Plenty of sheep and cattle would eat the rough – especially the cattle. They would have to. And that would give the more tender nourishing plants a chance. But that's been tried. And it doesn't pay. I remember in my young days when my father used to buy cattle in the spring, feed them on the rough grazing and then sell them in the back end of the year. But the dealers got wise to that. They knew we *had* to sell in the back end and soon we were losing on it. I remember a year when we sold in the late autumn for considerably less than we paid for the beasts in the spring. Not to mention the one that died on us.'

'Exactly,' agreed Iain. 'But if you could have afforded to hold off from selling, you could have got your price. The market was there. But you couldn't hold off – and so you were had. We come back to wintering again.'

'And what could you do about that?'

'Several things. But I'm only telling you now what other men have found out about it, dealing with ground like our own. I don't want to talk. Only I am satisfied that certain things – and I can tell you them – could be done whereby we could do our own wintering of our hoggs and put a lot of hardy cattle – not necessarily pure-bred Highlanders – on the rough grazing. And I don't mean cattle taken in for the summer grazing, but breeding cattle for all the year round. Then you could sell in lots, and in that way command your market. But even if we could winter our own hoggs, that would not only save us ten shillings a head, but, from talk I had with some of the farmers in Lower Strathorn, it would also do away with having to find outside wintering, and such wintering one day may be difficult to get at any price. Already the price is beyond reason and still going up. You know that. It's ruinous.'

'We know it. But how are we going to get our own wintering?' persisted Andrew.

'Och, I'm fed up,' said Iain suddenly relaxing and smiling. 'Come on, Mary, what about a song?'

'Mary will give us a song in a minute,' said Andrew. 'And if you can give us the wintering, we'll have a dance.'

Iain refused to go on. 'What's the good of talking?' he asked cheerfully. 'Anyone can talk. And I see Jock there with a sarcastic look in his eye. I think it's time we were in our beds. Anyway I'm off.'

'When you introduce your improvements in Torguish one day,' said Jock, 'we'll be watching you.'

'You'll watch a long time in that case,' said Iain, now on his feet.

'How that? Thinking of leaving us?'

'I might, you know,' said Iain, 'though it would break my heart to leave you, Jock. However, I'll see the lambing through first.'

'About the wintering,' began Andrew in his slow persistent way.

Everyone laughed.

'You see, no-one is really interested, Andrew,' said Iain.

'It's a "common" subject. The sort you want to get away from. You can see by the way we look up to those who get away from the land, how much we despise those who don't.'

'You seem to know a lot about it,' said Jock.

'I should,' said Iain. 'I am the man who came back to the land.' Then he turned away with a laugh. 'Good night, Ewan. Good night, Mary.'

Hamish and Hughie got up and went out with him.

NINETEEN

For a month Iain lived in a world of physical effort and intense interest. He had the full responsibility for the lambing on his hands and its continuous surprises and difficulties, thrills and despairs, were with him from sunrise until he dragged himself early to bed.

His keenness was a surprise to himself. He had never experienced anything like it, day after day. It consumed him. The sight of his first lamb had brought him to a standstill as before a revelation, a miracle. Heaven knows he had seen enough lambs in his time, but never a lamb like this lamb, newly born, swaying on its stilts, but hardy, for when he went forward a step or two out came its thin bleat and waggle went its tail with energy. Once in a jealously contested shinty game, Iain, playing for Kinbeg against the great Kinmore, had scored the winning goal in a last-minute wild rush on his own. He had known a sweet secret pride then. He knew it again now, but somehow more profoundly, for here wonder was added and a queer sort of gratitude. It was just after nine o'clock in the morning, far round the shoulder of the slope where small birch trees grew. The sun was shining and the purple bloom of the thin branches was a mist of delicate beauty. It was a sheltered spot and as the ewe moved, making it clear that she was not prepared to give much ground to man or dog, he saw a primrose starring the bank beside which she had given birth. April had still over a week to go. The first hill primrose he had seen and the first lamb! A brown wren, like a withered leaf, like a mouse, moved swiftly, stopped, and sang. The whole scene etched itself unforgettably on his heightened mind. Such conjunctions of the seen and the heard were normal enough. But as he took a step or two away, looking back, the faces of mother and lamb came through that arrested place and time. A whorl of grey over the left eyebrow invaded the small black mask. It turned away to fumble after life's needs. Swiftly the ewe sniffed her offspring, then as swiftly raised her challenging head. Iain went on, saying in a low vibrant voice, 'We've started, Heath; we're doing it, boy!'

Five more lambs within the hour. It was too easy, too good to be true. If this weather held the lambs would dry and frisk about like the birds. And why not? There was always a compensation in nature. The terrific snowstorm had tried to do its worst. Nature was no fool. Malign and destructive she could be, beyond man's understanding, beyond his endurance, but equally she could be lavish and lovely.

The snows had melted from the high hills, leaving white patches here and there, but there was still a fair rush of water in the burns. Under a vague apprehension, he had herded a few beasts away from one watercourse with its cataracts and tiny pools. A sick-looking ewe with drooping head, he had studied for some time: a gimmer, about to have her first. But he didn't convince himself about her health. From a little distance, he told her in rough friendly tones to keep her heart up, then went on.

Presently an insistent baaing drew his attention, and down he strode. He saw the capering ewe on the bank; the small pool, with the white splotch at its tail. A long leap and he was there. The lamb's head was caught between two stones and its body moved in the swift flow before the water tumbled over a yard-high falls.

He hauled it out. It was drowned, quite dead. He became aware of the mother, her head up, restless, wild-looking, baaing. Slowly his own face, darkened with blood, settled on her with a malignant look. 'You silly bitch!' he hissed. He handled the lamb again, a fine specimen. He could have wept.

Lifting the lamb by the hind legs, with the vague idea of giving the ewe a sniff and so perhaps making it easier to drive her towards the low park, he rounded a boulder and all but trod on a still-born lamb. There was no sign of the mother. He had heard of old ewes that were careless where or when they dropped a lamb. He didn't know. He just didn't know. Fifty yards farther on he came on a third lamb, strangled by a curiously horrible birth entanglement. He sat down and was nearly sick.

That night when he went in to report to his father he was dog-tired and glum. His father was still in bed, but eased up on the pillows. Iain, standing on the floor, his face towards the window, muttered a pointless remark about the lambing having started.

'How did you get on?'

'Very bad,' said Iain. 'Thirteen lambs – three of them dead.'

'It might have been worse,' said his father.

'No,' said Iain, whose brain had been full of sombre calculations. 'Only seventy-odd per cent – even if the living keep living.'

'I've seen it worse – much worse.'

'I don't know,' muttered Iain. 'One or two of the ewes were looking pretty sick.'

A husky sound came from his father's throat. Iain turned round. The slight dry smile was still on the face, a lightening of the weary expression like the coming of the living year he had seen outside. 'I was thinking of first days – real bad days, with a dead-born lamb at every turn. Don't tempt Providence. And you cannot expect this weather to hold.'

'I know that.'

'How about the ewes?'

'I didn't know what to do with the first one. I took her down and put her in the park. I thought if there would be a lamb without a mother – I might try and put the lamb on to her. She has milk. I managed to take a little away. The second ewe – I couldn't find her, though I tried. The third ewe – she's all right, but pretty exhausted-looking. I didn't want to take her down. She's fairly sheltered and I'll see her in the morning.'

'Well done,' said his father quietly, stirring slightly in the bed.

Iain did not look at him. 'I don't know much. I'll do my best. But—'

'Well?'

'If I could come and ask you things. If it wouldn't tire you. I'd like to make a job of it.'

'Surely,' said his father.

'All right,' said Iain and went out.

In the kitchen, he said to his grandmother, 'He doesn't seem ill-pleased.'

She paused. 'Ask him things,' she whispered, 'even if you have to make them up.'

He smiled. His father's 'Well done!' had gone deep. 'I won't have to make them up,' he replied. 'But oh, Granny, I would like to have a good lambing.'

'You'll have it, my dear boy, even if I have to come with you myself!'

He laughed. 'I believe you'd be game for it!'

'Give me a pair of new legs – and a new heart – and I'd take the hill yet like a lintie!'

'I'd give you the legs, but you don't need the heart.'

She shook her head. 'Your heart is so good you don't know you have one.' And off she went before him with the kettle.

Perhaps it hadn't been a completely disastrous day after all, thought Iain. His tiredness was lifting. As he towelled himself, he decided he would not only get some of the potato ground ready that evening, but also have a final stroll along towards the Island before it was quite dark.

The days grew more hectic as they went on. After the fifth, the weather broke. A cold wind came out of the sou'-west, with a small stinging rain. It pierced and was bitter enough for snow. His problems multiplied daily. He had always thought that maternity, the maternal feeling for the newly born, was a strong and invariable force. Now he encountered the ewe that showed no concern for her lamb, that walked away from it, stalked off, deserting it. He came on a lamb here, another there, two on one day, already deserted.

He hunted the mothers, rounded them up, cursed them as stupid brutes, did his best with them, and often – it would have been to his own surprise had he had time to think about it – with an endless patience, talking to them, cajoling them, feeling their udders, finding perhaps that there was little milk, perhaps sore or defective teats, relieving himself by cursing the lean months, but occasionally discovering nothing beyond a problem for his father.

His knowledge grew with remarkable rapidity. He not only assisted at births, pulling the lamb with instinctive care, but could tell at a glance when a ewe was near her time – the heaving flanks, the scraping with a forefoot, the turning round as if to make a nest, the sniffing and pause to settle, only to start the process over again, or even, if she had seen him, to clear off to some new couch. One of the crofters' dogs had this turning habit near the fireside, sometimes rising two or three times and going round after his tail before settling. They said it was 'the wild' in him.

He came home sodden but pleased. He had his tragedies – bitter they were to him – but from that first day his 'percentage' had mounted and was high. What if, at the great gathering about the beginning of June, when the flock was put through the fank and the lambs marked and docked, he could turn out a real final percentage of over eighty! He saw that it could be done, but he wasn't telling his father that. He was telling no-one. 'Oh, I'm struggling away,' he answered Andrew one night.

'Would you like me to have a look round with you?'

'No. You couldn't bring the army of the dead back to life anyway.'

'Not as bad as that, surely?'

'Bad enough,' said Iain. 'What sort of percentage should I get?'

Andrew looked at him.

'Why, what do you think you're shaping for?'

'I had a bad start. But I was thinking – if I could keep up – seventy—'

'This weather will clear. Your best weeks are to come. If

you're anywhere within sight of seventy-five to eighty at the grand assize, you'll hold your head high.'

'If only this weather would take off to give them a chance.'

'It could hardly be worse – short of the snow again.'

Then Iain had his run of bad luck. It was as if the bitter driving rain shocked some ewes into stupidity and kept the lambs from drying. The frail staggering mites got at his heart. He forgot himself entirely. Rarely now did he curse, and then only the combination of circumstances that seemed particularly malevolent. What amazed him was the persistence of life in the frail body, its capacity to withstand the cold, almost visibly to grow, to waggle its tail, if given the quarter of a chance. But once something happened to that inner vital thread of life, it was soon all over. He began to be haunted by the feeling that he might have saved one of the ewes had he known more.

It was during this stormy and ill-fated time that he for the first time skinned a dead lamb, clothed another motherless lamb in the skin, and brought off a new maternal relationship. It helped to brighten a whole day for him. In fact he was so proud of it that he was too shy to mention it to his father. Instead he asked what he should do to a sick-looking ewe whose afterbirth was still hanging.

'Leave her alone,' said his father.

'There was an old ewe on her back. She looked as though she had been there a fair time, judging by the mess her wool was in. I thought they didn't last very long like that?'

'Was she lying with her head up?'

'Yes. There was a slight slope.'

'Like that, and particularly if she can lie over on her side a bit, she'll last days. But if she's lying with her head down the way, or fair on her back, perhaps in a little hollow, she won't last a night. I remember . . .'

Iain found his father's description of an exceptional incident not only fascinating but full of illumination. It was given quietly, with a curious impersonality. All their talk had this impersonal matter-of-fact tone, unhurried and to the point. Often Iain's final 'I see' or 'All right' might have sounded flat or indifferent to listening ears, but to his father, as the guiding member of the business partnership, it clearly meant that his son had now solved his problem or got a grip on his difficulty.

One night his grandmother said to Iain, 'The doctor was in to-day. He's very pleased with him. He said he must be very careful for a bit for if he strained himself by trying to do anything, he would collapse at once. The heart wouldn't stand it.'

'Will he be all right?'

'Yes. The doctor said he has a grand constitution. He said his blood pressure was all right and – it's his own words – "He has the arteries of a young man".'

'I'm glad to hear that.'

'But he'll have to go very slow for a long time, and especially to be careful about the hill. But if he does that, he'll come all right. His lungs are clear. Isn't it good news?'

'Fine.'

'I found him smiling the other night to himself. I think it was over something you asked him, but he wouldn't say what it was.'

'Something I asked him?'

'I don't know, but I think so. Maybe you're not old enough to understand. But sometimes I would be listening at the door, because I wanted to hear how he would be taking it. If it went against him and he got worked up or angry – But anyway, what's happened is that he's got interested. He sees you're anxious to do your best and are relying on him. But it's more than that. Ach, if you were old as me you would understand!'

'Tell me.'

'I'm only an old woman now, Iain, but I've seen a bairn finding her ways. It's then you realize how many strange things and wonders and dangers there are in life, things you had forgotten. He was so used to handling sheep – for so long all by himself – that to him there was nothing in it. Do you understand me?'

'I – think so.'

'You'll be bringing back to him his own young troubles and fears. And he cannot show you by example. I mean he's not with you so that you could learn by watching. So he sees it all – in a new way. But I cannot tell you. To-day he was impatient with me for the first time.'

'What about?'

'"It's high time I was out of this," he said.' She gave a small quiet laugh. 'The nurse has been very good. She's going to help me up with him for half an hour the first fine day.'

'It doesn't look as if there was going to be any more fine days. It's awful weather. Enough to break your heart – up yonder.'

'Wait you! May is in now and you'll see the sun shining on the bonny green leaves before you know where you are. My heart is sore for you sometimes the way you're working, but I know it's no good saying anything. I'll keep the dry clothes on you. It's all I can do. For you're a headstrong thrawn young laddie – but you have a good heart.'

'Me headstrong? – and you ordering me about as I wouldn't order young Mat!'

'Now you're going to be fair mad with me,' she said, 'but I don't care. For I don't want the vanman to think I've started smoking at my time of life.' She put four half-crowns in a neat pile beside him. 'You'll buy your own cigarettes.'

He looked at the money and slowly flushed. 'I can't take it, Granny,' he said simply.

'Can't you? That's easy got over.' She lifted the coins and dropped them in his jacket pocket; patted him on the back and turned away. He got up and went out.

TWENTY

The weather suddenly cleared and the sun came out and shone on the bonny green leaves as she had foretold. He had twenty healthy lambs on a morning's round and never a casualty. The birches were awake in fairyland, more green light and fire than leaves. One solitary little aspiring tree took his breath. The ground held it by the ankle. There were new bird songs, from small fellows come all the way from Africa. He realized, as he lay and ate his piece, how little he knew about these birds; how little really any of the folk in Balmore knew about birds and wild flowers, mosses and plants, butterflies, about all the strange life so vivid and ardent around their doors and fields, on the hills. Listening to the song of the willow-warbler, he was entranced by its slow ease, its carefree perfection, as it came tumbling down, light as the celluloid ball on the waterjet at the circus side-show, tumbling from the branches, downward, with a lovely grace. A happy song, without strife or striving.

The wisdom of happiness. Was that why it appeared slow, even though it wasn't when you listened to it and thought of its being played? The mastery – that seems always to have plenty of time?

A desire for his fiddle stirred in him.

For three days, he had a run of remarkable luck without any real trouble. Only one ewe defeated him, and he decided to take lamb and ewe down to an enclosure where he could teach the careless obstinate brute some maternal sense. The lamb was not being fed, was trying to poach, got a butting from an inquisitive yeld ewe, and altogether needed attention.

His father's basic injunction to him had been not to disturb the ewes unnecessarily. Most of them would tend to keep low for the feeding, but again Blackfaces liked wild exposed places for lambing down. Persuasion and a good dog did a lot, but after many years on the same ground there developed a sort of flock sense. Guide it quietly and in time.

Iain had been conscious in his anxiety of making too many trips to the fank, of climbing up and down the broken slopes until the sweat was soaking his shirt while the cold sleaty rain stung his eyes.

But now – like the willow-warbler in song – he was developing a certain wise sense. When the recalcitrant ewe doubled back, he sent Heath after her. But she wouldn't be turned; she dodged, and went all out helter-skelter. He whistled and Heath stopped. Climbing up a little way to follow her intention, he suddenly heard a faraway bleating that yet seemed near, as if a lamb were crying from the heart of the earth.

It was a wild place of tumbled rock and for a moment he was touched by the uncanny as though the place had a face. Then he saw a ewe beside him. She pranced, baaing, in a way he understood. In no time he was flat by the upthrust of rock, peering down through a narrow slot. He could not see the lamb, but it was audibly there, in a small cavern. Taking off his jacket, he pushed the lamb he had been carrying into the wide poacher's pocket and twisted the jacket round it, leaving the protesting head clear.

For two solid hours he tried to get at the buried lamb, tearing turf and every movable stone away, until he had exposed bare rock and knew himself defeated. It was as though the great jutting slab had got pushed out at the base leaving its top leaning back against solid rock with its light covering of peaty soil. Opposite the slot or crack on the one side, he had uncovered a similar though smaller slot on the other side, also near the top. Once, after thrusting his crook down one opening and slapping it loudly, he had leapt to the other opening and fancied he had caught a glimpse of the lamb.

In the end he left, deciding to go home with the lamb he had and think out some tackle for getting at the buried one. His crook was too short and quite useless for the job. The one man who was knacky and inventive and had all sorts of gear lying about was Ewan. It was the kind of problem he normally delighted in. It would save time if he called on him first.

Seeing Mary over by a small walled field, he shouted to her and she came across to meet him. He was carrying the lamb under an arm, its head resting on his open hand. 'Your father in?'

'Yes.'

'Anybody with him?'

'No.' She came right up, smiling to the lamb.

'Look!' said Iain in the old friendly way, 'there's a lamb in a hole and I can't get him out. I don't know how long he's been there but he sounds a bit feeble. Are you coming up to the house?'

'Yes.'

'Come on, then.' On the way he told her his difficulty, and when Ewan appeared he began again.

'I'll take the lamb,' said Mary, interrupting him.

'Have you got – anything for feeding him? I mean a bottle?'

'I'll manage,' she said. 'He's starving.' She went away to the house with the lamb.

Iain explained the whole position earnestly and in detail, while Ewan thought.

'Listen!' said Ewan. 'What you want is a landing net, a big one. You also want a long switch, like a heather-burning switch. Poke the switch down one hole and sweep the lamb away – then have someone waiting at the other hole ready to scoop him up with the landing net.'

'Have you a landing net?'

'I'll make one in two shakes, if you give me a hand.'

Iain chuckled, all eagerness and delight. Ewan got a long piece of stout fencing wire, bent it into a round noose some two feet across, tied a simple knot, continued to wind the ends in and out in opposite directions until they met, whereupon he lashed them firmly to a hoe-handle. The double-strand of the noose stood out firm and strong. Onto this noose he laced a piece of herring net used for covering a stack of hay and reinforced the net with some stout string.

'It's a poacher you should have been,' declared Iain, laughing and neatly scooping up the ball of string from the ground.

'Now for a switch,' said Ewan. 'But you'd better cut one. It will be tougher and more pliable.'

'Thousands of them in the birch wood. This is great!'

'But you'll need someone with you.'

There was no-one in sight. 'There never is when you want them,' said Ewan, 'and I'm not much good for the hill myself.'

'Never mind. I'll get someone.'

'Mary! Wouldn't Mary do?'

'Yes, but och! I don't want to take her away.'

'Mary!' called Ewan.

In no time, Iain and Mary were on the way.

'It's a shame to bother you.'

'Nonsense,' said Mary. 'I'm glad of the outing.'

'The little fellow is bleating yonder enough to break your heart.'

'Is he? Poor thing!' Mary quickened her steps. 'How are you getting on with them?'

'Not bad at all. You needn't mention it, but things are going very well now, though I'm frightened to say anything. You never know what's going to happen next.'

'I know.'

'I would like to have a good season.'

'I think you will.'

'Do you? I have got some grand lambs. Real toppers. We'll go this way a bit.' On the edge of the Dell he cut a long birch switch.

Some way up the slope, Mary stopped, winded. Iain apologized for the mad way he had been racing on. But within half a minute, Mary was off again.

'How are you getting on yourself?' he asked, as the slope gave on fairly level ground.

'All right, I think.'

'You'll get your Highers?'

'So they say. But—'

'What?'

She hesitated. 'It's going to be a bit difficult at home. Father doesn't know that yet.'

'How do you mean?'

'Ina, my sister, won't come back. I know that now.'

'But she said she would – when you were ready to go?'

'She likes the city life. They're very good to her. She's a sort of governess now. She – she hates the thought of coming back to live here. She was at home for ten days when you were in Edinburgh. She told me then.'

'But – good lord! – what'll your father say?'

'I know. But I see Ina's point. Why should she sacrifice herself for me? And someone must stay with Father. He pretends to like living by himself when I'm off at school. But it's all wrong. I shouldn't be telling you this. Don't mention it.'

'Don't be silly, Mary! Surely to goodness we're old enough friends – many a scrape you got me out of. Hang it, I'm sorry to hear all this. Your father won't take it lightly.'

'I know. He thinks so highly of education and all that. He had set his heart on me going to the university. He has striven hard for it. And I know he'll drive me to it.'

'He'll hate failing.'

'Don't let us talk more about it. I love being out here.'

But Iain was following his own thought. At last he said, 'You may wonder why I don't come round so much, perhaps. But you see, I have failed – and I know how, in their minds, folk think about that. I don't mean your father would make any difference. Not for a minute. But – it's there.'

'I'm glad you mention it yourself. But I think you're wrong. Father is hurt that you don't come round in the old way.'

'I know that.'

They went on in silence for a little.

'Ach, don't let us spoil the day,' pleaded Mary.

'We won't,' said Iain, his brows gathering. 'But I'm fed up with all this – getting away and getting on and not. When Father is well again – I'm away, and I'll never come back. But I wish I could give some of them my mind before I left!

With all the work that's to do here – it does make you mad.'
He stalked on, switch and landing net over his shoulder.

Suddenly he stopped. There were ewes and lambs around.
'See that young rascal there?' he asked, pointing. She nodded.
'He was my first,' he said, smiling. 'Tough lad, isn't he?'

'How do you know him?'

'That's one thing that's surprised me – the way you get
to know them.' He went on talking eagerly, his eyes bright
in a woodland look, all human troubles forgotten. It was
like entering a new world, and Mary, only too anxious to
forget their talk, came alive in the moment.

When they reached the rock and Mary heard the bleating
of the buried lamb, her expression winced. 'Oh, Iain,' she
said, 'he's – he's weak.'

'I know. Now look here! this is what you have got to do.'
With a piece of string, he drew the thin branches of the
switch together, and having inserted it into the narrow crack,
he made her take hold of the handle. 'When I'm ready, you'll
push it right down and sweep slowly towards me. You understand?' He leapt round to the other crack, through which
the lamb must have fallen, and, flat on his face, with the
landing net sunk and ready, cried, 'Right!'

Mary did her best but no lamb appeared. Iain stopped
her and listened. Started her again, saying; 'Work it up a bit,
if you can. More yet! Yet!'

'I can't,' she said. 'It won't go.'

'Get down on your face and push it!' She did this and
struggled with all her might, but with no better result.

Iain sat up and thought concentratedly. 'Looks bad; looks
as if he's lying tucked away somewhere.' The bleating spired
once more. 'Oh, hang!' said Iain, as though it had pierced
him, 'I'll get at him should I have to blast the blasted rock!'
He got on his knees.

'What if he's hurt – from falling down?'

'I thought of that. If he had broken any bones, a leg or
anything, he should be lying below the crack. But he isn't.'
He thought for a moment. 'Pull the switch out a bit and
come here.' When Mary was beside him, he said, 'Lie flat.'

She lay where he had been lying. Beside her, he lowered the net. 'Now,' he said, their heads together, 'see the bottom there. That's where we want him. Keep the net up – just there – and should he appear, get the net behind him; don't let him back whatever you do.'

'I'll try,' she said.

He jumped up and went round to the switch. He felt the trouble – an outjutting ledge two feet down. 'No wonder you couldn't do it,' he muttered. Ten minutes after that, he had broken away a piece of rock from the crack. The switch had now a wider sweep. He did his utmost but no lamb appeared.

An hour later, it looked as if nothing short of blasting would be any use. Iain was all sweat and grime. Mary had helped, holding and levering at his orders, and was breathing heavily. They sat by the rock. There was nothing more they could do that day. By to-morrow, he decided, the bleating would have stopped.

'We'll try once more,' he muttered, getting up, as though there was something specially bitter in this defeat.

Mary could have cried. She got down on her face and inward in the intense heart of her own nature she cried silently for the lamb to appear, for the white body to be there like a miracle. So intensely did she desire this that she saw the lamb in her mind almost as clearly as if she had closed her eyes. For a moment or two she could not look. Iain was already flat and silent, listening for the bleat to guide his concentration of cunning. Then Mary grasped the long handle of the landing net, lifted it perpendicular, and looked. The lamb was there, swaying on its splayed legs, the black face tilted up towards her, and from its mouth came the spiring bleat.

For a moment every faculty in her was paralysed. She could not even cry to Iain. Then her heart began to throb chokingly, her arms shook, she made high whimpering cries to Iain and lowered the net, but not far enough, so that when she made an awkward pass at the lamb she merely hit it and knocked it down. At once distressed and sobered, she grounded the net to keep the lamb from getting back into the darkness. Now she cried out sharply, partly against Iain, who was already flat by her side, interfering with her, for the lamb was trying to stagger to its legs; she scooped the thin wire ring under him, taking the legs completely from him, and there he was tumbled into the net. 'I've got him!' she screamed. She did not hear Iain; she would not give him the handle. But he had got hold of it, was steadying it. Up through the crack came the lamb, and Iain guided the net gently to the ground.

'Oh, Iain!' she cried in a broken exalted voice.

He took her in his arms and kissed her in a wild gratitude. She was taken in the middle of her impulse to get at the lamb; there was a struggling and smothering; then he felt her giving way and in the same moment he released her and turned to the lamb.

The ewe was already at the net but stamped away a couple of yards from Iain, baaing loudly, and turned, circling restlessly, making enough noise to draw the world's attention exclusively upon herself.

Iain lifted the lamb out of the net and felt it all over unnecessarily. 'I think he's all right,' he said from his knees to Mary behind him.

'Is he?'

'I think so,' he said, half turning to make offer of the lamb but not lifting his face.

She got to her knees and took the lamb from him, into her arms, and looked into its face. Then she got up and went a slow two or three paces towards the angry ewe, now backing away and even stamping. Very carefully she put the lamb on its legs and backed away herself, whispering, 'Come on.'

Iain retreated with her and at a little distance they stood watching.

'Some of these ewes are great fools,' he muttered.

'Wait,' she whispered. 'She's excited. Give her time.'

Iain found time for some more remarks; then the little tail waggled with astonishing vigour and Mary smiled.

'That's better,' declared Iain. 'Look, I'll have to shut up

the cracks. I found a ewe stuck in one the first day I went round, in the snow. I won't take long.'

'Do,' she said.

As they moved, the ewe moved.

'Stop!' said Mary.

'Doesn't matter now,' said Iain, and off he went to unearth stones with which to block the cracks.

As he finished, Mary came back. 'They're all right now,' she said.

He shouldered the net and turned for home. 'That was a grand bit of work,' he said. 'I can't tell you how pleased I am. I hate losing a lamb.'

'Naturally!'

'It's awful how this kind of thing gets a hold of you,' he continued. 'I lost one ewe and awoke in the middle of the night and couldn't go to sleep for thinking of what I might have done!' He gave a chuckle or two.

'Your clothes are in an awful mess.'

'Och, nothing!' He brushed his arms and breast negligently.

'Not to mention your face.'

He wondered how she could have seen it, for they had not looked at each other.

'It'll wash off!' He laughed.

'What are you laughing at?'

'I suddenly remembered the time you spat on your handkie to wipe the blood off my brow.'

She laughed. 'An awful thing to do, wasn't it?'

'How, awful?' he asked.

'So – unhygienic.'

'Unhygienic be blowed!'

'And you were so impatient!'

'Funny how impatient a boy is.'

Now her laughter was full of delicious mirth.

'What are you laughing at?' he asked.

'You think you've stopped being impatient?'

'Why, haven't I?'

'Of course. It's very noticeable.' Then quite irrelevantly, she added, 'I knew it was going to turn out lucky.'

'What?'

'Saving the lamb. Do you know how?'

'No.'

'Because the first of your lambs I saw had his face to me. And when you said it was your first lamb, then I knew it was a sign.'

'Are you really superstitious like that?'

'Aren't you? Now be careful!'

He laughed. 'When did you see Mad Mairag last?'

'Not long ago. She's failing a bit.'

'Is she? You're awfully good to her.'

'Ach, poor old thing!'

'I often thought of her in Edinburgh. Particularly that time I was ill.'

'Were you very ill?'

'I was really. Off my head a bit. Do you know, several times I went to her drinking well. I saw it as clearly as I see you.' He was looking away in front of him. 'It helped me.' He staggered.

'Did it?'

'Yes. Queer, isn't it? And other things she said, too.'

'What things?'

'She said, *You must love the land.* Sort of thing you would never mention to anybody. But when I was a bit mad myself, I believed it. I mean it seemed to me as if all the talk about economics and improvements and that kind of thing was only on the surface. But down below was the real thing – like the lamb to-day – and she had it in the net!'

'Why are you laughing?'

'I'm not laughing at Mairag. But – I mean – ach, what's the good of loving the land when these fellows, who have the power, command the markets and can do you down? They merely take advantage of you. Loving, to them, is soft. And then, too, there's so much to learn and do. It's a big subject, I mean. But when your mind wanders off on its own it can see and believe queer things – like the drinking well. By the way, what's it like?'

She described it.

He nodded. 'The stone in front is a darkish slate colour, and one corner of it is broken off?'

She glanced up at him. 'Yes.'

'Queer. Because as far as I know I've never been there. I must go and have a look at it some time.'

'She often talks about you.'

'Does she?'

'Yes. Remember she said you would come back?'

'So she did!' He stopped involuntarily, then laughed and went on. 'I was bound to come back, off and on, for a time.'

'You should go and see her.'

'I will. Yonder's your father at the end of the house. He'll be wondering what on earth has kept us! Are you tired?'

'Not a bit. It was grand. And I'm so happy you got the lamb.'

'*You* got it. It wasn't me. You go first – and watch you don't slip, for it's steep for a bit.'

Iain waved the landing net as they approached Ewan. 'Got him! It worked!' He launched out on a full description of the whole episode. Quarter of an hour later, he left, still laughing and full of energetic movement, just as he used to be, refusing tea, refusing even to wash his face: 'The sight of it may keep Granny from giving me tally-ho!'

Then he was barging on, the lamb under his arm. 'I kept it up!' he muttered, smiling blindly like one who had come through a terrible ordeal. 'I kept it up!' On the uneven path he staggered like one half-drunk. There were buzzing noises in his head. His eyes saw the hills and the sky, gargantuan, vast. Screened by bushes, he sat down; then lay back. The lamb scrambled from his arm, its sharp fore hoofs dug into his chest. His eyes, wide open, had a glitter in them from the sky, while the awfulness of what had been revealed to him came fully upon him.

TWENTY-ONE

The spell of dry weather broke and drifting showers of small soft rain drew green from the earth and a riot of song from the birds. Lying on the hillside in the hot sun between showers, Iain's eyelids closed, but presently between iridescent lashes he was looking on the back of his hand. The skin was smooth and tanned, a warm yellow-brown, exuding stored sunlight from the pores. It interested him in a detached way as if this resting hand were not his own. The hand went slightly out of focus, and the tan and the stored sunlight and the smoothness belonged to Mary, was Mary, the smooth shoulders, the neck, the face, lying there – like all the hillside.

A hellish persecution, he thought, getting up and going on. He spoke roughly, angrily, to Heath, bursting at one stroke the delicate relationship between them. He did not mind, though it darkened him. He began to reason. After all, was he being fair to Mat? He left Heath at home next day and took Mat with him.

He could shout at Mat. He did. Mat became more erratic. Iain's brain narrowed in a precise anger. He would train the dog with an utter impersonality until he worked like a machine. Then, as he lay eating his piece, he offered part of it to Mat. Mat crawled on his stomach. 'What are you frightened of?' asked Iain coldly. 'Eh? What the blazes are you frightened of?' He fondled the dog below the ears and, suddenly smiling in an arid amused way, gave him the last bite. 'You're a bit like myself,' he said. 'And Heath, like Father. That's about it. What?'

He glanced ironically at the birch trees, all green fire in the burst of sun. Curious, he thought, the differences between dogs. He deliberately began to think of the many dogs he knew, and saw that they were very like human beings, each an individual full of his own peculiarities. There was that bitch, Nan, belonging to Hughie's uncle, so sensitive that one harsh word made her squirm. She was like a woman who, hearing a swear word, felt life blacken in horror, as if swear words were men's fists raised to strike. The 'unlawful' word! With a wink, Hughie could introduce a swear word into an ordinary remark about the weather and, right enough, Nan would spot it. It made you laugh. Then there was that dark-tawny collie of Jock's. Should anyone approach the house he circled round and came in behind, head down, hair up on the back of his neck, and his eyes . . . The killer. That's what he was. By nature, a killer. The sheep knew it. His paradise, a place for his fangs. Yet he would never go off on his own and be a sheep destroyer. The dog that did that was quite a different kind of dog, in comparison a frank and friendly dog. Iain remembered everyone's extreme surprise – he was a small schoolboy at the time – when the men took to the hill with their guns and came back, having shot Willie Gordon's black-and-tan Oscar. Then there was Widow Williamson's Tom, whose greatest delight in life was charging down the pasture field after gulls or rooks, bowfing for all he was worth. Iain smiled involuntarily, thinking about him . . . and at once got up, aware that he could not hold to his detachment any longer, that his obsession was coming in behind him.

Sometimes he had to take up a thought from the point where he had angrily dismissed it. Alan, for example. From the beginning, long ago, had he had some sort of premonition about Alan? . . . Nonsense! He could put Alan on his back any old time. He didn't dislike Alan, not really. It just happened that Alan somehow asked for it. Mary never came into it at all. And to prove it, Mary once was Angus's girl. He hadn't minded that a bit. If Angus and Mary had kept together and got married and so on, everything would have been absolutely all right. He would never have thought a thing about it.

Mary had been – oh, hang it, she had just run about with him. She was as natural to him as the daylight, the birds' nests, or whatever he had happened to be keen on. That was all. Because he knew her like that, there wasn't any silly love nonsense. And about the singing – that was natural enough. Why? Because, dammit, she could sing! If her face came to him now and then when he was under the influence of music, particularly these accursed Highland songs, well, what other face could come?

You're a simpleton, said the dark watching face in him. 'Ah, shut up!' said Iain aloud and went on, furious.

It irritated him acutely for that face to smile, to suggest that all the time, all his life, he had unconsciously been in love with Mary. It was so easy to suggest, so commonplace, so absolutely wrong. It made him mad. People were like that, all knowing and cunning, as if *they* knew! There was something sickening about the ordinary run of humanity . . . And then that awful uprush, that awful betrayal of himself, that utter weakening when, face down on the grass, he cried, 'O God, they're right!'

But he did not let the drowning luxury of defeat have its way. He fought it. He had to. He could not embroil Mary in this. He had too much experience of life now. Things could be too ugly. What was there in life for him, what lay in front? He was clearing out of Balmore absolutely and certainly. There was nothing else for it. Not now. He couldn't give in, hang about his father, make love to Mary on the sly, go on and on, with everyone thinking what they thought, in a sort of hang-dog way. He would sooner die. A betrayal of Mary, of Ewan . . .

For the awful thing was that he knew he had power over Mary. He knew it in that blinding moment by the rock. Heaven knows how he had kept up the talk, going along the hillside. His mind seemed to have divided in two, and the cunning part up above – not below, for there was only a boiling lava below – told him to keep up the old part of the natural friend, the boyish companion. And he had kept it up. He was certain he had deceived her. Talking to her father, too, in that laughing friendly way . . . So far, no damage had been done. No real damage. Mary might wonder, of course, but she was bound to see that it hadn't affected him much, that there was nothing in it. He could have power over her – but he hadn't used it.

The arguments were endless, and now and then he said and did extraordinary things. Once, for example, he swore to the solitary little birch tree that he would not mess up Mary's life. He swore solemnly, and felt the better for it, yet slightly ashamed – though of what, he did not know, and he mocked himself bitterly.

At times, he had a great longing for her. There was something about her, he thought, so natural, so friendly . . . a lightness of movement, a freshness of the skin on her face, a bright cleanness of her hair, a sunniness . . . something utterly known . . . tears in her eyes, on her lashes, that time with the netted lamb . . . and she wouldn't give him the handle . . . He felt her body in his arms . . . That was the way it generally ended.

He worked very hard. The potatoes were down, the corn pushing through, the grass coming away, the peats cut. There could no longer be doubt about his splendid crop of lambs. His father was up and moving slowly about. He would see a fine showing when the lambs came to be marked in June!

There was a deep satisfaction in all this fruitful labour for Iain. Once he surprised the thought in himself that it was a revenge. But that didn't worry him. Revenge or no revenge, the job would be done. He would do it for its own sake and ask no acknowledgements from anyone.

Then rather late one Saturday night, he went to Ewan's. As he hesitated at the door, he heard a voice say, 'And what's happened to the man who came back to the land?'

'I was half expecting him,' replied Ewan.

'I think there's someone at the door,' said Mary quietly.

At once Iain walked noisily in, his mind blinded by that repetition of his own description of himself – as a jocular sarcasm or nickname it was plainly already established! – even as the smile of greeting rose to his face.

Ewan welcomed him and Iain was gay and responsive.

'Sure as death, boy, you're getting thin,' said Andrew.

'You would be thin, too, if you did half my work. How are the peats drying, Sandy?'

Ten minutes later, Andrew was coming round in his slow way to the subject of wintering. 'They can say what they like – Jock and Alan and fellows like that – but the more I think over things, the more I am with you, Iain.'

'Why, what have they been saying now?' asked Iain, laughing. 'I'm prepared for a fight any time.'

'Well,' said Andrew after a moment's pause, 'I'll line up with you. We'll take them on, what?'

While the banter continued, Iain made up his mind he would let them have it. And when pressed to the point by Andrew, he began: 'The difficulty is getting these fellows, Andrew, to use common sense instead of prejudice – wintering is a matter solely of providing feed. Have we the kind of land that can do it? The simple way to find out is by having the soil tested. That's easy and costs nothing. The result of the test would show the deficiencies in the soil, what it needs to grow the right kind of grass. Have it drained properly and ploughed up. Give it what it needs, lime and phosphates or whatever it may be. Sow your seed. And then have it cropped properly, by beasts, by mowing machine, according to the way you decide to work it. Quite simple.'

Andrew scratched his head, while one or two chuckled drily.

'How do you mean – the way to work it?' asked Andrew.

'There are two or three ways,' answered Iain, lightly. 'If I had my way, I'd have plenty of cattle. Cattle and sheep – that's the old Highland way. The scientists are now finding out that our forefathers, before they were burned out of their homes by the landlords, knew what they were about. The landlords and their factors were not scientists: they were just money grabbers. However, that's an old story.'

'And a bitter one,' agreed Andrew. 'But go on.'

'Sow the right grasses and clover. The best kinds for our position are known – certain perennial ryegrasses, in particular. There are two phases in grass growing, what they call the vegetative phase, when you develop the stuff for eating, and the reproductive or seeding phase which you must keep in check if you're working on a grazing system. So graze all winter right up till about the beginning of May. By that time the hill is coming ahead, so take all your stock off the ground for a month to give the grass a chance. Then right through June and well on into August graze the ground with every cow and sucker you have and that will keep down the seeding phase. Take them off again in the middle of August, to give the grass a chance once more. Then by the middle of October, when we're now getting ready to send the hoggs away, you have your winter grazing waiting for you.'

Andrew rolled his head sideways in humorous wonder. 'As easy as that?'

There was a laugh.

'Anyway,' said Iain, 'it would be a change from seeing acres of fog and bracken. Don't you think so?'

'No doubt,' said Jock, 'no doubt.'

Iain joined in the laugh. 'Then there's another way,' he said. 'You could cut your grass at the right time and make silage of it. No bother about drying it – and you know how often much of our hay goes rotten with the wet. You can make silage of it *in the wet*. Very well. Make silage of it in pits. You then have the good green stuff to feed out to your hoggs in the winter. So you keep your hoggs at home, save the cost of wintering, and have better beasts. Again, quite simple!'

'You remind me', said Jock, 'of the fellow at the market fair at Kinmore when I was a boy. He would put a sovereign in the watch before your eyes and sell the whole thing for ten shillings. But when you opened the back of the watch there was no sovereign. What did you call him again?'

'A cheapjack,' said Iain.

'That's it,' said Jock. 'You remind me of him.'

'You remind me of the fellow who bought the watch,' said Iain.

Andrew threw his great head up and laughed.

'And who do you think is going to do all you say – find the money, plough the land, put up the fences, buy the grass seeds, drain the land, get the cattle, and so on?' asked Alan sarcastically.

'Not the landlord, I agree. Nor would his factor so advise him, nor the factor's assistant,' said Iain.

'Good, Iain, boy!' called Andrew. 'Don't spare them!'

'What's the good of talking like that?' asked Alan. 'Anyone can talk.'

'Can you find anything wrong with the talk?' asked Hamish.

'Well,' said Alan, 'who is going to put up the money? If the landlord was going to put it up, how would he get it back? Would you sink your money in something that wouldn't give you a return on it?'

'He could put up the rent,' answered Hamish. 'In fact if I know anything about landlords, he would put up the rent whoever sank the money. At the end of his term or lease, the farmer could be turned out whatever money he had sunk in such improvements. And you know it.'

'Wait a minute,' said Iain. 'Up to this point we're not discussing who is to put up the money. That's another matter. First: could it be done?'

'You can do anything if you're prepared to lose the money,' said Alan.

'You can't,' said Iain.

'Can't you?' said Jock. 'Give me the money and I'd let you see.'

'On your fields, Jock, you might grow oranges and breed giraffes – or pink elephants. I know.' Iain nodded solemnly. 'I was merely talking of grass and cattle and sheep.'

The fun went on. Hamish and Jock had a drastic passage. Alan appeared to withdraw from the talk with an amused tolerant smile. When Jock appealed to him he replied, 'Oh, I'm listening,' and smiled on.

'But about the money?' said Jock.

'I simply asked who was to put up the money,' replied Alan. 'What landlord, or any other person, would sink ten thousand pounds in something from which he would get next to nothing – and quite likely lose the whole ten thousand – when he could invest it with safety at five per cent? Would you? – or anyone else here?'

Jock thought for a moment, and laughed. 'That's put the kybosh on him!' and his eyes gleamed mockingly on Iain. 'Would you sink your thousands in the bog, Iain?'

Iain thought for a moment. 'I might,' he said lightly.

'Pigs might fly,' said Jock.

'I doubt it,' said Iain. 'It takes men to fly.'

'Good, Iain boy!' Andrew laughed.

'Besides,' said Iain, 'Alan is quite right. He can't see any other way of looking at it. And Highland landlords haven't got the cash, in any case. That's why they have sold our land to the sporting gents who make their five – or twenty – per cent elsewhere. What happens to us, to the Highland folk, to our land, doesn't, of course, matter a hoot.'

'Ah, rubbish!' said Alan. 'I asked who was to put up the money for your fancy notions and you can't answer. That's the fact.'

'I wouldn't say that,' replied Iain reasonably. 'What you have now shown is that we needn't expect the landlords to put it up – even if they had it. And we, the bold peasantry, our country's pride . . .' He turned to Mary. 'How does it go, Mary?'

At that moment Mary was counting the stitches on her knitting needle. Her finger slipped. 'You've made me lose my count,' she said, colour warming her face.

'Remember – the dear old "Deserted Village",' Iain prompted her.

'I don't remember,' she said, shaking her head and starting her counting afresh.

'"Ill fares the land, to hast'ning ills a prey,

Where wealth accumulates and men decay" – go on,' prompted Iain.

She went on counting.

'Still evading the fact,' said Alan.

'No,' answered Iain. 'Merely establishing the fact that the money will have to come from somewhere else – or our whole show is sunk. The only place left is the Government.'

'But that would mean—' Alan stopped.

'What?' Iain's eyes were on him.

'Working round to your Socialism! I see!' Alan's head tilted sarcastically.

'We were talking about where the money was going to come from,' said Iain.

'But how could the Government sink money in land without getting a hold on the land?'

'Well, how?'

'They couldn't.'

'That's the way it strikes me,' agreed Iain.

An hour later, when Iain sat on his bed, he swore to himself that he had paid his last Saturday night visit to Ewan's. Political talk was so full of niggling 'points' and Alan couldn't help getting heated. There was no vision, no belief. Even if they got the glen into their own hands, if it was nationalized or socialized, damned the thing would they make of it. He felt profoundly dispirited.

He saw Mary on her chair again, the warmth in her face. His head drooped. After a time, instead of getting up, he lay over on the bed.

TWENTY-TWO

The lambing over, there came a period of comparative ease. One Saturday evening, Iain stood at the window of his upstairs bedroom, looking out on the world. The wind had dropped and it was calm and still, an early June evening with a light that turned the young pastures into vivid emerald. His father was sitting down below, reading *The People's Journal*; his grandmother was knitting. The beauty of the evening touched his loneliness with an intimate sadness, a prisoning despair. All at once his mood was held with his breath in a death stillness, through which came the distant singing of a thrush like a singing across the fields of death. Suddenly his mother was there and he turned away. His eyes wandered over the backs of his father's, his grandfather's, books in the wall recess. Four fat green volumes of the Waverley novels. Two taller dark volumes of histories of the clans, with their coloured plates of the tartans. A volume of sermons. Burns. A translation of Virgil's Aeneid . . . His finger hooked out a tiny black book which he had never before noticed.

It was a diary of the year 1876, kept by his grandfather. The population of England in that year was given as 22,704,108. Scotland 3,358,613. For Monday, Feb. 7, the historic note was: 'Mary Queen of Scots beheaded, 1587.' Iain sat down by the window.

For a long time he became completely absorbed. The entries were short, only two or three lines for each day, but for Iain they were charged with meaning and pictures. On Jan. 5: 'Took down troughs and gave corn to tups for first time. Went to Balraid and came home with Donald Macpherson and stayed drinking till late.' On Jan. 6: 'Still fine weather. Killed Rorie's pig. Came home and went to

Cameron's house at night, stayed playing cards till 4 a.m. Had a hare hunt at Sorgil. David Williamson died last night.' The discovery of scab on some sheep, of three sheep 'drowned in a hole – must have been put in by dogs'; trapping, games of curling on frozen lochs; 'went through sheep in evening – looking exceeding well'; the arrival on March 2 ('rather stormy morning') of a box containing, '3 lbs tea, I lb coffee, 2 bottles whisky, 3 dozen porter, 2 lbs tobacco, &c.'

He did himself pretty well! thought Iain. The life of that older day began to swarm with interest. The journey for the hoggs at the beginning of April and all that befell on the way. And then a note that made Iain laugh: 'Still frosty. Had an awful job taking hoggs along to-day. Got drunk on broom last night and had to hire a cart to carry worst of them.'

The coming of the lambs – 'Many dead born'. Ewes had 'cast lambs in all places'. But he did not give numbers and Iain was disappointed, though distinctly left with the feeling that he himself had done astonishingly well.

'Cow got sick – gave her a bottle of train oil. Bought dress for wife at 15/-.' Clippings and dippings and a note about a neighbour having 'an awful spree' and 'breaking his machine on the road home'. (The older folk still called a trap or gig a 'machine'.) Veiled laughter of the kind here and there. And then a revealing note like, 'May 16. Went to sale to-day. Bought a lamp and some books.'

In June he was playing quoits and won a sweepstake. Somewhere he 'stayed late with the priest and drank a lot of porter.' For a staunch Presbyterian, it sounded very friendly! But two or three of the little communities he mentioned were now silent ruins. He came home from the sales in October to start the laborious business of smearing the sheep with tar. Expert smearers arrived from Fraserburgh. Iain's father believed that smearing sheep with tar – shedding the wool and rubbing the tar mixed with oil all over the skin – was still the best way of protecting them from vermin, if no longer practicable. Indeed when a sheep was 'struck' by the maggotfly, he still, after cleaning the infected part, liked to dress it with a mixture of tar and butter.

There was a separate section for Sundays. One entry read:
'Was at church. Preached from the text, John xxi, 15, "Feed
my lambs". Had an awful job taking a lamb from a gimmer.'

But Iain was now restless. The stir of that old country
communal life, with its responsibilities and games, its endless
variety and interest, had got into his blood. It might have
been a hard life, but they had their fun! He went downstairs, across to the barn, and pumped up the tyres of his
bicycle.

There were two or three fellows standing at the door of
Ewan's shop. He gave them a wave and swept on.

'Where away?' Hamish greeted him on the highway.

Iain leapt off. 'I'm fed up. Get your bike and let us go to
Kinbeg.'

They went.

Kinbeg was a scatter of houses with a large hotel for
summer visitors. The bar was round at the back and it was
full. Through the babel and the tobacco smoke, several voices
hailed them as they went in.

'Ha! the young champion from Balmore!' cried a man of
about fifty, grey-dark, with intelligent black eyes in a grey
face. He looked unwashed, was round-shouldered, and the
ends of his long pants bulged under his green knicker stockings. He shook hands with Iain and shouted, 'Two large
ones, Lachie!' In his day, he had been a great shinty player.
He was taking no refusals from anyone now, waved his arms
as though sending sheep dogs over vast hillsides, and swept
his way to the counter.

'You watch what you're doing, Francie!' said a man whom
he had elbowed away.

'Me! Watch myself from you?'

'You're in dangerous company,' answered the man with
solemn ambiguity. He was a known wit and there was a
round of laughter.

'By God,' cried Francie, 'if I couped you in the river I
wouldn't notice it.' He turned to Iain and clapped him heavily
on the back. 'What about playing for Kinbeg this coming
winter?'

'Oh, I don't know,' said Iain, smiling. He had not meant to drink whisky but found it impossible to refuse Francie, whom he knew quite well. On the occasion when Iain had scored the winning goal for Kinbeg, Francie had gone drunk for two days. He was reputed to have quite a lot of money and employed a shepherd. Now he would take no refusal from Iain. He would send the hotel car for him, he would fix up everything – leave it to him!

They became the centre of all interest, of every remark. 'That touch,' declared Francie, 'when you tipped the ball over his head and caught it on your club on the other side of him before it reached the ground – and let fly. Man, man, that was classic! I never did it better. And the goalie, still waiting for the ball and it in the net!' He shook his head. It was beyond any ordinary expression of delight. It was solemn. Francie's saying 'Shinty is *my* mistress,' had gathered a proverbial usefulness.

'You have maybe one weakness,' said Francie in a loud, confidential voice. 'I saw it that day. You played well all through, none better on the field. You worked. You did that. I was shouting at you. I'll admit it. You were our hope, and by God we were holding them level. Three minutes to go. "Hold them!" I shouted to you.'

'You were getting frightened for your money, Francie!'

'Money be damned!' said Francie, turning on the speaker. 'When your big-mouthed Farquhar from Kinmore offered me five to one that Kinmore would win I said I would take him on in twenty-pound notes. "We'll make it singles," he said. "That's more like the Kinmore spirit," I answered.' And Francie, amid laughter, gave the speaker his shoulder.

'"Hold them!" I shouted,' continued Francie to Iain. 'And then, by God, Kinmore Donnie fouled you. One of the dirtiest fouls I have ever seen on a shinty field – and I've seen a few. But there's a bad streak of blood in that family and you can't go against nature. It comes out. I relieved myself—'

'Hear! Hear!'

'I relieved myself of my feelings, but all the time I was

watching you. You got up. You stood looking at Donnie for a minute. Then you walked away. And it was then I heard some school loons beside me say, *Watch Iain Cattanach now!* And I watched, and by God you went through them with lightning in your feet and the hawk in your eye, and when you swung your caman in that last mighty drive—' Francie's suddenly outswung arm knocked a man's bonnet off and spilt his beer.

There was confusion for a little and much mirth, and Iain felt very embarrassed.

Francie, forgetting his reference to Iain's 'weakness' until he was prompted, nodded portentously. 'It's the weakness of the Highlander. Not a damn thing can he do until he's roused. But when he's roused – not hell itself can stop him.' He shook his head sadly.

'Nor floods nor factors,' a voice suggested.

Francie nodded, with a warm glint in his eye for Iain. 'By all accounts, you have been roused a few times since I saw you last. Good health to you, lad!' He drained his glass in compliment. 'The scribes and pharisees utter their condemnations. You'll always have Francie Colquhon to deny them. And if any one of the vermin tries to prosecute you—' he tapped Iain on the shoulder – 'come to me.'

'Why should anyone want to prosecute him?' asked Hamish.

'Eh?' said Francie. 'What?'

'It's time,' said Lachie the barman. 'Come on, boys, I must close up.'

'Time?' said Francie. 'Time for three large ones, you mean.'

'No. All finished. The police has been standing out there for the last half hour . . .'

Hamish and Iain got away at last.

'I seem to have a bit of a reputation,' said Iain as they pedalled along. It was a calm, lovely summer night.

'Ach, what's the good of listening to them,' replied Hamish. 'Anything for a yarn!'

Iain remained silent. After a mile or so Hamish said, 'Let's have a smoke.' He jumped off. Sitting on the bank by the roadside, they lit cigarettes and discussed Francie and the group in the pub.

'Did you hear before that it was I who pushed the factor in the river?' asked Iain.

'Heavens, no. They didn't mean that.'

'You know they did. Not that they blamed me, of course!'

'If someone has started that yarn, it must have been recently. I'll have a talk with Francie on the quiet. I don't understand it.' Hamish looked darkly annoyed.

'I almost got the impression,' said Iain with a wry smile, 'that I had pushed my father in the river.'

Hamish turned on him and said just a shade too quickly, 'Don't be a bloody fool!'

'So you heard it, too?' Iain seemed amused.

'I never heard it. And don't talk to me like that. Curse it, can't you understand that they are bound to talk about you? They mean nothing. What's the good of being upset about rot like that?'

'I'm not upset. And I've learned another thing, too. I couldn't have saved the hoggs at Tulchan bothy. It was the Devil – looking after his own.'

'Where did you hear that?'

'You needn't speak in that tone. I'm not a fool,' said Iain. 'Give a dog a bad name.'

'Ah, hell,' said Hamish, 'shut up!'

'They can say what they like for all I care,' remarked Iain. 'I've got used to a lot of things this last year. I understand. And after all, there was a warmth about the pub. We need more of that. I don't mean only in the pub.'

Hamish gave him a sidelong glance. 'You've grown old this last year.' There was something like gratitude in his dry smile.

'I've grown up, I suppose,' said Iain, with an equally dry humour. He looked around. 'It's a lovely night. And not a bad place. I may even miss it!'

'Where do you think you'll go?'

'As far as I can get. Australia, I think. For sheep. I'm going to write and find out about a passage.'

'They say they have "assisted passages".'

'No use to me. If I cannot get a passage as an ordinary seaman, I was thinking of asking about a steward's job. If you have a High School Certificate and been to the University, I believe it helps. I'll find out.'

'I would like to go with you.'

'You can't because of your mother. You know that. Lately I have been thinking of my own mother. I never understood her before. I never understood how a place can go against you. Even to the very grass.'

'It's all wrong,' said Hamish. 'It's all bloody wrong.'

'I know. That's the devil of it. But it's the men who have gone wrong. We should have the power to shape a place like this. You may think that I was merely getting at Alan and Jock and them for the fun of it. I wasn't.'

'I know you weren't.'

'I know the life in offices, sitting at desks, or in breweries or factories, in the big, dark tenement houses. For them who like it, it's all right. Often it's easy. You're sheltered. You go on doing the same thing day after day. But – take my job for the last two months. It's been gruelling work. But it did have responsibility, variety. Sometimes it nearly broke my heart. But some of these fine May mornings, when I found myself alone on the hill – it was lovely. No city person can ever understand. They think it's just scenery.' He paused. 'I have the awful feeling that there's no place on the world's surface – can be like it. Like that May morning, and walking on the hill.'

'Or at night – and the sound of the river in the throat of a pool!'

'People may laugh at Francie and his shinty, try to take a rise out of him, but he's right.'

'That bloody, grey, defeated laugh.'

'Like withered grass.'

Hamish stirred, looked about him, and smiled more naturally. 'It's good to be talking like this!'

'That's one thing you get in the city – talk. Good talk, too. But there's no reason why we shouldn't have it here.

Hang it all, you have only got to send a postcard to the county librarian for any book published, however expensive, on sheep, or farming, or psychology, or any subject under the sun, and it will be posted to you from Dunfermline. The only thing you have to pay is the cost of the postage back. That's all. We can do that sort of thing in Scotland still.'

'There's something gone wrong, wrong and small, with our old country.'

'The country is all right. We, the men, have gone wrong. I've thought a lot about it. I used to listen to some great talks in Edinburgh about Home Rule. There's the political blethers we hear at election time here and all that. I'm not thinking of that. What I do know, right in my blood, is this, that you'll never do a thing well until you feel responsible for it, as I was responsible, say, for taking the hoggs through the snow or for the lambing. It's the same for your country. Even for our music. We must feel – this is ours to make a job of. If that's lacking, you dodge and try to get something for nothing – and that's the history of the Highlands in a nutshell. We don't feel in our bones that Balmore is our land and as necessary to civilization as any other spot on earth. Depend on someone or some place outside – and you become dependent, in your blood.'

'And those who learn all that, and feel it in their blood – clear out.'

'They clear out – and the women drive them out, for the women smell the decay.'

'You think so?'

'I know it.' Iain paused and smiled, staring in front of him. 'You know Mrs Duncan, Archie Duncan's wife?'

'Yes.' Hamish glanced at him.

'She's a nice woman,' said Iain. 'I like her. Well, some time ago, it was in the gloaming, I was passing the house. Little Andrew – I suppose he'll be six or seven – went bawling round the gable-end. I don't know what he had been up to, but she was after him in a bit of a temper. They didn't see me. She gripped him and shook him. "You little good-for-nothing," she said, "it's another Iain Cattanach ye'll be".'

'Christ!' said Hamish. 'She didn't see you?'

'She did when she straightened up. But I was a little way off, so I gave her a wave and a good night, as if I'd heard nothing.' He added, 'In the Highlands we don't like to hurt people's feelings!'

'It's enough to make anyone bitter.'

They sat talking and smoking until the glimmer of the deep summer night lay on the quiet land. Then they mounted and rode on. On the grass field by the churchyard wall, two peewits swung up, crying. Iain looked at the tops of the headstones, and thought of his mother after Hamish had left him. Again, when he saw his home, he thought of her. The glimmer had deepened in a ghostly stillness and the house stood wrapped in its own strange silence. There was no urgency any more, and his mother was as the crying peewit, the cry all through the air and over the land, and understanding came upon him in a profound and reconciling way.

TWENTY-THREE

A strong element of fatalism got a grip of Iain in the weeks that followed. Once or twice he tried to argue himself out of it but could not. More and more he grew silent, avoided persons when he could, and spent his days on the hill.

The area of the hill which his sheep and lambs grazed became very intimate to him. Beyond its boundaries, even in the wild places, he at once felt the presence of the inimical spirit, the watching grey face. There were moments when he had an extreme apprehension, verging on clairvoyance, of the destructive power of that face, low to the ground, with the gossiping tongue subtle and sibilant in its mouth.

The gossiping word went from mouth to mouth; the eyes watched. He saw the spirit, the positive living spirit, being eaten by it, just as the maggots of the blow-fly or green-bottle ate the sheep.

The green-bottle had an unerring power of selecting its sheep. It flew around, sniffing, until it found some spot of fleece which the external world had soiled. There it laid its eggs. In one day the eggs hatched out into maggots. In two days the maggots were fully grown. From the first, the maggots had only one aim: to penetrate the skin and work their deadly way down into the sheep's vitals. The sheep went on living, rubbing or butting its sores against rocks and trees, until it was little more than a living shell. The brain became affected. It began to circle upon itself. Then it stood and looked upon the world for the last time; its head drooped; it got to its knees and lay over.

The first time Iain saw this happen was in the bracken patch on the slope below the birch wood. He had done his best with the ewe, cleaning the sores, wiping the maggots away as they came to the surface, treating her carefully to lessen the shock of the disinfectant. But the flies smelt the sores, grew excited in small clouds, followed the brute as though attached to her in a mysterious way. She went into the bracken to die. She died. He sat for a while beside her, moved not to the sorrow or rage that a year ago might have brought a youthful mist of tears, but to a dry-eyed bitterness that was remorseless.

For everything worked to the one end; green-bottles, maggots and bracken were all part of decay's conspiracy. The affected sheep went into the very bracken that sheltered the maggots and so became the happy breeding ground of the flies.

It was at such times that he had his most sweeping visions of reconstruction. Wipe the bracken away, wipe its green curse from the ground; destroy the growths that shelter the parasite and encourage the good plants that give strength and health, for the maggot-fly smells not health and strength but uncleanness and decay.

And through it all he saw that as it was with the sheep so it was with a community of people. Men said that women gossiped. But men themselves gossiped in a more deadly way. A hint and a nod and a certain kind of laugh. They set the maggot to eat its way into the vitals. Let any man try to do something beyond his fellows, beyond the circle of living they command, and the sly maggot-men get after him.

Iain had his triumphs, particularly at the great June gathering of the sheep, when ewes and lambs were brought to the fank and the lambs were marked, docked, and counted. Iain knew now what good lambs looked like, and as he saw them, sturdy and healthy in their hundreds, flowing on into the confining stone walls, he could not help a deep emotion of pride. There, at least, was his work for all to see, and he observed his father stand and look at them, and knew that no other eyes in the world could more accurately assess their value as stock. Though he was aware that it went deeper than that, for in his father's eye for a living beast was a final assessment beyond any market price.

The hoggs he had brought home through the snow were

shorn for the first time. The fank was a centre of riotous activity, lambs being shed from ewes, male lambs from female lambs, and yeld ewes being 'drawn' to the clippers. Baaings and bleatings, barkings and snappings of crofters' dogs, the circling of the whisky bottle as the day wore on and vigour needed its traditional stimulant, the jamming of a castrator and the use of the human teeth, loud shouts, jokes, an occasional roar of laughter. Iain was working himself dizzy. There was no time for thought. At such a moment, the common effort in fruitful toil seemed to bring out what was natural and best in man.

But Iain had his triumph. The whole day worked up to that. All the lambing days, the days of struggle and toil, now found their moment of reckoning. Docked tails were counted.

Iain's percentage of lambs from his ewes worked out at eighty-seven.

There was chaff and compliment. The characteristic dry humour shook its head over mention of miracles. Hamish and Jock had an uproarious passage. Iain felt confused and moved. But inwardly, singing in him, was the thought, 'I've done it!' At least he had done this. He had finished the job.

Said Andrew to his father at the end of the day in a voice loud enough for Iain and others to overhear, 'Well, Duncan, I'm thinking it's about time we retired and left the young ones to carry on. It's beginning to look as if they could do without us.'

Iain's father smiled as he turned away. 'It's been a good day,' he said.

Hamish winked to Iain. 'You've done it on them to-day!'

There was something so penetrative, so triumphant, in Hamish's wink that a great surge of feeling came over Iain, a desire to break out of the bitter ingrowing ring of loneliness and find the warmth and music of living that was native to his spirit. On Saturday night, Hamish, Hughie, and Iain cycled to Kinbeg Hotel. Francie was there, and Iain drank a little more than was good for him.

Thereafter, day after day he worked ceaselessly, high up on the hill with his sheep, carrying a pair of hand-shears unobtrusively to clip soiled spots from his flock, watching them carefully, spending hours with a scythe among the bracken, noting the ways of the maggot-fly which a spell of damp warm weather seemed to encourage, lying on his back like a deer-stalker with staff and telescope and sweeping distant places slowly, or, for long tranced minutes, watching a near bird or butterfly or dragonfly which had been deceived by his stillness. Then occasionally, when his feet of their own accord took him to a certain spot, he would lie flat and turn his glass on Ewan's cottage. The High School was closed for the summer recess and Mary was at home all day.

Sometimes he had an ardent desire to stay out all night – in some bothy, like the Tulchan bothy. The desire would sharpen to a craving as his legs wearily began the homeward trek. The sight of his father working about the steading or along the river reaches often actually stopped him and he had to force his feet to move on.

But on Saturday evening, washed, shaved, and freshly turned out, he mounted his bicycle and set off for Kinbeg with Hamish and Hughie. One night a mixture of whisky and beer induced on the road home a violent drunken sickness. It was two o'clock in the morning – Sunday morning – before he opened his own front door and tackled the stairs to his bedroom.

But the following Saturday night they were in Kinbeg again, and when Hamish made even a tentative effort to control Iain, Iain turned on him with a mocking intolerance. There was a noisy hour in the pub that night, but no violence beyond some strength-testing horse-play, and on the way home, when they got off their cycles for a smoke, Iain looked at Hamish with a smile far back in his eyes and said, 'There are two fish in the Red Pool.'

Hamish's eyes met Iain's and between them leapt the flash of friendship. In a moment they were alive with energy and a warm, exciting humour that completely consumed the troubled estrangement in the pub. Hughie saw what was happening, saw the sunlight licking up the mists, and said 'No!' strongly.

'No?' repeated Hamish laughing.

'Why not?' asked Iain, amused, already on his feet.

'Because the river is being watched,' answered Hughie. 'And you're not to go.'

'He won't let us,' said Iain to Hamish.

'Come on!' said Hamish.

'No, you won't,' said Hughie.

'You going to stop us?' asked Hamish.

'Yes,' answered Hughie. 'Now, don't be damn fools. The river is being watched.' His features sharpened as he turned on Iain. 'I know they would like nothing better than to catch you.'

'Who?'

'Finlay. And Major Grant behind him.'

'How do you know?'

'Never mind. I know. I'm not about the big house for nothing. They haven't forgotten. And you haven't done your best to help – with Major Grant.'

'To hell with Major Grant! Come on, Hamish!'

'No, you don't!' cried Hughie. 'If you do, I'll tell the world.'

Iain walked away, followed by Hamish. Hughie put his fingers in his mouth and let out a piercing whistle. They turned on him. He ran, and as they chased him they fell and choked with laughter. At last Hughie sat down. 'It's all very well for you,' he said.

'How for me?' asked Iain, weak with laughter. Then he saw the strain behind Hughie's smile.

'You know what they're saying – you could hear it in the pub – about who pitched the Major in the river.'

'I know. But what do I care?'

'You may not care. I do. If they catch you poaching – then I warn you that I'll tell it was me who did it.'

Iain's expression narrowed dangerously. 'If you did that I'd break every bone in your body.'

'Don't be so sure you could.'

'Couldn't I?'

'No.'

'Don't be two young fools,' said Hamish. 'You're quite right, Hughie. There would be no damn sense in walking into their clutches.'

Iain laughed sarcastically. 'You're game, I must say!'

'It's all very well for you,' said Hughie. 'But if you think I'm going to shelter behind you, then to hell with you. I'm getting a bit fed up with it.'

Iain looked at him and his features softened. 'Sorry, Hughie.'

'Oh, it's all very well,' said Hughie, his eyes staring in front, angry and hurt.

Hamish gave Iain a warning wink. 'After all, Hughie,' he said, 'you did it to save Iain. But for you Iain would have been caught red-handed. He's sheltering behind *you*. We were all in it, and if you're going to take it like that, you're going to make me feel pretty awkward. Poachers should hang together.'

'I'm prepared to hang all right,' said Hughie, with a grim humour. 'Only, I – when I hear them say things about Iain, it makes my blood boil. I very nearly let Finlay have it the other day. I'm afraid it'll come spouting out of me. I'm thinking of clearing out. I'm fed up with this rotten hole.'

They talked for hours and this time it was after two o'clock on Sunday morning before Iain got home.

On a Saturday night towards the end of July, when the sheep-shearing was over and men were taking their ease, the summer in their blood and harvesting ahead, it was Hamish who lost his wits in the pub and struck a man who had irritated him more than once with his hidden, insinuating humour. Lachie, the barman, was a powerful fellow. As Hamish was forcefully held, his antagonist was cleared out and, in fact, disappeared. No damage was done and Iain did his best to soothe Hamish.

'If you fellows from Balmore don't know how to behave yourselves,' said Lachie, breathing heavily and redly angry, 'you'd better keep away from here.'

Iain looked at him. 'We know how to behave ourselves all right,' he said.

'We'll have no lip from you,' said Lachie. 'We know you. Clear out! And do your dirty work where you're used to it!'

'If you touch me,' said Iain, 'I'll smash your face.'

Francie intervened, getting in front of Lachie. Hamish, suddenly sobered, said, 'Come on. Let us go.'

'Come on, Iain,' said Hughie, taking him by the arm.

They went out. The summer daylight lay around as they mounted their bicycles and pedalled away, followed by a laugh or two.

This story reached Balmore in a wildly distorted form.

Iain's restlessness grew. He had now stopped going to Ewan's cottage altogether. As August came in, his father more and more wandered about his sheep. For hours on end, Iain would lie concealed on the hillside, Mat beside him. The young dog had become his slave, and understood Iain's moods or orders in a way no-one could have foreseen. One day when Iain, lying alone on the hillside, broke down and wept, for he was secretly leaving in two days and Mary and his fate had been haunting him, Mat licked his ear once, then sat back on his haunches, quivering and whining. Presently as Iain looked at Mat's face he saw the suffering behind the mask.

He could not bring himself to speak to his father. In this he knew he was to blame. But what, after all, could he say? There was nothing to say except that he was leaving. Once discussion about working the sheep was over, Iain had drawn into himself. Things had happened which could not be washed away.

On his way home, drained of emotion by his breakdown on the hillside, he decided to tell his father that he was leaving the day after to-morrow. That would get it over and he would have a last day to himself. It might also make things easier at home; might give his father and grandmother time to understand and accept. He would like to part decently from the people he cared for. That would be a help to him, would lighten the future. Perhaps they were just waiting for him to break this awful aloofness, this instinct to avoid them, to be by himself. He realized that somewhere deep in him he had a great respect, even a strange wordless fondness, for his father. Once or twice he had had a swift intuition of all his father's life. Torquil's words about 'the great nights' they would be having; his father's struggles; the crippling loss of Torglas; the debt; his mother's increasing obsession; the long, grey years; his final quietude – with pride hidden, the old Highland pride, hidden but still there, as it would be until the end. Good stock! The real stuff! thought Iain, feeling the response in his blood. That his father had been shamed by his own son before men like Major Grant and Mr Cunningham could not be forgotten. It was a shame in the blood. Iain understood this.

He went to the post office and bought a packet of cigarettes. As he was leaving, Sandy Morrison, who drove a small lorry, said to him, 'What about a run to Kinmore to-night?'

'When?'

'About eleven. I'm picking up some late goods.'

Iain hesitated. He liked Sandy, and the outing would be a small adventure. 'Afraid it's a bit late.'

'Not at all. There and back. Anyway, you'll find me at the garage.'

'All right; but don't expect me.'

Iain could not help grinning to himself as he went on. He had been ready, in an instant, to avoid the talk with his father! And here he was now, going back by the hillside, to avoid Ewan's cottage! The grin twisted. The match broke as he struck it. His mind hardened. I'll speak and get it over, whatever happens! he thought, and the cigarette smoke was hot and bitter in his mouth as he sucked it in. But he knew he was going to speak.

TWENTY-FOUR

Iain sat silent, lost in a sickening wonder at his grandmother's stories of drinking and fighting in the Kinbeg pub. Drunkenness and physical assault, ugly and brutal.

Not whole stories, but bits, smeared with blood and sin, as though she could not bring herself to fill in the detail.

'He said he was only warning me. He said, "I'd advise your grandson not to go back there".' She was referring to the Kinbeg vanman who came once a week with some groceries and household goods and took away her eggs.

He stirred. 'Does Father know?'

'Yes, though he has said nothing to me. But I thought I should tell you, for he may speak.' Then she added, 'Everyone knows.'

'So the vanman said I wasn't to go back there?'

'He said that. He said they would "get you" if you did.'

Suddenly he became aware of a quietness in his grand-mother's voice and manner, a friendliness as of an ally. Not once had she asked him why he had done it or begged him never to go back to Kinbeg. He lifted his head and glanced at her and saw that she had something else in her mind. She was sitting before the fire and sometimes turned her face towards him as she spoke.

'Torquil Macfadyen from Altbreac was in this morning,' she said. 'He was asking for you.'

'Was he?' His head lifted sharply.

'Yes.' But she did not look at him. He knew now that the real trouble was coming.

'He had a great word for you. I heard it all.'

'Oh?'

'Your father did not say much when Torquil praised you. Torquil was full of his own laughing, telling him how you played the fiddle. Then he saw that your father had something on his mind. So he laughed more than ever. He hit your father a great wallop on the shoulder and asked what he was glooming about, for boys would be boys, and if you shoved the factor in the river, wasn't it the very place for factors. Torquil kept on about it. Your father sat down. Then Torquil saw that your father had not heard that story.'

Iain sat quite still. When his grandmother had composed herself, she went on in the same quiet voice, as though relating something that happened long ago. 'Torquil said that it was just a yarn that was going the rounds and he was sorry that ever he mentioned it, for likely there would be no more truth in it than in most yarns. Your father said nothing and I pressed Torquil to have something to eat but he said he couldn't because he had to get to Kinmore. Your father gave him a dram and asked about the people of Strathorn. Then they went outside. Sitting here I could hear the rumble of Torquil's voice and now and then great swear words rose out of it. At last I got to the door. Torquil was stalking off, still shouting an angry word or two, but your father had turned to the byre and his face was dark.'

In the silence, Iain was aware that his grandmother's face turned to look at him, then turned away. He had had nothing to say. His body sank down and got clamped.

'I'm telling you all that, Iain, so that you may be prepared. For things have come to a pass, and angry words never yet mended anything.' She lifted her face and turned it towards him, towards the window, the light. 'Your father went out just before you came in, and I have been sitting here thinking about my life. It came upon me to tell you about it, I don't know why.' Her eyes were back on the little yellow flame that lazily licked the edge of a peat and her right hand smoothed the dark cloth of her skirt.

A desire to get up and go away shot through him like a tongue of fire, then it died down and went out.

'It's not easy to tell you,' she began, 'but maybe you will understand it. For I know that whatever you may have done, you did not mean to do harm. You have a good heart, Iain.

I know that. I'm near the end of my time, and all I have learned, I sometimes think, is only just that, whether the heart is good or bad. I am not the one who could ever sit in judgement on you. For I had a hard time of it once. It was very, very hard, and the sun went out on me for many a day.' She paused. There was no sorrow in her voice and suddenly she looked at him and smiled. 'You may not think it,' she continued, 'but once I was young – as young as yourself, Iain. I was even younger, I wasn't yet nineteen, when a man came into my life. He came from the sea, from a ship, from one of those ships with tall masts and many sails. What was I but a foolish lassie, and he was the morning sun to me. He was tall and slender and to this day when I see the sun on the yellow corn I hear him laughing. I was in service at the time in the house of a man who was a ship chandler in Fraserburgh. He had come with his family on holiday to Lower Strathorn and taken a furnished house there for the month, and I was the servant engaged to help in the house. The family took to me so much that nothing would stop them but they must have me back to Fraserburgh with them. My father had only a small croft, but he did outside work, for he was a good-living man and when he had a job to do, mending dykes and fences, he did it well. I was the youngest of five and the others were all out at work, and I was sorry to leave my mother. Often and often since these days, I have seen her eyes looking at me as if they cradled me in their sight. She was a good mother to me in the hard, silent days . . . Yes, she was a good mother. Oh, Iain, she had lovely eyes.' She smiled and the tears went trickling down her wrinkled face. 'It's easy to weep when you're old. Don't mind me.' She wiped the tears away with her hand and her face seemed to lighten, to lift, with a strange touch of youth or memory upon it. 'It was a trading schooner, trading to the Baltic. I would know when she was leaving, and whatever I was doing I would find time to run up to the high attic window to have a look at her, standing away to the sea with all her sails set. Lovely she was, like a ship in a dream, and indeed whatever cargo she carried with her, she carried all the dreams of the lassie who was looking at her. All of them, for oh! I loved him dearly. Oh! I was fey for him. I remember that last time when she was setting out. Something overcame me and I fell on my knees and I prayed. Never before did I know what praying meant. And maybe never again. For it was weeping I was, as if my heart was broken, and my hands were hitting the hard wall as though it was a stone face that could not hear me, that would not promise . . . Hard, hard is the rock to a lassie's hands then. Maybe I had a fore-vision. I don't know. Maybe I was just frightened, because everything was so near I might miss it, for when the ship came sailing home again we were to be married. My mistress found me sitting there in the attic and she comforted me with good sense – she was a very sensible woman. I admired her because there was nothing soft about her. She was always just and fair. I did not tell her everything because I was frightened. Before, when the ship sailed away, I knew she would come back. This time . . . she didn't come back.'

There was silence for a little while.

'I never saw him again. She was an old ship and some said she went down, but some said she was sold to a trading firm in Finland and had her name changed. I waited and waited, for I knew he would come to me if he could. But he didn't come. Then my mistress began to question me. She had a young family, the oldest a lassie of sixteen still at school, and she didn't want them – to see – to know – oh, love's shame is more bitter than any shame in the world. It was a terrible time, that. Then I made up my mind that I would do away with myself. For I could not bring my shame back to Strathorn, to my father's house. Death would be easier than that. There was a lonely place of rocks and the sea where once we had loved each other. Perhaps I was a little wrong in the head by that time, for I remember the night when it came over me, with a strange calm, that it would be easy to do. It was like giving myself to the sea and to him. In the queer notion I had – maybe I dreamed it – though the queerest dreams I ever had came to me with my eyes open – I had the queer notion – I saw myself going down under the sea, and away far under the sea, walking to where he was. Then just as I saw him at a little distance, I would cry out with gladness – and come to myself ... It was the night before, the night before I was going to do away with myself, that my father came. Perhaps the master and mistress had been getting a little frightened for me. I don't know. She was a just woman and would not turn me out of the house. So she had sent for my father. He took me home. Terrible is the righteous wrath of a father. If silent wrath could have slain me then, dead I would have been before I walked in at the door of my home and saw my mother's white face in the gloom.' She paused. 'It was within that home, barely two months later, that your mother was born.'

The silence came from far away, through the evening silence now upon the world, and the ticking of the clock had no meaning in time. Iain stirred and had the strange feeling of lifting his limbs out of a heavy sea.

'I thought I would tell you that,' she said. 'I don't know why. But I feel you are planning to go away. It is a terrible thing – to go away.'

He leaned forward, his forearms on his knees, staring into the fire. 'You got married after that.'

'Yes. The man who married me had known me always. We were at school together and he said he had long loved me. At first, life was not always easy. He would have dark moods on him. But I understood that and there was nothing I would not do for him. And as time went on and his own child was about his knees, we grew happy together.'

'You forgot the first man.'

There was a little silence. 'Yes,' she said softly.

He felt the heat sting his face. 'I did not mean that,' he muttered.

'I know,' she said. 'You never forget. In all the lands of the world – you'll never forget. Things will remind you always – as you remind me.'

'How?' His voice was low and harsh, but gentle.

'When you gather your brows as you did just now. You

have a certain look, a flash. You walk upright and lithe. One day – you were walking past with the dogs – looking ahead ... you put the heart across me.'

'Where did he come from?'

'From the Western Isles. And that's another thing. When I heard Mary Cameron singing his Eriskay song, I looked at her – and I saw myself. I saw the braes and the rocks, and the wind was in my face, and the sea was hitting the rocks ... You'll think I'm a foolish old woman, but that's not the way it is, Iain. When you grow old you grow quiet, and the fears and the feelings matter no more. But you don't forget. I can see little Seonaid now – for that's what he called me, for though I was baptized Jessie, it's Seonaid in the Gaelic. I can see her playing about me. She was slim and very quick. She had the prettiest ways in the world, and made daisy chains, and had a quick temper. Then she went to school, and one day she came home and her clothes were torn and she had a scratch of blood on her cheek and I could see she had been fighting. But she would not tell me what had happened but kept to herself in a strange way. Then in the deep gloaming of the summer night when I was putting her to bed – himself was out – she said to me, "Mammy, what's a bastard?"'

A harsh sound came from Iain's throat as the chair creaked under him.

'You're not allowed to forget. You know that already,' she said.

'The maggot-folk,' he muttered.

'But she held her own against them and she had a great loyalty, especially to her little brother when he began to go to school. Once she fought a boy over him, and there was talk about it and they said it was the bad blood in her. But there was no bad blood in her. Only she could not stand cruelty. Even to birds or beasts. It always put her beside herself and then she would do a thing in the flare of the moment. That was all. And though I may not have been like that myself, I loved her for it. She grew up into a fine girl; wilful, I admit, and proud beyond what should be, but maybe that was just the need to hold her own. It's only now I'm seeing that maybe that never left her, though when she married your father I thought it was all over and by with. Perhaps what you suffer in your youth never leaves you. I don't know. But in the end it came out and warped her a little. I think it did.'

'How do you mean?'

'When things began to go wrong, and the Torglas sheep were smothered in the snow, and her family was growing up, I think she began to fancy that the land would get her children, and the poverty of the land. She was saving you – from things she never forgot. We were poor enough when my man died and that was when she was fourteen years old. She was a good scholar, but she left school then. It's difficult for me to tell you . . . I can't put words on it.'

'Did my father know—'

'Oh yes,' she interrupted him. 'The first year or two he came about the sheep, I said nothing. Indeed, there was nothing to say, for your father was always a modest man. He had a light in his eye and great fun in him, but he was mannerly, and oh Iain, I liked him. You cannot know how a mother feels. Your father came of fine Highland stock. When I saw that he was fond of her, I made up my mind. I was not proud, but – I could not be less than him. It was hard on me, but the time came. I can see him now. He was sitting on the chair by my fire. Seonaid had not yet come in. I began – but the words would not come to me. Then he looked at me – in a shy way – like a boy – and smiled – and said—' Her voice broke. She could not go on. 'He said – oh, he just said – he said, "I know".' Then she completely broke down, moved as she had not been by anything she had yet told him.

The evening light was growing dim in the kitchen. When she had composed herself she arose and went to the window. 'I don't know what's keeping him,' she said. As she turned to the dresser where the lamp stood, Iain got up and went to the window. The summer nights were closing in. The sky was overcast with grey, sad cloud. The hens had gone to roost and the silence lay about the steading accepting the darkness. He got an impression of his father, standing alone by a grey dyke. Then suddenly he saw him coming. He was walking slowly, an embodiment of dark thought and power, of the falling night, coming to the house in a fated and fatal way. Something purposeful about the slow figure came against Iain's breast like a flat hand, pushing him back from the window. Without a word, he turned to the stairs and went up to his bedroom.

He listened till his mouth went dry, then moved about to show that he was there and that he was not listening. He did not know what to do. His mind was blank, with the muffled sound of a voice crying aloud in it. But not his own voice, nor anyone's voice. He sat on his bed. What was he going to do? Had his father nothing at all to say? The silence was taut, like a trap, a black, terrifying arch, towards which he could never move.

There was nothing to do. It was too late now.

The darkness thickened in the room and about his body which had grown heavy, but though it was heavy it was yet held on nervous dagger-points of feeling which now and then thrust at it, until at last he could no longer remain there and remain himself. A decision was made somewhere and now he was walking, thoughtless, to the stairs and down the stairs, steadily. Taking a deep breath, he went into the kitchen. The lamp was lit, his father was sitting by the fire, his grandmother looked up at him from her darning. Suddenly he did not know what to do, so automatically he turned to the door and took his cap off the hook.

'Are you going out, Iain?' she asked in a quiet, normal voice.

'Yes,' he answered. Then, strangely compelled to add something, he said in an indifferent voice, 'Sandy Morrison is going to Kinbeg and asked me to go with him.'

His father's body turned solidly on its chair. 'Have you not gone enough to Kinbeg?'

Iain realized that his tongue had betrayed him, for Sandy was going to Kinmore, to the railway station. But the tone of his father's voice made any correction impossible. He stood with his cap in his hand, looking at it. His father arose.

'Have you no shame in you at all?' asked his father. 'Is there no end to the disgrace you can bring on yourself and on your home?'

Iain looked at the cap as his hands turned it slowly. He had nothing to say. He would take his punishment. He would never speak. When his father had finished, he would go away quietly.

'Coming home here on a lie, thinking we would never find you out! Is there no manhood in you at all? Can you use nothing but your drunken fists? Can no-one rely on you?'

His father's voice, harsh with contempt, had also a terrible menacing quality in it.

'Were you at the river the night Major Grant was thrown in? Answer me!'

Iain remained silent.

'Answer me!' The voice exploded with extraordinary force.

'Yes,' answered Iain.

There was silence, then his father's voice came, low-pitched, marvelling through a sort of horrible finality, 'So you were there! So – you – did it!'

Iain was too beaten, too mauled, to attempt to explain anything. But his mouth mumbled indistinctly, 'I didn't.'

The vague sound, as of a boyish petulance, pierced his father's restraint and the whole body tautened and lifted with a jerk. 'At the very time your mother was begging for you, begging – from the man you tried to murder!'

A low, moaning sound came from his grandmother that rocked the kitchen and swung black shadows of agony through the light.

His father took two steps towards Iain, to wipe out the evil from before his sight, to cleanse the house of what stood before the door. As he stopped, his rounded burly body seemed to swell. 'Is the blood in you so black, so bad, that nothing – nothing – will ever clean it?'

Then Iain lifted his head and looked at his father, straight into his father's face, and he said, 'There is no bad blood in me.'

There was a horrible long moment when they stared at each other, then the father, sensing the dark implications in Iain's utterance, appalled and blinded by its dreadful challenge and meaning, strode forward and with his open hand hit his son's face a smashing blow.

With a cry, the grandmother came to them, crying, 'Duncan! Duncan!'

Iain gathered himself from the door and again stood before his father, his hands by his side. The sight of his exposed defencelessness, with its awful waiting, but with the features drawn, the brows gathered, was too much for the father, who now must break what he saw before him, but the old woman had him by the shoulder, was shoving herself between them, crying, 'Duncan! Duncan! What are you doing?'

'Leave me, woman!' he shouted.

She hung on to him. 'Iain, go away!' she cried.

'I'm going,' said Iain, 'don't worry.' He turned for the door. 'I'm going – for good.' The broken, sobbing anger in his voice choked it. As he went upstairs, he was trembling violently. He heard the voices down below, but cared no more, did not listen. His fumbling hands found his purse of money in the small trunk. He wanted nothing more, nothing more, nothing. He stumbled downstairs, outside, and was going away. He heard his grandmother coming crying after him, crying, 'Iain! Iain!' But he held on by the park dyke. 'Iain!' she cried, in a final, high, dreadful way, and then he was going on, and no-one was coming after him, nothing about him but the night, and its darkness grey about his feet.

O God, it was a terrible way to be going! The anger, the hopelessness, the misery of it, broke in him afresh as he struck the main road. His grandmother's cry pierced him. Her life's story went through him like a spear. He might have stopped for a moment and comforted her. He might have done that. Damn, he might have done that. It wouldn't have cost him much.

His eyelashes blinked the hot tears away. The night rose about him, charged with the past things of his life. Sorrow and a crying wildness were in his head like the crying of moor birds, and his going away had their distant notes within it. The telegraph wires turned to gossamer, but he could not think of the car that was coming, nor care; then in an instant as the car, cornering at speed, shot its headlights upon him, he was blinded and could not in that instant remember where he was, and stood, and suddenly remembered, and instinctively swung away from the lights that had swung round on him. There was a terrific screaming of brakes and tyres and he was hit with a crashing, crumpling thud and softness that flung all consciousness from him as his body was lifted and pitched over the roadside ditch.

PART FOUR

THE DRINKING WELL

ONE

The notes were not the notes of any bird that sang. In savage and disconnected scenery they fell like drops of water, round and pellucid, and turned into pure sound as they struck and vanished. Note after note, in curves of sound that rose and fell like the onflowing branches of a creeper, of a flowerless honeysuckle, so pure in line that the line itself was the flower. He waited for it to stop. But it didn't stop. It could not. Just when it was going to stop, it began to rise again, to rise higher, to reach up for some final unimaginable hold on the branch of pure space, and, in the very instant of attainment, there it was, curving over and down again, but onward, festooning in aerial lightness the dark, fathomless chasm.

Waiting for it to stop became a faint agony. It was like the Celtic pattern that interlaced and went on, exquisite in its subtle line, but without end, with the awful tyranny of the endless; the Celtic pattern that wrought its music on the upright stone, turning the stone and its arms to sound and aspiration, to an evocation of holiness so absolute that it remained quiet and simple.

Then in a moment he knew that at last, at last, now, it was going to stop, and like beauty that had utterly fulfilled itself it did, in fact, stop. Silence became a suspension of faculty within the utmost world – and here, along an invisible corridor quite near to him, soft footfalls approached, like heartbeats. They, too, stopped. A door began to open very slowly. He saw it open, and waited. Round its edge with a profound effect of stealth a face appeared. It was a young woman's face, lovely as the face of an angel. The golden hair curved and curled, close to the head, away from the smooth brow, and the containing line of the face went down to the chin and up again in a perfect oval. The eyes, wide-set, were large under the thin pencillings of the winged eyebrows and the mouth was red.

Surprise opened the mouth slightly and widened the eyes. 'Oh!' she said. She came into the room in a long, close-fitting green dress, approached the bed hesitantly, and regarded him with living light and colour. 'Are you better?' she asked, and the question in quite a different way came from her eyes.

His eyes watched her with a curious fixed glitter, looking upward a little from under the eyebrows. The bedclothes came to his ears. He never moved. He did not even blink, so warily did he watch her.

She swayed, uncertain. 'I'll tell Nurse,' she whispered, smiling. She looked again at him from the door, then vanished.

Her silk dress fled like a wind along the corridor. 'Oh Nurse – oh Uncle David,' she cried in an intense whisper, 'he's alive!'

'You mean he's conscious?' said the nurse, looking up at her.

'Yes, yes. At least – I think so.'

The nurse and her uncle, who had now reached the top of the stairs, stopped before her dramatic doubt.

'His eyes are open, but—'

'I'll go along and see him,' said the nurse, filling in the pause sensibly, and she went. Evelyn drew her uncle into the room with the open piano.

'Why did you go to his room?' asked her uncle.

'I don't know,' she answered, looking at him with her face wide open. She caught a lapel of his jacket and then stood thinking and listening within herself.

'We were coming up to stop you making that row on the piano,' he said.

'His eyes – they did not seem to recognize me.'

'They wouldn't, naturally.'

'I don't mean that. They seemed – not blank – but – I can't explain. I have the awful feeling that he has lost his memory.'

'Don't be absurd.'

'He looked at me as if – as if – I was going to pounce on him.'

'Sound, sound fellow!'

'Please, David, don't be silly.' She tugged the lapel and let it go. 'It would be awful, wouldn't it, if his brain was permanently affected?'

'It would indeed.'

She sat on the piano stool. 'I wonder what's keeping Nurse? She is always so terribly matter-of-fact.'

'Give her a chance,' said Mr David Henderson. 'And as for being matter-of-fact – you know you shouldn't have gone to his room.'

'I know. But – I was playing, and Bach makes you feel, believe – I don't know, but I suddenly had the feeling that if I saw him I should know. So I went – very, very quietly. And his eyes were open, like the eyes of an animal – in its hole.' She glanced at him and smiled, but anxiously, searching his face.

'Did you speak to him?'

'Yes. I asked him how he was. But he did not answer, though his eyes never left me. I backed away carefully.'

'And he probably didn't believe it. Now listen to me, Eve. I know something about concussion. As I told you, I've seen many recover from it. I've been knocked out more than once myself. We know he's a tough young Turk. We know that his skull pan is all right. The doctors have told us. It's now a matter of time. That's all. So you must stop worrying. You definitely must – or I'll be annoyed with you.'

'I've had horrible dreams.'

'Naturally. For the only two times you've seen him blood was gushing about.'

'Yes, but—' She hesitated, her brows netting. 'I was to blame,' she murmured.

'If you say that again, I really will be angry. We have gone into it all over and over – ah, Nurse, well?'

'There isn't much change,' answered the nurse with professional calm.

'But his eyes?' said Evelyn.

'He seems to be sleeping, as usual.'

There was a short silence.

'But he was,' protested Evelyn. 'I saw him. His eyes were open. They watched me.'

'Yes, yes,' said her uncle. 'He will come round in blinks like that. Everything is going excellently. Fine . . . hallo! there's a car.'

Mr Henderson's house party was beginning to arrive. The car brought two of his guests, Mr Cunningham from Edinburgh, and Mr North, a London surgeon in his thirties. Presently, over a drink, their host said, 'Seems we can't get away from that young apprentice of yours, Cunningham. You know, the local boy?'

'Cattanach?'

'Yes. We all but killed him the other night. With the car. When I picked him up, I thought he was away with it.'

'Good heavens! And what—?'

'He's upstairs – just coming round. Evelyn was driving. We were a bit late, though not speeding really. Only naturally she's taken it a bit to heart. Oddly enough, nothing seems to be broken, though he's got a bad one here,' and he put his hand to his head, 'though not deep.'

'Extraordinary!' said Mr Cunningham.

'The last time – the only time – I saw this young fellow,' Mr Henderson explained to the surgeon, 'he was pitching one of Mr Cunningham's staff through a glass door – with particularly bloody results.'

'He may thrive on it,' suggested Mr North.

'We're hoping so.'

They smiled. 'Only the local medical seen him?' Mr North asked.

'No. As it happened, we nobbled a Glasgow brain specialist at Kinmore yesterday. At least the local doctor did. He was having him through for a case at the hospital. A good fellow, the local doctor. Sensible chap. The consultation was favourable. Questions of shock, X-ray, and all that, but they have it in hand, I think.'

'Good,' said Mr North. 'I'm not a brain specialist, but anything I can do—'

His host thanked him, but added firmly that nothing 'professional' was to interfere with his holiday. If, however, North cared to have a talk with the doctor, had a look at the patient, and *then* assured Evelyn that everything was all right, that would be very helpful. 'For some reason she trusts you.'

'No explaining those things,' Mr North agreed, with a merry touch of confusion. Of medium height, rather ruddy in feature, he had, and emanated, an immense vitality. At times he glowed with merriment. His career had been very brilliant.

'He never made any effort to get back to your office?' Mr Henderson asked Mr Cunningham.

'No. Never even wrote me.'

'An odd crowd.' David Henderson, six foot two inches, nodded thoughtfully. His head of strong, neatly brushed hair was dark grey, his features lean and steady, with a selfless penetrating look in the grey eyes. 'I like 'em. His father is steady as a rock. Says little. I rather fancy there had been a spot of trouble with the boy. That night, I mean.'

'He seems to collect trouble,' said Mr Cunningham. 'But I must say I rather liked him, too.'

His host nodded again. 'You get fellows like that. Usually there is something to them. Not always. Evelyn called on the old lady – the lad's grandmother. I don't know what witchery the old woman put over. Then I had a long talk with Major Grant. Things are pretty complicated. It seems the young devil has been drinking a bit. And the story is accepted locally that it was he who pushed Major Grant in the river. The worthy Major, anyway, is satisfied he did – but I think he has rather a down on the lad. Perhaps with good reason. He may be a young rip. On the other hand, Evelyn has a remarkable story about what he did with sheep. The whole thing rather fascinates me – particularly as he was plucky enough on this occasion not to get killed.'

'It was certainly considerate of him,' the surgeon agreed.

'My God, it was,' said his host with some fervour. 'However, all this is to warn you that you needn't expect me to fuss about. Everything is yours. I hope you enjoy yourselves. But if you see me stalking the local people or rounding up sheep, you'll know I have my own game on hand.'

'Been working things out?' suggested Mr Cunningham.

'I have.' He turned to Mr North. 'Cunningham is referring to extensive surgical notions of mine.'

'Really! And the body?'

'The old earth.'

'Not the Conservative Party?'

TWO

Iain was acting like an animal and knew he was. He had to keep inside his sluggish brain and the awful pains that shot through certain parts of his body when he moved. If he lay inside them long enough, then one day they would open out, break apart like a chrysalis, and he would be free. At first he felt this with the extreme thinness or weakness of a fly. He lived so far back within himself that his body and brain did not yet belong to him. Then his brain began to form within the region of his head and movement of its thick matter got clogged in so exhausting a way that a dull throbbing pulsed through it until it discovered its echo in his left ear. After that, it spouted up by the left ear as through a miniature trunk pipe, and spread its flushings over innumerable branches, until the whole brain was intolerably weighted with the blood-flow and drowned. Then a knot of pain formed in the brain like a nest in the branches, and he knew he had got to be very careful.

He also learned a lot about his body. In fact, the central knot of consciousness became at times extremely cunning about certain parts of it where the pain lay in ambush. The pain did not belong to the sharp edges of broken bones. He satisfied himself about that in subtle interior ways. The pain came from bruisings and the bruisings wanted to be left alone, to lie low, like himself. When he disturbed them, they shot blinding arrows, and these arrows were the pain.

So he lay low like an animal. The nurse's attentions were at first a nightmarish ordeal, but he soon learned to deal with them, to get over them with the minimum of movement, keeping his eyes shut and letting his brain go completely sluggish. Not that he *had* to do this. His eyes and his brain did it themselves.

But the evolutionary process into himself could not be stopped. There were lucid moments, vague and quickly clouded, but they grew. They got mixed up, however, with sections of dreams, formal patterns that moved like sombre-faced dead bodies through the air.

Evelyn's face began to haunt him. At first he was quite certain she had been real immediately the door had closed. Then something familiar about the face had worried him. This familiarity belonged to dream, to another plane of experience, to a visionary world. This visionary world had the curious intense reality of all things conceived in the brain. She was alive in her own right, in that world, in that way. And he knew he was afraid of her.

The next time he heard the music, the silence, the soft foot-falls, and saw the door beginning to open, he closed his eyes. There was an extraordinary effect of light coming from the open door that made his eyelids flutter, so his head lay over and he breathed heavily. The door closed. No extra light could have come from the door, of course. This annoyed him. He wondered if he would be able to hold out.

From the nurse's talk, the doctors' visits, he knew now where he was and what had happened. He was perfectly aware that Mr Henderson, the laird, had come in to see him in the company of a new doctor. He had answered the doctor dully, stupidly, but with enough sense to make it clear he wanted to be left alone. No visitors were allowed. The plan in his head was perfectly simple. Have as little to do with these people as possible, keep them beyond the barrier of illness, until his body knew the time had come; then clear out. Once, as the blood went threshing through his head, his voice muttered, 'I'll beat it then!'

The next time he heard the music, he listened to it objectively and wondered who had composed it, wondered, at least, what had been the composer's idea. It was afternoon and the house was quiet. The music stopped. The footsteps came. They terrified him and he closed his eyes. He knew she had gone to the window. Time passed with so slow an intensity that he wondered if he had fallen asleep. He opened his eyes. She was standing by the window, looking back at him.

'Are you awake?' The voice was gentle and she came lightly to his bedside. There she stood smiling down upon him, an eager tenderness in her face. As though aware she was too tall for him, too distant, she sat down on the chair near the head of the bed, moving it slightly as she did so. 'Nurse is resting, and I said I would keep watch. Do you mind?'

He could not close his eyes now, but he did not answer.

'I mustn't tire you. Is there anything you would like?'

'No, thanks.'

'Are you awfully tired?'

'A bit.'

'But you feel you're getting better, don't you?'

'Yes.'

'Oh, I'm so glad. Thank you for speaking to me. I mustn't tire you.' She got up. 'You're sure there's nothing I can bring you?'

'No.'

She hesitated. 'Would you like me to – play for you?'

'No.'

'Oh, I'm so sorry!' Her face flushed as if she had committed some egregious error.

The blood-throbbing started. He felt the sweat beading on his forehead.

'You must forgive me. They told me you liked music, played the violin. You will forgive me, won't you?'

His hand came up of its own accord and wiped his forehead. Quickly she brought a sponge and a small linen towel. 'Please!' She sat on the bed and leaned towards him and wiped his forehead gently. Never had he seen any face so distinguished, so unique in its beauty before. Its familiarity came from some other land, some other time. It was flawless, classical, living; breathing and moving; arched over him. She sat back and smiled into his eyes. 'Now! Is that better?'

'Yes, thanks.'

Her head moved a little to one side with a light grace, as

though from a deep understanding she would draw the smile up out of his face. The corners of her lips spoke their woman language. Her eyes drew away, smiling in silent talk. She got up.

His eyes lightened and he smiled to thank her, but not looking at her, preparing himself to rest. Yet he had to say something, for his 'No' to her question about the music had been impolite. The burden of it! 'I liked the music.'

'What's that?' She stooped.

'The music – what – was it?'

'Oh! A Bach chorale. Did you like it?'

'Yes.'

'You like Bach?' Her eyes shone above him.

'Don't know. I – don't know about music.'

'But you play, don't you?'

'Just Highland music, a little.' His head moved and lay sideways. He tried to relax all his body to keep its incipient trembling from her sight. If she did not go soon, his head would explode, his body burst into bits.

She sat down on the bed. 'When you are properly convalescent,' she said, with a shyness in her lovely smile, 'you will play your violin and I'll accompany you. I'll get some Highland music. Tell me! What shall I get?'

'I – can't remember.' His brows gathered.

'Please don't try. I'll get some. You do remember, don't you?'

'No. I – I can't remember.'

'Don't you remember – anything?'

His eyes closed. 'I can't – tell you.'

She caught his wrist gently. He tried to keep it from shaking, could not do so, let it go, and felt it rattle within her light clasp. He drew it away. 'Sleepy,' he muttered.

He did not hear what she answered, but she was going. He opened his eyes. The room was empty of her. He let go everything, his jaw, his trembling flesh, and sank out of consciousness.

THREE

'It goes much deeper than that,' said David Henderson. 'Granted, I may be influenced by my Colonial experiences – but why shouldn't I? The simple fact is that that young fellow up there, when he does go to Australia or New Zealand, will turn up trumps. He is precisely the kind of chap they want. Why, then, should we lose him here?'

'Well, we don't want to lose him. Why should we?' Sir George Paddock smiled. 'After all, if the Conservative Party has one fundamental concern, it surely is the land.'

'I wonder! I mean is it really the land – or their ownership of it?'

'Now! now! That kind of heresy is too easy. You must learn that that is the kind of socialistic claptrap which is thrown at us as a matter of Party warfare. You must understand that. Otherwise they'll trip you up in no time.'

There were four of them round the smoking-room fire after a day on the hill, a bath, and a good dinner. Cunningham and North were clearly prepared to be interested and amused.

'I rather fancy they're going to trip me up,' said Henderson, with thoughtful good humour. 'So I'm trying to think it over. As far as I can gather, the Highlands turned violently against landlords because of the way landlords treated them at the time of the Clearances – evictions, burnings, and so on.'

'That's an old story; and becoming really a bit tiresome,' interposed Sir George. 'After all, we do evolve. If we are forever going to be held responsible for what a few of our ancestors did, well—' He shrugged.

Henderson smiled. 'I understand. But I am merely trying to get it clear, not any particular theory, but the actual thing. The fact seems to be, then, that the people of the Highlands, after what had been done to them, went Liberal or Radical in mass. It was their political protest against their actual treatment. They are still Radical. The term has now evolved, in the industrial centres, to the word Labour or Socialist. But, underneath, it's the same kind of protest against the owning class. Anyway, rightly or wrongly, it exists – here. As far as I can see, if I were to stand as a landlord Conservative for this constituency, I shouldn't have a dog's chance. Even though the people themselves are very conservative in habit and thought.'

'But you needn't necessarily stand here.' Sir George Paddock looked at him through his cigar smoke.

'That's just the trouble. At least I know something about this place now. If I can't work the big magic here – I mightn't be interested.'

'If it's personal, like that, well, of course! Though even then, all the more reason why you should have a shot at it here. We thought of that. You are a man who can talk to them about the Colonies at first hand. That could be extremely important, in this way. As you say, the best of the Highland lads clear out and make their way in the Colonies. You can tell them about that. You can say you have seen it, describe it to them. And presumably it's not roses all the way! But it does give an outlet for the individual spirit. They go because they are born individualists prepared to fight. Well, your programme would be that you were prepared to offer them that individualism and that fight at home, right here, on your own estate. Facts and figures. Realities. Hill sheep farming, for example, and what needs to be done and what you, as a landlord, are actually prepared to do whether you are returned or not. That would square with your basic philosophy which, I take it, wants to encourage the individual and the individual spirit – individual expression – rather than the regimentation of that spirit by a bureaucratic machine.' Sir George Paddock was a man of fifty odd years, with the pleasant manners, the guiding suavity, of a chairman of many committees. He was a good shot still, though now inclined to talk at times when Finlay, over-conscious of the lying stag, would mutter, 'Not so loud, sir.'

'That's where you have me on the cleft stick,' Henderson admitted. 'Basically and philosophically and all that – fine. But they are not dumb muts, whatever they may appear. They will merely see us up to some new tricks in order to save our own, to save our landlordism. A rather shocking history has taught them the old one about the leopard and his spots.'

'But we can change the spots,' answered Sir George. 'There is a whole science of camouflage – for the grimmest of all human business. Thus do even fables change.'

'Proving that the more they change, the more they are the same thing,' suggested the surgeon with lively eyes.

'I don't get you.' Sir George looked at him.

'Modern version: beware of the leopard when he changes his spots.'

Sir George smiled. 'We are all leopards.'

'That's good and honest,' agreed Henderson. 'Let us test it practically. There was a poaching affair here some considerable time ago when our local factor, Major Grant, a decent fellow, was pushed into the river and very nearly drowned. I happen to know with certainty who two of the three poachers were. The lad upstairs is supposed to be the one who pushed the Major in. These three poachers, if you like, are the leopards. Now in my reclamation schemes, these are the three to whom I should like to give the work or the sheep farms where initiative, guts, real staying power is needed.'

Paddock laughed. 'You'll excuse me,' he said. 'I really do have a fairly wide experience of poachers. All this sort of silly romance that's grown around them – it's bad. They are generally quite worthless characters, unstable, and certainly the one thing they haven't got for any job is staying power. Fundamentally, they are anti-social. I am not talking to you politically now. I really do appreciate what you intend doing here. And I would warn you to watch what you are doing – I mean in the people you employ and your tenants. If you don't, you'll come one terrific cropper.'

'Thanks. I appreciate your advice. For long-established

conditions in a place like the south of England, which you really know, you may be right. I don't know. From my own experience of human nature in the raw in many parts of the world, I should say you may, all unconsciously, be prejudiced. However, I am concerned with this spot and I have been looking about me for a year or two. And that's the conclusion I have come to.'

'It's dangerous romance.' Sir George Paddock was moved to flick ash off his cigar. 'I warn you. I am prepared to give odds now that they are Red to a man. They'll milk you, ask more and more, until finally they achieve their ambition of turning you out neck and crop.'

'You may be right,' said his host. 'An interesting gamble. But you go a bit fast. The average poacher in the Highlands is a fellow who wants a bit of sport and can't get it. He belongs to a sporting country, a sporting people. He is primitive in that way – like all of us here now. But we deny him his outlet. Whether in sea-fishing, rearing sheep or crops, he still in large measure has to depend on chance. The sporting gamble. It's in his blood. Give him that sporting chance – and he has staying power far beyond the normal. You see it in the stalkers and gillies. You know perfectly well that nine times out of ten they are far keener than the sportsmen they have to guide and even prod on. Well, the problem now for me is how to direct that psychological stuff into fruitful channels.'

'Irrespective of the outcome?'

'Oh, no,' answered Henderson. 'The outcome would be a reclaimed and fruitful land. That would give me a personal satisfaction. That, if you like, would be me at last cultivating my garden!'

'Well, of course, that is a personal affair.' Sir George, smiling, shrugged very slightly.

'Everything is a personal affair', said Henderson, 'in the end. When it ceases to be personal, it becomes impersonal – the bureaucratic machine you talked of. I thought that was where we agreed.'

North, whose spirits were irrepressible, laughed quickly.

After much talk about 'principles', Cunningham suddenly asked, 'Do you actually know if it was young Cattanach who pushed the Major in the river?'

Henderson looked at him with a quizzical smile in his eyes and remained silent.

'All right. I'm not asking.' Cunningham smiled.

'I shouldn't tell you,' said Henderson slowly. 'But I think I will. You must promise me meantime to keep it to yourselves. Actually it was so remarkable a happening, I can't get over it. I was walking home with Finlay to-day. There was also a certain young gillie. I know you will be good enough never to ask his name. I was talking to Finlay, with the gillie walking just behind. In quite a natural way, I worked the talk round to the drowning affair. This, roughly, is what happened.' And he went on to describe fairly accurately how Major Grant was pushed into the pool. 'Finlay, you will observe, was careful not to mention personal names, so in the same conversational tone, I said, "I know young Cattanach is a tough customer, but surely he didn't mean to drown the Major?" And Finlay at once said, "I am not accusing him of that. I never said he meant it." "But you are quite sure he did it?" I asked. At that direct question he went a bit dour in the Highland fashion, then said, "I am not accusing him." And when I probed him gently a bit further, he said, "He's never denied it anyway," and that's all I got out of him. I left Finlay and on the way here was waylaid by the young gillie. He said, "Excuse me, sir, but I would like to say something to you." He was in an obvious state of suppressed emotion, but with a flash in his eyes. I told him to go on. "Young Cattanach did not shove the Major into the river," he said. "Didn't he?" I asked. "How do you know?" He took a moment, then said, "Because I was there." "You were one of the three poachers?" "Yes, sir." Now I could see it took a fair amount of courage for an estate worker to tell his employer that he had been poaching his river in rather criminal circumstances. "This is interesting," I said. "Can you tell me who pushed the Major in the river?" After thinking for a moment, he said, "No, sir." "Don't you know?" I asked. "Yes, sir, but it was not Cattanach." "Then it was either you or the third man?" "Yes, sir." In this way, I'm afraid I trapped him into making it clear that Cattanach was at the river. When he saw this, he became distressed, for he was obviously an honest lad and a bad liar. Then I spoke to him in a friendly way and told him if he made a clean breast of it to me, no-one should hear about it and no-one suffer. I had to repeat it. He looked right into my eyes, and then came away with it. He was the lad who pushed the Major in the river. The Major coming along the edge of the rock, was just about to shine his torch on Cattanach – when the whole business of Cattanach's going to your office, Cunningham, his sick mother's ambitions for him, everything, would have been wrecked. The gillie saw this in a flash and, on impulse, tipped the Major into the river. Being tipped into the river merely meant a ducking. And that's all it should have meant, but for the extraordinary fact that the Major got entangled in the net. And now the interesting part of the story comes. For the Major was really drowning. Young Cattanach's ear caught the choking sounds. He came back to the pool. Flashed the Major's torch on the water and, grabbing the net, pulled the Major ashore. In short, Cattanach, who had only been inveigled into the fun, was in simple fact the lad who, beyond any question whatsoever, saved Major Grant's life.'

'That's very interesting.' Cunningham spoke slowly, looking closely at his host.

'As a study in loyalties,' Henderson said, 'I think myself it is rather remarkable. I thanked the gillie for his confidence, and said I realized how difficult it had been for him to say anything earlier. "Yes," he answered; and then added, "Cattanach said he would break every bone in my body if I told it was me who did it".'

North laughed outright.

'Well, there you have it,' said Henderson. He looked at Sir George Paddock. 'What am I going to do about it?'

'Seeing you said you were going to do nothing, what can you?' answered Sir George.

Henderson looked bewildered for a moment. 'Good God, man, not that! I mean about the land, about fellows like that for my schemes.'

North jumped up and turned his face to the door. They looked at him with some astonishment. The door opened and Evelyn came in.

FOUR

Iain did not think of himself as suffering from delusions. He knew that everyone was kind, that he was receiving the very best attention. He even saw that it might have been awkward for them had he been killed; at least they would naturally have felt uncomfortable about it. The remaining nurse – there had been two of them to begin with – was a Kinmore woman, and he had got from her the details of the accident. Yet he could not get rid of the feeling of being pursued, of being the cornered animal that the stalkers would in due course close in upon. He would have to escape; give them the slip when they were least prepared for it. This became a profound secretive preoccupation with him, and the two most deadly stalkers were Mr Henderson and his niece Evelyn.

Occasionally, too, he was uncertain whether a thing had actually happened or whether he had dreamed it. The incident or dream of tearing the clothes from Evelyn's back was extremely vivid. It had seemed to him – and this certainly suggested delusion – that someone was playing the piano, but then in a moment other themes were started by other players, there was even a distant but ominous band playing one of Mary's songs with a sadness that was the very essence of peril. In all this there was something of the nature of a concealed but horrible competition, though, in a way beyond explaining, each theme was privy to the competition and kept its invisible eye on Iain to note the effect.

As Evelyn, suddenly materializing, bent over him, he struggled wildly and his left fist, gripping her dress behind her neck, ripped it away. He did not see her body; she was the secret enemy; all the themes rose in a tearing madness, collapsed inward, and he fainted.

He was left with the feeling that something like this – the

actual struggle at least – had really happened, if not with Evelyn then with someone else. More and more he dreaded Evelyn's appearance in his room. She absolutely exhausted him. She came in a golden mist of tenderness and sympathy and wanted to talk, to draw him out. Her manners were charming and sensitive. She behaved like one who was falling in love with him, who loved him in some degree already. She was like one making a romance of what had happened, floating about in its golden mist, moved by its strange and new sensation. It was terrible!

'I do feel I was to blame. That keeps haunting me,' she explained. Now that the actual accident had at last been mentioned between them, she became absorbed. She sat on the bed.

'You weren't,' he answered. 'As I say, I saw you coming and should have got off the road.'

'It's awfully sweet of you to say that. I did my best. I really did. It was a dreadful moment when I saw you standing in the lights. I did not know which way you were going to go. I had to decide in an instant. I shoved both feet out with all my strength. And I'm pretty strong. I am, you know. And thank goodness these hydraulic brakes do really work. Uncle David broke the windscreen with his head! Did you know that?'

'No.'

'He did. Quite ruined his best hat.' She had a rich, gurgling chuckle. 'But the awful moment was when you went the wrong way. I mean when you went to the same side as I did. O God, it was awful!' Her hands struck sharply together and pressed. He saw that in fact she was strong, full of a lithe, physical strength.

He said nothing. The appalling weariness and fear she induced were gripping him; the heat was beginning to smother his body; the sweat would burst out soon.

'Odd, isn't it, that we should always meet in blood?' She regarded him in an amused, fascinated way.

His eyes opened upon her in a full stare.

'Didn't you know?'

His mind went completely blank so that he had to grope for its substance, its edge.

'You don't remember seeing me before?' She was teasing him now. 'I remembered you at once. Whenever we got your face in the light, I knew it was you. I even remembered your name. I cried out to Uncle David, "It's Iain Cattanach!"' She gave him time, smiling. 'You can't remember?'

He could not speak.

'You stared at me enough,' she said. 'In that Edinburgh office.'

His hand came up to his forehead. She dived for the sponge and towel. She wiped his eye-sockets as well as his forehead, gently but firmly. 'I do forgive you for not remembering.'

'I do,' he muttered.

'Do you? You are politely pretending now; being the Highlander!' She finished the wiping.

'I thought' (his mind wouldn't work) 'you were a dream.'

She sat quite still, arrested in a sort of tranced beauty. A blatter of rain hit the window. Her uncle came in.

'I hope this young woman is not tiring you?'

'No,' breathed Iain, aware of the tall man's cool eyes.

'He's just been telling me,' said Evelyn, 'that I wasn't to blame. Don't you think that's noble of him?' She sat smiling to her uncle in a rather remote way as from the heart of a consummated miracle.

'I think it's perhaps more than you deserve,' answered her uncle, eyeing her.

She did not protest.

'Glad to know you're getting on,' he said to Iain. 'Don't let these people worry you. When you feel able for it, I'd like to have a talk with you, about real things, like sheep and farms. I'd like your opinion. Now, Eve – out! A little of you goes a long way. Come along.'

When the door closed, Iain looked about him. His breathing grew rapid as he tried to push himself up. But he was too weak yet, too hurt, too sickeningly tired to get away. They would beat him to bits, they would break him, if he didn't escape!

Within his collapse, his mind became cunning, not for his body – he could now raise his hips to start the pain – but for itself. He hated being in this house, he feared and hated its owner and his niece. They stalked in upon him. Everything surrounded him. He was trapped.

In the Edinburgh offices the term 'persecution mania' had been a fashionable joke for certain queer, timid clerks. Apparently a person gave way to that kind of thing. An obsession. He argued it out. But it made no difference. It was somehow as though people here were symbols, stood for more than themselves, for landlords, for the past. The laird's tallness was in itself a whole vision of power. He came walking up corridors.

Damn them, they were not his people, he wanted to be rid of them, that was all! What the blazes were they to him? Couldn't he get clear of them? Wasn't he free?

Sometimes, when his mind got into a tempestuous condition, he had heightened moments of extreme clarity. He realized perfectly well that Miss Evelyn Henderson – her father, whom she had adored, had been killed in the Great War – was a beautiful, friendly young woman, anxious to do her best, and grateful that he made no fuss about the accident. (As if he would! As if he would tie himself up about that!) But in these moments of extreme insight he saw her whole behaviour, the very springs of her charm, her movement, as a blossoming of pure selfishness, an insatiable loveliness that sucked his strength out of him, reminding him of a school story he could not quite remember about a siren. This was absurd, even fantastic, but when he shifted his ground (secretly holding, however, to his insight) and saw her as a figure of love and romance, a creation in golden mist floating above physical assault and blood and wavering death, his reaction was even worse. The figure became possessive in a vampirish way. Its demands, its appalling orange-golden thirst, could never be satisfied.

His heated mind worked over this, not at his wish, but by a fatal involuntary attraction, for it was part of what was hemming him in. Sometimes his vision achieved extreme penetrations, starting often from a point of pain. And once, when things were ominously upright, the walls, every part of the strange landscape, he caught Mary Cameron by the wrist and said in a low voice, 'Come on!' and they stole away, step by step, while he was ready with the blow and the feet that would run.

He did not 'love' Mary Cameron. There was no romance about Mary Cameron. She was there like his own blood. He could grip her by the wrist and hold her as he held his own breath. And she wasn't a hindrance. He hadn't to save her. Nor had she to save him. But together, in the treacherous moment, they made one invincible force that nothing could stop. Through the wood, and the still menace of the wood, and the faces behind trees, and his eyes were watching, and his body ready for the thrusting arms, ready to smash them down, to clear the way, and within him was double his own strength. She doubled his strength, and because of her and with her, he knew the way.

The dangers were being passed, paralysed within their own darkness, the bodies stiff, the branches frozen, unable to strike, smitten to a staring enchantment, and his head was beginning to turn back over his shoulder, keeping them there, when Mary's voice said in a clear, sweet wonder, 'Iain, the drinking well!'

And there was the well on the open hillside with the green grass running from it, and the smooth flat stone. Crystal the water was, and he saw that it was the water of life, welling up and running over.

But he could not drink, he could not move, and stood there in the light which was everywhere, for within him his voice cried silently, 'It was so like her to find the well!'

It was so like her – O God, I am weak! – it was so like her, that his eyes brimmed.

FIVE

Mr Henderson stood with his back to Iain, looking out of the bedroom window for a moment. Then he turned, his manner easy and friendly.

'I don't suppose you know what these famous old *black cattle* of the Highlands were like? I was talking to your father, but he wasn't certain. No-one seems to know. Do you really think they were black?'

'No,' said Iain.

Henderson looked at him. 'I wondered. The camouflage sounded wrong. They were always these picturesque fellows with the long horns?'

'No,' said Iain again. 'I don't think so.' He pulled the bedclothes from his throat.

'Afraid I'm tiring you.'

'No,' muttered Iain politely. Then he added, 'The colour was dark brown.'

'That's more like it. Ever seen one?'

'I have read about them. Like great stags, straight thick back, deep in the rib. The horns were blue or yellow, small, with black tips.'

Henderson nodded thoughtfully. 'Where did you read about them?'

'In a book called *The Grampians Desolate*. It's a poem – with long notes. Published about 1800.'

'Interesting.' He glanced out of the window, then took an idle step or two in the direction of the bedroom door. 'I should like to see the right breed of cattle on these hills again. I believe you think the same?'

'Yes,' said Iain without any stress.

'Tell you what I have been wondering. Just what proportion of cattle to sheep would the ground carry? Any ideas?'

Iain did not answer.

'Didn't happen to say anything in that book you mentioned?'

'Yes. Two black cattle to every twenty sheep.'

'Two cattle – to every twenty sheep! Are you sure?'

'Yes.'

'Did you say he was a poet?'

'He was also a landlord.'

Henderson gave a short laugh and glanced searchingly at Iain. Iain felt the warmth coming up over his body and the sweat beginning to break.

'Let me see – how many sheep have you on your place?'

'About five hundred ewes.'

'That would mean – a whole herd of cattle!' Henderson moved restlessly. 'But look here – did it pay – away back in – when was it?'

'About 1798. He – the landlord – introduced improvements – in houses and the land. He ran the farms in a sort of joint-stock way, but with each tenant holding his own share. They became well off.'

'How do you know? Did he give figures?'

'Others offered four times the rent to get into the farms.'

'Ah! So the landlord turned the old tenants out?'

'No. He put up the rent.'

Henderson chuckled again and glanced at Iain. 'The old story!'

Iain said nothing and Henderson realized he could not break through the boy's defences. He took a small diary from his pocket. 'Can you give me the name of that book?'

Iain gave it to him.

'Thanks. Everything seems to turn on money.' He put the diary in his pocket. 'Supposing you had a landlord who would improve – without putting up the rent?' he asked in his friendly voice.

'That wouldn't solve the whole question.'

'On the basis that one swallow doesn't make a summer? But it would be a beginning.'

Iain said nothing.

'You're a bit sceptical? In the case of landlords who couldn't put up the money – you think the Government should? Say exactly what you think.'

'Who else could? Who would sink money that would not give him a good return?'

'Not many, I agree. But if the Government put up money, then they would have to see that things were run well.'

'Yes.'

'What would that mean – to the fellow who would have to work the land – say, like yourself?'

'It would be all right.'

'For things could hardly be worse than they are?'

'No.'

'I agree.'

'Then—' began Iain, and paused.

'Yes?'

'The Government could not waste public money. They would have to see – I mean, the prices – they could not let selling prices go too low – they would have to do something about marketing, about minimum prices.'

Henderson's lips parted then gathered in a soft whistle. 'By God, that's a point!'

But Iain could hold on no longer. With his palm, he wiped the sweat from his eyebrows. His eyes glistened, stung with the sweat.

'Here, I am sorry,' said Henderson. 'I forgot. Did not mean to trouble you like this.' He came to the bed. 'You take it easy. Take it easy. And if there's anything you want, for heaven's sake, ask.'

When the door closed, Iain got up on an elbow. There was a bottle of sleeping tablets somewhere. His brain was going to bits. He could see a bottle on the dressing table. But his elbow gave under him. His hands shook. He was quivering all over. 'O God!' he cried, trying to hold on. His head fell back and gasping breaths came through his wide-open mouth.

SIX

'It may not be an easy walk for Jack North,' said Mr Henderson drily, as he watched the surgeon and his niece disappear round the rhododendron bushes.

'He also has a mind of his own,' Mr Cunningham suggested.

'He'll need it. The fact is, I'm afraid, she has been vamping that young man upstairs.'

'He's not coming down?'

'No. He mistrusts us. He now knows you're here, too. And I could see that Eve had already told him about the meeting. I rather suspect she has told him a lot.'

'What do you think he'll do?'

'Heaven knows! They're an odd lot. But I like them. The stuff is there – if only I can get it going. But it's really one hell of a problem.'

'And it's going to cost a lot.'

'I don't mind that. And Paddock may be right – I don't care. I'm through with politics – for the time being, at least. In Paddock's eyes, I'm not a pukka landlord, Cunningham: only a Colonial!'

'It's a pleasant change.'

'Paddock must think of landlords generally. They all haven't my cash. I know. That's tough on them. But I'm thinking of the land, and the excellent human material that's dying on it, dying out. Very well. If landlords cannot find the money to put the land in heart, then someone, the Government, the nation, must. All I have got to do first is to prove it can be done.'

'But if the Government is going to put up the money, where is landlordism going?'

'Where it deserves to go, if it cannot do the job. It's been

damned selfish. It's drained the land. "Extractive farming"
– I should think so! The whole thing has been a scandal.'

'But if there is not money in farming—'

'There *is* money in farming, as in everything else, if you
do the job. And anyway, take Paddock and his Conservative
or Tory Party. Haven't they been in power often and long
enough to ensure that farming got a fair show? If there's no
money in farming, if the bread of life isn't even worth a
political deal, what the hell have they been up to? However,
I'm dealing with things I see and know. I hate regimentation. I'm a Colonial. But Paddock is enough to drive me into
the Socialist Party, if only to keep the demagogic thing
human!'

Cunningham smiled.

'That young fellow up there – he's made me think. He's
made it clear as the nose on my face that the root of this
business is the human material. He has guts. Plays the violin
and poaches. He is important, not only because he has the
right ideas, but because he has life.'

'But do you think that type is general?'

'In Australia, in South Africa, I have met scores – hundreds
– of them. I know what they can do. No-one can tell me.'
Henderson paused thoughtfully. His face was lean, the skin
weathered and tough, and there was the slightest suggestion
of a stoop about his shoulders. His eyes were clear, could
hold their look – and move quickly. 'There's been a long
connection between your firm and our family, Cunningham.
You know how things went.'

'They went that way pretty well with most landed families in the north.'

'I've been thinking about it. There were a few of us in
the family, so it was a case of a good education and find
your own feet. But when I hit out for the Colonies, my
mother felt it – much the same, I fancy, as any mother on
a croft does. I mean – there is the parallel between the sick
lad upstairs and myself. I'm an older edition of him.'

Cunningham glanced at him.

Henderson continued: 'I had contacts – and luck. Also,

perhaps, a wider knowledge of the kind of men who rule affairs and make money. I mean I knew when to borrow to the limit on farm and stock and wade in on the frozen meat shipping side. I got the tip – sized it up – took it. It came off. That was my luck. But it is not the usual picture. It is balanced by the failure. But there *is* the usual picture – of the man who makes good in a sound way. No more than that – and no more, I am convinced, than he could do here *if* he got the chance and showed the same grit and energy.'

'You think so?'

'Working things. Making them go. It's the only way for the ordinary fellow to be creative. Anyway, I'd like to see these fellows stirring. They've gone soft. They've forgotten how to help themselves. It's no good *giving* them things. They've got to be stirred up. They're of my own blood and I like 'em! It fascinates me – and there should be a fight in it!'

'But would young Cattanach come in on your plans?'

'That's my problem. And, dammit, I have a hunch that if I solve this business between his father and himself, he will. Everything depends on how we pull off this meeting. I'm going to be frank and friendly and dead straight. But I'll guide the talk with some guile. There's one thing about the Highlander – get him on your side and he'll stick to you beyond the last ditch. I'm on the boy's side. That's my trump card. It's the boy who will finally dominate the game. You watch.'

'You look like sitting down to a poker session.'

Henderson's expression eased. He smiled slowly. 'Honest to God, Cunningham, I would like to put more into my native soil than my own long body.'

There was a moment's pause. Henderson took out his watch. 'Our prospective glen soviet is late. Typical, I suppose.'

'There they are,' said Cunningham.

They stepped back a pace or two from the window.

'They rather look like four prisoners being brought to the bar,' Cunningham added.

'Suspicious of us. Probably thinking we have laid a trap. What an amount of history comes there!'

A maid showed them in.

Cattanach came first. His host shook hands with him; and then Cunningham, shaking hands with him, said, 'Glad to meet you, Mr Cattanach. Very sorry to hear of your son's accident.' Then big Andrew had his turn of hand-shaking, followed by Ewan Cameron and Hamish Macpherson.

'Make yourselves comfortable,' said their host, 'and we'll all have a drink. Cigars here, and cigarettes.'

Cunningham, smiling in the friendliest way, helped them to cigars. They each took one. Henderson, pouring whiskies, hoped the weather was going to clear up, and Cattanach first, and then big Andrew, told him with slow calm that it was. He asked them if they would like soda in it and they thanked him. About to squeeze the syphon, he paused. 'Sure you wouldn't prefer water?' Well, perhaps water would be better. He smiled and handed the water jug to Cattanach, who gravely handed it to Andrew, who passed it on to Ewan, who gave it to Hamish, who rose and put it back, undrained of a drop, on the table. When Henderson laughed, they all smiled.

'They put that much water nowadays in it as it is,' explained Andrew.

Henderson told them a story of the Australian backwoods, a story of tough drinking in which he had taken part. 'I'm afraid I had more strength than sense then. I always remember one fellow – he was a Skyeman. He gave me a tip. "Always," he said, "drink plenty of water – *in between*".'

'He wasn't far wrong, that fellow!' Andrew agreed. 'Otherwise it dries you up. Not that I have been dried for many a day.'

Henderson eyed him. 'I don't know that I would be prepared to take you on yet.'

'It would be easy now,' answered Andrew. 'But though I should be ashamed to say it – I have seen the day!'

'Well, here's to many more days! It was very good of you all to come round.'

They politely returned his toast and drank. They lit their cigars, Andrew puffing away at his as though his pipe had clogged on him.

Ten minutes later Henderson had told them of some of his farming experiences in the Colonies, of Highlanders he had met, and how many of them had often wished they were back in the old home, though as they always added, 'There's nothing yonder.' This had made him think, and he had decided that if ever he got the chance to do something back home, he would do it. And now the time had come.

Sitting there in his chair, he talked to them in a friendly way, contrasting conditions in the Australian sheep world with conditions in Scotland, asking questions and drawing them into the talk. He showed not only a first-hand knowledge of working sheep in the Dominions but a wide grasp of the shipping and marketing sides. Then presently he was sketching the broad outline, as he saw it, of the industry in Scotland and placing hill sheep farming in its proper perspective. In the first place, about seventy per cent of the agricultural land in Scotland consisted of rough grazing. It was therefore of immense importance for the future of the country's farming. In the second place, it was from the hill sheep farmers that the low ground farmers depended for replenishing their stocks. Cheviots and Blackfaces, with the half-breds or cross-breds, made up the bulk of all flocks. To keep the industry going there had to be a continuous flow of breeding ewes from the hills. 'You know all that better than I do. I am merely trying to show you how important I think your part of the industry is. It is the fountain-head of the whole thing. It is not only important to you, it is important to the country.' That raised political implications, not to mention questions of organization and marketing, of research. He told them of the many first-class research organizations in Scotland, all ready to help those – who were prepared to help themselves! He had visited several of them. He explained some of the things they had done and were doing. And he did not forget to ask questions.

'Here's one thing I don't understand and perhaps you can explain it. On the hills here we rear Blackface sheep. Now Blackface mutton in sweetness, in flavour, beats any mutton I know. How does it come about, then, that the hill Cheviot wether, though about the same weight as the Blackface wether, sells at nearly double the price?' He looked at Cattanach.

'I have often thought of that,' said Cattanach, 'but seemingly the butcher prefers the Cheviot. I think it may be because the Cheviot fattens a little more quickly, though he doesn't fatten so well.'

'And so you are half sunk at the start. And the Cheviot will try to oust the Blackface. And the public will lose the meat with the finest flavour in the world!'

Even Hamish, who had come with the utmost reluctance, who had sworn at the last moment in Ewan's shop that he would not go, and after ten minutes decided to go only because there might be a trap for Iain, was now interested, if still suspiciously waiting for the trap to be sprung. But he liked the man, liked his cool eyes, the friendliness, the easy manners, that had no trace of condescension. It was beginning to look as if he was the real Colonial! He listened to, he even seemed to look at, what was said; weighed it open-mindedly, nodding only when he got the pith of the matter. It wasn't going to be easy to fool this man! Hamish found a curious secret pleasure in the thought. In a tight corner in the backwoods he had used his fists to some purpose, decided Hamish with respect.

When Henderson turned next to an examination of the estate of Balmore, its agricultural decline, the increasing poverty of the soil through 'extractive farming', the kind of farming that 'took everything for a present profit and let the future go hang, putting little or nothing back into the soil, letting the flat ground of the river valley, through lack of proper drainage, turn into bog,' the spreading bracken, the increasing fibrous nature of the rough grazing everywhere, the haphazard heather-burning, he drew a picture which interested them to the point of a dumb uneasiness. He saw he was 'getting hot', and straightway instanced an area of some fifty acres which could be reclaimed – drained, broken up, ploughed, limed, manured, and sown to the proper kind of grass – and then asked them how many hoggs, for instance, such an area, with the crop properly and richly saved, could winter. He looked at Cattanach.

Cattanach took his time. He spoke slowly, asking questions, showing the complications of the problem, the labour involved, hesitated about coming to a conclusion, then came to a tentative conclusion reluctantly, as though he were far from being satisfied about the practicability of the affair. 'It means a big change,' he concluded, 'and a big expenditure.'

'Forget the expenditure,' said his host. 'That's my side of the problem. As landlords, we have been drawing rents long enough without doing much for them. If I am to continue to draw a rent from the soil, then I am going to put that soil into first-class condition, or as near it as I know how. I owe that to myself as well as to you. If you are satisfied with your present rents – right! we'll fix them for as long as you like. If a man is prepared to put his heart into the job, the profit will be his. The more he thrives the better I shall be pleased. There's no catch in all this. So let me hear your opinions. What do you say, Mr McAndrew?'

'I hardly know what to say,' replied Andrew slowly. 'It's a bit new to us. I am getting old and – I don't know. It's like a breath of life in many ways. I would like to see the young ones getting a chance. I would indeed. To tell the truth, I have been thinking a lot about it.' He leaned back. 'At first I thought it was just talk. I couldn't believe there would ever be anything in it. And there will be those – and I'm not forgetting myself – who will take all they can get for nothing! We have become a bit suspicious-minded, maybe, and not only of the landlords! But there are still some reasonable ones left who could take a chance when it comes their way.' He paused. 'To tell the truth, for it's what was in my mind as I listened to you, there's one young fellow in this house, Iain Cattanach, who has all your ideas and has spoken of them more than once among us.' Andrew stared before him as if it was all very strange. No-one looked at Cattanach. The eyes of Hamish and Ewan were on the landlord's face.

'I know that,' answered the landlord. 'Among the younger men, he is my central hope.'

Andrew drew a heavy breath. 'I am glad to hear that,' he said.

'Now listen to me.' Henderson looked steadily at Andrew. 'Why is he? Not merely because he has the ideas, but because he has guts. He is keen. He can take responsibility. He'll see a job through. He is the sort of lad who has given the Scots Colonial his reputation. We needn't boost ourselves by saying it's the highest reputation. But we can fairly say that there's none higher. And you had better get me quite clear now. That's the kind of spirit I want here. The spirit that will have a pride in its job and will do it come hell or high water.'

Andrew was so moved that he stretched unconsciously for his empty glass. Cunningham filled all the glasses.

'What do you think, Macpherson? You're a young man.'

'About Iain?'

'Well?'

Hamish looked into his glass, then lifted his eyes in a quick dark glance. 'He's a bit of a nuisance sometimes,' he said in a casual way. 'Last spring he drove our hoggs home through a snow-storm. We were a bit worried because we knew he would die on the job rather than give in.'

Henderson kept looking at Hamish for a moment.

'Perhaps I might add a word,' said Cunningham, pleasantly. 'There's a good lot of pride in you Highland people, and when your pride is hurt you have a habit of keeping your mouths shut. From what I have been able to gather, the lad upstairs is no exception. Frankly, then, as far as I am concerned, if Iain Cattanach wants to come back to my office, I shall certainly take him. Or, if he would prefer another office, I can find him one. I have complete confidence in him. In fact, a letter was written to him, making that clear. You may know that?' As he looked round the faces, he saw that no-one knew it.

'Tell them the story,' said Henderson suddenly.

'Oh, well, it's just an office story,' said Cunningham. 'The lad was provoked, pretty badly, by one of my staff. But he took it all in good part, until one day the question of your compensation, Mr Cameron, over Balrain, cropped up. Iain found out that there was an old entry in the estate records which in itself completely justified your claim. There need

have been no gathering of evidence. Unfortunately the
member of the staff who was dealing with the case accused
him of sneaking and apparently said some other nasty things.
It happened that there was a glass door near them, and that
proved unlucky for the other man. Mr Henderson saw it
happen. I didn't.'

'He dusted him,' said Mr Henderson simply.

Hamish involuntarily laughed, then quickly lifted his glass,
drank, and choked a little. He looked as if he might suddenly
get up and go away to enjoy himself properly.

'He never told me that,' said Ewan rather grimly.

'Perhaps he never told you that he hauled Major Grant out
of the river and saved his life. But that's another story! Have
another cigar, Mr McAndrew.' Henderson held out the box.

'Do you mind, sir, if I have my pipe? I think I would
enjoy a smoke now.'

Presently their host said, 'Now to get back to business.
For unless real things get *done*, I am not interested. Let me
put one concrete proposition to you. And let me say you are
not just here at haphazard. Sheep farming, crofting, and the
local trades or crafts are all represented, including a repre-
sentative of the younger men. Don't be offended if I say that
I first satisfied myself that you are about the best I could
get. If you cared to co-operate and help as a sort of advi-
sory body or committee, that would be very helpful all round.
But we'll talk about that again. Meantime let me see how,
say, Mr Cattanach here would react to this concrete proposition, this actual beginning. We'll go into all questions of
finance, stock, agreements and so on later. Only my aim will
always be this, that I don't want to create servants of the
estate. I like men who stand on their own feet. If I can help
them to do that, I shall be repaid enough. If our children,
or their children, want to run the whole affair as a social or
communal concern, fine! That will be their problem. Now,
Mr Cattanach, you once had the farm of Torglas?'

'Yes.'

'I have had it surveyed. You certainly had an eye for possi-
bilities. You had a bad run of luck.'

'It could be a good farm. I knew that.'

'But it needs development. When I see all these remains of cultivated patches, not only by the stream but up on the hill-sides, telling the old story of vanished crofting communities, I feel it's pretty sad. Sheep *and* cattle: that was the old way. You in Torglas had all your eggs in the one sheep basket; the ground had gone back; and the snow took its chance – when you weren't there. With borrowed money, you had no margins to work on. Now what I would like to do – what I am going to do – is tackle Torglass in a pretty thorough way – ploughing, sowing, fencing, sheep *and* cattle. Assume for a moment that this will be done, and the man to whom it will be given will have a chance to thrive. Now I am experimenting in human material as well as in soil. I would like to give Torglas to your son, Iain. But he's young. He's only twenty-one. And you don't have experience at twenty-one. He would need someone now and then to fall back on, to ask advice from. You know the farm. Would you be prepared – to advise him? I don't mean you to give up your farm here, of course. You would need help. That's easy. Young fellows must learn somewhere. You have experience and stability. They need that. Would you?'

Cattanach did not speak for a moment. He had sat somewhat solidly, like an outcrop of his native rock, and they had been conscious of his presence because of the hidden trouble about his son. His manner and speech had been calmly impersonal.

Now as he began to speak, they knew he was deeply moved. 'I was not prepared to excuse my son for anything that had happened. You make it difficult for me to say much. You are very generous, sir. He is my boy, and I felt responsible for him. When Mr Cunningham spoke – and said he would take him back – that came very near to me.' He paused for a moment and looked down at his hands, then he lifted his face. 'He saved my life in the river. When I was ill, he came every day and asked my advice about his difficulties with the lambing. He worked the sheep well. None ever did better. That's – that's all I can say.'

There was complete silence for a few moments. The strength of Cattanach's sincerity, his personality, filled the room.

'You give me hope, Mr Cattanach,' said Henderson quietly. 'And you will excuse me, for I must get this clear. Do you mean that you would like your son to go back to Edinburgh?'

Cattanach looked at him almost with a trace of bewilderment. 'No. That Mr Cunningham would take him – that's what I meant. We can now begin again. I forgot to say that any advice of mine, or anything I can do to help you, now or at any time, in any way – you have only got to ask me. Should it so happen that my son would make a success of Torglas, where I failed, that would lighten the end of my days.'

The lights had long been on. The informality of the talk, the tobacco smoke, the extreme interest of the subject-matter, the curious interfusing of the personal, the sense of 'Colonial' freedom and frankness, with portentous events impending, had induced a complete forgetfulness of time. But now as Henderson was about to speak, they heard quick footsteps coming to the door. The door opened and Evelyn looked at them, looked round the room, in a breathless way.

'Isn't he here?'

'Who?' asked her uncle.

'Iain. He's gone. He's not in the house.'

They all stared at her, and the silent question sprang like a trap: were they too late?

SEVEN

Ewan Cameron stood on the road above his cottage, listening. The night sky had cleared and the wind was soft again out of the south-west. Neither voice nor footsteps came on the wind and he went down to his cottage. Opposite the lighted window, he paused, but the silence from his kitchen was absolute. Because he had not expected anything else, hope died within him, leaving its secret place arid.

As he entered, Mary arose. 'Anything wrong, Father?'

'I don't know.' He looked about him in a worried, embittered way. 'Has anyone been here?'

'No. Father, what is it?'

'It's that fellow, Iain Cattanach. Heaven knows why he should go on making it difficult for himself.'

'What's happened?'

His limp was very pronounced as he gripped the chair arms and sat down with a thud. 'Plenty.'

'Won't you tell me?'

'What have I to tell you except that the laird spoke of him so highly you would think he was the only young fellow in the whole place.' He listened. 'Offered him the farm of Torglas, cattle and sheep and ploughing and thousands spent on it. All that Iain was saying should be done himself. Everything.'

'Did he refuse?'

'Everything he wanted. And I said to myself: he'll show them now! He showed them all right.'

'Father, won't you tell me what happened?'

He looked at her, then his eyes lifted.

'What are you listening for? Who's coming?' Her voice rose.

'Hamish Macpherson. He went over with Duncan

Cattanach to his house. He'll be looking in. I'll tell you what happened.' He told her what happened at the meeting in a dry objective way, his voice gathering a sarcastic emphasis as he pictured at last the scene in the Edinburgh office over his own compensation case. 'You see, he would feel a loyalty to me. It was too much for him.' His shaven lips, which were mobile and sensitive, twisted. 'Mr Cunningham said he had the utmost confidence in Iain. He said he would take him back. Duncan was moved!' Two soft snorts of breath came through his nostrils.

She saw he was hardly listening to himself. He was putting in time. Something had happened which he did not want to tell her. Presently he got up and went to the door. 'I'll be back in a minute.' He closed the door behind him.

She stood on the floor and heard the silence everywhere going up to the sky, planes of silence, and she moved on her toes to the door to keep them from falling and crashing, knowing Iain was underneath. Quietly she drew the door open. Her father was in the barn. She could not move, but so intently did she listen that she heard her father's low searching voice: 'Iain! Are you there?'

Now footsteps were approaching on the road above. Her father was coming up from the barn.

'Is that you, Ewan?' called Hamish.

'Yes. Have you found him?'

'No.' They met at the door. 'He's not at home. I had a look round the outhouses and went the rough path to the bridge. I fell in the bloody burn.'

'Come in,' said Ewan.

'Is that you, Mary?' asked Hamish, as he all but stumbled into her.

They stood in the kitchen.

'What's happened?' Mary asked Hamish.

He saw she was very pale. As he smiled his eyes glittered. 'When we were all talking down below in the big house, Iain cleared out. No-one saw him go.' He spoke lightly, like one on a poaching foray with the enemy at hand. In his dark face was something incalculable, dangerous, and swift.

'I can't think where he would have gone,' said Ewan to himself.

'It's a poser right enough,' Hamish agreed. 'But we'll have to find him, and soon. Otherwise it will be all over the place, and that would be a pity.'

'Just when things were shaping so well. You would think he had no sense at all.' Ewan looked about the kitchen floor and then sat down.

'He hasn't much,' Hamish agreed. 'He didn't come this way. I am pretty sure of that. Hughie would have spotted him. Hughie was waiting up here on the road for me since the first of the dark. He thought there would be news about Iain . . . There was!'

'Where is he?'

'I sent him on past the big house on his bike. Iain would never have taken that road. But you never know.'

Mary left the kitchen without a word.

Hamish listened to her going into the parlour. It was dark in there.

'And things turning out so well for him. What will they think?' muttered Ewan in a forlorn harsh way.

'We've got to stop them thinking. And that big Colonial has sense in his head. When I said to him that we would find Iain all right and that it would be a pity if anyone else started searching or said anything, he looked at me and nodded. I thought more of him for that than all his talk about the sheep.' After a moment he added, 'All the same, if we don't find him by the morning they'll start dragging the Bridge Pool.'

A curious choked sound came from the parlour and Hamish knew Mary was standing in there with the door open.

'What are we going to do now?' asked Ewan.

'I've been thinking,' said Hamish. 'There's no house he would go to. That's plain now. I don't think he would be hiding about. That's not his spirit. He would hit out into the hill to get away. His head may not be as clear as usual. In that case, he'll drop in his tracks. All the same, he would have a place in mind. The only thing I can think of is this – he's taken the hill path for Strathorn.'

'Strathorn!'

'Yes. He often spoke to me about his trip there. Torquil Macfadyen urged him to come back. Jamie's last word to him, at the time of the snowstorm, was an invitation to go over for a day or two. Iain once suggested I should go with him. And there's always the Tulchan bothy to rest in.'

Ewan looked at Hamish, and the drawn grey expression showed how deep lay his anxiety.

'So I'll hit out there,' said Hamish, as though ever since he had come into the house he had been pursuing deep in him a secret line of thought. 'Have you a torch?'

'Will you go now?'

'I'll go pretty fast,' answered Hamish. 'Where is it?'

Ewan got up and began hunting about the dresser. Mary came in and gave Hamish the electric torch.

'That's fine,' said Hamish. 'If he turns up before I come back, for God's sake hold him. Too much depends on him now, for all of us. He'll take the young fellows with him. They like him. I'm not a landlord's man, as you know. Iain is less. But there's a fight here, a real chance, and heaven knows where it might not end.'

'What power have I over him to hold him?' asked Ewan with bitter irony.

'More than you know,' answered Hamish swiftly. 'And the line to take is this. Tell him he'll be a bloody deserter to go now. If he doubts the landlord and the whole thing – right! let him call the landlord's bluff. But the fight is here – not at the end of the earth. I see it at last. The maggot has been in us too long. And if he tries any running-away stuff on me now, he's for it!' He swung away. The laugh came over his shoulder and he was gone.

When Ewan saw Mary putting on her tweed jacket, he asked, 'Where are you going?'

She could not speak but she turned her face to him for a moment, her lips drawn over her teeth, glanced at him with eyes that told her secret story, shook her head pitifully like one who could no more command her fate, and went towards the door.

Ewan stood long looking at the closed door; then a groan came from him and he sat down, for Mary was more than the sun's light in his home.

EIGHT

The stars were shining but there was as yet no moon. After Mary had gone a little way, her feet gained confidence, and soon she was crossing the fallow field to the edge of the Dell. As she came among the small birch trees she stood and listened, but heard only the wind in the hard leaves. It was very dark down in the Dell. The place was like a den. She groped her way down, and stood, and in a low voice called, 'Iain!' A scurrying of some beast in the undergrowth quickened her to a sharp cry. When she had hold of herself again, she became aware of an ominous waiting in the invisible about her. A body could lie in a heap, and death was simple and final. The leaves told the wind. 'Iain!' Her voice rose. She stumbled forward, tearing through the invisible, tearing out of the dark den. Nothing came after her, and she went on.

As she took the slanting path along the heathery slope towards Achmore, she suddenly thought: What if he has gone to Achmore! She stood as in a private revelation.

But she could not believe it. She was trying to make him feel as she felt, act as she acted. He had never gone to Achmore since he had come home. Why should he go now? Her feet quickened. Twice she went off the narrow path and fell. She began to run. She had no fear at all. Mad Mairag might tell her something. *He's there!* she thought. This was madness. She tried to feel her disappointment when he wouldn't be there. But she couldn't. She hadn't time.

There was no other house for him but Mad Mairag's. None. It was true! But terrible for her to delude herself like this. Terrible.

She came over the breast and saw the window light at a little distance. She stopped. Why wasn't Mairag in her bed? What was she doing up at this hour? She couldn't go on.

Now her feet were going, quick but stealthy. No-one must know she was coming. Nothing must be frightened away. She had difficulty with her breathing. As she came by the end of the cottage, she stopped again and strove to control herself. Now! It was now! She went slowly on. There was no blind on the little window. She looked in. Mairag was sitting alone before the fire, bent forward, utterly still. The cat was asleep in the rocking chair. A trickle of steam rose lazily from the spout of the black kettle.

The cool stone of the window-ledge came against her palms. She pushed at it to keep herself erect. The enchanted and desolate stillness of the kitchen wavered on her film of vision. Mairag rippled slowly like a witch in a wave. Her forehead hit the window-ledge, and so quivering and broken a breath came from her that its moaning darkened her own eyes and told her that all had been mockery and hopelessness. Softly and heart-brokenly she began to sob against the shelf of stone.

She felt the hand under her arm, heard the old woman's voice saying quietly and gently, as though the world might overhear, 'Come away, my darling. Hush! Come you!'

Mary let herself be led towards the door, caring no more about the old woman, or about the sounds she made, or the blinding tears. The old woman led her past the door of her dwelling, led her to the next door in the long narrow cottage. The goat bleated. 'Be quiet, you old fool!' said Mairag in a harsh voice. The goat bleated again. 'She's annoyed because she didn't hear you coming,' Mairag explained, a laugh in her voice. Mary could now see a dim whiteness, like the whiteness of a ghost. 'Would you like to sit down, my dearie? . . . Here! Sit you there!' Mary found herself sitting on a low stool. There was a strong smell of goat; a quietness of conspiracy, of wild necromancy. Mairag still spoke in a low voice, as though 'they' might overhear.

'I was wishing you to come,' said Mairag. 'And you have come! Isn't that fine?' Her low cackling laugh was friendly. 'He won't hear us here.' She was delighted as a child playing a cunning game of make-believe.

'Who?' Mary could hardly breathe.

'Who do you think?'

Mary could not see the old woman's face, but she imagined the cunning eyes, heard the weird cackle being held. The teasing was an intolerable madness. 'Who?'

'They all come back to Mad Mairag,' answered the old woman, with knowing triumph.

Then Mary's skin ran cold with thought of the dead.

'They all come back, one way or another. But his feet were heavy feet, and Nancy heard him going to the well. I found him there. Wasn't that clever of me?'

'Who? Tell me!'

'Hush! He's sleeping. Hush, calm you, my darling. He's sleeping, your own lad, and Mairag got him for you. Wasn't that clever of her?'

'Where?'

'At the well. He had his face in the water—'

'Where is he?' Mary's voice rose to a half scream.

'Hush! He's in my bed.'

'Is he—?'

'He's sleeping. And his brow is cool now. He's lying there like a child. Bonny he is to look at, your own lad, with a fine brave face on him. Wise you were in your choice, my pigeon. In all places he will walk with light feet. The hawk is in his brows, but tender is his mouth. Go with him and he will go with you, and many a wonder he will bring into your days. Many a wonder. For dearly he loves you, and where love is, wonder is born.'

Mary could not bear any more. Every word of the old woman's would be ambiguous now, for she could talk of the dead as if they were living. To probe her was to increase her enigmatic talk, to indulge her cunning love of surprise. Dread, a choking sense of horror, lifted Mary to her feet.

'Would you like to see him?' asked Mairag.

It was the awful question the relatives of the dead asked.

Mary did not answer and stumbled out of the door. She was no longer capable of understanding what Mairag was saying as she walked beside her. At the door, a low laugh from the mad mouth turned her blood cold. Mary went on, against the light, against the rocking chair with the sleeping cat, the black kettle with the feather of steam at its spout, turned to the bed, went to it, and met Iain's open eyes.

'Mary!' Iain got up on an elbow.

Mary could not move, could not speak. The effort at controlling herself had been too great. Her body suddenly broke and she fell forward on the bed, to bury her face, to hide herself. Her whole body began to shake in a spasmodic sobbing.

Iain heaved himself up and leaned forward. 'Mary!' A hand went to her head. Except for his jacket and shoes, he was fully clothed. He was caressing her hair. 'It's all right, Mary. I'm fine.' The bed-cover was in his way. He got his legs free of it and swung them to the floor and turned to her. 'Don't cry like that.' He put an arm round a shoulder to lift her away, but she would not be lifted. He put out his strength, but she would not show her face, and blinded it against him.

'I thought you were dead,' she said and gave way completely. 'Leave me.' She made to turn from him but he held her.

'Did I mean all that to you?' he asked.

'Oh yes!' she said. She was ashamed, ashamed of having broken down, and struggled to get away from him.

'Mary!' As he tried to lift her head, her mouth, Mairag's face appeared and smiled to him. Mary felt his involuntary stiffening, broke away and turned. But Mairag had withdrawn.

'It's that mad woman,' he said.

'She's not mad,' murmured Mary, stilling her sobs.

'She's as mad as a March hare,' said Iain. He staggered over to the rocking chair and tipped the cat out of it. 'Sit down here.'

'No. You sit.'

The rocker swung him so unexpectedly that he gripped it. He let his head lie back and closed his eyes. The emotional disturbance, the fight within him, exhausted him. Moreover, this trembling of the flesh, this quivering in the brain, had assailed him when different planes of experience had got mixed. He opened his eyes and watched Mary. She was, of course, absolutely real; there was no doubt about it. She even had the teapot in her hands. But in an instant, and with an effect of extraordinary clarity, he saw her there, involuntarily standing still, before his eyes, saw the breath held in her mouth as she looked at him, and he was aware of the plane of entrancement.

'Do you think this is real?' he asked.

She did not speak.

'I have had some awful dreams. I don't know that I am quite right in the head yet. Do you think I am?'

Love and concern made her face extraordinarily vivid. He was watching her in a curious steady way. She got down on her knees before the fire. 'You know you are.'

He leaned forward and touched her; then he leaned back. 'It's this rocker,' he said, steadying it. 'I think it's bewitched.' He smiled with a remote almost cool humour. 'But you have a habit of leaving me – at the last minute.'

'I never have,' she said simply.

'Oh yes, you have. Once we were going through an awful place. I had you by the wrist. I was watching for the dangers and suddenly you said, "Iain, the drinking well!" And there it was in a sunny place. But – you were gone.'

'You know you were dreaming.'

'When I left the big house and was coming along here – I was very tired – and lay down. Then you were with me, and again – again – it was the well. And my face was in the water. And your hands lifted me. But in a little while I saw that they were not your hands – but the hands of that mad woman.'

'She's not mad.'

'Oh yes, she's mad. She gave me a drink and the best sleep I ever had. She seems to have brought you, too. But I expect you'll leave me again – when I wake up.'

She looked into his eyes. 'You know you are teasing me.'

'Will you leave me?'

She looked at the teapot, cupped in her hands. 'You know I will never leave you – if you don't want me to.'

Then he stirred and the earth-life came into his face. 'I am not being fair. It's because there is no pith in me. It's awful to be weak.' His expression twisted, his eyes glistened. 'You see, I'll have to go away.'

'Why?'

'Why? You can ask me that?'

'They don't want you to go.'

'They? Who?'

'My father told me. At the meeting they had. The laird. Your own father. Hamish is looking for you.'

His expression slowly narrowed in suspicion. 'What for?' He was all human now.

'Iain – please – will you listen to me?'

'Go on.'

'Don't you trust me?'

'I don't know.'

That pierced her, but she did not show the hurt, though she could not speak for a moment. He waited. Then, because the hurt remained, in a quiet, unemotional voice, she began to tell him what her father had told her about the meeting.

'My father said the laird spoke for a long time about all that, about improving the land and having sheep and cattle. He said the laird had all your ideas about that.'

'He's going in for politics,' said Iain with a withering humour.

'I don't know. My father did not say anything about that. Then big Andrew said that you had all these ideas, and the laird said that he knew that. He said he looked upon you as a leading figure among the young men.'

'What for?'

'For carrying out his schemes. He said you had spirit and – and guts. He said he had seen you throwing the man through the door. But that was after, I think.' Mary paused in her calm recital to try to recollect precisely. 'Yes. Mr Cunningham told what happened in the office, how the man who was dealing with my father's legacy did not give some information and how you found this out. The man called you names. Something like that. But Mr Cunningham said he had every confidence in you and would be glad to take you back if you cared to go.'

'He said that, did he?' Colour began to seep into Iain's cheeks.

'Yes. He also said that you dragged Major Grant out of the river and saved his life.'

'Who told him that?' Iain's brows gathered darkly.

'I don't know. But my father said that the laird was amused. For all he can think of are his schemes. He wants to give men a chance. Then he put a plan to your father.'

'Well?'

Mary was sitting back on her heels, looking at the fire. She told him about Torglas in the same even voice.

'What did Father say?'

'He said he would help you if he could. He said that if you made a success of Torglas, where he had failed, it would lighten the end of his days.'

Iain's breathing had quickened. He recklessly got up.

Mary leaned forward to the kettle and tilted its spout over the tea-pot. There was only a small dribble of water left in it. She looked round. Iain was standing on the middle of the floor staring at the window. Mairag came in with a bright tin pail and a jug. 'I've brought some water from the drinking well,' she said, looking at them from under her brows.

Mary smiled and thanked her. Mairag put three jugfuls of water in the kettle; as she did so, she gave Mary a sly nudge and whispered, 'I was listening!' Then she brought her lips to Mary's ear and added in a very low whisper, 'And I wasn't the only one!' Whereupon she withdrew with her pail and her secret joke.

'Madder than any March hare,' said Iain, looking for his shoes.

'She is not mad,' said Mary.

'She loves the land!' said Iain. 'And the little feet going to the drinking well! And birds singing in the rain! She makes poems on trees!' He laughed.

She glanced at him. He swung round, 'Mary, you're the only one I can trust in this world. Don't let them put me through it again!'

She controlled herself, did not move, though his cry had pierced her heart. 'You know you must do it,' she said. 'It's what you have dreamed about. You must speak to him, and find out. What does it matter who offers the chance? A beginning has to be made. This may be the beginning of new life in the glens. He's not the old kind of landlord. He's a Colonial.' Her voice rose despite herself, and then with a cry: 'O Iain, wouldn't it be lovely if you got things going, and all the young fellows, and the girls, too, were in it, happiness and work, and your fiddle going, and dancing! And one day – it would be the people's glen.'

'Dreams!'

'Wherever we go, what have we at the end of the day but our dreams – and our hands? What has any people, whether in Australia or Russia, but just that? Haven't I heard you say it? The Highlands will never be anything – but what we make them.'

'I did not know – you thought like that.'

'How could I help it, listening to you?' But there was no humour in the words. Then in a remote colourless tone she added, 'And it's more than that.'

'How, more?'

Her head made a restless movement. 'I know you would never be happy unless you were doing that.' It was the woman's final judgment. It went deeper than all theories. It sounded sad, yet did not accuse him of seeking his own happiness. It was the hidden level where the seed germinates from which life grows.

'You're only thinking of me?'

She shook her head, and in doing so felt she lied, for she had been thinking only of him. She had no way of telling him, or of telling herself, that the thinking had been only in her head.

The shaking of her head at once disturbed and stilled him. 'What could one fellow do? It's far bigger than that.'

She pulled her resources together. 'Once Goldie – the English master – said – "Utopia is one man's dream".'

'But he was sarcastic. Surely you saw that!'

'Yes.'

'Well! What was the good of saying it?' He had been drawing life from her, and now her stupidity hurt him. He could not bear much.

She did not answer.

'Sarcastic, that's what they'll be. All the maggot-men. If you mentioned "dreams and hands" to Goldie, he would grin at you. A country simpleton, a sentimental fool, he would call you. Surely you can see that.'

His talk hurt and confused her, but she would not let herself break. Not looking at him, as if her words might again be wrong but were her words, she said, 'He was sarcastic because he was afraid to fight. He had given in.'

Iain stood quite still. His breath stopped in him. 'Mary!' he said in a low voice that was a cry. She saw the life in his face, the life that would fight and never give in. Its hill strength weakened her. He was coming towards her. He took her in his arms.

Presently, 'Never mind me!' he said, for he could not control the trembling of his flesh. She hurried to get the tea ready. He closed his eyes and let everything sink deep within him, sink deep for a few moments in utter peace and renewal.

Iain came to himself. The cat was on his lap. From the steaming kettle, he looked around the kitchen. His hand went up to his head and his eyes stared. 'Mary!' he cried in a loud voice, getting to his feet and spilling the cat abruptly to the floor. 'Mary!'

Mary came quickly in. 'I'm here, Iain. It's all right,' she cried brightly. Mairag was behind her.

He looked at them, breathing heavily – and slowly smiled. 'I must have been asleep.'

'You have been asleep – but you are awake now.' Mairag considered him with her cunning smile, as Mary hurried to make a fresh pot of tea.

He sat down. His heart was beating strongly and he felt its flush in his brain, but apart from a cramped feeling in the groin, he had no pain. He looked at Mairag teasingly. 'Great traffic to the well to-night?' The old banter was in the voice.

She gave her cackling laugh with delight. 'You drank of it yourself!' she accused him.

'I know you!' he said. 'You think you'll have Mary and me coming to it now.'

She clapped her hands, quickly glanced at Mary and back at him, as if her head swung on an oiled pivot. Then her look steadied on him, but sideways. 'It's the well of life,' she said.

'Well! Well!' he said.

She was delighted and bustled about.

When tea was finished, Mary said, 'Now, Iain, I have got to go home. They'll be wondering where we are. I must tell them. Then I'll get Hamish or Hughie to come with your own horse and you can ride home. Until then, you can have Mairag's bed.'

Iain gave a solemn tilt to his head and addressed Mairag. 'She's wanting to leave me already.'

Mairag laughed.

'Now, do be sensible, Iain. You're weak yet. You know that,' pleaded Mary.

'If she thinks she's going to get rid of me as easily as that,' said Iain to Mairag, 'she's wrong.'

Mairag clapped her hands again and swayed. To this young man, even the path to her well was not a solemn place; it was full of life and fun and quick feet.

'Mairag, you said you'd help me,' urged Mary.

'His feet are on the way,' said Mairag.

Iain laughed. 'Where's my cap?'

Mairag brought him his cap.

'Thank you for all your kindness.' Iain put out his hand. His voice dropped a tone – 'And mind! I'm going to keep my eye on you!'

Impulsively she worked his hand up and down with both

of hers. Suddenly he embraced her. 'You have been very good to us. I'll never forget you.'

At that she was overcome and said 'Och! Och!' shaking her head and lifting her hands like two wings and beating him with them as he turned and went before her.

At the door, Mary kissed her.

'Be going, my darling,' said Mairag. 'Be going with him – and watch his feet in the darkness.'